WAREHOUSE DREAMS

THERESA HALVORSEN

NBBP

First edition published by S & H Publishing, Inc 2020

Print ISBN: 978-1-955431-01-9

Ebook: 978-1-955431-00-2

*To Brad—you've made me happier
than I ever thought I would be.
To Talen and Connor—I'm grateful
each and every day to be your mom.*

CHAPTER ONE

I FUCKED UP. Horribly. Like going to lose my job screwed up.

I looked around my director's office at Phillip's Academy for the Advancement of Wilds. My hands left sweaty imprints on her desk. I pulled them into my lap, lacing the fingers together to keep them from shaking.

Hell, since I lived at my job, I'd be homeless too. I'd lose friendships, the roof over my head, and the most rewarding work I'd ever done. Holy-mother-of-god, how could I have been so phenomenally stupid?

I'm on the girl, Daniel thought. *She's in the cafeteria. In the kitchen. She's raiding the walk-in frid— Gone. She's messing with us.* Daniel's mental voice was thick with his southern roots.

"I know..." My voice was creaky. I tried again. "I know you wanted me to stay put," I said to my director, Miriam. She sat, curled into her comfortable chair, her eyes closed to focus on the conversation in her head. "But can I please go look for her?"

Miriam nodded, a single movement, and I teleported to the school grounds, searching for the child. I rubbed my aching chest, my fingers shaking. Maybe I was having a heart attack. That was possible, right?

People under forty could have heart attacks? Maybe if I had one, I wouldn't get fired.

Any idea where she went? I asked Daniel.

She's back in the cafeteria, he thought. *Pinging to the pantry, the snack shelves, the walk-in fridge. Never seen anyone teleport so fast.*

We're going to find her halfway through a wall. Miriam's thoughts sounded tired.

Hell of a way to be woken up. A sigh echoed through Daniel's honey-colored shields.

How old is she? Miriam asked me. Telepathy wasn't a strong Gift for her, and her normally magenta shields, her mental protection from other telepaths, were gray around the edges.

Around twelve, I answered, sweat trickling down my back. It was summertime in Chicago, and even at midnight, humidity hung thick in the city.

I doubt she's only twelve, Daniel snapped. *She has too much control.*

The girl is deaf, I snapped back. *She might be older. It wasn't like we did a full introduction or anything.* I was pretty sure the girl was deaf. I hoped she was deaf— I mean, not that I wanted someone to be disabled, but I hoped I hadn't misread the situation that much.

I sighed, a quick puff of air in the night. It didn't matter whether or not she was deaf. I had brought home an unknown and potentially dangerous Wild, with teleporting skills beyond those of any adult.

Who was stealing everything she could get her hands on. And no one could catch her.

There was no way I'd fix this. I was done.

Where is she? I asked Daniel.

I'm watching her teleport all of the snacks from the cafeteria, he thought. *I wonder where she's hiding them. I'm going to— Hell, she must have sensed me. Jumped away again.*

She's probably trying to find a place to eat. I used my Gift to scan the school grounds for the girl's thoughts. She had to be somewhere. *I got the impression she was hungry. And hurt, scared and confused.*

And deaf? Daniel thought. *That's a hell of a perfect grift. She played you. And we don't have the money to replace all the stuff she's stealing.*

She can't get out. The wall will stop her. I wished my chest would stop hurting so I could think. I'd never, ever misread the situation so horribly before. I mean, after fifteen years working with Wild teens, I know how to read them without actually reading their thoughts, because no one wants to see the thoughts of teenagers.

If I was her, Daniel thought, his shields glittering. *I'd be panicking, realizing I can't get out. My next step would be to hack into the transport pad or try to get the gate open.*

I'm going to wake the rest of the faculty, Miriam thought. *They need to pair up and go building-by-building and room-by-room to find her.* Miriam's voice changed slightly as she opened a mental channel to all the adults living at Phillip's Academy for the Advancement of Wilds, nicknamed the Warehouse. *All staff meet in the admin conference room immediately.*

I pulled myself out of the channel, blocking out the sleepy telepathic questions and the explanations from those already awake.

Kendle, please come back to my office.

With a sigh, I teleported to Miriam's office and stood in front of her desk, my hands behind my back.

Miriam fished around in a drawer and pulled out a bottle of painkillers. Her magenta shields were now threaded with gray. She was a second-generation Bred, back when the geneticists were still figuring out how to manipulate the genetic codes of unborn babies for the parents who could afford it. Miriam's parents had given her intelligence, a take-charge personality, beautiful aquamarine eyes, and psychokinesis as her primary Gift. Miriam's telepathic Gift was weaker as her parents hadn't had much money left for it. It was a mistake the geneticists had learned from. Now parents chose equally strong psychokinetic and telepathic Gifts. Those who couldn't afford both, didn't have Gifted kids.

She was angry with me. I could just see the emotion under the surface of her shields. What was I going to do without the Warehouse? Without my home, my work? I loved my tiny apartment and beat-up office, loved the daily chaos and juggling all the mismatched pieces of the Warehouse together so the other teachers could focus on helping the Wilds. And I loved my co-workers. We were each other's family. Every day was hard and stressful, but I was grateful to be here.

A glass with two fingertips of amber fluid appeared on the desk in front of me. I sniffed— whiskey. Blech. I much preferred gin.

"Sit down," Miriam said. "And drink it." She took off her glasses and polished them on her pajama pants.

"No thanks," I said.

"You're having an anxiety attack." Miriam held her glasses up to the light, made a face and polished them again.

"Am not." And with that, I could add immaturity to the list of things I'd done wrong tonight.

"You're pale and literally shaking," Miriam said. "The water in my vase is moving, which means you're leaking and losing control of your Gift. If you don't calm down, you're going to shatter the vase."

"I haven't done that in years." I never knew why liquids were the first thing my Gift latched onto when I was emotional.

"Drink," she said. "Or I'll have the RN give you a sedative. It's going to be a long night, and I need you to be at your prime."

"Why?" And did I still have a job?

"Because you're our strongest teleporter and we may need you to catch that child."

Somehow, that made me feel better. I wasn't going to get fired on the spot at least. I didn't sit down, but I picked up the glass and tossed down the whiskey, choking and sputtering at the hated burn. But the knot in my chest loosened, and when I wiped my hands on my jeans, they didn't grow damp again. The water in the vase was smooth. I could do this. I could prove I was valuable, and Miriam shouldn't fire me. Right? I hadn't even been written up, except for that one time Miriam had almost expelled me my second—

I slammed the door on my meandering thoughts. This wasn't helping. I took some deep breaths, grounding myself in this reality. I counted five things I could see. The green lamp on Miriam's desk, the wilting marigolds, the pattern of browns and blues on the visitor's couch, the rip in the brown Pergo flooring and my own muddy sneakers.

I moved on to four things I could hear. The hum of an air conditioner, my thumping heart, voices outside on the pathway between the admin and dorm warehouses and a dog barking in the inner-city neighborhood surrounding our school.

My heart slowed, and my brain kicked back in.

We needed to find the Wild teen before morning.

CHAPTER TWO

YOU GOT A MINUTE? Eeva, my best friend, had asked me two hours ago, her telepathic voice cutting in and out. Telepathy over long distances was difficult even for Quality Breds, and Eeva, a Wild, was two time zones away in the foggy Bay Area.

I smiled at the touch of her sunny blue shields that reminded me of spring days in Chicago.

Of course, I responded. *Call me.*

Then I had to hunt through my desk drawers for my rarely used cell phone. I generally only used my cell to speak to the Reg parents of our students or friends like Eeva who lived too far away for easy telepathic conversations.

"What's going on?" I asked. "Need me to pick up a shift at Mt. Olympus?" I asked, naming the Bred bar Eeva managed.

"We're closed for remodeling," she said. "The owner is re-theming it again. This time it's a 1920s speakeasy. Should be pretty snazzy when it's done."

"Snazzy? That what the hip kids are saying?"

"You tell me. You work with them."

I laughed. "Pretty sure we weren't hip when we were here. I think you've gotten old." I leaned back in my chair, putting my feet up on my desk and hoping Miriam wouldn't walk by.

"So if Mt. Olympus is closed, what's going on?" I asked, changing the subject. "You okay?"

She was quiet for so long I thought I'd lost the call.

"Eeva," I said into the receiver. "You okay? Do you need money? Tell me your boss is paying you during the renovation." I hated talking on phones. I missed being able to tell what people were feeling and thinking through the colors moving in their mental shields.

"I'm fine. I'm actually busier now than when Mt. Olympus is open. Nothing to worry about. But I've been seeing this Wild kid hiding in this plant nursery close to my apartment. I think I've seen her every day for about a week. Tiny, dirty, skinny. You know how it goes."

I did. Wilds don't have predetermined genetic codes. Our parents are Regs—people without Gifts who couldn't afford or didn't want to choose our genetic codes. Only Breds are supposed to be telepathic and psychokinetic. And yet here we are. Unlike Breds, there's no party when, around twelve years old, we know our fathers are sneaking away from work to drink beer in movie theaters. There are no presents from proud grandmothers when we realize our mothers are exhausted and fantasizing about leaving all of us. Checks don't arrive in the mail when we embed a fork in a wall two inches from our brother's head during a whose-turn-is-it-to-do-the-dishes fight. We terrify our parents, who ground, beat, beg and bribe so we won't read their minds or float our beds three feet off the ground during a nightmare. Our teachers and principals expel us, and coaches kick us off sport teams, citing safety concerns and telling our scared parents we need to be home-schooled and not be let out of the house. Until Miriam founded the Warehouse, there were no teachers to show us how to control and use our Gifts.

Many Wild teenagers run away or are kicked out of their homes, to live on the streets, begging and stealing. Some band together for safety and others form thieving gangs, making some neighborhoods unsafe. Law-abiding Wilds on the Gifted Registry can't get jobs or complete school because the Regs don't want us around and the Breds don't want to deal with their "weaker" cousins. And Wilds not on the Registry, the ones who manage to find jobs and pay rent, are in hiding, desperate not to use their Gift where Regs might see because they'll get fired or worse, institutionalized.

So Eeva seeing a skinny Wild kid on the street wasn't anything new.

I sighed. "Miriam said we can't take any more kids off the streets. They can't pay tuition, cause too much chaos, and generally don't succeed. We have to expel them and turn them over to the Guardians. And then they're locked up and drugged." I disagreed with her decision; the Warehouse should help all Wilds, but I kept losing the argument. "I think I have a contact in San Francisco County," I continued. "Maybe we can get her set up with some food vouchers. No shelter will touch her in that county though. And don't do anything stupid like taking her in yourself."

"I know," Eeva said. "The thing is…I saw her teleport. A few times. And she has this bloody wrap around her arm. You really can't help?"

"You sure she was teleporting?"

"I'm sure," she said. "I wouldn't have contacted you for just a Wild child living on the streets. I know Miriam's rules."

"Don't start."

"She's a bitch. She doesn't care anymore."

"A bitch who saved my life." It was an old argument and one I hoped she wasn't going to start.

"Please Kendle. This girl is so lost and confused. She has no shields and no control, but she's teleporting constantly. It's going to kill her."

I sighed into the receiver. "Moving Day is next week. I'm completely swamped getting ready. I still have to deal with all the room assignments, do the cleaning—"

"You guys always keep one or two slots open for mid-year students," Eeva interrupted. "Don't you have any left?"

I sighed again, a sigh that blew my white bangs out of my face. I did have one more spot for a girl, but if I took on this Wild, it'd mean no more girl students this year.

Please, Eeva thought, reaching out across the states.

I shouldn't, I remembered telling myself. I was too busy, and it was almost ten o'clock at night anyway.

"Which nursery?" I said.

"Seriously? You're really going to go?"

"Yep."

She gave me the address.

"I'm only going out to bring her a supply backpack. And I'll talk to her. Try to get her some help, but won't be able to bring her to the Warehouse."

"Thank you. I'd meet you, but I have a work meeting with the contractor and the owner."

"Now?"

"It's only eight here."

"True. Okay. Got it from here. Let you know how it goes."

"Miss you," she said. "Come see me soon."

"I will." I lied, but she knew.

I pushed the off button on the phone and pulled on a jacket. I used my Gift to grab a black backpack out of the supply closet and teleport it to myself. All I would do is make contact with the girl, offer the pack, come back home and be asleep before midnight.

CHAPTER THREE

JESUS, it was quiet here, even though I was in the middle of San Francisco. The nursery plants must be absorbing the city noises. I kept my phone flashlight pointed at the ground, walking between the rows of plants. I stayed away from the building housing the cash registers, and garden implements. If there were a Wild here, she'd be hiding in the plants, not the building full of cameras and people during the day.

My heart pounded, and I had to take a few deep breaths. My imagination turned ornamental hedge bushes into hiding spots for monsters wanting to grab me. A bullfrog bellowed close to my feet and I jumped.

Nurseries sell plants, not monsters, I reminded myself.

I crossed into an area filled with potted fruit trees and roses. The sickly-sweet smell of the flowers filled the air. I walked a little further, my feet crunching on gravel, searching with my Gift.

I'm not sensing anything, I thought to Eeva. *Are you sure she was at this nursery?*

Positive, she responded, her sunny blue mental shields darkening like the sun had gone behind a cloud. *I tried to speak to her telepathically, but she teleported away.*

Shit. She's not here now. I'll try—

I stopped. I sensed someone in front of me, their thoughts tinged with the apricot mist of pre-shields. I sighed. She was definitely Gifted. The mist proved that.

I lifted my phone flashlight. Twenty feet away was a child, her red hair matted and filthy, wearing sagging jeans belted around her waist with a rope and a too small pink sweatshirt, its sleeves ripped to make room for her arms. The shoes were mismatched, and one had a sole held on by rubber bands. Her left arm was wrapped with filthy rags, cradled against her body.

Hi, I thought, uncertain if she could receive my telepathy. *My name is Kendle.*

I waited to see what she would do. It was too dark for her to see my white hair and purple eyes marking me as a Wild, but I hoped she'd realize I wasn't a Bred.

I was like her.

She stared, not moving.

"Hi," I tried verbally. "Are you hungry? I can get you some food."

She just stood, her thoughts circling. I tried not to read them, but her mist-like shields couldn't hide them. She had recently lost someone she loved and was completely desperate. Willing to do anything for food and to feel safe, for a few minutes. I remembered that feeling, the painful craving for an angel to save me because I couldn't save myself anymore.

"I work for a school called Phillip's Academy for the Advancement of Wilds," I said. "That's a terrible name, so we call it the Warehouse because our buildings are all warehouses. It's a school for Wilds like you and me. We teach Wilds how to use their Gifts, so they can get a job, and a home when they're adults. I can buy you some food and we can talk more."

She shook her head and signed something with her hands, though it obviously hurt to use her arm.

My heart sank. On top of everything else, she was deaf?

I switched back to telepathy. *I'm sorry. I don't understand. Are you deaf?*

She nodded.

Can you speak telepathically?

She shrugged. I didn't know what that meant.

But you can hear me?

Another shrug. She was hearing me a little, at least. Communicating with her would be hard. I'd have to be careful there weren't any misunderstandings.

My heart broke. Eeva was right. This girl would die on the streets if someone didn't teach her to use her Gift.I used my Gift to move the backpack halfway between us. Inside I'd packed water, a toothbrush and toothpaste, soap, granola bars, spare socks and a blanket.

There's food and some supplies in there. It's yours.

She teleported to grab the bag and then back to her spot in just a few seconds. Holy shit! I'd never seen trained Wilds teleport back and forth that fast.

Be careful. Teleporting is dangerous.

She rolled her eyes.

I almost smiled. Teenagers always thought they knew everything, even hungry ones kicked around by life.

If it's okay with you, I'd like to come back to see you tomorrow night, I told her, hoping she understood me. Maybe I could convince our nurse to do a field dressing and give her some antibiotics. Anything would help.

She shook her head and signed something to me. She was so broken.

I'm so sorry. I don't understand.

She twisted two fingers together and then mimed walking, grimacing in pain when she used her hurt arm. Her mind roughly touched mine, and I caught an image of the admin building at the Warehouse, a picture from our internet page. *You want to come with me to the Warehouse?*

She nodded, her head bobbing up and down quickly. I was surprised.

That's not how it works, I thought. *We don't normally take Wilds off the streets. I'd have to run it by the director.*

She shook her head and stomped her foot. I understood that.

Yes, we have taken students off the streets, but it's rare. Phillip's Academy isn't the best fit for everyone. We have lots of rules and expel students if they don't follow them. And we have to learn more about your Gift, to make sure the Warehouse is the best place for you.

She signed at me, then winced, holding her arm, frustration leaking through her thoughts. I felt her reach out to my shields, trying to speak telepathically. I could almost hear her question.

...an audition?

Sure, I answered. *Or an interview. Like for a job. But even with that, we might not have room for you. But I can buy you some food for now. And maybe get someone to look at your arm tomorrow.*

The mist surrounding her thoughts turned blue-gray. She'd believed I'd save her.

My heart constricted and I had to take a deep breath. I so wanted to help this girl. She walked toward me, the sole on her broken shoe dragging in gravel. Up close, her cheeks were gaunt with hunger, her eyes sunken in her pale face. A swollen belly sticking out under her sweatshirt told of a diet of whatever she could find, most past its expiration and unhealthy. Dried blood caked the rags she'd wrapped around her left arm.

She signed at me again, tears running down her cheeks.

I shouldn't do this. I couldn't do this.

She was so powerful and so untrained. She could do a lot of damage without meaning to.

So scared and hungry.

A car pulled into the nursery parking lot, and voices rippled out as the driver and passenger got out. We froze. Then a giant flashlight shined between the potted roses. The girl and I dropped to the gravel.

"This is the police," a male voice said over a loudspeaker. "Cameras have picked you up. Come out immediately or we'll come in after you."

Fuck, fuck, fuckity-fuck.

Do you know where the nearest transport pad is?

The girl nodded.

Can you transport there?

Her expression told me, "duh".

Meet you there.

Thirty seconds later, we stood in front of the transport pad and I had a one-sided telepathic argument with a deaf girl who may or may not be able to understand telepathy.

I'm not letting you teleport twenty states away from here, I told her when she refused to get onto the pad. *It might kill you.*

She rolled her eyes and held up six fingers.

Fine, I thought. *It's six states away, but I'm still not letting you do it. We're going to take the transport pad.*

She shook her head and stomped her foot. I sighed and concentrated on what she was trying to tell me. The Warehouse was exactly what she needed because she had to get better at telepathy ASAP. I just had to talk Miriam into it.

Transport pads are very safe, I thought. I pointed at the metal circle, powered by our Gift. *Safer than teleporting. Do you know how many Gifted have died teleporting themselves? Besides, our fence around the school has metal in it that blocks people from teleporting in. You have to take the pad if you want to get onto the grounds.*

Finally, she nodded, and I was able to enter the coordinates into the touchpad that would take us home.

CHAPTER FOUR

WE APPEARED AT THE WAREHOUSE, and I breathed through the nausea caused by the transport pad until it passed. I hated transport pads. But the girl next to me seemed perfectly fine, her thoughts excited and covered by that apricot mist. I could almost see the pretty adult she'd become, if she had food and someone caring for her.

You're just staying here for the night, I told her. *I'll get you some food, have someone look at your arm. You can't stay, not yet. We choose each student very carefully.*

She squared her jaw and nodded once, looking at the warehouses around her. I sensed determination in her thoughts.

Miriam and Daniel had opened the Warehouse over twenty years ago in the middle of Chicago's industrial area. They'd bought the run-down warehouses of a failed tech start-up with the last of the life insurance payout from Miriam's dead husband. They'd put the wall up first, protecting us from homeless Regs and Wilds, and hiding the warehouses from the boarded up or barely hanging on businesses.

Then she and Daniel gutted the warehouses and built classrooms, dorm rooms, offices, a cafeteria and apartments for the staff. The three-story dorm building was probably my favorite, shaped like a giant brick and covered with colorful murals. While we never had enough money or time, we did promise a different future to our students. On hard days, I imagined that hope seeping into the metal and stone of the buildings so everyone could feel it.

I let the girl take it all in, including the giant grassy area, the rock garden and the vegetable patch.

Let's head to the cafeteria. I'll get you some food and have the nurse look at your arm. I'd have to find out how much of my mental communications she picked up on. She was probably missing nuances like when you were only semi-fluent in another language.

I didn't even know her name.

Okay, food first, then a piece of paper and a pen.

I glanced around. She was gone. I reached out with my Gift and found her in the cafeteria. Guess she couldn't wait for food.

I teleported to the girl and spotted her stuffing bags of chips into the backpack I'd given her. She saw me and teleported away.

I reached out again, searching. She wouldn't be able to leave the grounds, not with the wall and the gate closed. I felt a tremor in the admin building, on the first floor, in the staff offices.

Was that her? What was she doing there?

I teleported to the admin building and went into Daniel's office. The girl was in the midst of grabbing books off shelves and sliding them into her backpack to join the bags of chips.

Wait a minute!

She used her Gift to slide Daniel's screen across the desk and included it in the backpack as I ran toward her.

"You can't take that," I said verbally and mentally.

She teleported away, taking the backpack with her.

Oh no.

———

After Miriam woke everyone, I met the other teachers and the overnight nurse, Jasmine, in the admin conference room.

I took my normal seat, my eyes down, while everyone else sat, their colored shields spiking, circling or flowing around them depending on their personality, and mood.

"It appears we've been targeted by a powerful teleporter Wild," Miriam began. "She's currently stealing everything she can from the cafeteria and our offices. We can't catch her."

"And we've been trying," Daniel drawled.

Franny, the science teacher, raised her hand. Miriam nodded at her.

"How did this happen?" she asked, running her fingers through her dyed purple hair, trying to work the sleep tangles out.

"Long story short, Eeva told me about this child, living on the streets and teleporting all over the place. I was trying to get her some help," I said. "You know, a backpack and resources. But the cops showed up, threatening to arrest us." I shrugged. "She was injured and hungry, so I brought her here. It was just for some food and for Jasmine to look at her arm. I didn't realize she was playing me."

What the hell were you thinking? Daniel thought in a private mental channel to me. *You should never, ever bring an unknown Wild into the school.*

My stomach tightened even more, my heart physically hurting. I tried to take a few slow breaths without being obvious.

I do it all the time, I responded. *I wasn't planning on having her stay. I just wanted to help her feel safe for a night.*

Well, it was stupid.

Noted.

Seriously? That's all you have to say? Noted? Daniel's hard shields filled my mind for a second. He was so pissed.

Kaya, the English teacher, passed me a water bottle.

"Sorry everyone," I said, popping the cap and taking a sip. I forced the water inside the bottle to stop moving, breathing deeply.

"We all make mistakes," Kaya said, patting my hand.

"That's true," Franny said, yanking her hair into a ponytail but missing half the strands so they flopped around her face. Her shields were a light violet and ebbed toward pink when emotional. "The other day I was trying to do that experiment where you mix different chemicals and the colors switch back and forth. I made my mixture, thinking I would just get a pretty turquoise color and ended up stinking up the whole lab. Turns out the freaking kids had mixed up the labels. So I tried to fix it but set the table on fire."

I liked Franny, but she was a Value Bred; the perfect example of a

Bred whose Reg mother didn't have enough money to fully build a child's genetic code, yet the geneticists had taken the money anyway. Her mother had paid for Franny to have telepathy, psychokinesis, a fast metabolism, and intelligence. She'd wanted her daughter to be a scientist or a teacher at a Bred school, like Seagull's Landing. But had lacked the money for personality modifications like leadership, charisma, or good judgment and hadn't requested any unique physical features. The result was a plain-looking Gifted woman, smart like a Bred, who tended to say and do the wrong thing at the wrong time. She wasn't a scientist and Seagull's Landing wouldn't touch her.

"We're going to table the conversation for another day," Miriam interrupted. "Though I'm unhappy there was a fire I didn't know about."

"It wasn't a big fire," Franny said with a flap of her hand. "I sucked the oxygen from around it, and it was fine."

"Focus people," Daniel said, thumping the table. "We need a plan."

"The dorm is locked down, right?" Miriam asked.

"Yes," Kaya said. "I double checked. But anyone can teleport in and out of the buildings. We never worried about it before—so few of our students can teleport. We always assumed the wall was enough."

Miriam rubbed the bridge of her nose. "I want this child caught within the next hour. Kaya and Jasmine, please stay in the dorm area so you can protect the students. Everyone else pair up. I'm going to assign each team a location to stay at. If you spot her, I want her sedated to stop her from teleporting. Last thing we need is for her to get hurt. Understood?"

We all nodded.

"Kendle, you're going to be our runner. I want you—"

Someone jabbed my mind and I winced. A poorly constructed thought inserted itself in my mind.

See...power... right?

Excuse me? I asked the small voice.

...looking...passed...? Can I stay?

CHAPTER FIVE

TEN MINUTES LATER, I sat in Miriam's office with Jasmine, Miriam and the girl. Everyone else had gone back to bed. Jasmine, her light green shields moving like growing plants, gently cleaned and bandaged the girl's cut and infected arm, while the girl stuffed trail mix into her mouth.

Hi there, Miriam thought to the girl. *My name is Miriam Phillips. Are you deaf?*

The girl nodded.

And mute?

The girl nodded again.

And you can hear us? Miriam tapped her head.

The girl lifted up her uninjured hand, pinching her fingers together to indicate a little.

Can you speak telepathically?

...hadn't tried... The thought was too sharp and pierced my mind.

Miriam winced. *Please don't speak with telepathy.*

You're hurting us, I clarified.

The girl gasped, her cheeks turning bright red.

It's okay, I told her. *A lot of first years don't know how to send thoughts properly.*

...stay...?

I rubbed my throbbing head. This girl had too much power. She needed to learn control.

Let's talk first, Miriam thought, fishing out more pain pills and passing me the bottle. *Do you write with your right or left hand?*

The girl raised her uninjured right hand.

Good, Miriam thought. She used her Gift to bring the girl a piece of paper, a pen and a clipboard. *What's your name?*

"Becca Nikolaev," the girl wrote.

Tell us why you stole from us tonight.

Becca leaned over the piece of paper writing furiously. "Kendle said I had to audition. I'm really strong."

Did you? Miriam asked me in a private mental channel.

Have I ever forced a student to audition? I asked her.

Miriam raised an eyebrow.

Of course not. I told her it was like an interview. Remember, she's only picking up on some of what we're saying.

Becca kept writing. "This is the only school for Wilds. I researched it. I have to come here." She underlined the word "have" twice, forgetting Jasmine cleaning her arm and wrenching it away from the nurse.

Jasmine touched Becca's shoulder and made eye contact. "I need you not to move so I can fix your arm," she said, enunciating each word. "Do you understand?"

Becca nodded.

Sweetie, I said to Becca. *I said the Ware— Phillip's Academy may not be a good fit for you. Any Wild under eighteen, regardless of how weak or strong their Gift is can come here. You don't need an audition or even testing. But we have many rules. Students must work very hard on their studies. Some Wilds don't want to do that.*

Becca's thoughts shifted with anxiety and she disappeared.

"Dang it," Jasmine said, sitting back on her heels. "I wasn't done. She took my entire roll of bandages with her."

"Where'd she go?" Miriam asked.

"I've got her," I said. I was getting the hang of finding her apricot thoughts. "She's just outside. I don't think she has good control when she's upset."

Miriam's lips tightened and reds of anger shot through her magenta shields. I'd really fucked this one up. I shouldn't have brought Becca back with me. I knew better.

There was a knock on the door. Miriam opened it with a wave of her hand. Becca stepped inside, the roll of bandages from her arm trailing behind her. Then she disappeared and reappeared next to the window. There were tears in her eyes. She tried to sign something, but her bandaged arm got in the way.

It's okay, I thought. *Sit down. Let's try some relaxation techniques. Close your eyes and take some deep breaths, breathing all the way down to your belly.*

Becca tried, her eyes open, locked on mine, but the clipboard with her paper shot off the table and flew past her to hit the wall.

Becca moaned.

No worries, I thought. *We're used to that around here. Look at the walls.*

Becca craned her head, taking in the patched and repainted dings and scrapes. All of our walls were gouged, especially in Daniel's psychokinesis classroom.

I used my Gift to give her the clipboard back.

"How's her arm?" Miriam asked Jasmine.

"Near septic. Looks like she cut it on some metal, maybe barbed wire? I'll give her a tetanus shot, a shot of antibiotics and an oral dose too. If that doesn't work and it may not, she's going to need IV antibiotics. She could've lost her arm."

Miriam sighed and Becca paled, having lip-read Jasmine's words.

You did the right thing bringing her here, Jasmine thought only to me.

I'm not sure Miriam sees it that way. I really messed up.

Depends on if you think saving someone's life is more important than getting in trouble at work. She winked, taking the sting out of the words.

I breathed deep. Jasmine was right. I'd done the right thing, even if I'd get into trouble for it.

Jasmine cut away the bandage with leaves and twigs in it from Becca's arm. *Miriam has to see the big picture. She uses us for the details. But I don't think this girl is a danger. She's too innocent.*

How long have you been on the streets? Miriam asked Becca.

Becca's story was the same as so many Wilds. She was born deaf to Reg parents working multiple low-paying jobs to make ends meet. Her parents loved her though. They wanted what was best for her and sacrificed their mental and physical health to keep her fed, get her a sign language teacher, and purchase good shoes and clothes so the other kids wouldn't make fun of her. Becca had only realized she was a Wild six months ago after she'd been teased for being poor and had teleported instead of running away. Her school had immediately expelled her for "fighting."

And then her parents moved and moved again so Becca could go to schools that didn't know she was a Wild. They told her not to use her Gift, to try again and again not to do something that was instinctual.

Did your parents know it was dangerous not using your gift? I asked.

She shook her head, her blue eyes big. "How?" she wrote on her piece of paper.

Have you heard about Wilds imploding? Exploding cars or buildings? People being hurt because of Wilds?

She nodded.

We have to use our Gifts. We have to empty out our batteries, or our Gifts just keep building until it explodes when we are under stress. Like how a balloon pops if it's overfilled. So, it was a good thing you couldn't stop using your Gift.

Eventually Becca's parents pulled her entirely out of school, saying they would move in the summer and try a new school. But then a careless driver killed them as they crossed the street on the way to work. Because they weren't on work property, their employer refused to pay any workers comp. Becca didn't know how to access her parent's savings account and didn't even know if they had one. Though a social worker said they would put her in foster care, no one ever came. She ran out of cash within a week, food after two. She started stealing, using her teleportation Gift to get in and out of stores without being caught. She was out stealing the day the landlord had her apartment cleaned, throwing all of her and her parent's things into recycling bins and having a moving company take away the furniture. Becca had managed to fish out a few family pictures, but the landlord had taken anything of value.

Becca's tears dotted the paper as she wrote.

I was so tired of this story; the same as so many Wilds. My life after my mom died had the same plot points. No one cared enough to help us.

Except Miriam and everyone that worked at the Warehouse.

I guess I don't understand, Miriam thought. *If you knew about us, why didn't you just contact us when your parents died?*

Becca wrote, "You would've let me come here?"

We would've figured out a way to help you, Miriam hedged.

Becca disappeared out of her chair, the bag of trail mix falling to the floor and spreading bits of raisins, cereal and tiny crackers all over the place.

Jasmine sat back. "Luckily I was done with her arm."

Becca reappeared, standing on a couch in Miriam's office, and quickly jumped down.

Her thoughts were gray. She was getting tired and that meant less control and more mistakes. *I'm sorry, I'm sorry, sorry,* leaked through our shields, bruising our minds.

No worries, I told her. *Sit down and focus on your breathing again.*

We have to take her, I thought to Miriam. *She literally has no one.*

An institution will keep her fed and safe.

And drugged and with no future until she dies. She could be the strongest Wild we've ever had. We have to teach her.

Becca, Miriam began, *While I understand your desperation, there are steps we have to take before we allow a student to come here. If nothing else, we have to have a place for them to sleep—*

Becca's pen scratched so hard, she ripped the paper. "I'll sleep anywhere. The floor, or a closet, in a basement. Or a tent outside in a sleeping bag. I'll even—"

Miriam put power behind her words, *Becca. It's the middle of the night and you need sleep. Kendle and I need sleep too so we can make good decisions and have good control.*

Becca's thoughts went black. *Please don't make me leave. Don't make me go back to the nursery. Bugs crawl in my hair when I sleep, and I'm so scared they're going to crawl in my ears and—*

You'll spend the night here, Miriam responded. *Go with Jasmine. There's a bed in the infirmary for you. I'll let you know if you can stay in the morning. But for now, sleep.*

Becca's eyes were sad, her thoughts dark. This poor child was completely desperate. I'd done worse things because I had no choice. And Miriam had let me come to the Warehouse.

Things will look different in the morning, I told Becca. *Trust us. We'll do what's best.*

CHAPTER SIX

THE DOOR CLOSED behind Becca and Jasmine. Miriam took off her glasses and tossed them onto her desk. They landed glass down, but Miriam didn't notice. She pressed her palms into her eyes.

"I can't have this conversation with you right now," she started, her eyes still covered. "But you need to spend some time reflecting on what you did wrong, so this doesn't happen again."

"I understand," I said.

"You can't put this school at risk because you feel bad for a teenage Wild on the streets. Anyone coming from the outside should be scanned to make sure they're not going to steal or hurt us."

I kept my face composed and my shields from shifting. I hated scanning—forcing myself into deep thoughts of Regs and Gifted, trying to figure out what they were capable of. It felt like a huge invasion. But it was one of Miriam's rules.

I wanted to argue, explain that Becca was only supposed to stay one night, and I hadn't felt the need to scan her. But I knew better. Miriam was right. I should've done my job.

"Bringing on a child with Becca's Gifts and her disability is going to strain our resources, which have been close to breaking for years," she said. "We can barely support the students we have."

"I know," I said.

"It's summertime and we're nearly out of money until the paying students come back for the school year."

"I know," I said again. I was responsible for the budget. We were living off vegetables we grew ourselves, in addition to flour, sugar and rice I bought in bulk. And if Becca could stay, I'd have to find the money for sign language lessons for me, so Becca could keep up her skills for when she left the Warehouse.

I'd always wanted to learn another language.

"I don't think I can look at her tomorrow morning and tell her she can't stay," I ventured. "Where would she even go?"

Miriam looked at the framed picture of her dead husband on her desk. She'd named Phillip's Academy not after herself, but him. "I scanned her while she was writing her story. She's telling the truth and is very innocent and sheltered. I'm amazed she survived on the streets. Make it happen."

The pain in my chest released. "You got it. Thank you."

Miriam opened up her screen and opened her calendar. "And I want to meet with you at eleven tomorrow morning to discuss your mistake further." She clicked a few buttons and I knew I had a calendar invite pinged into my email.

"Understood," I said.

Miriam squinted at her screen.

"If it's easier," I started. "You can owe me a paycheck a week late. I know things are tight."

"I already owe you two paychecks," Miriam said, not taking her eyes off the screen.

Three. But who was counting?

"Get some rest," she said, still not looking up. "You're exhausted."

"I'm going to go tell Becca she can stay."

"She's probably asleep." Miriam finally looked up, grabbed her glasses and gave me a limp smile. "She looked more tired than you."

I shook my head. "She's still awake. I would be." *Will I still have a job after eleven tomorrow?*

Miriam closed her eyes. *You didn't make that big of a mistake,* she thought. *Though there will be discipline.*

The next morning, at exactly eleven, I ducked into Miriam's office, my screen held against my chest.

"Ready for me?"

She nodded and closed her screen. She'd replaced the wilting marigolds with chrysanthemums, huge multicolored blossoms. Other than the flowers, her desk was clear except for a stapled piece of paper in front of the visitor chair. Sweat broke out under my arms and my heart hammered. I could do this. It was just a write-up and it was completely appropriate. I'd fucked up and had to pay the consequences. I was lucky I still had a job.

I'd spent the morning showing Becca where she'd sleep, introducing her to the other first years, and giving her a tour of the Warehouse. I issued her uniform—two pairs of pants, a skirt, five shirts and a hoodie. Most of the kids rolled their eyes about having to wear a uniform, but not Becca. She was so happy to have clean clothes she could wash in a washing machine. Then she and I spent an hour on the internet shopping for non-uniform clothes, underwear, socks and bras for her. I stretched the budget to the breaking point and bought a few things to personalize her dorm space. Then we went "shopping" in the storeroom, finding a cover for her bed, and an old lamp with a rainbow shade. I even found frames to fit the beat-up family pictures she'd somehow held on to.

She glowed when I handed her the frames, thanking me with sign language and clumsy telepathic thoughts.

The telepathy teacher will show you how to use your Gift better, I told her after one of her thoughts rattled through my shields and left me with a minute of vertigo.

Of course, that was assuming we'd hire a telepathy professor before school started. Or I'd have to sub for that class. It didn't matter what I did at the Warehouse, I reminded myself, as long as I could stay.

"Stop stressing," Miriam said when I sat down in her visitor chair. "I'm just putting a clarification of my expectations into writing." She handed me the paper. The document stated I would run any recruiting decisions past her before bringing a potential student to the school. I was also to think more "big picture" and understand my decisions had larger implications.

I signed the statement after skimming it over. I wasn't going to think about it anymore. I'd already been up all night telling myself how stupid I was. Today, I needed to move on.

"Done," I said, pushing the document toward her.

"Do you want a copy?"

"God no."

Miriam smiled. "You're a valuable member of the team. I don't know what we would do without you. This was just a small judgment mistake I know you won't make again. Right?"

"Right. Appreciate the butt kicking."

Miriam chuckled. "Don't make me do it again. I dislike doing these." She did, I could see it under her magenta shields.

"I won't." I stood.

"Oh, one more thing," Miriam said. "Changing the subject. I do need to take you up on your offer to delay your paycheck, if it's possible."

"Anything," I said sitting back down. "What do I need money for anyway?" It was true. Miriam couldn't pay us much but made it up with free room and board.

"But I will pay you back, as soon as the parents pay tuition when classes start," Miriam said, ignoring my question.

"I know," I said with a smile. "I trust you and know where you live."

"Indeed," she said. "Thank you. I'm sure you have things you need to do."

"I do. It's almost Moving Day, and I have to build a schedule for..." I trailed off. Miriam was still looking at me, but I could tell she wasn't listening.

"Anyway," I said. "I'll let you get to work."

"See you around."

CHAPTER SEVEN

I USED my Gift to press the buttons on the keypad to the Warehouse gate, timing it so I didn't stop my jog for the gate to slowly slide open on its rusty track.

I mistimed it and had to turn sideways, tucking in my butt so the gate didn't catch me. I'd have squealed, if I'd had the breath. My feet pounded on the asphalt path to the admin building, and I waved at the students weeding the vegetable garden. I got one wave back—not bad for teenagers during the summer at eight a.m. Of course, there should've been at least five or six more of them out here, instead of the...I counted quickly. Four. There were four of them out here? Seriously? If I let them tend the garden at ten and sleep in, then it was too hot, and I was torturing them. But apparently eight was too early? Could. Not. Win. I'd have to assign different chores.

Yay me.

It was a week until Moving Day, the official start to the school year. Becca had settled in and I'd learned some sign language along with her roommates, despite working ten-hour days. But I needed a daily run to keep my Gift from leaking.

At the admin building, I went up the clanging metal staircase to my apartment on the second floor, stopping in the hallway to catch my breath. I had smoked too much pot last night and my lungs were tight. I coughed, sweating profusely inside the air-conditioned building, and lifted a corner of my shirt to wipe my eyes, leaving damp and dirty stains on the hem. The temperature outside was pushing eighty degrees and the humidity was over one hundred percent. I caught a whiff of myself and grimaced. I'd forgotten to put on deodorant again.

I pushed my hand against the lock to my apartment door and went inside, letting the door close behind me.

Hello?

Well, that was a new voice.

I stuck my head out of my apartment and saw the boxes lining the hallway. The door in the apartment next to mine was open. The new telepathy teacher must be moving in.

My sense of observation was on fire today.

Hi, I thought to the owner of the charming turquoise shields flowing back and forth across his thoughts like ocean waves.

He stepped out from the apartment next door and I joined him in the hallway, closing my door behind me. He was so gorgeous my mind stuttered. Pale green eyes, unique to Breds? Check. Black almost blue hair? Check. Tanned skin so perfect he didn't have pores? Triple check! Six feet tall and the perfect meld of slender muscle? Yummy. His parents must have spent a fortune on his genetic code. He had to be a Quality Bred.

What was he doing at the Warehouse?

His eyes ran down my frame, taking in all my dirt and grime. I wondered what he saw. That I was barely 5' 4", in a world full of Bred women no shorter than 5' 10"? My frizzy white hair normal in women over seventy, but a mark of a Wild in a thirty-two-year-old? My bizarre purple eyes, which weren't violet, but bright purple? Oh! And I was sweaty, dirty, and stinky.

I scowled.

He greeted me by touching his shields to mine, a typical Gifted greeting. I'd never seen shields that reminded me so much of the ocean. There were even dots of orange and red almost like tiny fish beneath the surface—mild anxiety of being in a new place.

I knew my way of seeing shields as colors was unique, though not unheard of. Most Gifted saw or 'felt' walls around other telepath's minds. But I had to be unique in a fucked up Wild way. I got to see shields as colors and movement linked to health, emotions and personality.

The Bred held out his hand and I reached for it, realizing too late I should've refused, telling him I was too sweaty to touch another human being. His skin was smooth, like he'd spent his life rubbing expensive lotions into it and his nails were even manicured. I sighed. What on earth was Miriam thinking? He wasn't going to last here.

Kendle May.

Stephen. I think you're the last one I haven't met yet.

He'd met everyone else? When?

Do I have something on my face?

"What?" I said out loud.

"You're staring," he said. His voice was perfect too, smooth and mellow with a hint of humor and a faint New England accent to add just the right amount of culture.

"Sorry," I said. "I must have left my brain outside when I was running. Nice to meet you. I should shower." I placed my hand back on the palm lock of my apartment.

"I'm the new telepathy teacher," he said, not meeting my eyes as more reds and oranges dotted his shields. My weird eyes must have thrown him.

"Figured. It was the only open spot we had. Welcome to the Warehouse. I'll check in with you later when I'm not so sweaty." I opened the door, but just a crack, hoping he'd get the message and go back into his place. I didn't want him to see my banged up and mis-matched furniture.

More oranges and reds leaked into his shields.

I was being rude.

And god, he really was breathtaking, some defiant part of my brain whispered.

"I'm sorry," I told him. "I must have woken up cranky and left my brain outside. I work in recruitment, do all the administrative stuff and run the before and after school classes and clubs."

"That must keep you busy. What kind of clubs?"

I smiled. I loved our clubs, the huge number of them and how engaged the kids were. "Whatever the students want and will put time into. We have a botany club, a baking club, a book club—"

"Only clubs starting with Bs?"

Funny. His parents must have checked the "sense of humor" box when paying the geneticists. The kids would destroy him.

Though I guess technically it's not a book club, it's a reading club, I thought, pretending to ignore his comment.

There's a difference?

According to the third level requesting the name change, it's huge. She spent forty-five minutes in my office explaining it to me.

Which is?

In a reading club, you read whatever you want and talk about it, but only if you want to. In a book club you get assigned books you "have" to read and then you "have" to talk about it.

He leaned on the door jam, looking like he belonged in a commercial for cologne. "So, she and her friends just want an excuse to sit around and read."

"Pretty much. But it still counts as a club. They have the best attendance record."

He grinned and my heart sped up. Stupid hormones.

"Anyway," I said. "I need to shower and start work."

"It's Saturday."

"And I have work to do. Reading club doesn't run by itself." I shrugged. "Actually, it does, but the S&M club doesn't."

"S&M?"

"Sugar and marshmallows. They make candy treats, like chocolate-covered marshmallows. What'd you think I meant?"

His eyes laughed at me and his shields turned a bright turquoise. I'd never seen anyone's shields shift so much. *Did they pick that name?*

A door opened and Kaya came out from her apartment. She spotted us and sashayed in our direction. Kaya's Bred parents had given her mahogany skin, high cheekbones, bright blue eyes and dark hair surrounding her face like a sunburst. They'd designed her genetic code so she'd become a famous dancer. She wasn't a Quality Bred, but she wasn't a Value one either. She was somewhere in the middle, like most Breds. She should've been spending her time choreographing, or featured in music videos, internet shows or the theatre, making millions instead of teaching Wilds English and dance on Tuesday and Thursday afternoons. But somewhere along the way she'd either developed or been given a streak of independence. She did whatever she wanted, whenever she wanted to do it. And she didn't want to dance.

"Stephen," she exclaimed with a giant smile, focusing entirely on him. She gave him a full body hug, ending with a little back rub.

Oh God, I forgot she did this every single time, Stephen thought to me.

Have you met Daniel yet? He loves her hugs, I thought with a wink, so he knew I was kidding.

Young Polynesian guy or older guy with the Southern accent and curly hair? Older.

I can only imagine. He grinned.

Stephen was really charming and flirty. I wondered if his parents had chosen it for him.

Kaya turned to me, and tried to give me the same hug, her typical greeting for everyone except the students. I sidestepped.

"I'm so gross and stinky from my run."

"You know I don't care," she said, embracing me. Her orange, red, and yellow shields flickered like a friendly campfire as they touched mine, but her perfect nose crinkled slightly. I'd warned her.

"It's so good to see you again," she said to Stephen once all the hugging was done. She turned back to me. "Stephen and I taught together at Seagull's Landing before I came here," she said, naming the most exclusive Bred school.

"I'd forgotten you taught there," I said.

"I only lasted one year." Kaya frowned, which looked weird in her normally smiling face. "I hated it."

"When I heard about Phillip's Academy, I contacted Kaya," Stephen said. "She told me about the opening for a telepathy teacher."

"What did you teach at Seagull's Landing?" I asked, giving up on the idea I'd take a shower anytime soon.

"Telepathy. Same as here."

Daniel came up the clanging stairs, holding a cup of coffee from the cafeteria. "Did you run behind a dirt truck?" he asked me. "How'd you get so dirty?"

Oh goody. I had to deal with asshole Daniel again.

Daniel had always been the psychokinetic teacher, even when I was a student. My first few years at the Warehouse, my Gift had burst out of me when I was happy, sad or angry. I'd gouged the walls, shattered plates, broken windows, and snapped screens. One time I'd managed to crack the metal stairs up to the second floor of the dorms after a boy I'd liked had told me I was dumb, and no one liked me. Daniel had spent hours helping me learn to control my PK.

I owed him. Without all his work, I would've been institutionalized years ago as a safety risk to myself and others. I'd tried to thank him over the years, tried to get him to see me as an adult, not the child he'd helped. But nothing worked. He still treated me like a misbehaving student.

Daniel held out a hand to Stephen whose turquoise shields swirled with more reds and oranges. "Daniel Kaminski. We met when you interviewed."

Where was I when Stephen interviewed?

You were out investigating a potential Wild in that Colorado high school when he came by, Kaya told me, in a private channel, knowing me better than she should. Miriam was so excited. She hired him on the spot. It was a great move; he's an amazing teacher and his students adore him.

I shook my head, though the people around me weren't a part of the conversation. *I doubt it. He's too used to weekends off and assistants to grade his papers and—*

Kaya shrugged. *We'll see. I did tell him how hard it is to work here. How there's no real down time and how...beautiful and challenging the kids can be. He was excited. I think he was bored at Seagull's Landing.*

Of course he was. He can have anything he wants. Anyone he wants. And he's bored?

He wants to help Wilds. His family is very angry that he came here.

And another reason he won't last.

"I'm going to shower," I said. "See you all later." I pressed my hand against the lock and paused. I still didn't want Stephen to see the inside of my apartment. Not only was the furniture old but my bed was in the main room, and I didn't even own a couch or a screen; just a beat-up armchair where I read, my feet tucked beneath me.

"I've something for you," Daniel said to me, escaping Kaya's hug. "Mr. Sparklebutt was at my door again. Keep him more under control."

This has to be a joke, right? Stephen's voice laughed in my head. *You guys are just hazing me.*

Nope, I thought, meeting his laughing eyes. *That's actually the cat's name.*

"I don't have a cat," I protested. "Mr. Sparklebutt was Eeva's. She told him to watch me when she left. I can't keep him away." Though I had to admit he spent most nights on my bed, and I had a special food and water bowl for him.

"He probably comes to your door because he knows you hate him," Kaya said.

"Maybe you should feed him," I said. "That way he knows you like him, and he'll leave you alone."

"No one should be feeding him. We shouldn't have pets," Daniel snapped. "Keep him under control or I go to Miriam."

What is your problem this morning? I thought in a private channel to Daniel. *You're being an ass.*

But I slammed up a shield so he couldn't respond telepathically. "Good to meet you," I said to Stephen. "Welcome to the Warehouse." I flung open my apartment door, no longer caring if anyone saw the inside. At least it was clean, I'd made the bed before going for my run and didn't have underwear sitting in the middle of the floor.

CHAPTER EIGHT

A WEEK LATER, I put my foot in front of a suitcase zigzagging across the grassy area and traced the psychokinetic energy back to the owner. Finding it, I nudged his immature shields.

Your suitcase is over here.

Thirty seconds later, I said "Hi," to a kid running towards me. He was brown skinned with a Hispanic or Mediterranean background. His clumsy shields were thick in some places and thin in others, but already taking on a greenish cast like new spring growth. In a few months of working with Stephen, his shields would be shades of green, moving sharply into jagged peaks when emotional.

I'd met him and his parents a few months ago. They'd just found out their son was Gifted, and lickity-split had enrolled him in the Warehouse, being one of the few families paying full tuition. His telepathy was weak, and he'd probably struggle to send and receive telepathy. But his psychokinesis was pretty strong.

What was his name?

"Mateo," I said. "Let's hold off on the PK until you've had a few days in class."

"Yes ma'am," he muttered, his shields darkening to a forest green of embarrassment.

"Do you know where you're supposed to go? Are your parents here?"

He pulled a crumpled sheet of paper out of his pocket. I recognized the letter I'd composed for new students, welcoming them to the Warehouse and telling them what to pack.

Today was the official start of the new school year, Moving Day, the day when walking across the grassy area was an adventure in avoiding bruises. On Moving Day, everything came out of the dorm rooms. The kids used their Gifts on suitcases, trunks, and boxes, making items move suddenly and appear and disappear at random.

Once everything was out, the cleaning crew gave the dorms a thorough cleaning. A few days ago, after looking at the budget, Miriam had asked if I thought the staff could do the cleaning this year, but with some supply ordering finesse, I managed to find room in the budget for the cleaning crew. There was no way we had the time to clean on top of everything else.

After the cleaning crew was done, the kids moved back in, but could move back into different rooms, or change roommates without causing a ripple effect. It took me hours each year to go through the requests and figure out who was rooming with who.

I grabbed Mateo by the arm just as a cardboard box appeared half in, half out of the grass right where he was standing.

A fifth year, Jameson, his lapis blue shields wrapped around his thoughts and his copper colored hair bright in the sunlight, ran over. "Fu— Rats," he said.

"Gosh-dang-darn-it-all," I responded, inspecting the box. He'd done a poor job teleporting and the bottom half had completely merged with the grass and dirt, a foot down. We'd have to dig it out.

I rephrased my thought—he'd have to dig it out.

"Do you know what you did wrong?" I asked Jameson. I hadn't recruited him and didn't know him well. Jameson preferred to spend his time video gaming in his room, not on the extracurriculars I ran. I knew he was a strong psychokinetic though, and in his last year, he should've known how to teleport the box better.

"What happened?" Jameson's roommate, Weldon, ran over, his silvery shields stretching like a balloon around his thoughts.

Jameson shrugged and looked at the random books, papers, and weird items that had exploded out of the box, his shields turning gray.

"What did you do wrong?" I asked again.

"Didn't think about the items in the box, just thought of the box," he muttered.

"Partially correct," I said. "I bet you'll find you left some of the things behind. But you didn't think about where you were putting it. That's why it ended up halfway in the grass. Have you managed to teleport anything correctly yet?"

Jameson shook his head, streaks of black appearing in his blue shields.

"It's not a big deal," I told him. "I once put a book halfway through a closed window. And I left the pages behind. Destroyed the window. When you're teleporting, you have to think about where you're going to put the item and make sure there's nothing in the way. That's why it's so hard to learn."

"And why you're not supposed to teleport yourself," Weldon said.

"Yep," I said. "Go get a shovel from the gardening shed and clean this up."

"Yes ma'am," Jameson muttered.

Weldon smiled at Mateo as Jameson ran off. "You'll like it here, dude," he said, doing some sort of a complicated fist bump with Mateo the other boy somehow knew. "Name's Weldon if you need anything."

"Mateo."

"Cool dude. See you around." He ran back off toward the dorm with a wave.

"I forgot where we were," I said to Mateo. "Do you have the piece of paper with your dorm room assignment?

He waved the welcoming letter at me.

"Not that one." I said. "The one with the map on it?"

He searched his pockets, then pulled open the suitcase. I spotted his parents standing outside the dorm building and waved them over.

"Welcome to Phillip's Academy officially," I said, shaking their hands. "Now that it's the first day of school, do you have any questions?"

The mom glanced at her husband, the sun absorbing her dark hair, and I tried not to read their thoughts. But of course, it was impossible. They were Regs. They were sad their son wouldn't live with them, anxious about having an empty house, happy their son wouldn't accidently out them as being related to a Wild, and guilty about the thought. And of course, wondering if their son would be happy and safe here.

After another glance at each other, the mom asked the question.

"I can't answer whether or not Mateo will like it here," I said. "Being a teenager is hard. In brain development terms, teenagers are a lot like toddlers. They're testing limits, need others' acceptance and don't want to be told what to do, all combined with hormones. Add in a challenging curriculum and inadvertently reading the thoughts of others. These years will be hard, for you, and for him. But we're the only school for Wilds in the world. We genuinely care about our students or we wouldn't work here. Our teachers are highly trained, many of them Breds. I know we're a little run-down, but we'll help turn him into a successful adult in whatever way that means to him. Hopefully Mateo will be happy during his time here."

I watched his parents' thoughts swirl. I hadn't made them feel much better, but they needed to hear this. I couldn't let them go home with unrealistic expectations for their son's future.

Luckily, I had another speech.

"I know I wasn't as reassuring as you would've liked, but Phillip's Academy has been my home for nearly twenty years. I was a student and never left. Mr. Kaminski, the psychokinetic teacher, was my teacher. I've learned more than I could've imagined, made friends I'll cherish forever and have a career I wouldn't have had without this school. I'm amazingly lucky Director Phillips allowed me to come here."

The dad reached for my hand, vigorously shaking it with his calloused palm. "Thank you so much," he said. "He's our only child and we want to do the right thing."

We didn't know what else to do with him," the mom said. "He's gotten difficult this last year."

"Mom," Mateo hissed.

"I remember lying in bed, hearing my mom's thoughts. She was so worried about me," I said. "I'd promise not to use my Gift in school or where others could see me. But I didn't have enough control not to use it."

They thanked me again and following Mateo's found map, headed toward the cafeteria. I rubbed my temples, trying not to hear the thoughts of the new students and their families.

So many Wilds. I didn't think there were this many. We'd been told it was rare. There has to be over fifty here...

...box almost hit the kid. Is he okay? Oh wait, maybe all this stuff flying around is normal? Should...

... sort us into houses. No that's stupid. This isn't Harry...

I pulled out a bottle of blockers, pills developed to numb our Gifts, and dry-swallowed two. While I liked the numb and high feeling the pills gave me, they dulled my Gift too much and I tried not to use them. But I also hated to hear the thoughts of others, if they didn't want me to.

The bell rang, announcing lunch and half the people on the grass jumped. Miriam came over the loudspeaker and invited parents to join their child for lunch.

I pointed a few lost families toward the combination cafeteria, multi-purpose and industrial kitchen warehouse. When we'd moved onto this site, that warehouse was windowless with giant rolling doors. Ten years ago, we'd taken out the big doors and added windows, letting in sunlight and fresh air. We'd unbolted the circular, rectangular and square tables so they moved around the room depending on how the kids wanted to sit together. At the end of each year, we'd paint the walls a soft white and then let the students design and paint a mural. Last year, each student had painted a hummingbird. Some were huge and multi-colored, while others were tiny and plain. Most of them had names or inspirational quotes in the wings, or below or above them. Between the hummingbirds were flowers, trees and stars. It should've been chaotic, but it was beautiful and cohesive.

And was my favorite mural in years.

Today, the windows were open to the summer heat, letting in faint breezes off the lake and letting out the smell of cooked food and the verbal chatter of parents and the teens.

I grabbed a seat next to Kaya at the staff table. Her eyes were unfocused, but she gave me a quick smile before returning to her telepathic conversation. I was hungry but didn't want to wait in the line zigzagging out the door for food. Instead, I watched the kids grab food trays and find seats, smiling and laughing with their friends and family, showing off their Gifts, floating food and eating utensils around the room or into open mouths. We were always one tiny step from a food fight.

The colored shields and fogs floating around the room shifted. Stephen snaked through the student tables toward the staff one. He held a nearly empty tray of food, only salad, balanced by his Gift. I wondered what he was used to eating at Seagull's Landing. Steak? Sushi? Today we served grilled cheese or chicken salad sandwiches with chips and a green salad. There was Jell-O or thick slices of homemade chocolate cake for dessert. Nothing special, but it was filling, cheap and the kids liked it.

I put my elbow on the table, chin in hand and watched the other students watch Stephen. A fifth year untied her hair and shook it out. Other girls stroked on lipstick or giggled as he walked by. One of the fifth years even pulled the V-neck of her top down revealing even more cleavage.

Did you see that? Kaya asked.

Sue Beth? I asked, naming the girl showing an impressive amount of cleavage and willing Stephen to look her way. *She's always been...*

I didn't like to call the kids names. They'd been through enough and even if it was only in my mind, it was distrustful.

Flirtatious, Kaya added for me.

Stephen reached the main table and met my eyes. My heart rate increased. It was almost Pavlovian. No wonder the teenage girls reacted to him—I was old and jaded but still alive.

You get used to it, Kaya said. *The other girls will too. He can't help it. He doesn't have any control over what he looks like.*

I looked at the other teachers. Franny hid behind a book, Daniel stared out at the students and their parents, and Seiko the math teacher, stared at Stephen, a small smile on his lips.

Wipe the drool off your chin, I thought to him.

He startled, his striped emerald shields cracking like glass and then rebuilding. He winked. *I'd seen him on the internet but didn't realize until a few days ago how beautiful he was.*

I watched Stephen pick up a bite of salad coated with the ranch dressing I ordered by the barrel and could barely keep in stock. He made a face and put down his fork.

Guess he was going to buy his own dressing.

On the internet? I asked Seiko. *Doing what? Didn't he work at Seagull's Landing?*

Oh sweetie—he's a Rune.

My chin fell out of my hand, and I almost face planted onto the table.

Well, that wasn't embarrassing. Not at all.

He's a Rune? I thought to Seiko. *His last name is Rune?*

Where have you been? That's why Miriam's so excited to have him here.

What the fuck is a Rune doing here? He has plenty of money, he doesn't have to work.

Unless you're making more money than me, he's not doing it for the money. He's always at a charity event or volunteering. And, if you think he looks good in jeans, you should see him in a tux. Seiko stood up and paced to the back of the room. He must have spotted one of the kids about to break a rule.

But working here is different than paying a thousand dollars to eat steak and lobster somewhere, I thought.

Seiko shrugged. *You should ask him why he's here.*

No point. He's not going to last. Did you see his face about the ranch dressing?

No adult likes the—

A piece of chocolate cake launched off a tray and stuck to the ceiling. Fourth and fifth years rolled their eyes and went back to their lunches. The second and third years laughed, pointing, and the first years and their parents either looked shocked or amazed.

Daniel put down his coffee and Franny slid a bookmark into her novel, standing up. The cake fell off the ceiling and somehow landed on a table fifteen feet away from where it should've. The girls at the table squealed and their chairs scraped on the concrete floor as they stood up, shaking cake crumbs out of their hair.

I heard plates slide around on tables. The entire room paused for a breath.

Daniel stood up. "Enough," he said verbally and telepathically. "Lunch is over. Go get your rooms unpacked."

The chairs scraped on the concrete floor as trays were gathered, trash was thrown away and we herded the kids and their families out to the grassy area.

"Do you think the kids got enough food?" Franny asked. "Maybe we should serve a snack at three. Something fun."

"I think I saw some marshmallows and graham crackers in the pantry," Stephen said. "If we have chocolate, we can do s'mores in the microwave."

Yes! Franny thought. *Ever seen a marshmallow blow up in the microwave? We could make it a Moving Day tradition. Have a contest to see how big the marshmallows get before exploding.*

I envisioned the mess.

Maybe you should do that in a class, I thought. *I think the kids are fine. I'll make sure the dorm snack shelves are full.*

Sounds good, Franny thought. *I'll plan a lesson around exploding marshmallows though.*

Sorry, Stephen thought to me as we followed the kids outside to the grassy area.

For what? The s'mores? It's a good idea. Franny just has no filter. Whatever she thinks is what she says.

She's definitely a Value Bred.

She has a good heart and is an awesome teacher. The kids love her. She's not any better or worse than any of us.

That came out wrong, he said. *I think Franny will be amusing to work with. She's honest and loves her job. That's more than a lot of Breds I know.*

A window in the dorm building broke and a small fishbowl launched through it to land on the grass, miraculously intact, still full of water and with the fish barely disturbed.

I got it, Daniel thought, grabbing the bowl and marching into the dorm.

I'll get the window replaced, I thought. I kept stacks of them in the supply room. They were only single paned and let in lots of cold during the winter, but we went through too many to afford the expensive ones.

CHAPTER NINE

A FEW WEEKS into the school year meant established routines. The first years learned when to wake up if they wanted hot eggs in the mornings and what time we'd set all the leftover dinner desserts on tables in the cafeteria. They found out what time to shower so they had the most hot water, the absolute latest they could sleep if they wanted to get to class on time and how late they could sneak out of their rooms before the teacher on dorm duty caught them and told them to go back to bed.

I launched the clubs held after school and during lunches. Some students proposed new clubs and I restarted the clubs we'd paused during the summer. All of our clubs were student run, but I still had to make sure they did something, even if it was just drawing Anime in a classroom together or building an internet channel only watched by the Wilds at the Warehouse.

I also restarted the after-school classes. Kaya taught dance, Seiko art, while I taught theatre and music. Anyone could join, but they had to commit to classes twice a week for a month before they could stop. The only thing we didn't have, despite lots of begging, was sports. Miriam had outlawed them twelve years ago after the cheating got too out of control. It was just too easy for some Wilds, especially the fifth years, to manipulate balls and goals. But we let them play informal games of soccer or baseball in the grassy area, as long as there was no fighting or cheating.

Our school year started at the same time the Regs' did. Reg principals and teachers were on the lookout for Wild teenagers trying to hide their Gifts. In the fall, I usually got at least one email a week from a school suspecting they had a Wild and asking me to come out and evaluate. Most of the "Wilds" were difficult teens the administration wanted to expel. I loved telling those they didn't have a Wild, just a student that needed help.

But sometimes, they did have a Wild. And some of those kids joined us at the Warehouse, while others were removed from the Reg school to be homeschooled by their parents. Or their parents moved, telling their child not to use their Gift in front of others, hoping to get them through the school years without anyone realizing.

It was a normal day when I'd come out to Eagle Valley High School in Idaho and met the principal, Whaley. It was a few weeks before Halloween, and cars with hastily scraped frost still clumped on windshields waited in long drop-off lines.

Whaley was a huge man, and his hands swallowed mine when we shook. He wore jeans and a bright red t-shirt decorated with the school's mascot, a flying Eagle. His muscles stretched the seams of the shirt and his thoughts told me he doubled as the weight training coach.

The kids' and parents' thoughts and feelings washed over me, despite my shields. I sighed and tried to block some of it out.

...blood cells fight infection, white cells carry oxygen. Wait. Is it ...

...angry this morning. My arm hurts. Hopefully he went back to bed. What if he's still awake...

I fished a bottle of blockers from my bag and gulped two more. A floaty feeling already muddled my thoughts, making it harder to use my Gifts, but I had to do something. I couldn't tell which thoughts were mine and which were someone else's. This was an easy identification gig. I'd be fine. I'd figure out if there was a Wild, talk to the parents, see if the kid was a good fit, and head back to Phillip's Academy by lunch. Easy-peasy. I'd done it a million times.

A group of ninth graders passed by, looking tiny and immature compared to the seniors, interspersing the word 'fuck' with every other word. Seeing Whaley, they switched to 'freak', and 'frack'. I bit my lip to hide a smile. Reg kids, Wild kids, Bred kids—some things were the same.

"Sorry," Whaley said.

"About the cussing? I work with teenagers. That was nothing. Imagine being able to read what they're thinking."

I shouldn't have said that. Whaley's thoughts turned dark and he stepped away from me.

Fucking blockers.

A car driving past the school slammed to a sudden stop, the brakes screeching. The car behind him skidded into the oncoming lane and another car went up onto the sidewalk, narrowly missing a group of teenage girls. Everyone leaned on their horns as the girls squealed and tottered away on too high heels. A boy's backpack flew open, papers taking flight in the autumn wind.

Uh oh.

A Wild was leaking, affecting everything around them. This was completely uncontrolled and probably unconscious.

"You have a Wild," I told Principal Whaley. "And a strong one. Any idea who?"

He shrugged. I wished I couldn't read his thoughts. They binged back and forth between observations of the kids walking in, and concerns about having a Wild next to him. He also wanted a second cup of coffee, though he was trying to cut down and was sore from his morning workout due to 'tweaking' a muscle a few weeks prior.

Then his thoughts focused. "You won't turn him in, right? I mean, you swear you're from Phillip's Academy?"

"Yes. I won't give him to the Guardians or sell him into human trafficking. Do you want to come by Phillip's Academy sometime? Check out the students? They're pretty much like other teenagers."

"No, thank you." He said it automatically, turned off by the idea of being around so many Wilds. "Actually," he said. "I will think about it." And he would. He was trying and I appreciated that.

His mind gave me the image of a small ninth grader with brownish blonde hair and acne dotted cheeks. I almost said the boy's name but caught myself. Whaley knew I could read his mind, but I shouldn't be obvious.

I spotted the boy matching the principal's mental image, though his hair was dark with grease from not showering. If I focused, I could see the waves of psychokinetics coming off him like purple tentacles. Where the tentacles reached, the chaos went. I'd never seen anything like it.

"That's him?" I asked.

"Promise?"

"I do." I wished there were more Regs like Whaley. It was rare to meet one that cared this much about his students regardless of whether they were a Wild.

"His name is Leo Watson. Now what?"

"Let's bring him into the office and call his parents. I'd like to talk to them about his Gifts. I promise—if there's this much chaos here, there's more at home. They know he's a Wild."

"He lives with his dad. His mom ran off several years ago. As far as we know, they've had no contact with her. Do you think she was a Wild?"

Probably.

I shrugged and pulled out a set of mental cue cards. "Hard to say. There's definitely a genetic component to being Gifted. The geneticists creating Breds have proven it. But I think for Wilds, there has to be an outside event or stimulus to make our Gifts manifest."

And it was increasing. There were more and more children coming out as Wilds each year. And more and more Wilds with weak psychokinetic and telepathic Gifts, but irregular physical characteristics like my white hair and purple eyes. And then there were the kids with the extras, like Becca's skill with teleportation. I swore there were Wilds who could make plants grow and talk to animals, though Daniel assumed I was crazy.

"Leo," the principal bellowed. "Come here." I resisted the urge to stick my finger in my ear and wiggle it around. Leo turned toward us just as a redheaded girl pushed another blonde girl hard enough the blonde girl fell forward, her arms outstretched to catch herself. She landed painfully, calling out.

My stomach seized. It was impossible.

Regs always feared the Gifted, especially Wilds, because we were their children, their siblings, and their co-workers. There was always the fear we could manipulate thoughts and force people to do things they didn't want to. The Bred scientists said it wasn't possible.

But I'd seen Leo's purple tentacles coil around the redhead, just before she'd pushed the other girl. I gently scanned Leo, hoping he wasn't strong enough to notice. Leo's surface thoughts were full of guilt. He not only knew he was Gifted, he knew he could control others, but didn't know how he was doing it. He hadn't meant for the redhead to push the blonde, not really. But the blonde had laughed at him for something stupid he'd said the other day in English, and he was so embarrassed. But now the blonde was hurt, and he'd done that.

His dad was going to kill him.

I'd normally take him back with me in a heartbeat. I wanted to. His thoughts broke my heart. But if he could control others, there was no way. It was too risky. But someone needed to teach him how to use his Gift. Papers, leaves and hats flew around him in a manufactured wind. He was already leaking more than I'd ever seen, and someone would call the Guardians soon. I couldn't leave him here.

I tapped one of the tentacles with my shields, a gentle knock. *Hello.*

He froze. Then he ran.

Seriously?

"I'll be back," I said to the principal. I walked after Leo, refusing to run. Where did he think he was going? The school was in a neighborhood surrounded by houses and parks. He couldn't hide.

A kid with dreadlocks came at me, swinging his backpack like a bat. I used my Gift to slam up a physical barrier for the backpack to hit. The backpack fell and I jumped over it. The teen blinked, picked up his pack and headed toward a classroom. I walked faster, using my Gift to track Leo's purple tentacles. He was running across the football field.

You're safe, I tried thinking to him. *I won't hurt you. I'm here to help.* I wasn't sure how much he could understand, but I figured if he could control people, he was a strong telepath.

A custodian came at me, waving a mop—I ducked beneath it,

turned around and grabbed it away from the man. He blinked at me. "What?"

I handed him back the mop. "Sorry," I said. Someone, probably me, was going to get hurt if I didn't stop the boy. I teleported to Leo and projected a physical barrier in front of him. He ran into it and dropped to the ground, cradling his nose.

Whoops. I helped him up, checking out his nose. It wasn't broken, just bruised and barely bleeding.

"You're okay," I said. I pulled a spare towel out of my bag and handed it to him.

"How'd you appear out of nowhere?" he asked around the towel. "Thought you weren't supposed to do that."

"Practice. But it's dangerous, so don't try."

Now what? I knew he could control people with his Gift. But I couldn't take him with me, not without Miriam's permission. I didn't need another write-up.

I wracked my blocker-fuzzed brain. We couldn't stay here. I should take Leo home, explain what happened to his dad, and then ask Miriam what to do.

"My name is Kendle," I started. I pulled off my beanie so he could see my white hair. "I work at a school called Phillip's Academy for the Advancement of Wilds."

The purple tentacles were twined around the boy, creating a bubble of a shield around him. It was incredible. I wondered what else he could do.

"We teach Wilds how to control their Gifts in addition to general education," I said.

I always felt a bit like Hagrid in Harry Potter when I told kids this. Unfortunately, I wasn't offering a magical castle and yearly bouts with He-Who-Shall-Not-Be-Named. I was offering a second option in a world without many options for Wilds.

"I could go there?" he asked.

Great. Here was where I fucked up with Becca. "Maybe," I said. "We'd have to talk to your dad."

"My dad won't care. He doesn't like me anymore."

Wow, that was a lot to tell a stranger. I wanted to tell him it wasn't true, but he'd probably read it in his father's mind. This kid was going to need lots of counseling.

"Okay. But I still need to talk to him. You can't just disappear. Does your dad know you're a Wild?"

Leo shrugged, his eyes on the ground.

"How about we call your dad and talk to him?"

"I didn't mean to have Skylar push Ivy," he said, the words running together. "I just think of things and people do them. But not always. Like this one time, I tried to get my math teacher to draw a happy face on the board, just to be shit-faced funny, but she—"

"Leo."

"Sorry," he said. "I shouldn't have cursed. Are you like a teacher at the Academy place?"

"I'm a recruiter. I promise, I'll answer all your questions, but—"

He froze, his purple tentacles turning tarry with fear. I glanced over my shoulder. Black uniformed Guardians headed in our direction.

Fuck-fuck-fuckity-fuck.

"Don't run again," I said both verbally and telepathically. "It'll make it worse."

"But what—"

"I'm going to teleport us away. We'll figure out where to go from there." I hoped the blockers wouldn't interfere too much. This could really hurt. "And then we'll go talk to your dad. Don't be scared and don't pull away."

Before Leo could say or do anything, I took his clammy hand and teleported. Teleporting was hard, teleporting others was really hard, but teleporting under blockers was nearly impossible.

The world swayed as we reappeared in the middle of the street.

A horn blared and we jumped out of the way of an oncoming car. The driver shouted "Fucking GAFUs" out the window and flipped us off. Swell. He was probably contacting the Guardians. I wiped my nose, my hand coming back red. I felt blood dripping from my ears.

"Oh my god," Leo said. "He called us GAFUs."

I had a killer headache and was bleeding from my nose and ears. And the kid next to me was freaking out because someone called him a GAFU, which stood for Genes-All-Fucked-Up, a horrible slur for

Wilds. On top of that, I didn't know where we were, and I was lucky I hadn't hurt Leo. I felt cold. I could've killed both of us. Maybe Miriam was right. Maybe my decision-making sucked.

Leo held out the bloody towel I'd given him. I wiped my nose and ears on an unused corner.

"Okay, dude," I said. I pulled up a map on my phone. We were a few blocks from the school. "We're safe for the moment. Do you have a phone? Can you call your dad? I need to talk to him."

"What do I tell him?"

"Tell him my name is Kendle and I'm from Phillip's Academy. He can look up our website. We need to figure out what to do with you."

"Am I expelled?"

"Probably," I said. "Someone called the Guardians. They won't want you there anymore." I started walking away. We needed to get far away from the school before the Guardians found us.

"So, yes I'm expelled?" he asked, his tentacle shields pounding in time to his heart. It didn't make my head feel any better.

"Yep."

"Can you call my dad for me? He'll be too mad." He held out the phone, the purple tendrils reaching out toward me.

"No," I said using my physical and mental voice. *And don't ever do that again.*

Leo paled, the tentacles circling around his thoughts. "I didn't mean to," he whispered.

God, this kid needed someone to teach him control before he hurt someone.

"Call your dad," I said. "We'll figure this out." I stepped away to give him some privacy.

I reached out with my Gift, and it made my head hurt worse. *Miriam, I have a question.*

Miriam's magenta shields were faint. *Unless it's an emergency, you'll have to wait. There's a situation here.*

What's going on?

Nothing we can't handle, but I need to focus. Unless you've been arrested, you'll have to wait.

I'll connect with you later. Change of plans; I would talk to the dad and then Miriam.

Leo stuffed his phone into his pocket. "I left a message. No answer."

"Do you know where your dad works?"

"Duh."

I raised my eyebrow.

"He works at a hospital," Leo muttered.

"Doctor? Nurse? Tech?"

Leo looked off into the distance, red creeping to the underside of his shields.

"Leo?"

"He's an assistant."

"Like a P.A.? Physician's assistant?"

"Like a director's assistant. She makes him work really long hours. Even the weekends. He's always taking calls from her." Leo thought an admin assistant was a girl's job. And he hated his dad's boss. I wondered if it was Leo that hated her or his dad.

After some more back and forths, I used my phone to order a car to take us to his dad's work. Even with the blockers muddying my thoughts, I wasn't stupid enough to teleport both of us again.

The car found us a few minutes later and as a bonus, the driver didn't say anything about our blood-stained clothes. His thoughts told me he figured we needed a hospital. I looked down at the blood from my nose on my new pink blouse. Awesome—just how I liked to meet parents.

CHAPTER TEN

"WHERE TO?" I asked Leo once we'd been dropped off at the hospital entrance.

He shrugged. "Don't know."

"Can you try calling him again, please?"

We stepped into a corner away from the noise of the hospital lobby. I thought it was weird how hospitals made their lobbies look like a living room, with soft, padded couches, coffee tables and fake flowers everywhere. But it couldn't change the fact that hospitals were places of bad news. Mists of reds, oranges, rancid greens and dark navies swirled everywhere, tangling up in hair, riding on shoulders and twisting around ankles. I didn't know how anyone could stand to work here.

Leo stuck his phone back into his pocket. "No answer."

I was getting annoyed.

"Do you know the name of the director he works for?"

"Indira someone?"

I pulled out my own phone and went to the hospital's website. Luckily, Indira wasn't a common name and I was able to find her on a 'Meet our Directors' webpage.

"Her?" I asked Leo, pointing to a picture.

He shrugged. "Maybe."

I was going to strangle him. Quitting my job and moving to a Caribbean island to bartend sounded perfect around now.

I walked over to the information desk and smiled the professional smile I used on parents. "Hi," I said to the older woman in a pale blue uniform sitting behind the desk. Her badge told me she was a volunteer and that she spoke Patwah. She was also upset Debra got the best location to sit at, and she was stuck in the stupid ER where she had to see way too much blood. I pushed her thoughts out of my head.

"Can you help me? I'm looking for Indira Dewan. She's a director here. Can you point me toward her office?"

I was to take a right, then immediate left, straight for a while, take the third right in the circle kind of like a roundabout, and if I hit a door saying employees only, then I should turn around and take the second right. I finally asked her what Indira's office was close to and if there were signs pointing us there. She told us her office was close to Pharmacy 2, but not Pharmacy 2A, which was in an entirely different building.

We passed nurses and doctors in scrubs with booties over their shoes and their hair in fluffy white nets, thinking about their coworkers or worrying about their patients. We passed rooms named after donors and slightly faded quotes from staff reminding patients the hospital really did care about them. And through it all, the smell of cleaning supplies tried to cover up the scents of blood, sewage, sweat, sadness and fear.

I hated hospitals.

We turned a corner and saw a Guardian standing next to a patient in a wheelchair. The patient was obviously sedated. He wore a hospital gown and bands, dull gray metal and plastic bracelets that sedated your Gift and tightened painfully if you tried to use it. The scars on mine, Daniel and Seiko's wrists were from bands. I ran my thumb across the raised ridges and swallowed, pushing back the memories of the Gladiator Ring and the gang I'd joined before coming to the Warehouse.

Leo stuttered to a stop.

"Let's see if we can find another way," I said. We backed down the hallway and went through a service door to the parking lot. From there, we found a different entrance and a different volunteer who actually walked us to Indira's office.

I knocked on the door as the volunteer went back to her desk, and then again when there was no answer. I tried the door—locked.

What would I do if his dad was in a meeting or off site?

We heard the clack of high heels approaching. Two people turned the corner, one older and graying in a wrinkled shirt with a bag over his shoulder and a notebook in his hand. The other was a woman, beautiful and perfect as only a Bred could be. Leo's father worked for a Bred.

Of course he did.

CHAPTER ELEVEN

"Leo?" The man said, surprise echoing in his thoughts as he shifted the bag onto the floor. The flap popped open and I saw it was stuffed full of notebooks, two screens and post-it notes.

The Bred gently touched my shields with hers, greeting me. Her shields were an exquisite golden color with tiny jewels of turquoise, sapphire, ruby and emerald throughout. Her surface thoughts glided between the jewels, peek-a-booing just a bit. And she was physically beautiful too, with clear fawn skin, huge dark eyes with thick eyelashes and high cheekbones. I wondered if she looked like her parents or if her parents had checked the Bollywood box when paying the geneticists.

She ran her eyes down my body, taking in my white hair and bloody shirt.

"Is this your son?" she asked the man. I fought not to roll my eyes. She had an English accent, which had to be fake because Europe completely condemned the creation of Breds.

The man took a deep breath. "This is my son Leo and..."

"I'm Kendle May," I said, shaking both their hands. "Leo had a bit of a...situation at school and we wanted to talk with you about it."

You're not a Bred. You're a Wild.

Holy shit. The accent was even in her thoughts. What. A. Fake.

I work for Phillip's Academy for the Advancement of Wilds, I told her and winced, wishing the name was better. I hated this instinctual desire to impress her, to make her like me.

I steadied myself by thinking of her parents sitting in a room with a geneticist, telling him they wanted their daughter to have so much charisma people would want to worship her. She must have been a horrible teenager.

I think I've heard of that school. It's supposed to be...shoestring...quaint and perfect for Wilds. She'd mentally crossed out the word shoestring, but I still heard it rippling through my mind.

We do our best, I responded. *But funding is always a problem.* My mental voice was sugar sweet. *We're a non-profit and always looking for donors. As I'm sure you know, there's a tax incentive. Here's a brochure.* I pulled one out of my bag and offered it.

She raised an eyebrow, while the jewels in her shields sparked out. She wasn't used to being spoken to that way.

I'll talk to my accountant. She gave me a sympathetic smile. *It seems like you've had a rough day.*

You have no idea. I offered a small smile and dropped my eyes to the ground. Then I wondered what I was doing. I wasn't going to let her charisma control me.

And it can be difficult for Wilds to do things we Breds take for granted, she continued. *I understand lifting small objects or even basic telepathy can cause trauma to your Gift, such as nosebleeds. I can find you a scrub top if you'd like.*

Fuck her—I'd teleported two people on blockers, without killing us. Let's see her do that.

Meanwhile, Leo and his dad were having a hissing discussion about what had happened and who I was.

So, Charles's son is a Wild? Indira asked me.

I can't confirm that.

She smiled at me, a smile without teeth, a conference room smile. *I understand,* she thought. *That's disappointing though. I'll have to let Charles go.*

Why?

Because I can't have someone who is related to a Wild working for me. I'm responsible for the research arm of this entire health system. I handle sensitive information and need someone one hundred percent focused on their position. I can't worry the boy would overhear something confidential in his father's thoughts and tell his friends.

I couldn't believe it. She'd actually fire someone for having a Wild child? Were things really at this point?

But being a Wild isn't something we have control over, I thought. *And Regs can't control if they have a Wild child. If Charles is doing a good job, then his son being a Wild shouldn't change things.*

Bloody reds leaked through Indira's golden shields, winking out the jewels entirely.

I also have had a terrible day. What I do with my employees doesn't concern you. Having a Wild family member isn't a protected class.

But if you fire him, we can't charge tuition for his son. Know how we're "quaint"? It's because we keep having to offer free tuition to everyone because Regs related to Wilds can't get jobs.

The jewels blinked back again through the blood. Indira nodded, a quick bob. *Fair point. I will think about it. If you take the child with you, would he have contact with his father?*

Only what they both want.

And presumably you're teaching the students ethics and morality of using their Gifts?

Some of Kaya's English assignments were about ethics and morality and we claimed it was a part of the curriculum. But our primary focus was on teaching the kids control before they destroyed the buildings or read our thoughts.

Of course, I said. *We do it through class discussion and reading assignments. Have to sneak it in or they're not responsive.*

I guess that makes sense. You are dealing with students without a lot of education. I'm sure their parents don't explain the responsibilities accompanying our Gifts.

Why did everything she said about Wilds in her fake English accent have to be insulting?

Their parents weren't expecting their child to have Gifts.

Exactly. Very well, if you take the child, I will continue to employ Charles. He has been a decent assistant and I would hate to lose him.

Great! Now I just had to convince Miriam to take on a student who could control people with his Gift.

Totally doable.

"Charles," Indira said. "Why don't you take the rest of the day off? Use the time to figure out your family situation."

Charles paled. "We have a presentation to prep for tonight. I just need a few minutes."

She shook her head. "Your family is more important." She went into the office and closed the door behind her.

Liar, liar pants on fire.

Charles stuffed his hands into his pockets, looking down at his shoes. Leo mirrored his pose, his purple tentacles gray and wrapped around himself.

"Let's go outside," Charles said. "There's a coffee cart and some benches to the left of the parking lot."

Leo and I found the benches in a little alcove cut off from the parking lot by potted trees while Charles waited for coffees. The leaves had fallen off the trees and lay around the pots in wet clumps of brown mush.

Leo sat, drooped over, his hands hanging between his knees, fighting tears.

"We'll figure this out," I said. Then I cursed myself. I shouldn't have promised that. I couldn't bring him back with me. I had to follow protocol, talk to Charles, leave Leo with him, then go and talk to Miriam. He may not be able to come to the Warehouse—Miriam may not let him.

Miriam?

Not now. I'm expelling someone.

My chest froze. I hoped it wasn't Becca.

Who?

Jameson.

For what?

I'll explain later, but I have to focus. She broke the connection.

Now what?

Charles came back with a coffee for him, a tea for me and a soda for Leo. He was more resigned, his thoughts carefully constructed. Someone had taught him some meditation techniques.

"Explain again what happened," he said to Leo.

Leo told how he'd run away from me and accidentally outed himself as a Wild to the school. He left out the part about forcing the redhead to push the blonde.

I jumped in. "The school already knew he was a Wild. That's why they'd called me in. Yes, this could've gone differently, but in the end, we'd still be having this talk today and he wouldn't be going back to school tomorrow."

"And who are you?" Charles asked.

"My name is Kendle May. I work for a school called Phillip's Academy for the Advancement of Wilds."

Charles nodded. "I actually looked you up the other day. I was thinking of giving you a call." He took a sip of his coffee. "What is it you do?"

"Recruitment, admin duties and after school activities."

"I saw on your website there are a lot of clubs."

"We have over fifty different clubs, all student run," I said. "Then we have classes like music, dance, art and theatre in addition to the regular curriculum. Our students leave with the equivalent of a high school degree and learn how to control their Gifts."

"I read all that on your website and agree it's the best place for Leo. Unfortunately, I can't continue to care for him and keep my job. You have my permission to take him, and I'll pay whatever tuition my income requires. Send me the paperwork and I'll write a check."

Leo looked like he'd been slapped, and the purple tentacles of his shields stretched out toward his dad.

Don't, I told him.

The tentacles retreated.

"Dad, can we—"

"This sounds like the perfect place for you. I'll pack his things tonight and send them to the school," he said to me. "You can take him with you right now; there's a transport pad in front of the hospital. But I really do have to get back inside. My director needs me."

Wow, Indira had fried his brain with her charisma. No wonder Regs were so scared of the Gifted.

"Unfortunately, we don't accept every student. Safety is a huge concern and—"

"Wait, after all this, you may not take him?" Charles stood, looming over me. "He was expelled because of you and because you came here, I might lose my job."

"Wait, you're not going to take me?" Leo had gone white. "But you have to. He doesn't want me anymore."

"Leo, we have to choose each student very carefully," I said. "Not everyone—"

"You heard him. Work is more important." Leo stood up and my coffee cup trembled. A phantom wind blew my hair into my face.

"Leo," I said verbally and telepathically.

The display of napkins and coffee stirrers on the coffee cart fell over and full bags of chips whipped into the air.

I touched Leo's arm. "Leo, I need you to get control."

The glass doors to the hospital cracked. "Leo!" I fished around in my bag. I carried emergency sedation syringes for this reason. "Take some deep breaths or I'll have to sedate you." I pushed him down to the bench and linked my eyes with him. "Breathe and tuck your Gift away," I commanded.

Leo held onto my eyes and we breathed in and out together. The breeze died down and he looked away.

I pushed my tangled hair out of my face. "At the risk of causing more problems, I have to tell you Leo's Gift is unique," I said to both of them. "I've never seen anything like it. It's danger—"

"Which is why you have to take him with you," Charles said. "You don't understand what you did bringing him here.

"Actually I do, but—"

Guardians appeared around the building and headed toward us.

Fuck-fuck-fuckity-fuck. They'd found us. They must have assumed I would go to Leo's only family and gotten the address from the school.

The Guardian in the lead was tall and slender with her blonde hair shaved on the sides, and the rest pulled into multiple thick braids.

I'd dealt with her before. She'd "detained" me a year ago for being out in public, claiming I was using my Gift without approval, which was a lie because I was on the Registry. As long as Wilds were on the Registry, they could use their Gift in public. But for some reason, her scanner wasn't working, so she arrested me to "confirm" the information. The Warehouse lawyer had gotten me out, but I'd spent hours locked in a cell, handcuffed with bands tightening on my wrists.

They'd never let Leo go once they figured out he could control people.

Hello Amanda. I stood and greeted the Guardian. I barely resisted calling her Amanda-the-Ogress-Hag to her face, as I'd renamed her in my head. Amanda was a Value Bred proven by the faint acne scarring on her cheeks and the basic rust colored bubble around her shields.

May. What's going on here?

Just doing some recruiting.

Were you over at Eagle Valley High School this morning?

Sometimes recruiting takes me into the schools. It's permitted, if I'm invited.

And were you?

Of course.

She looked at Leo and Charles. "Are you Leo Watson?"

Leo nodded, his purple tentacled shields stretching everywhere. The park bench under him vibrated.

Awesomeness.

Deep breaths, I told him. *Think about something you like doing, like video games.*

"Amanda," I said. "He's an untrained Wild and you're freaking him out. You know what could happen."

"People like you shouldn't be out in public," she said. She turned to Leo. "I understand you caused a disturbance at your school. We can't permit that."

Charles grabbed my hand. "Please, help him."

"Sorry Amanda," I said. "His father just signed the papers to enroll him." Miriam was going to kill me. "We were just finalizing the details. Once the kids are enrolled, you can't touch them."

"He should go on the Registry."

"That's not mandatory."

My boss is working with the OOG to get the rule changed.
But it hasn't happened yet. You can't touch him.
I could arrest you. And him.
For what?
Being Wilds. That's enough now. God only knows what you're doing to these poor scared Regs, she sneered. She hated Regs too, thought the world should be Bred only.

"Is there a reason the Guardians are here?" Indira asked, stepping outside, a wallet in her hands.

"I'll get your coffee." Charles jumped to his feet.

"There's no need," Indira said, with a smile of a princess to a favored servant. "I needed a breath of fresh air. Can I help you with something?" she asked again, looking at Amanda, her smile strengthening. Amanda smiled back and dropped her eyes.

"Not at this time," Amanda said to the ground.

"Then please leave. You're causing a scene."

Amanda nodded, and backed away, not turning her back on Indira. She disappeared behind a building, probably heading for the transport pad.

"Thank you," I told Indira.

"Has the situation been resolved? I could use Charles' help if he's not going home."

"Yes," Charles said.

"Yes," I said and fished the paperwork out of my bag. "Sign away. And I'll need to come back tonight for further paperwork," I said to Charles. "The director may want to meet you. Will you be at your house at eight tonight?"

He looked at Indira.

"I will make sure he's home by then."

"Thank you," I said, touching her beautiful shields with mine.

It was not a wasted interaction, she thought. *I've never thought too much about Wilds, and you've raised some fascinating areas for reflection.* "Good luck, and I will be in touch for a donation."

I nodded, resisting the urge to drop my eyes, bow and back away.

CHAPTER TWELVE

LEO and I stepped off the transport pad and onto the Warehouse property. He had his school backpack full of books he'd no longer need and his shirt, his only shirt right now, was still bloody from his nose. Leo's shields pulsed with anxiety, fear and sadness.

Charles had tried to give Leo a hug, but Leo had stepped away, refusing to look at his father. Charles locked his emotions away, and left, carrying his boss's coffee back into the hospital, secure with a job he'd almost lost.

I hated it.

"Are you hungry?"

Leo shrugged, though his tentacles flashed red at me. Must be a yes.

"Let's head to the cafeteria then. I have to talk to my director, but I'll have another student do a tour and we'll find you a room. Okay?"

He shrugged and used the movement to wipe his eyes and nose on his shoulder, pretending he had an itch. Fifteen-year old boys don't cry.

I acted like I didn't see it and started lecturing. "Phillip's Academy for the Advancement of Wilds was founded twenty-two years ago by our Director Miriam Phillips. Phillip's Academy for the Advancement of Wilds is a terrible name, so we call it the Warehouse, but not in front of her," I cautioned.

We moved down the path away from the admin building toward the cafeteria. "In the beginning the Warehouse was an after-school program, a place where Wilds could go to control their Gifts. But Mrs. Phillips quickly realized Wild children needed more. Too many of us were expelled from schools, ran away or lived on the streets and a supplemental after school program wasn't enough. So, she talked her Bred friends into either giving money or teaching here. She fought for accreditation, for the licenses to house and feed Wilds here. Two years after she started the school, we moved to this location and gradually moved into all the warehouses, buying and modifying them however we wanted."

As I spoke, Leo's tentacles calmed down, wrapping around his thoughts, the color mellowing to lavender. He wasn't really listening, but that was okay. I just wanted him to think about something else.

We entered the bright cafeteria; its windows open to try to catch a breeze off the lake. Sunlight lit up the mural, highlighting the hummingbirds and the words of hope. Classes had just ended and half the tables were full of kids eating snacks and studying. I heard verbal conversations and felt the ripples of telepathy. Books, screens and board games floated around the room, along with the occasional pair of sunglasses or lipstick.

The word "cool" pulsed through Leo's thoughts.

"Grab something to eat," I told him. "We don't charge for food. If you're hungry, just take it."

I walked over to a table of fifth years as Leo inspected the snack shelves.

"That's Leo," I told them, pointing him out with a head bob. "He needs a tour. Do you guys know where Weldon is?" Weldon was great with first years.

The kids at the table exchanged looks and I felt the echoes of their thoughts.

"What happened?" I asked.

"So, basically, it's like this. Jameson was selling stuff," said Samantha, a pretty Wild with blonde hair, blue eyes and sunny shields.

"What kind of stuff?" I asked.

Samantha shrugged. "Like alcohol and pot." She held up her hands. "I never bought any. None of us here did."

The kids at the table nodded, but their shields told me differently. Great. I'd have to tell Miriam.

"So, he's like not here anymore," Samantha said. "And Weldon's pretty upset, so he's in his room."

"Gotcha," I said. "Listen, I have a favor to ask. Leo's new here and just came out as a Wild. He got expelled today. Can one of you take him on a long tour? I have to meet with Mrs. Phillips."

Tom, a fifth year with shields like cotton candy, raised his hand.

"I'll help too," Samantha said.

"Thank you. He's had a rough morning," I said.

"That's pretty normal for our first day here," Tom said. "But then it turns into our best day."

I smiled. A social worker had contacted me about Tom as she was processing him for an institution. His parents had turned him over to the Guardians—a scared and skinny boy who'd never wanted for anything, until during a typical argument about doing the cat's litter box, he'd shattered their enormous saltwater fish tank. His parents had driven him to the nearest Guardian station and dropped him off without a suitcase or even saying goodbye. He only had a weak psychokinetic Gift, but it spiked with his emotions if he didn't use it constantly. As long as an employer didn't check the Registry, he'd be able to pass for a Reg when he graduated.

One more thing, I thought to Tom. *And please try to keep this to yourself. Leo can...be careful...his Gift is odd. Please let me know if you see him doing anything...different.*

Different how? Tom asked, with a frown.

Just weird. You know how us Wilds are, I thought. *Thanks again.*

I introduced Leo to the others. Leo was guzzling his second soda and munching on spicy Cheetos, his fingers already red with the dust. Samantha laughed and handed him a napkin.

"Nice. I have a spicy Cheetos obsession too," Tom said. When I left, Tom was telling Leo which day the groceries were delivered (Wednesdays) because it was the day the best snacks came out.

I crossed to the admin building and knocked on Miriam's closed office door.

"Come in," she called out. Stephen and Seiko were inside, sitting in the chairs before her desk. As always, it took a few seconds for my brain to stop stuttering in Stephen's presence. I couldn't wait until I got used to his good looks. Seiko winked at me, though his normally emerald shields were tinged with a sad blue. Miriam sat in her desk chair, her shields subdued and wrapped around herself. She was tired and worried.

"You didn't have a choice," Seiko said. "A suspension would've sent the message his behavior was fine. Then others would've tried the same thing."

"I know." She took off her glasses and set them next to her, rubbing her palms into her eyes.

"Kendle," she said. "Were you having a problem?"

"Yeah, and I need to talk to you."

Miriam nodded at me. "I think we're done," she said to Stephen and Seiko.

They said their goodbyes and left.

I'm going to hit Atomic later tonight, Seiko thought, naming a Wild bar in the middle of Chicago. *I need a drink, wanna come?*

No thanks, I answered, though I knew I'd need a drink later, too. But getting dressed up and leaving the Warehouse didn't sound like fun.

Let me know if you change your mind.

Invite Stephen. At this point he should be an alcoholic like the rest of us. I sat down on the chair vacated by Seiko.

Or a pothead.

Or both, I joked.

Can you imagine him at Atomic? He wouldn't be able to swallow a time-suck-bomb.

He made faces at the spaghetti on Thursday night, I thought. *We should totally do a field trip sometime. It'd be good for him.*

Do we have to invite him? I mean he's total eye candy, but he's no fun. He just works all the time.

Sounds like the rest of us. I'll talk to you later. I closed the connection.

I crossed my legs in the visitor chair before Miriam's desk. My head pounded as I came off the blockers, my Gift gradually returning to full strength.

The flowers on her desk were shades of blue today, varieties I couldn't name, but they went from near white to near black and everything in between.

"Do you want the good news or the bad?" I asked.

For a second Miriam's shields crumbled, turning gray and ashy before rebuilding.

"I'll take the good news first," she said. "Though it looks like you had a hard day."

"I know," I muttered, picking at a bloodstain. "I really liked this shirt. Anyway, we have a new student."

She sighed. "Without running it by me? I thought we talked about this with Becca."

"Yes, and I tried a few times to contact you."

I explained how Leo had run, how someone had called the Guardians, how we'd gone to his father's work and Charles' reaction to us showing up. Then how the Guardians had threatened to arrest Leo.

"I had to use our get-out-of-jail-free card, or he'd be with them now. And even then, the Guardian didn't want to let him go. It was that Bred I've had problems with. Amanda-the-Ogress-Hag. You may get a complaint."

"I remember her from last time. But it sounds like a tricky situation."

"I didn't know what else to do. And I did try to contact you."

"I know. If there's a complaint, I'll handle it. Running from the Guardians and having his father turn him over to us to prevent an arrest isn't the best introduction for that boy."

"Yeah, he was crying when we got here."

"Poor thing." I wasn't sure the label worked for a fifteen-year old boy, but I let it go. "Where is he now?" she asked.

"Tom and Samantha are giving him a tour."

"Those are good kids."

Miriam stood and went to the window. I could just see her thoughts. She was worried the hot water heater in the dorms was going out and of the leak someone had reported in one of the classrooms. She was disappointed and sad about having to expel Jameson.

"What happened with Jameson?" I asked.

"I hate you reading my thoughts." Miriam didn't turn back from the window.

"I know. So, what happened?"

He was running a black market. Miriam's mental voice was so tired. "His brother, his Reg brother, was shipping in alcohol, pot and prescription drugs. Then Jameson sold them to the students."

I groaned. "And we don't inspect packages from family members."

"Which is going to change," Miriam said.

"Naturally." I could see my workload increasing already. The kitchen and janitorial crew wouldn't have the time. "The kids haven't been acting drunk or drugged or anything, though some of the ones in the cafeteria lied about not buying anything from him."

"There's a drop off spot in the cafeteria so the kids can turn in their purchases without consequences. Then we'll inspect the dorm rooms. Seiko, who discovered it, thinks it just started." Miriam turned back from the window and sat down. She moved the picture of her husband by an inch. "So, to summarize, you went out of order bringing Leo here without checking with me." She put her hand up as I protested. "Though I know you tried. And you think he'll be a good fit here? You did scan him, right?"

"I did. And there was nothing. But his Gift is...different. I've never seen anything like it."

"So that's the bad news?"

I swallowed and ripped off the Band-Aid. "I think he can control people with his Gift. That's why I couldn't let the Guardians have him."

Miriam's shields exploded in colors of magentas and grays. She stood up and paced back to the window, staring out into the grassy area in the middle of the campus. Her shields were paper thin with exhaustion. Everything was cracking and she was out of tape to hold it together.

"If the Guardians took him, they'd never let him out again," I said. "Never. He's fifteen. And scared."

Miriam bowed her head.

"I tried to contact you. I didn't have a choice. His father won't take him back. If we kick him out, he's just another Wild teenager on the streets and he'll be dangerous one day if he doesn't learn control. He was leaking already. This is the only place for him."

"So, you put a child that controls others with a bunch of emotional teenagers who are telepathic and psychokinetic?"

"We can teach him to manage it. And his dad can pay tuition."

"And you didn't run this past me?"

"I did try."

Miriam leaned her head on the glass. "So your two choices were to bring this child here, putting our entire campus, the students and us at risk? Or allow the Guardians to detain him and then go through the proper channels to try to get him back, assuming we felt we could contain his Gift safely?"

"We never would've gotten him back."

"We never would've risked our students. I'm becoming concerned by your decisions, Kendle. You're not thinking of the entirety of the school, you're only thinking of the individuals."

"But that's what we do. Every Wild is an individual and no one cares about us, except...us."

Miriam came back to her desk and took a sip of water not saying anything. She was thinking about what to do with me.

My heart pounded and the familiar pain in my chest started. I took a deep breath, and another trying to calm down. The water in Miriam's vase sloshed back and forth.

"I agree I messed up with Becca," I said. "Bringing her here without doing a superficial scan. But she was just desperate. She's only thirteen."

"Becca teleports out of her classes at least once a day, which distracts everyone and then she has to run back from wherever she went to, which is further distracting. We're lucky she hasn't destroyed the molecular stability of our buildings."

"We've had students with harder Gifts. There was that firestarter five years—"

"Who I nearly expelled after the third bed he set on fire."

"Nearly. He worked so hard with Daniel and me to learn control and now has an admin job at a Reg firehouse. And he's a volunteer fire-fighter." My hands were sweaty. I twisted them together. "He's a perfect example of what Phillip's Academy can do for Wilds."

Miriam's shields turned crimson. "Consider yourself under proba-tion," she snapped. "You may not bring any student here without my permission and you will run all recruiting actions through me before doing anything. Any. Thing. Am I clear?"

"Yes."

"When recruiting you will have another teacher with you to aid in your decision-making skills."

"But— "

"I cannot have you continue to put the lives of our students in jeopardy by only thinking of the individuals. You're lucky I'm not asking for your resignation. Am I clear?"

My stomach dropped and black spots appeared in my vision. I had tried, but I just couldn't leave Leo. "Yes," I managed.

"Go find a bed for your new student. Then finalize the paperwork and bring it to me. I will go tonight to talk to the father and get the final signatures. Am I clear?"

"Yes ma'am."

CHAPTER THIRTEEN

IT WAS after midnight and I couldn't sleep. I'd gone back to work and triple-checked all my work. Then I'd gone for a run until my legs shook. I'd come home, showered and tried to watch an internet show. But none of it helped the anxiety clawing at my chest or the tears randomly falling. And my Gift leaked. I couldn't stop liquids from whirling around me. So I'd retreated to the roof of the admin building. Over the years, the faculty had found the flat roof a good spot to hide in an overcrowded campus without much privacy. Eventually, we'd moved camping chairs, lanterns and even a mini-fridge out. We kept it locked in case the students stumbled on our hideout, but none ever had.

I took a pull on the joint I'd snuck up, breathing the smoke into my lungs and blowing it out. I waited for the numb feeling, and for the anxiety to release, but it didn't come. I took another pull and watched the smoke disperse, wiping my tired eyes on a tissue. I wondered when I would run out of tears.

I couldn't believe how angry Miriam had been. I'd tried, I really had. I'd learned from my mistake with Becca and contacted Miriam about Leo. She wasn't available. I spent the whole morning saying Leo couldn't automatically come to the Warehouse. But when Amanda-the-Ogress-Hag showed up, I just couldn't leave Leo.

Right?

Fuck, fuck, fuckity-fuck.

A feather brush to my shields made me sit up in my camping chair. I used my sleeve to wipe my runny nose and eyes; my tissue had fallen apart a while ago. Stephen stood outlined in the security lights of Chicago businesses, holding a bottle of wine and a single glass.

Do you want company? I can leave if not.

Company actually sounded good. And from him. Guess miracles could happen.

I used my Gift to slide another chair out from under a storage tarp and set it next to me. *Join me. The stars are really bright tonight.*

He sat down, leaning back. *The ones we can see are. There's a lot of light pollution here. But Venus and Jupiter are out.* He pointed out two bright stars.

I didn't know we could see Jupiter without a telescope.

Only on some nights. He's not always visible. A second wine glass appeared in his hand and he passed it to me. *Seems like you need this.*

Why not? It wasn't like the pot was working. And I'd take anything that might help right now.

I passed him the joint, but he waved it away. I pinched it out and stuck it into a pocket for later.

Do you want to talk about it? he asked, the turquoise and green shifting like waves in his shields.

I'm sure you already know. I took a big sip from my wine. The flavor of sweet grapes with an undercurrent of raspberry exploded on my tongue. I took another sip. I'd never tasted anything like this; it was like drinking an alcoholic jam. *I'd rather talk about something else,* I thought. *What do you think of the Warehouse?*

I hate it here.

I knew it. Knew he wouldn't be able to handle the long hours, the Wilds, and the shoestring budget.

I can't believe you're admitting that already, I thought to him. *Though I get it. This is a hard place to work.*

Wait. What am I admitting? The transition has been a little more difficult than I expected, but I'll adjust.

Whoops. I'd seen a private thought, only visible through his shields because he was thinking about it constantly. Well, this was embarrassing. I took a giant sip, the thick wine coating my tongue.

Sorry, I thought. *I think I saw something you didn't mean for me to. Sometimes I just get through shields, some sort of a Wild thing. Be careful what you think around the kids.*

I've been teaching for a while. I know how to shield my thoughts.

Obviously.

I took another sip of the sweet wine. I lifted up the bottle to look at the label like it actually meant anything. It was a port, which I'd never had.

What did you test at for your telepathy? he asked suddenly.

Wilds don't test.

That's right. I'd forgotten. I'm going to talk to Miriam about that. We should test at the beginning and end of each year to see if the students improve.

We know they improve when they stop breaking things.

His thoughts chuckled at me. *True. I would've guessed you're strong at psychokinesis. You can teleport almost as well as Becca, and you have more control.*

I snickered and didn't know why. My wine glass was nearly empty, and he topped it off. *Everyone has more control than Becca.* I stretched my socked feet in front of me. A toenail with chipped polish poked out of a tiny hole. I put my other foot on top of it. *You can teleport right?*

Of course.

He was quiet, taking a small sip of his wine and holding it in his mouth before swallowing. I was probably committing some offense slugging the wine. Knowing Stephen, port was probably expensive.

There's no music tonight.

What?

Someone plays music at night. Or several someone's. Sometimes there's multiple instruments. I can hear them in my living room or up here if they have their window open.

Whoops.

Um, that's me, I told him. *I'm sorry. I try to play quietly so not to bother you and Seiko.*

So that's why the apartment next to yours was open. He refilled my glass.

I winced. *I switched my bedroom and living room and play in the bedroom space so I didn't keep Seiko up at night. You shouldn't be able to hear me in your bedroom. Have I been keeping you up?*

It's my favorite part of living here.

A puff of air escaped from my lips. He hadn't meant for me to hear that thought either. Maybe he'd been drinking before he'd come up here. I shouldn't be in his private thoughts so easily.

You're amazing. And can you play multiple instruments with your Gift?

I'm sure some Breds can too.

You'd be the first I've heard of. How many years did it take you to figure that one out?

It's weird. I took another sip and the stars blurred. *I can pick up any stringed instrument and know how to play it, with my Gift and without.*

He turned his head toward me. *That's not weird, it's amazing. Why are you here? Why aren't you a professional musician?*

But as he said the words, I could tell he knew the answer. *Because you're a Wild.*

Home run. My blood buzzed pleasantly, and I wondered what I'd been so upset about earlier. Everything was going to be FINE. Nothing bad would happen. Miriam had just been stressed lately. I would just talk to her in the morning. It'd fix everything.

He refilled my glass. When had it gotten empty? And when would we run out of wine?

How's Leo? I asked.

Amazing, in a frightening way. I've never seen anything like him. It shouldn't be possible to control another human without their consent. There have been rumors in the S&M communities, but in the end, it's about consent. Yes, the...participant was being controlled, but if they withdrew their consent, it stopped.

Really, Stephen? S&M?

There was enough light for me to see him roll his eyes which made him attractive, not mind-blowingly handsome.

I did a bunch of research about Breds being able to control people with their Gifts. It came up.

Whatever you say. I closed one eye trying to get the two Stephens to merge into one. *But Leo needs control,* I thought, trying to focus my brain.

He does indeed.

I had to bring him here. I couldn't let the Guardians...we'd never get him back. They'd put him in the bands, drug him and house him in one of those institutions.

Our glasses were nearly empty again and he used his Gift to refill them, not moving from his inspection of the stars.

"The Warehouse isn't for everyone," I blurted out, my voice loud in the night air.

I know. That's why Miriam is so insistent on not bringing in challenging students, like Leo.

Well, that was borderline nasty. I drained my glass, telling myself I was being too sensitive.

"Sorry," he said, his voice loud in the quiet night. "I'm just tired." He was too. His shields were gray tinged. Off in the distance, a helicopter rattled, and we faintly heard the loudspeaker demanding someone put their hands up. *This is just so different than I expected. I knew it would be hard, but not like this.*

Why'd you come here?

I was bored.

Seagull's Landing has an unlimited budget and rich students. We're so broke I had to cancel our dairy shipment for next week.

"We're not going to have milk next week?"

"Not next week. I have to find a new supplier."

He pressed his lips together. "That's ridiculous. We need a better source of income. Maybe a fundraiser or something."

"Tried it once. Didn't help."

"Maybe you didn't do it correctly."

I nodded. He was probably right.

We're not for everyone, I tried again. *We've had a lot of teachers leave, some after only a few months. It's not going to get any easier. Winters in Chicago are cold, and the buildings are hard to keep warm.*

Are you saying I should quit? I've never quit anything in my life.

There's a first time for everything. I pulled the thought back before I sent it to him and hoped he didn't see a hint of it in my shields. Instead I shrugged.

You probably think only Wilds should work here.

Nope. I finished the last of my wine. *But I do think Wilds understand Wilds better than Breds. And Wilds need the jobs.*

What about the exposure of having me, a Rune, working here? Having me here will increase donations.

You can do that anywhere, even back at your job at Seagull's Landing if you wanted. You could go back to eating steak and lobster every night, instead of chicken casserole made with frozen chicken and peas bought by the pound.

We didn't get steak and lobster every night.

I bet you got nights off and had a lounge, not on a rooftop with broken camp chairs.

He finished his wine. *True.*

If you don't like it here, go back to your life. It's not going to get better.

He stood up, the camp chair squawking in the night. *I won't quit. Why don't you want me here?*

I stood up too. The world tilted and I floundered, finding the back of the camp chair so I didn't fall.

"I was trying to help," I said out loud. "Stay and be miserable. Leave and be happy. I don't care." I crossed to the stairs and clumped down, too drunk to teleport. Out of the corner of my eye I saw Stephen throw himself back into his camp chair with a frustrated groan.

It was a terrible day.

CHAPTER FOURTEEN

I SAT at my desk in my office, my head in my hand. I had already taken four ibuprofen and was on my second cup of coffee. I had forced some dry toast down to absorb the meds, and surprisingly, had not thrown it back up.

What was in that wine?

Leo had spent the night on a cot in a two-person room and that wasn't going to work for tonight. I needed a new plan. I tried to focus on shifting students around to find a bed for Leo among the other fifteen and sixteen-year olds.

Holy shit, I was going to throw up. I used my Gift to shift the trashcan and leaned over. My stomach lurched and settled back down. False alarm.

A knock on my door frame made me look up. Stephen stood there, his ocean-like shields wrapped around his thoughts.

I think I owe you an apology for last night. A beautiful bouquet of flowers, with tiny purple blossoms, and big yellow sunflowers in a crystal vase, appeared on my desk.

For what? What had happened last night?

Hasn't anyone given you flowers before as an apology for being a jerk?

I tried to think past my headache. Had anyone? My relationships had always been casual and argument free. What had he done that made him a jerk? And what I had done?

"I'm sure someone's gotten me flowers," I said out loud, my head pounding in time with my words. "I probably owe you an apology too, though I don't remember much."

He grinned, the expression turning him human.

I like him better this way, my libido muttered.

Have you ever had port before? he asked.

I shrugged and tried to focus. *Probably not. I'm not much of a wine drinker.*

Then I owe you double the apology. Port is strong and not meant to be drunk in one sitting, even shared. Can I get you some pain pills?

I took a bunch already. Why aren't you hung-over?

He hesitated. *At risk of arguing again, my genes don't let me.*

Again? Oh no. I must have gone off about Quality Breds versus Wilds. Whoops.

I have to drink a lot to get and stay drunk, he continued. *My parents increased our tolerance and metabolism to alcohol. They thought it would allow my siblings and I to enjoy work functions and expensive drinks without embarrassing ourselves, but instead increased our chances of becoming alcoholics. But that's beside the point. And I have a class in a minute. But I'm sorry if I offended you last night. You were just offering advice and trying to help.*

I was glad he thought so. What had I said? "Don't worry about it," I said.

But I'm not leaving.

Had I said that? It was pretty shitty of me, even if I did think he wasn't going to last long.

Sounds good, I thought. *It's hard on the kids when their teachers leave mid-year.*

He raised a perfect eyebrow. *That's not what you thought last night.*

Maybe I owe you some flowers too.

He laughed and my heart thumped. Stupid hormones.

It's all good. We'd had a rough day yesterday. Feel better and enjoy.

Thank you. I will.

He left and I moved the vase to my windowsill, shifting the angle so the largest sunflowers looked out at me. I couldn't think of anyone bothering to get me flowers before.

CHAPTER FIFTEEN

THE SEASONS HAD OFFICIALLY CHANGED, and the mornings were cool. Leaves skidded through the doors and gathered in slippery puddles. We ate on tables too close together, the clearest sign to me the seasons had changed. Half the cafeteria had been turned into a haunted house for Halloween, built, maintained and staffed by the students for the other students. The room reeked of paint, plywood and canned tortellini.

So, you've never been to a haunted house? I asked Stephen. *You didn't do one at Seagull's Landing?* I couldn't imagine Halloween without a haunted house in the cafeteria.

Never. The students put on costumes and jump out at people, right? In addition to all the blood and spider webs? I can't wait.

The haunted house can be pretty dorky, I thought. *The kids work really hard on it, but sometimes they go too far with the fake blood and body parts.*

And we have to patrol it and make sure no one is using a dark corner to make out, Seiko added. *And then the kids try to scare us.*

I laughed. *This one time Franny—*

An echo rippled out through the cafeteria and the faint chatter of thoughts increased. It was October, so shielding was better, but the thoughts pinging around the room were red and orange tinged. Kids gathered around those with screens.

"Something happened," Seiko said, standing up. I pulled out my own screen, a red bar telling me there was "Breaking News."

Filling my screen was an image of a building on its side. Police and ambulance lights reflected on the dust floating through the air. Emergency personnel ran around, pointing, shouting, and helping dusty and injured people out of the rubble. In the corner of the screen, a perfectly made-up female reporter spoke into the camera from the news studio.

"—appear to be survivors. We thank God for our emergency personnel. We'll be talking to some of those heroes soon. We do not have a casualty or survivor count yet—"

I took a sip of my iced tea, wishing they would just come out with what happened, rather than trying to make things as dramatic as they could be.

"—Guardians are here, at last. We—"

"Oh no," I said. "Not another one." I knew what had happened. Someone had imploded from not using their Gift. They'd bottled it up, until it exploded out of them, destroying the building and probably killing people. Someone had either been pretending to be a Reg or had lost control.

"We should tell the kids to stop watching this," Stephen said, rising.

"Why?" Seiko asked. "It could be their future." But he also rose, his emerald and black striped shields shattering and rebuilding.

The camera crew moved the lens in close to the Guardians carrying a limp someone out of the rubble. He or she, it was hard to tell because of how covered in dust they were, was handcuffed, with the dull gray bands and had a chain connecting their feet together.

"—haven't identified the perpetrator, but it does appear as if the Guardians have made an arrest." She touched her earpiece, frowning. "I'm pleased to announce the perpetrator of this terrible act has been identified, but seeing as how he's under eighteen, we will not release the name until his family is notified."

"Enough," Stephen said to the suddenly quiet room. "Put down your screens and head to your next class."

I'm sending the students to their classes a few minutes early, he told Franny, Miriam, Kaya and Daniel. *They shouldn't be watching the news.*

This is so horrible, Kaya thought. *I'm grabbing my stuff and will meet the kids in my room.*

On my screen, the Guardians went to move the person into a van, where he'd be taken to a transport pad. For an instant, we saw his face, blood and dirt distorting the features.

My heart dropped and I paused the feed.

"Oh my god," Daniel and I thought together, for once perfectly synched. *Jameson,* I whispered in my co-workers' thoughts.

Seiko's shields went fully black. *What?*

I think it's Jameson, Daniel thought.

A bunch of fifth years gasped, staring down at their screens. They'd seen Jameson too.

I stood up and clapped my hands. "Everyone head to your classrooms."

"But Ms. May," Weldon said, tears in his gray eyes and glacial-like shields pale and unmoving.

"I know," I said. "Head to your class and we'll talk there."

The kids went to their classrooms, quiet, their shields blue and gray. The other teachers canceled their lesson plans and let the kids talk, yell and cry in the classrooms. They talked about Jameson, about the Guardians and about implosions. Then classes were dismissed and the kids either sat in their rooms or went to the cafeteria or dorm common areas to talk more. I checked periodically on the kids in the cafeteria. They'd watched their screens, talking quietly or crying. But there were lots of hugs and students with arms around each other too.

Later that evening, we met in the admin conference room, watching our screens for more updates. We'd reached the interview point of the disaster, with experts pulling apart the details and offering their opinions.

"I have with me Director Jenkins from the OOG, the Office of Gifted, to talk about this incident and previous implosions of Wilds. Director?" said a news anchor.

The camera cut to the handsome Quality Bred director, his amber eyes contrasting with his dark skin. "This sad event highlights the importance of something I've been working toward in the OOG." He folded his hands on the table, next to the required coffee mug, proving how serious he was. "We need more federal protections placed against Wilds. It's not safe for them to be in the general population. My current goal is to introduce legislation to test for Wilds in schools, removing them from the Reg population as soon as possible, to protect—"

Seiko used his Gift to throw a pen where it embedded in a wall. I jumped. "But what the fuck will you do with us, once you've removed us from schools, you idiot?" Seiko shouted.

Kaya pulled the pen out of the wall. "Seriously," she muttered. "You're as bad as the kids."

"Wilds can't be trusted around the general population," Director Jenkins continued. "And we can't continue to risk our buildings falling down because a Wild gets angry or—"

"Then propose funding to help us learn," Seiko screamed. "You monkey-fucker. How about legislation to send Wilds here instead of locking them away?"

"So, what is the OOG proposing to do with Wilds once they're removed from the schools?" the anchor asked.

"Unfortunately, the best way to control Wilds is to institutionalize them, as we've always done, with people who are a risk to themselves or others."

"A risk to themselves or others?" Seiko yelled. "All Wilds are a risk?"

"But the expense would be astronomical. And the taxpayers would be responsible for it," the anchor stated. "And what about the Wilds already in the general pop—"

Miriam's voice cut through Seiko's yelling. "That's not helping," she said, coming in with Daniel. Her magenta shields looked like the rest of ours, dark and heavy. Her cheeks were pale with new lines etched in her face. She looked ten years older. We all did. We turned our screens off.

We had to expel him, right? Seiko thought to me. *I had to say something to Miriam? I couldn't hide Jameson's black market.*

Of course not, I thought. *You did the right thing.*

I said he should've been expelled. What if I was wrong? What if I caused this?

You did nothing wrong, I responded. *Jameson was turned over to his parents. They obviously weren't letting him use his Gift or he wasn't using enough of it. But it's not your fault.*

I looked around the table. Kaya's face sparkled with tears and Stephen's arm was around her, his shields a dark gray. I put my arm around an openly weeping Franny and Seiko leaned on me. I put my arm around him too.

Miriam cleared her throat and swallowed. "I..." she licked her lips. *We need to keep it together.* "I mean..."

Daniel spoke. "I know we're all feeling confused, sad and angry. But we don't know why this happened. We don't know what caused him to implode. We don't even know if he caused the building to fall." Kaya reached for Miriam's hand as Miriam took a deep breath. But Miriam moved her hands off the table, leaned back and raised her chin.

"You did tell the family, right?" Seiko said. "About what could happen if he didn't use his Gift at least a little?"

"Of course I did," Miriam said. And in that moment, I saw her shields pulse with the lie. She couldn't remember whether or not she'd said it. She'd been so furious with Jameson, she couldn't wait to turn him over to his family and search for all the drugs and alcohol.

"Our number one priority is our students," Miriam said, her chin still raised, and her words calm and measured. She straightened her glasses, pushing them up her nose. "We can get the kids to counselors if they need them, but I think we should be prepared for any students wanting to talk to us. Meeting over." Miriam stood up.

Daniel took a deep breath, his honey-colored shields thick and blocking his thoughts. "So do y'all want to have classes tomorrow? Normal routines? Or cancel them and let the kids do what they want?"

The debate lasted twenty minutes as Daniel intended it to and gave us something to think about, to discuss, to bond over and make decisions. In the end, we decided to have classes, but let the kids talk about Jameson and the office of the OOG if they wanted.

Miriam dismissed the group again and as the others grabbed their screens and jackets, I touched Daniel's shields with mine.

Thank you.

We all just needed some grounding. We're a good team and here for the kids. Don't worry about what the asshole from the OOG was saying this morning. No matter how scared Regs get, the government won't let them lock us up.

But in the past, others had been locked up for being different, for causing problems, I wanted to say. But I chickened out.

I nodded at Miriam's empty chair. *Is she okay?*

Daniel and I walked out of the room together. *It's not for me to say,* he thought. *But things are going to be bumpy for a few months. Hang in there.*

Anything I can do?

He turned to look at me, really look at me, his brown eyes searching my face. For a second, I thought I felt his honey shields lean into mine.

Just keep doing what you do, holding us all together.

CHAPTER SIXTEEN

THERE WAS a snowstorm the first week of November, which was early for Chicago. I pulled jackets, scarves, hats and gloves out of the storeroom for kids without the money to buy any. We broke out the board games for the weekends and evenings with games of Monopoly, Risk and Munchkin spanning several days in the cafeteria. Seiko promised to protect them with his life and put a locking cover over them to prevent anyone from messing with them while the players were absent. I had one of the crafting clubs come up with a trophy for the winners, which kept them busy, too.

The dorm hot water heater finally died, but a healthy donation from Indira Dewan helped us buy a new one. I sent her a nice thank you card, signed by all the kids and faculty. Stephen said he would take care of thanking her further. Apparently, he knew her from events they'd attended together.

Small world.

A mixture of rain and snow pattered against the windows in the conference room as we met for our weekly meeting to go over issues we were having with students or the facilities. The conference room was my favorite room in the Warehouse. On the walls were giant presentation size papers with post-it notes of ideas all over them. A few years ago, with the help of a freelance project manager, we'd organized all our ideas on post-it notes, written with different colored pens, creating a patchwork of colorful ideas. It was too bad we'd never had the time or money to make them happen.

"Last item on the agenda," Miriam said, looking up from her screen. The meeting had lasted four hours, it was after eight p.m. and we were all brain-fried, tired and hungry.

"It's a quick item," Miriam said, shooting Daniel a dirty look when he obviously stifled a groan. "Do we do the shopping trip this year?"

"Why are we even asking?" Seiko said. "Isn't it part of the curriculum?"

Miriam rubbed her eyes behind her glasses. "It is, but I worry about safety. The anti-Gifted agenda seems to be growing. There are more and more protests about keeping the Gifted, even Breds, away from Regs."

"There was the one Wild family found murdered in the park," Franny said, looking up from the doodle on her screen.

"But Regs have and always will hate us," I said. "The kids have to adjust to that before they graduate."

"But it's getting worse, or at least the media is focusing more on it," Kaya said.

"It's always been that way," I said with a wave of my hand. "We've always had to watch out for Regs. Nothing's changed."

"Do you even watch the news?" Daniel snapped.

"When was the last time you left here?" I snapped back.

His honey colored shields flickered, hurt rippling across them.

"Sorry," I said.

He rubbed his forehead. "No, I'm sorry. I was rude first. Miriam, it's time to stop. We're all too tired."

"Five more minutes," she said. "I hate leaving things on our agenda. And we have to make a decision about this."

"What is the shopping trip?" Stephen asked.

"We're not the 'real world'," Seiko said using finger quotes with an eye roll. "A lot of the kids don't leave until they graduate."

"So there's transition challenges," Kaya said, her long earrings swinging back and forth with the movement of her hands. "To help, we take kids with good control out several times a year to a casual place for lunch, a mall and a grocery store. They learn not to use their Gifts under any circumstances, and how to interact with Regs."

"It's an important part of the curriculum," I said.

"But our biggest priority is to keep our students safe, so I think we should eliminate it until things in the real world," Miriam nodded at Seiko, "Calm down."

This is not a five-minute conversation, Seiko thought to me.

Nope.

I'm so tired. She should just put it up to a vote, not have a whole debate. I have all this grading to do.

I'll help.

You're beautiful. Appreciate it.

"Miriam raises a good point," Kaya said. "We did have the Guardians called last time."

"That's because we took all the fifth years," Seiko said. "All sixteen. Even when we split them into two teams of eight, it was too obvious. A smaller group this time would be better."

"I'm not a fan of the Guardians," I said. "But the kids have to learn how to talk to them. Follow instructions, don't argue, don't do anything threatening. That type of thing."

"Bottom line, the kids need to be taught how to be out in the Reg world," Stephen said. His voice was deep with exhaustion, which only made it more melodic. My libido asked what it would be like to wake up hearing his voice. I blinked and refocused. God, I was tired.

"Right," Seiko said, pointing at Stephen. "So they need the shopping trip."

"They're with one of us, right?" Stephen asked. "We're not just dropping them off somewhere?"

"Two of us go with them," Daniel confirmed. "Any more brings too much attention. And I agree with Seiko," he continued. "Our students need the tools to succeed and the shopping trip is a tool."

Miriam's shields spiked and her lips turned down. She looked around the table. "Does anyone agree with me?"

"I think the shopping trip is a good idea," Kaya said.

"Me too," Seiko and Franny chimed at the same time.

"I understand the safety concerns," Stephen said. "However, our students have to deal with those after graduation regardless. I think if we take precautions, they'll be safe enough."

Miriam looked at me. We hadn't talked much since she'd put me on probation, though I'd never received a formal document or anything. But I was scared of making a mistake and giving her a reason to be done with me.

"Kendle, your thoughts?" Miriam said. "You go out into the real world all the time. We ended up with Leo because a Guardian was going to arrest both of you, am I right?"

"True," I said. "But I think the kids need as many tools as we can give them. Our goal is for our students to succeed in the real world. Interacting with Regs is part of that. I vote for the shopping trip."

God, I hoped she wasn't too mad at me.

Miriam pursed her lips. "Here's what we're going to do. I'm only sending four students and two professors. Kendle and Seiko, you're voluntold."

"What?" Seiko said. "Kendle and I went last time."

"And you can go this time." Miriam stood up. "This Saturday morning, please take four students out. Kendle, I want the list of the stores and the city you're going to go to, on my desk at eight a.m. tomorrow, along with the list of which students you'll take, how long you'll be gone and your travel plans." I looked at my watch. It was nearly nine p.m. now. If I used last year's plan it wouldn't take too long and I could get a few hours of sleep.

"Wait," Daniel said. He looked at Miriam, and I felt the echoes of telepathic conversation. Everyone else stood, stretching and gathering their screens.

This sucks. I have a comedy gig on Saturday night, Seiko thought. *I was going to work on my set that day.*

We'll be back in time. Or see if someone will trade with you, I thought. *Maybe Stephen.*

Seiko looked at the telepathy teacher, his shields turning more emerald. He was crushing bad on Stephen. *He's too handsome. Everyone will know he's a Quality Bred.*

Then Franny.

You want to go shopping with Franny? He raised an eyebrow.

"Ten is fine," Daniel said as Miriam swept out of the room, not saying anything to the rest of us.

"What?"

"You can get the lists and stuff to Miriam at ten tomorrow." He rolled his neck and left.

"Anyone want a nightcap?" Kaya asked. "My apartment?"

I shook my head. "Promised I'd help Seiko with his grading. Next time."

"I, too, have grading," Franny said.

"Why not?" Stephen said to Kaya. "But just one drink. It's getting late. And I probably have grading too."

"What do you grade?" I asked Stephen as we walked out of the conference room and went up the stairs to our apartments. "I don't think the last telepathy teacher did anything that required written homework."

"I have them write essays on the ethics of using telepathy."

Well I guess that answered Indira's question about anyone teaching ethics.

CHAPTER SEVENTEEN

BENEATH OUR FEET, the metal hummed and then we were on a transport pad in a small town in Maine. Traffic buzzed around us, and even with recent environmental laws, sent pollution shimmering up to the tops of the tall buildings. Reg pedestrians hurried past, either glancing to see who appeared on the pad, or ignoring us outright.

Seiko and I had chosen Samantha, Tom, Weldon and Leo for the shopping trip. Seiko and I had a long debate about allowing Leo to come, but we needed a Wild who was older, had recently spent time around Regs and would be able to help the others understand why Regs did what they did. And Leo was stable—as far as any of us could tell, he wasn't controlling anyone. It was like he'd figured out how to shut down that part of his Gift, without any help from us. We'd take it as a win.

Vertigo from the pad kicked in and I grabbed onto the rail. I wasn't the only one—the other kids and Seiko held on, breathing deep. A Guardian clutched my elbow, steadying me.

I jolted and he smiled.

"Thanks," I said, surprised.

"Happens to a lot of people." He was young, probably in his first year as a Guardian. His parents had chosen blond hair, skin that tanned easily and big chocolate eyes mimicking his shields. He wasn't a Quality Bred, he was good-looking in a normal way and not handsome in the god-like way Stephen was.

"I hate transport pads," I said.

"Me too. And you wouldn't believe who I've seen throw up after using one." He bumped my shields with his chocolate ones before letting go of my arm to help the teens off the pad. He checked our names off his list.

"Kendle May, Seiko Kalani?" He glanced up from his handheld at us.

"Kendle," I said just as Seiko said, "Guilty."

The Guardian snickered, then checked the four kids off his list. "You're all from Phillip's Academy?"

The kids nodded or shrugged depending on how they felt about a Guardian speaking to them.

"Where are you heading?" he asked.

"Shopping. We're going to leave through the transport pad up on 5th street," I said.

"I need a list of where you're going."

I pulled out my screen and pointed out the coffee shop, mall, restaurant and grocery store, all in a five-block radius. "Do you really need all this?" I asked him as he stared at my screen.

"I do."

Sorry, he thought to me. *They're getting really strict with Wilds.*

This is ridiculous, Seiko thought in a private channel. *We're not doing anything wrong.*

I know. Hold on.

What do we do if they don't let us off the transport pad?

Talk to Miriam and head out next weekend.

We should've brought a Bred with us. His black and emerald shields looked muddy.

The Regs hate them too. And the idea is to let the kids feel what it'll be like when they graduate. They won't have a Bred with them and need to figure it out.

I know. But after our meeting I started watching the news. Did you hear about the Wild teenager lynched and hung off a playground? This grandmother with her two—

The Guardian handed back my screen. "I appreciate you letting me look at the list. It seems appropriate for Wilds."

"No worries," I said. *If something goes wrong, can we contact you?* I asked.

He nudged my shields with his chocolate ones, and I realized, too late, he thought I was hitting on him.

Of course. I'm done today at seven, if you want to meet for coffee later, ummm...I'm sorry, I forgot your name. His cheeks flushed and he looked at the screen again. The colors in his shields shifted. *I mean, I'm sure you're busy. I mean, I see you're on the Registry for Wilds. I hadn't noticed...I mean...* He squinted again at the screen. *I mean you're not even a teacher, you're like a secretary...isn't that what an administrator is? Sounds like a really busy job. You're probably pretty busy. I mean, totally get it if you're too busy.*

Jesus. Guess his parents hadn't spent money on his personality. Must be why he was "just" a Guardian. I took a deep breath, pushing my temper down. I couldn't get angry with a Guardian. *I am busy and I love my job. Thank you for the offer, but I wouldn't be able to meet you. I have to get the kids home.*

Relief flickered through his shields.

"Let's go," I said to the kids.

We moved off the transport pad and through the gate into the pedestrian traffic.

The kids moved slowly down the sidewalk, window-shopping in the touristy downtown, until we hit a traffic light and had to wait our turn. The traffic roared past us and the kids were subdued. Even Tom, who normally laughed at everything or made everyone laugh, was quiet.

Don't forget to use your verbal voices, I thought to the teens. *Most Reg teens aren't this quiet.*

What happened? Seiko asked.

Nothing, I told Seiko. I wanted to forget the conversation. I felt so slimy. I wasn't interested in the Guardian but felt like I'd done something wrong.

Not even a teacher. Seriously?

Seiko touched my shields, a virtual hug.

He thought you were a Bred, didn't he?

I don't get how. I look nothing like them.

You're pretty, like the value ones are. And with your eyes behind contacts and hair hidden, you could pass for a Bred. Not Quality, obviously. But you could pass.

Is there a compliment somewhere in there?

This time he did put his arm around me, a quick hug. *You know I adore you. Don't worry what some crappy Bred thinks. Besides, you wouldn't want to date a Value Bred. If you're going to sell your soul, go for a Quality one.*

————

We entered the mall through the huge glass doors, pausing off to the side, watching the Regs hurry in. Some wore designer clothes, clacking by in their heels, looking for the next fashion, while others slouched in oversized sweatshirts and torn jeans. Couples strolled hand-in-hand looking for something to do. On this Saturday morning, moms and dads pushed strollers and dragged toddlers.,. A group of teenage Regs passed by us, laughing loudly. The mall echoed with voices, and was scented with the food court processed food, plastic clothes and perfume. The Regs' thoughts broke against our shields and I let the kids acclimate to them.

...entrance? It's so far away from the can...

...behave this time. God, I should get a coffee first, so I don't fall asleep. That was so emb...

...a pink dress. No wait, pink looks awful with my hair. Should I get my hair do...

I have blockers if you need them, I thought to the kids. *But use this time to work on your shielding. Blockers numb your Gifts, so you may be unable to defend yourself or find out if someone is targeting you.*

Take some deep breaths, Seiko thought. *Push the Reg thoughts away but stay open so you can learn if someone suspects you're a Wild.*

The kids' shields gained strength and became almost wall-like, each of them in their own way. Weldon's looked like an ice wall, Tom's looked thick, pink and sticky, Samantha's like a garden maze and Leo's was a giant purple bubble, the tentacles carefully wrapped around his thoughts. Stephen was doing his job well.

"Let's go in here," I said, indicating a store popular with teens, carrying shirts, hats and other pop culture paraphernalia. They went in eagerly, moving down the crowded aisles, oddly silent. I focused and felt the echoes of telepathy. Tom pointed out a shirt, with a double entendre stamped onto it and Samantha laughed, her hand over her mouth.

Don't forget to use your voices, I reminded them.

Fifteen minutes later, Weldon and Leo had purchased shirts, hats or magnets they thought Seiko and I didn't understand and couldn't wait to show their friends. Leo had bought hair dye and make-up for men. Samantha had raised her eyebrows at the purchases and refused to buy anything.

Boys are weird, Samantha thought to me.

"Boys are weird," I said out loud with a meaningful look. "That never changes. But they usually stop smelling once they hit eighteen."

"Dude," Weldon said. He fist bumped me and grinned.

We went to a few more stores then took a break at the food court, standing at a tall table to munch on cinnamon and chocolate chip cookies, still warm from the oven. Our kids watched the Regs in the packed food court or stared at the brightly colored moving ads trying to get our attention. It was noisy, verbally and my head ached with the effort of tightening my shields against the thoughts of the Regs. I was seriously considering taking a blocker, just to numb things a little. But if something happened, I wouldn't be able to help as well.

So far, so good, Seiko thought to me.

Everything is fine, I responded. *We overreacted for no reason. Two of us for a whole four students is definitely overkill. Next time we should bring eight and split into two groups.*

A tall thin cry from an infant cut through the noisy chaos.

Weldon craned his neck. A baby wearing a pink dress with a fat matching bow on her head screamed in her stroller. The mom moved the stroller back and forth trying to sooth the baby while she ordered a toddler to "please, please just eat one more bite of food."

"Poor thing," Weldon murmured. "That baby has an ear infection and is in a lot of pain. I can just see it."

"That's terrible," Samantha said. "I'm going to tell the mom." She stood and started to move toward her.

"No," Seiko and I said at the same time.

"But—"

"Sit back down," I said.

"You can't," Weldon said. He put his arm around her, like a boyfriend talking to his girlfriend and whispered in her ear.

"But I can feel it," she whispered back. "How can you stand it?"

"Because it's the only way you survive," Seiko said. "We can't let the Regs know who we are."

"But we're not doing anything wrong."

We're not supposed to use our Gifts where others can see, I thought. *They'll call the Guardians and you could get arrested. Let's go.*

We balled up our trash and headed to the next store. I looked back at the family. The mom had weak pale blue shields around her. They were poorly constructed, holey and rimmed with exhaustion. She was waiting for an older child to finish a birthday party and knew her daughter had an ear infection but couldn't afford the co-pay to see the doctor. Her judgmental mother-in-law was bringing some baby Tylenol and God, she was hungry. She'd only had enough money to buy lunch for the toddler. And he wasn't even eating. What was she going to do for money? She was on the Registry and no one would give her a job.

I pulled out of the Wild's thoughts with a faint gasp, my heart breaking. I rubbed my chest. I wished I could just wave a magic wand and fix this family's life. There had to be something we could do. I should bring it up to Daniel and Miriam. Maybe we could offer adult classes on shielding and controlling psychokinesis. Might be a good revenue stream.

In the next thirty minutes as we headed to the third floor of the mall, the kids' energy level faded. As did their shielding. I passed out blockers to Samantha, and then gave one to Seiko.

I'd forgotten how bad it is, he thought, dry swallowing the pill. *I don't think I can handle being around this many Regs.*

"Last store before lunch," I said, leading the group into a clothing store full of cheap, but fashionable trends. Seiko disappeared into a bathroom, while I stood off to the side, watching the teens grab clothes and hold them up deciding whether or not they'd try them on, or put them back on the rack.

An older woman approached me and stood, watching the kids. I gently probed her thoughts. She had teenage grandkids and wouldn't be spending any time with them at the holidays. Her daughter had just started a new job and couldn't get the time off work. The woman was sad, but proud of her daughter's career.

"Are they all yours?" she asked.

I chuckled. "None of them. I promised my sister I'd take my niece and one of her friends out shopping. All of a sudden, there's four teens crowded into my SUV."

The woman giggled. Her hair was gray but cut close in a trendy and attractive look that went with her sharp blue eyes. "Teens can't go anywhere without their friends. Last year I wanted to take my grand-daughter out to dinner, just the two of us."

"Fun," I said. *Pretend I'm your aunt if this lady's still talking to me when you're ready to go*, I thought to Samantha.

"But somehow I ended up with my granddaughter, her boyfriend and their best friend."

"Auntie," Samantha interrupted in a fake English accent. "May I please purchase this?" She held up a truly awful jacket covered with fake flowers.

"It's your money, my dear," I said, not missing a beat.

The woman watched our interactions with a small smile.

"I'd best get back to them," I told her. "Nice talking—"

A laughing Tom held a pink blouse to his chest and asked if it made him look beautiful. He backed into a display of jewelry, and it fell.

Let it—

Too late. Tom and Weldon caught the display with their Gifts, one of them sliding the jewelry back into its spots and the other moving the rack into place.

The entire store stopped, the tinny rock music the only sound echoing through the store.

"We're leaving," I said, my hands raised like they'd all pulled a gun on me. The thoughts of the Regs hit against my shields. One person thought we should wear a sign or something like a giant W or a G for GAFU. After all, he thought, you really couldn't tell just by looking at us, unless we had some weird hair or eyes. And one man thought of a family member, a brother he hadn't seen in years, who'd been kicked out of their house for destroying their father's high school football trophies with his Gift.

Samantha put down her armful of clothes, while the boys put their hands in their pockets, hunched their shoulders and headed toward me. I only had four students, but I still counted heads before moving into the crowded mall.

I contacted Seiko. *We had an incident, nothing big, but we're going straight to lunch. Where are you?*

What happened?

I told him what Tom had done.

Glad you guys are okay. It took me forever to find a bathroom. I'm pretty close to the restaurant. Meet you there.

Sounds good.

I'm so sorry, Tom thought at me, his cotton candy shields looking like burnt sugar.

I know. It was an accident. The reason we do this is because mistakes happen, and Mr. Kalani and I won't always be around. Let's go to lunch. It's not a big deal.

A full two minutes passed before I realized we were being followed. I glanced over my shoulder. A man from the store, his twenty-something daughter and another man followed us, their thoughts full of hate.

Fuck, fuck, fuckity-fuck.

Change of plan, I thought to my kids. *We're heading to the transport pad and back to the Warehouse.*

Oh no, Samantha thought in the open channel to me. *I'd checked out the menu for lunch and I was so excited to try their 951 burger.*

Ms. May, please don't punish the others, Tom thought just to me. *I'll go back to the Warehouse, by myself. It's okay.*

Wait, dude, why? Weldon glanced over his shoulder, his icy shields pulsing with his heart rate.

Are they following us? Leo asked. His purple shields popped, and the tentacles released. *I can stop them.*

Absolutely not, I thought. *Then they'd be right to be scared of us.*

But Ms. May—

I said no.

Well this couldn't have gone worse.

Even if they're following us, we're doing what they want, I thought to the kids. *We're leaving. So, it's not a big deal. Everyone calm down.*

I glanced over my shoulder. The group was closer. I didn't hold back and slid into the thoughts of one of the men. He was going to make sure we left the mall. He didn't want our kind around him.

I fell back, putting myself between my kids and the Regs. Tom increased his pace and the others fell into step with him.

Don't run, I ordered. *I got this. We're going to be fine.*

I opened up a channel to Seiko. *Meet us at the transport pad on 5th. We're being escorted out.*

By who? Security?

Some Regs. They're following us.

Jesus. Where are you? His emerald and black shields flared in my mind's eye as he reached out to make sure we were safe.

Third floor, heading toward the closest exit to the 5th street pad.

I'm heading to you.

We're fine. We're leaving. It's going to be fine.

If I kept saying that, it'd be true, right?

Roger Dodger. Keep the connection open. I'll find a way to get to you if you need me.

I glanced over my shoulder. There were more Regs now, two more women and another man. What the fuck? Did a memo go out that there were Wilds in the mall?

The Regs thoughts behind me felt like a hurricane on the horizon. I glanced over my shoulder. There was one more man, making a grand total of seven. They followed us, their thoughts boiling with hatred. Was it somehow obvious we were Wilds?

Escalator, I thought to the kids. *Keep your shields up and for God's sakes don't do anything that'll bring any more attention.*

They stepped onto the escalator, peeking over their shoulders at the people following us. My back felt exposed, like someone was about to push me down the stairs.

We reached the bottom and Samantha and Tom started trotting, their arms at their sides.

Just walk, I reminded them again. *People will think you stole. We're fine.*

Just as the thought was through my shields, a coffee cup flew through the air heading for Leo's head.

I used my Gift and the cup fell to the ground behind us. Unfortunately, the top flipped off and the hot liquid spilled, making one of the men slip.

He yelled out, "Stop them! We don't want them here. Fucking GAFUs." The storm at my back increased and we were still another floor away from the exit.

Take this escalator, I thought.

It's an up, Tom thought. *We need to go down.*

Use it to go down. And say excuse me.

The kids weaved back and forth through the Regs trying to go up the escalator. The mob followed, some taking the same escalator and others, full on running to the down escalator.

I opened a mental channel to the Guardian at the transport pad.

Hi there. This is Kendle May. I came across the transport pad earlier with the four teens. We're having a bit of a problem at the mall and could use some help.

What kind of problem?

We have, I glanced over my shoulder, *seven Reg adults following us.* Another coffee cup came at us, this one empty. I deflected it without even thinking and winced when other Regs turned their head to stare. I guess I should've let it hit me.

One of the Regs yelled, "Get the fuck out of here, and don't come back. GAFUs don't belong around normal people."

Samantha's breath hitched and she hunched her head into her neck, her arms wrapped around her chest.

They're throwing things at us, I continued to the Guardian. *We're trying to leave but need an escort to the transport pad.*

One moment.

Tom glanced over his shoulder and almost fell across a stroller. He danced around it. "Sorry," he gasped to the mother, who stared, outraged at him.

"Watch where you're going," she yelled. "You could've hurt my baby."

"He's sorry," I said, slightly out of breath myself as we moved past.

"He's a Wild," one of the men shouted.

The woman swooped forward to protect the stroller, yelling, "He could've killed my baby. Stay away from us!"

"Love to," I muttered.

Excuse me, I thought to the Guardian. *Any word on when we can get help? We're ten minutes out to the transport pad, but I'm not sure we're going to make it.*

One moment. Then he closed the connection entirely.

Fucking bigoted idiots.

Keep moving, I told the kids. *Don't stop and get to the transport pad. I'll catch up.*

I'm going to need help, I thought to Seiko. *Where are you?*

I'm at the transport pad.

Thought you were meeting us at the exit.

Thought you said transport pad. Heading back. God, I wish I could teleport. You'll have to call in the Guardians.

I did. I don't think they're coming.

What?

I slowed down and let the mob catch up, giving my kids a chance to get ahead. "We're leaving," I turned to tell them, my hands up. "You're welcome to walk with us, but please stop throwing things. They're just kids and you're frightening them."

My heart hammered in my chest and I didn't know what to do with my shaking hands.

"We don't want you around us." The Reg feared we'd know what she did with the body, tying cinder blocks to the ankles before throwing it in the pond behind her aunt's house. She was thinking it so loudly, it was all she thought of.

I yanked myself out of her mind. I hated being around Regs.

"I know you don't want us here," I said. "That's why we're trying to leave."

"You should be locked up where you can't read our thoughts. One of you stole my identity last year." This was from a tired and skinny looking man with a flabby belly. And he was right. A Wild hooker had stolen his identity. And then his wife had enough of the alcohol and hookers and left him. And of course, in his mind, it was the Wild's fault, all of our faults.

"Just let us leave," I said. "Please. We're not even from around here."

"Then why are you Wilds here? Why would you come here?"

Someone screamed and Regs ran toward me.

Holy fuck, what happened now?

Kendle!

We're going to die.

I teleported myself the hundred feet or so in front of the kids. They'd made it to the front doors, but were blocked by a Reg.

A Reg with a gun.

"Holy God," I said out loud. I was standing between the man with a gun and my kids. A gun. An actual gun. My brain shut down. Behind us, Regs screamed and ran away. Except for the mob. They hemmed us in, blocking our way back out.

This was not happening.

Seiko, we really need some help.

I thought back to the Guardian, but his mind was completely closed to me. I reached out, trying to find any Guardians.

To anyone in the vicinity, I thought, opening up as many channels as I could. *My name is Kendle May. I'm an administrator at Phillip's Academy. I have four Wild children with me. We're being threatened by a Reg with a gun. Please help.*

No one answered.

I touched the mind of the man with the gun. His name was

Richard and his thoughts were layered, complex and mixed with emotion. He flashed back and forth between the present and the past, blaming Wilds for his marriage, money and career problems, but everything was muddled. It was hard to tell what had happened to him and why he thought Wilds caused it. But he felt completely justified ridding his world of a few more Wilds.

I flung a physical barrier up around the kids, a bigger barrier than I'd ever held before. I had no idea if it would actually stop a bullet. The kids all had their hands in the air, frozen in place.

I sent another message to the Guardians, but there was no response.

Seiko. There's a Reg with a gun. We need help.

I'm coming. Miriam and Stephen are on their way too. Stephen is going to teleport to you.

"I want all of you to concentrate," I told the kids. "Concentrate on using your psychokinesis to put a physical barrier around you. I have one in place but go ahead and practice putting up another one. Help is on the way."

Leo's purple shields broke into tentacles and reached for the man. *No,* I told him. *It's still wrong.*

But Ms. May—

Could I live with myself if one of the kids died because I wouldn't let Leo use his Gift?

Okay, keep it ready, but only if it seems like he's going to shoot us. Leo's tentacles circled around, but didn't touch the Reg.

Samantha sobbed and Tom put his arm around her. He concentrated and put up a small barrier around the two of them. The other students tried to do the same. I had to tell Daniel to start teaching this.

Assuming we survived.

"Hi," I said to the man with the gun. "Richard, is it?"

I realized my mistake as soon as I said it. The only way I'd know his name was if I'd read his mind. He raised his gun, cocking the hammer back. I put up my hand to stop Leo.

"Look," I said. "These are just children. I'll stay here and you can let them go." I pulled off my beanie. "I'm a Wild. I'm only thirty-two but have white hair. My mother worked in an insurance company and we lived with my grandmother. All three of us, in this tiny apartment with a little balcony off of it. The dog slept out there." I had no idea what I was saying. All the kids were crying, big tears falling down their cheeks. Someone behind me breathed out, a scared sobby sniff. "Please let them go," I begged. "They didn't choose to be born this way."

He shook his head. His thoughts were so layered and horrible. I wasn't even sure he was fully capable of speech.

My nose felt cold. I put my hand up and touched blood. My head hurt. It was taking too much effort to keep the barrier up.

Stephen? I need help. I can't do this much longer.

Here.

Richard yelped as Stephen appeared. He pointed his gun at Stephen.

I dug and reached out with my Gift to enclose him in the barrier just as Stephen slammed one up. Our barriers merged and everything changed. I could still see the colors in shields, but also taste and smell them.

This is new. The thought echoed back and forth in both of our minds and we didn't know who had spoken it and who had heard it.

But keeping the barrier up was easy.

Miriam and Seiko ran to us.

We're fine, Stephen and I thought to them. *Get the kids to the transport pad.*

Together we strengthened the barrier around Richard, a dome sparking with our Gifts. Miriam and Seiko grabbed the kids and sprinted off with them. Richard fired at them, but the bullet glanced off and fell to the ground.

The mob screamed and hurried away.

We kept the dome up around Richard, letting him fire his gun again and again against it, until the chamber was empty. He let out a yell and pounded his fists against the barrier. Stephen and I watched him, not speaking, until the Guardians showed up.

―――

It was surprisingly difficult for Stephen and I to unmerge, but we managed, after realizing both of us saying the same thing at the same time unnerved the Guardians. They took the Reg into custody and he went without saying or doing anything. His thoughts seemed almost blank. He barely even registered he was being arrested or he'd failed to kill any Wilds.

I tried to explain to the Guardians what had happened and why we were at the mall, but they didn't want to hear it from me. They waited for Stephen to repeat the exact same thing, their eyes on his, their lips pulled down into their serious thinking looks, showing how important he was.

I finally quit and moved away to sit down on the ground, my back against the wall. The Guardians barely noticed. My shirt was another loss, blood from my nose smeared down the front. I pulled a packet of tissues from my purse and tried to clean up my face. No one had offered me medical help other than Stephen.

Kendle? Stephen's voice vibrated painfully through my shields. They'd like a description of the Regs that chased you.

I tried to get to my feet and Stephen was there, his hand out to help me up. *Almost done, love.*

I gave the Guardians a description of the seven Regs and within a few minutes they'd moved off, thanking Stephen, and only Stephen for his cooperation.

"Jesus," I muttered. "I'd forgotten how subhuman I am compared to a Bred."

Stephen sighed. "I don't want to fight again."

I touched my bruised shields to his. "I'm not trying to pick a fight, I promise. It's not your fault."

He smiled at me and touched my arm. *Glad you're okay.*

Me too. And the kids too.

Ready to go home?

Please. Can we teleport? I don't want to see another Guardian for a while.

Of course.

But I hadn't anticipated how drained I was and fell to my knees when we appeared outside the gates of the Warehouse. Things went gray and voices muttered around me.

"For god's sake Kendle, next time take a transport pad," said Daniel. "Why'd you let her teleport herself?"

I tried to open my eyes, defend Stephen, but it was too much effort.

"Dr. Evander is in the infirmary looking at the kids," Kaya said. "Let's get her there."

I struggled to speak, but I was so tired, and the ground was soft and comfy. Turquoise shields surrounded me, and I let it all go.

CHAPTER EIGHTEEN

SUNLIGHT MOVED over my closed eyes, offering brightness and shadows. My body was warm, and a cool breeze blew through my hair. I inhaled deeply, smelling salty air. This was not the Warehouse.

I shaded my eyes against the glare. I stood on a beach, an ocean beach. I'd never been to the beach in my life and this one was better than any I'd seen in movies.

The sand sparkled with pinks, whites and blacks. I picked up a soft handful and released the glitters to the breeze. I walked toward the water, the swells gently washing up and over my violet-painted toes. The water was a perfect balance between the heat of the sun and sand, silky on my skin.

I frowned. I almost never painted my toes, lacking the energy or desire. No one ever saw them other than me, even in the summer.

Where was I?

It was sunset and the clouds were pink, purple and orange, prettier than any I'd ever seen. A flock of pelicans flew by, one diving to scoop up some fish. Dolphins played in the waves.

I couldn't have picked a more perfect spot if I tried.

This was not a normal dream, not with the purple toes and the... gauzy skirt I wore.

Okay, this was going too far. I'd never owned or wanted to wear anything as ridiculous as a white skirt. I really should be wearing shorts and a t-shirt. And then, I was. I looked down at the red shorts and black t-shirt and smiled. Now I got it. Whatever I thought of, happened.

Nice.

A shadow on the sand moved toward me.

"What are you doing here?" he asked. "This is my spot."

"I have no idea. But I can leave."

"Not yet." He pointed off to the horizon and the sun melted into the ocean, the sky full of oranges and purples reflecting off the water. A tiny sliver of a moon rose, and bright, bright stars filled the sky.

Stephen took my hand and raised it to his lips, his pale green eyes on mine.

My heart paused, and I had to take a breath.

"There are few things better than a sunset with a beautiful woman."

I laughed and he looked down at me, his eyebrows raised.

"Does that line normally work?" I asked

He grinned, becoming human. "I wasn't thinking of it as a line, but you're right. It was terrible. Honest, but terrible."

I pulled my hand away and walked a few steps from him. With the sun mostly set, it should've been cold, but the sand was still comfortably warm on my toes, the waves running over them.

Suddenly the world shattered in bright colors of turquoise, green, blue, gold, violet and sage pulsing in time with a loud sound.

I rolled over and hit the snooze button on my alarm. In the low yellow security lights from the outside, my apartment looked small, shabby and dark. The dream released as my mind went down worn, but dusty paths, wondering what my life would look like in twenty years. At this rate, I'd still be alone and in this apartment, barely a memory in most of the students' minds I'd tried to help.

I shivered. The covers had fallen off my bed at some point and I used my Gift to wrap them around myself. My alarm went off again. I had to get moving—kitchen supplies would be delivered in a few hours and I had to take inventory before the staff moved them into the pantry and walk-in fridge and I had no way of knowing what was new or old.

But I couldn't focus. I didn't want to look back at my life in ten, twenty years and wonder what went wrong. Wonder why I was alone with an apartment full of musical instruments, thousands of books on my screen and no one to share those things with.

I yanked the covers off and got up, shivering against the cold. Those thoughts didn't help, and I had work to do, Wilds to help.

CHAPTER NINETEEN

THE NEXT EVENING, I tossed my notebook onto the big table in the conference room and sat down in my seat, kitty-corner to Miriam's seat. I stretched, my hands over my head, as the other faculty members arrived. I looked at the giant papers on the walls with their sticky notes. So many ideas to make the Warehouse better. We should plan a meeting to go over them again. I sent myself a reminder.

Stephen came in and took out his screen. "Do I just plug my screen into..." he looked around. "Don't we do a presentation?"

Kaya released Franny from her welcome hug and went over to Stephen, putting her arms around him. "We do, but we don't do a PowerPoint." She tugged his mussed hair down.

Tonight was our quarterly check-in about the students. For the next two nights, we'd discuss each student and tweak their educational plan, making sure they had what they needed, and the team was supporting them. Daniel had always taken the discussions the most seriously of all of us, building a full report for each student, noting their skills and setting goals for them.

At least, he'd taken it the most seriously before Stephen.

Stephen's shields grayed and I saw the orange and red anxiety thoughts swimming beneath the surface. He'd worked hard on his presentation and was excited to show us.

How does he find the time? Seiko thought to me. *I mean, seriously, he's making all of us look bad.*

Right, I responded, watching the reds and oranges.

And what's he going to say? 'I think this student will have effective shields in two months, whereas this student still needs to learn how to send his thoughts.' Why is that a PowerPoint?

Right, I thought again. *Wait, are you angry with him? Thought you liked the eye candy.*

He's just so...perfect. It's exhausting.

I looked at Stephen. There were new shadows under his eyes I hadn't noticed before. His shields were still turquoise, shifting into grays and greens depending on his mood, but there were more grays now. I wondered if he still hated it here.

Kaya pulled out a projector, untangling the cords so Stephen could plug his screen in. Stephen touched her arm and smiled, thanking her. For a second, just a millisecond, I wished I'd gotten the projector out for him, so he'd smile at me like that.

I shook my head. That dream had messed me up. It was probably some weird side effect from the merging. Stephen and I should probably talk. But what would I say? 'Hey baby, you been having any weird dreams about me?'

Yeah, I was totally going to do that. I barely resisted eye rolling. Hopefully the dreams would just stop on their own.

Franny came into the room, spilling papers everywhere, talking loudly about how sorry she was for being late, and it was because of a little accident with acid in the lab, but it had only stained one of the tables...

"Miriam's not here yet," Kaya interrupted. "You're fine. Take a few deep breaths."

"Thank God," Franny said, dropping into a chair with a dramatic sigh. She kicked her shoes off and used her Gift to slide all her spilled papers into a pile.

Seiko passed Franny a water bottle, and then said to me, *Besides, I don't think I'm the only one with a crush.*

I don't have a crush, I thought, pushing away a quick image from a dream, Stephen wrapping his arms around me, our feet in the surf. I'd felt so cared for. I pushed the image away. I took care of myself. *Stephen's like art on the wall in a museum or playing a song I didn't write,* I responded. *I can look at it or enjoy it, but not want it as mine. Does that make sense?*

Seiko chuckled. *Whatever. Just don't do anything stupid.*

You too.

Not a concern, even if he swung my way. Breds and Wilds can be friends, or good for a quick bang, but we're too different for a partnership. I'd lose more than he would.

I reached out for his hand, touching it. *Then what are we doing? There has to be hope for things to be more even. People like Franny, Miriam and Kaya are trying to help us.*

What? You think love conquers all? He thought it in a singsong voice. *Come on, you're smarter than that. At the end of the day, a Bred, even a Value Bred, won't understand why we're the way we are.*

"Everyone is having a conversation without me," Franny said, looking around the room. "I hate being left out and you all promised you'd stop."

"We weren't talking about you," I said.

"We were figuring out our presentation," Seiko said, as Miriam came in and started the meeting.

CHAPTER TWENTY

THAT EVENING, I curled up in my armchair, staring at the reflections of my apartment in the window, not doing anything. I was so tired. Miriam had loved Stephen's presentation and wanted each of us to do something similar. For tomorrow. I didn't know where I'd find the time. None of us did. The kids kept needing us.

And after Miriam's instructions, Stephen had sighed, his beautiful turquoise shields turning a dark gray as he unplugged his screen and put it away. He knew we weren't happy with him.

It wasn't his fault. I knew that. It was a good presentation and he was just doing what he thought was best, what he'd learned to do at his Bred school.

But where would I find the time to build an entire presentation?

I lifted a joint and put it between my teeth, using my Gift to light it. I breathed in, my fingers in Mr. Sparklebutt's fur. I puffed out, twining the smoke around my fingers with my Gift, and sending it out the open window. I guess I could work on my presentation now. Put in an hour or something. I'd feel less anxious in the morning, at least. And then I could take a few minutes to play before I got some sleep. Maybe spend a few minutes with the first instrument I ever played, my cello.

Do you have dorm duty tonight?

Eeva! Long time no talk. How's it going? Her voice cut in and out with the distance and I asked her to call me.

A minute later, she answered, "Things are good. A lot going on, but things are good. I do have a favor to ask though."

"Sure! Whatever you need. Though your last favor got me written up."

"You brought a scared thirteen-year-old back to the Warehouse. What did you do wrong?"

"I got where Miriam was coming from. It was a fair write-up."

"Miriam's a bitch who uses you. I don't know why you're so devoted to her."

I took another hit off the joint. I didn't want to have this conversation again. Eeva brought it up periodically, usually whenever I mentioned how tired, or how broke I was because Miriam had withheld my paycheck again.

"Sorry," Eeva said. "I don't want to fight, and I really need that favor."

"Sure. What did you need?"

"Are you doing anything tonight?"

I couldn't tell her I was going to work on a PowerPoint presentation for the Warehouse, not after she'd already called Miriam a bitch. "Not much. Just going to read."

She was quiet for a minute. "You were going to work, weren't you?"

I took another hit, though I was starting to get dizzy. "Probably."

"Well I have something you'll actually get paid for."

"A gig? I haven't played in front of anyone in months. Are you serious? And it's paid? What's the venue? What kind of music?"

I could feel her embarrassment through the phone lines, even without a telepathic channel open.

"Never mind," I said, eyeing the joint. It had taken away my filter. "What's the favor?"

"One of my girls called out. We just reopened, we're packed, and I can't find someone to cover."

"I haven't bartended in over a year. And it's a Monday night. How busy can you be?"

"I know, I know. But it's only seven and I'm turning people away at the door. It's nuts and we can't keep up. You know how it goes. This needs to be perfect. Everything needs to be perfect."

God, I really didn't want to. Yes, I could use the money—the holidays were coming, and Miriam now owed me eight paychecks, with only promises to pay me as soon as she could. My eyes felt grainy and my skin hummed with exhaustion.

There was a thump behind me. I let out a screech.

Sorry, sorry, sorry, sounded a voice in my head tinged with apricot. I inhaled wrong, coughed and transported the joint to the kitchen sink.

Becca stood in my apartment, shaking.

"What happened?" Eeva demanded in my ear as other voices, the other teachers, echoed in my head, *what's wrong, do you need help?*

I'm fine, I told all the voices.

It's okay, I told Becca who looked like a puppy caught peeing on the floor by their owner. *It's not a big deal.*

A knock sounded. I went to stand up, but the cat dug his claws into my pajama pants and skin.

"Son of a bitch," I screamed half in, half out of the chair as he dropped with a yowl and bolted under the bed. I leaned into the chair to keep my balance and the rickety leg I'd been meaning to fix snapped. I overbalanced and fell to the floor.

That's it. I was just going to live here. The old carpet was surprisingly comfortable.

Oh my god. Becca ran over to help me up, while the knocking continued.

"Kendle, you okay?" asked a voice with a southern drawl on the other side of the door.

"Fine," I called out verbally and mentally. My armchair was broken. I righted it and it tipped over again. Mr. Sparklebutt growled from under the bed and I rubbed my leg. He'd ripped my pajama pants.

"Kendle, are you okay?" Eeva yelled in my ear.

"I'm fine," I said into the receiver. "I'll call you back in a minute," and hung up.

I took a deep breath and used my Gift to open the door. Mr.

Sparklebutt went running out, stopping to hiss at Daniel who flipped him off.

"I'm fine," I told him. "Becca appeared and it surprised me. Then the—cat ripped my pants. Then I broke my chair."

The tears prickling my eyes surprised me. I loved that chair. It had been my first purchase with my first paycheck from Miriam.

Becca was frozen in the middle of the room, her shields gray, her thoughts circling with fears about getting kicked out, how upset I was, and why she couldn't control herself no matter how hard she tried.

I put my arm around her. *I'm not mad at you.* I stepped back, to sign, "I promise. It's okay. It's not a big deal."

Daniel stepped in and inspected the chair. *I can fix it for you.*

It's probably time to be replaced anyway. I rubbed Becca's shoulders. She took a deep breath and another. She was trying so hard for control and not to teleport away.

Don't be stupid. If you love the chair, I'll fix it. He opened up his mental channel. *Come on Becca, let's get you back to the dorms.*

Am I in trouble? She asked.

Was it intentional?

She shook her head.

Then no, Daniel thought. *We've talked about this. Tomorrow we'll see if there was a trigger, but not tonight. We're all too tired.*

I nodded and forced a smile for her. *It's not a big deal, sweetie. You just startled me. And I'm frustrated about my chair, not with you.*

She left with Daniel, who closed the door after him. *I'll come back and look at your chair.*

I took another deep breath, kicking the chair with my toe. It was so dirty and stained and had a rip along the back I normally hid with a blanket. *Don't worry about it,* I thought. *I have to go to Mt. Olympus.*

Tonight? It's after nine.

But only seven there. Eeva needs the help, and I need the money.

Daniel's shields homed in on mine. *How much does Miriam owe you?*

It doesn't matter. I don't need much. And she'll pay me back once she has the money. The grocery bill is more important. I know that.

Don't let her do that to you. You deserve to be paid for your work. And leave your door unlocked, so I can fix your chair.

He must have hit his head. He wasn't normally this nice to me.

He disconnected from the conversation before I could thank him.

I picked up the phone and dialed the number for Mt. Olympus. Eeva picked up on the first ring.

"Please Kendle, I've tried everyone else. If we get complaints about slow service, the owner will fire me."

He would too. He was a Bred who owned exclusive Bred bars in almost every major city and they practically printed their own money. Each bar had a theme, but it was classy and trendy and spurred new fashions so the Breds could be in character when they went. The drinks were carefully built concoctions, perfectly balanced with their own unique glasses, ice and garnishes. And because the bars only allowed Breds, they were the place for political and business deals in addition to the place your partner begged you to take them.

"Can I leave by midnight your time? I'm so tired."

"I'll get you out by eleven. Pinkie promise."

I fished the joint out of the sink, making sure it was out before putting it into a drawer. "I'll be there in fifteen minutes."

"Thank you so much. I owe you dinner some night. Pick a day. We'll drink a bottle of wine or two and catch up."

I couldn't help but smile. I missed her so much. "Agreed. See you in a bit."

I showered quickly, tying my white hair into a ponytail. I stroked brown shadow onto my eyebrows to darken them to a more normal shade and added a few coats of mascara. I glanced into the mirror and made a face. It was the best I was going to get.

And it didn't matter. I was just a Wild girl serving drinks.

CHAPTER TWENTY-ONE

Not only did Mt. Olympus only cater to Breds, but they didn't allow Wilds or Regs as patrons and the servers were all Wilds. The owner wanted the Wild servers to use their Gifts to deliver drinks and anticipate orders without reading minds.

When I got there, Bred bodies packed the bar, the tables and the booths. The 1920s bar was giant, taking up one full wall, polished with carved details I could barely see through the crush of bodies around it. A huge mirror with sparkling accents provided the backdrop for dusty bottles of liquor with names like Sarsaparilla and Absinthe. The mirror was even slightly wavy to mimic the way old glass flowed over time. Chandeliers with fringe and red shades over electric candles provided flickering light. There was even a piano, where a Wild wearing a fedora played modern songs with a 1920s feel. The female staff wore flapper-like costumes with tight bodices and fringed skirts hitting mid-thigh with fishnets and heeled boots underneath. The men wore tight pants with suspenders and a white or pale blue shirt and fedoras.

Eeva had decided to put me in the men's costume, and I was pleased I didn't have to show off my pale legs, even in fishnets. The men's pants were skintight on my hips and while the shirt was baggy, the collar was open enough I'd have to be careful when I leaned over, especially once I'd added the suspenders. Lovely. At least I'd remembered a bra.

"Bartend or wait tables?" Eeva asked. She wore a uniform too, but it was pants, with a low-cut top and a short emerald jacket, highlighting her red hair. She looked enough the 1920s part to be able to fill in any gaps, but customers would know she was the manager.

I glanced at the menu of craft cocktails.

"Wait tables," I said. I was still feeling the effects of the joint, and waiting tables was easier than mixing drinks I'd never heard of. I was handed a cocktail tray and told who to telepathically send my orders to. The trick to waiting tables at Mt. Olympus was prioritizing all the telepathic requests for drinks, who sent them and where they were.

Within five minutes of hitting the floor, I was sending multiple trays and glasses through the air to the Breds who ordered them.

I drifted over to a table, my Gift open to pick up on any orders. One of the Breds, a woman with bright copper hair, flipped through a menu before asking, *Which one is your favorite? Oh. I guess, these drinks are expensive, so you probably haven't tasted one. Though maybe they give you a script or something to follow?*

Jesus, her friend with fashionable twenty-years-ago turquoise eyes thought. *I'll have the Ghostly Widow,* she thought to me. *It's good, just have it,* she thought to her friend.

The copper-haired Bred, her perfect rose-gold shields swirling like silk, read the description and made a face. I pointed to one right below it. *The Medusa's Tail is very popular. Absinthe and champagne.*

Sounds fine. I know how hard...I really support Wilds. It's just terrible how society is treating you. I'm glad you can get wo—.

Oh for God's sakes, her friend snapped. *Stop talking to the help.*

I wondered if her friend knew I could hear her.

I'll be right back, I thought and actually walked to the bar, giving my order verbally to the bartender, who looked at me like I was crazy. *I just need a second,* I told him. He shrugged and turned away to mix my drinks.

"What the hell?" the bartender asked, picking up a bottle where a mini whirlpool swirled. I took a deep breath, tucking my Gift back and waiting until I was in control enough to float the drinks to the Breds.

The woman with the rose-gold shields smiled and lifted the drink, taking a quick sip. *You're astute. This is exactly what I wanted.*

Enjoy, I responded, knowing my smile was strained.

I'll make sure to leave you a big tip. I'm sure you need it.

Thank you, I thought back, hoping my smile didn't look as rigid as it felt.

Fucking-A, was it eleven yet? Could I go home?

Eeva's voice broke into my thoughts. *VIP group coming in. All wait staff focus on them. Let's have their drinks ready before they sit down.*

A smiling Eeva, being the perfect hostess, showed five men and two women in. I focused on the shields, hoping the Breds were thinking about what drinks they would want. Breds like these would want their drinks to be perfect. The colors of their shields, gold, violets, turquoise and greens swirled in my mind's eye.

A champagne cocktail, with flavored gin, I told the bartender, checking one of the men off.

I focused on the next set of shields, golden with jewels. Where had I seen those shields before? *A bourbon drink, something with honey and some flower...maybe lavender,* I thought.

I analyzed the movement of one of the men's shields, before realizing his swirling turquoise and green shields were familiar. *A port,* I thought to the bartender, wishing I could disappear into the floor.

Seriously? Tonight, he had to come here?

Could this day get worse?

I watched the owner of the golden shields, Indira Dewan, run her hand up and down Stephen's arm and wondered why I'd tempted the universe. The hot spurt of jealousy surprised me, and I had to take a few deep breaths to make it go away.

Well, that was new.

Eeva, I don't want your other guests to feel neglected. You never know. One of them could be a reporter. Should I let the others focus on the VIPs and—

No way, she thought, her sky-blue shields turning red. *Do you know who these people are? They're Runes. One of them is the head of R&E and one of the women is Senator Rune. Sen-a-tor.* She enunciated each syllable. *In my bar. And the other—*

Yes, I know, I interrupted. *And one of them is Stephen Rune who works at the Warehouse. He lives next door to me. And you have me in this ridiculous and humiliating costume.*

Seriously? What's a Rune doing working at the Warehouse?

A question I ask every day, I snapped.

Fine, she snapped back. *Focus on the other guests.*

You so owe me dessert with my dinner.

Just be perfect. It has to be perfect.

I will. I know what's at stake.

At ten thirty, I reminded myself I only had thirty more minutes of this hell. The Rune group had put away an impressive four to five drinks each and Benjamin, the CEO of R&E, the genetic company creating most Breds, had downed seven. He shouldn't be standing, but there he was, talking loudly and with lots of arm flinging, but mostly coherent. Stephen hadn't been kidding about he and his siblings' ability to enjoy alcohol.

His parents had obviously wanted their children to look alike as they all had the pale green eyes and blue-black hair. But Senator Rune's skin was icy pale, and she had thick pink lips and high cheekbones, whereas Benjamin was darker skinned, with a strong jaw. Stephen was a merge between the two, with golden skin and large eyes, so much larger than his siblings.

He and Indira were well matched and seemed like lovers, trying each other's drinks and laughing together. She touched him constantly and while I noticed he didn't touch her back, he didn't seem bothered by her either. No wonder he'd wanted to thank her personally for her donation.

The jealousy spiked again. So I'd had a few erotic dreams. He didn't belong to me.

At exactly eleven, one a.m. my time, I went to Eeva. "I'm done," I told her. "I'm wiped." I gave her my handheld. She grunted and ran it through the computer, showing me the amount of tips I'd made. I'd done well. It would be nice to have some money in my bank account again.

Thank you for helping out. I don't think we would've done as good a job tonight without you. Especially not with the Runes being here.

You're welcome. That dinner had better be amazing. With steak.

Steak? I was thinking chili and cornbread.

That'd be good too.

She touched my arm. *You okay? You look exhausted.*

It was a hard day. And it was weird seeing Stephen here and essentially waiting on him. At the Warehouse, we were colleagues, but here, I served him because I was a Wild and he was a Bred.

I'm sorry, Eeva responded. *And then I had to ask you to work when you probably needed an evening with a novel.* She gave me a hug. *Get some sleep. Things are always better in the morning.*

I went into the back to change and was halfway into my sweatshirt and yoga pants when oceany turquoise shields tapped mine. Hard and uncontrolled. *I saw you.*

Of course he had.

You sent me the port when I arrived. I thought it was an odd choice, but then I noticed you hiding in the corner, doing all the work.

He was completely shit-faced, at the point where his metabolism stopped absorbing the alcohol. Indira had left an hour ago, but Stephen had remained with his siblings.

There were a lot of people trying to keep you and your family happy tonight, I thought.

I know. I saw them too. It's so boring and fake. They're all fake. My entire family is fake. I wondered if he knew he sounded like one of the teens he taught.

Why are you here? he asked. *Doesn't the Warehouse keep you busy enough? A friend needed a favor. Why are you here?*

I saw the answer though he tried to push it down. *You wanted to be around your own kind,* I answered for him.

It was a shitty day, he thought. *I wanted a drink, friends, my family and—*

People that understood you, I added.

Of course they're all fucking assholes, which I am not. So they were no help whatsoever. And they're being assholes about where I work. I get why you hate Breds so much.

I stuck my head back into the bar, making sure I stayed in the shadows so the other Breds couldn't see me. Stephen's hair was sticking up again and he finished his drink in one long swallow. *So they were no help,* he repeated again. I wasn't even sure if he knew he was still talking to me, or simply thinking loudly.

I'm sorry.

Why is it so hard to do the right thing? I'm not trying to show off or make things worse for others.

Ah.

I'm just trying to do the best I can. And doing a presentation about each kid so we can come up with the best plan for them isn't a big deal. We owe them so that they have the best outcomes. I thought that's what today was.

Everyone at the Warehouse wants what's best for the kids. And not doing a PowerPoint doesn't mean they don't want that.

I know, I know, I know.

I was so tired. *Look, last time one of us was drunk we fought. I'm too tired to fight and you're too drunk.*

Will you be home later? The question was oddly intimate, like a lover asking if he should wait up.

The Warehouse is my home. Where else would I go?

To someone else's home. The idea was like a jellyfish, just floating through the connection.

Go back to your family, I told him.

I hate being bored and they're so boring. My life is boring.

He flung himself backward on the wing-backed couch he sat on, and his brother gave him a dirty look before continuing his conversation.

Wait, no it's not, he continued. *Not since the Warehouse. The Warehouse is terrible, but not boring.*

Good night, Stephen, I thought. *Drink lots of water before you go to bed.*

He looked over at me, meeting my eyes, though I still stood in the shadows. There was a glint I hadn't seen before. *Wanna come over? It'd be fun.*

It would. Somehow, I knew—

I shut the thought down. There was no way I would win in that scenario.

Good night, I thought again.

You'll come over.

No, I won't, I clarified.

Not now, but at some point.

You're rambling. You're going to be embarrassed if you remember this conversation.

True, he slurred. *But you'll pretend it never happened.*

Good night, I thought and broke off the connection.

CHAPTER TWENTY-TWO

THE NEXT MORNING, I was interrupted by a faint nudge from Stephen's turquoise shields as I stepped out of the shower.

Here we go, I thought to myself. I'd come home last night and gone immediately into my instrument room. Stephen had come home right after me, his shields still foamy as his body processed the alcohol. I could just hear him moving around his living area, probably grabbing some water and a screen to read or watch a show. I'd picked up my cello, placing it between my knees. Should I or shouldn't I play? I needed to, needed to release my Gift and music was the best way. But there was something so intimate about how he thought of my music, like it was for him, not for me.

I pulled the bow across the strings and felt his attention through the wall. I played until my wrists were sore and he was asleep. Until nearly four a.m.

Now it was six a.m., and I regretted everything.

Did you need something? I asked Stephen, wrapping my towel tighter around my breasts, which was ridiculous, because it wasn't like he could see me.

Are you awake and coherent?

Mostly. That's what coffee is for. How are you feeling?

Not hungover which is a bonus. Um, did I ... say—?
Nope.

I felt the rumble across his shields. Had he known I'd lied? Or was it relief he thought he hadn't said anything? *Those drinks were really strong,* he thought. *And I get drunk so rarely. My sister tells me I tend to just ramble about whatever pops into my head.*

Your sister is right. I added cream and sugar to a giant cup of coffee and used my Gift to float it into the bathroom with me. *But you didn't say anything important.* I took a giant sip, scalding my mouth, and willing the caffeine to work. I felt like shit. *What did you need?*

I have to head out of town today and need a sub. Is your calendar free?

I pulled the towel turban off my head and my white curls exploded around my face. I started the process of smoothing them down. *Today?* I'd planned on building a PowerPoint presentation for each club, so I didn't feel like such an uneducated, unprepared idiot tonight. And then I'd do one for each student in the extracurriculars like dance and theatre, outlining where they were competency-wise. I definitely didn't have time to sub.

Just for the morning, he added. *The Level One and Twos. I can talk to Miriam if you want.*

It's just—

I don't have a choice, he thought. *They told me last night, I have to meet with the family lawyer, and I have a bunch of papers to sign. And today was the only time everyone was available.*

Jesus. What are you signing? Did your family find the lost crown jewels? Is it nuclear codes? Are you secretly aliens from another planet bent to take over our corrupt government, but you've found it's too much work so you're going to head back to your home, but not before having to take a bunch of—

He laughed, so loud I heard it through the wall. *What is wrong with you?*

Apparently, I ramble when I'm tired. I took another sip of my coffee.

I have to sign paperwork related to my mother's will. It's taken us five years to get to this point, but her estate has finally been decided.

I'm sorry.

Thank you, he thought. *We weren't close. She wasn't close to any of us. She just paid for her children's genetic code. She even used a surrogate. Being pregnant would slow her down too much.*

Wow, I thought, not sure what else to say.

You were close with your mother, right? He asked.

I think so. It's hard to remember.

Your mom was pretty. She looked like a fifties pin-up model with her brown hair, tied up in a bandana, blue eyes. Tattoos of flowers and butterflies on her arms. She was tired a lot. Am I right?

Do you see dead people? I asked, trying to keep my tone light, while my chest froze.

He chuckled. *I saw her when we merged. You were thinking about her when we stopped those bullets.*

I had no memory of that, but he knew what the image I held of her looked like. My eyes filled with tears. I missed her so much.

I swiped at my eyes and took another sip of the coffee, spilling half of it as it sloshed back and forth in my mug. I was just tired, I told myself. I pushed her image away and took a deep breath and another willing the coffee to slow down enough to drink it.

I'm sorry, Stephen's voice echoed across the open channel.

It's nothing, I responded. *You just caught me off guard.*

Want me to come over? I can bring some coffee. I think I have some slightly stale coffee cake in my fridge.

I looked in the mirror. My towel had slipped halfway down my breasts, and my hair stuck up Einstein's.

I just got out of the shower. Absolutely not.

He chuckled across our mental connection, oddly intimate.

I took another sip of coffee, the sloshing slowing. *If it's just your first two classes, I can sub.*

Thank you.

———

I was late to the telepathy classroom, which pissed me off. My plan was to be there ten minutes before the first bell to prepare calmly for the day, review Stephen's lesson plans and greet each student with a smile, asking them how their morning was.

But the Regs standing outside the gate with anti-Wild signs, a bull-horn and chants wrecked it. The Regs held signs saying we didn't belong in their neighborhood. Signs saying we, all Wilds, should be locked away. Signs about protecting their families against us. We 'd had to call the Reg police and escort the students from the cafeteria to the classroom building. We didn't want them to hear the Regs and the horrible things they shouted.

The bell had rung when I'd followed the last student in, and I had to race to the classroom. I figured it would be chaos, but the kids all sat, chatting quietly in desks fanatically lined up. I frowned. I didn't think I'd ever seen rows that straight at the Warehouse. But the tops and legs still had carved or drawn graffiti from bored kids. Tall, double-paned windows let in lots of light and drafts during the winter. There was a whiteboard against the front wall and a large selection of colored markers beneath it. A projector was set up to show notes and diagrams to the students.

"Sorry," I told everyone, plugging my screen into the projector. I signed a quick good morning to Becca who grinned and responded with the same. "Mr. Rune is out for a few hours. He said to spend the next hour working on shielding. Sound good?"

The kids nodded. There were a few "yeahs", "yeps" and one overzealous "yes, ma'am!"

It was amazing to see the kids in their desks, wearing the same uniforms I had worn fifteen years prior. It was the same gray pants, or gray skirts if they wished. The same black, white or blue collared shirts, with hoodies or sweatshirts over the top. We allowed the kids to accessorize however they wanted, so there were lots of beanies, base-ball hats, colored socks, bright shoes, painted nails, heavy makeup and colored hair.

"Okay, first things first. Let's get these desks out of the way."

The kids frowned but a couple shrugged and stood up.

"You guys do shielding in your desks?" I asked, surprised.

They nodded.

Weird. Everyone else I'd worked with started with relaxation exercises, so the body was comfy when the mind was so heavily used. In fact, one of my more popular early evening classes was yoga because it prevented cramps and stiffness from sitting in one place too long.

"Let's try it my way and tomorrow you guys can go back to Mr. Rune's way."

A desk shot halfway across the room, and Leo jumped out of the way.

"Use your arms and legs to push the desks please," I said. "Or you'll have to patch and repaint the walls."

Becca disappeared with a squeak. I ignored it, but figured I'd raise the alarm if she wasn't back in five minutes. It wasn't like she could get through the outside wall.

I had the kids sit and teleported a bunch of floor pillows into the room from the storage closet and joined them on the floor, my knees popping loudly. I tucked my legs into a traditional lotus position.

"Grab a seat however you're comfortable. Criss-cross applesauce, kneeling, sitting with your legs out. Whatever works. You guys do this in psychokinesis right?"

Again, there were a few nods. "Then just sit down however you're comfortable."

Becca reappeared, walking through the door. *You're fine,* I told her. *Grab a seat.*

There was lots of shifting around as the students moved into their comfortable spots. Mutters of conversation and thoughts touched my shields.

...break from the asshole before he...

This is stupid. I'm never going to...

...like sitting on the floor. This makes...

I pushed their thoughts away. "Focus on your breathing. Put your hands wherever they're comfortable."

There was a giggle and a boy shoved a girl's hands away. "What," she asked, her eyes innocently wide at me.

I glared at her. *Would you want him to do that to you?*

No. The word was spotty, but there. She lowered her eyes, her cheeks flaming.

"We're going to start breathing, in and out through the nose," I said. A set of blonde identical boy twins glanced at each other and I felt the echoes of their conversation. Mateo leaned in. The twins were lightly Gifted when they started three months ago but had somehow jumped to the head of their classes in psychokinesis and telepathy. We'd talked about them last night. Daniel assumed it was a twin thing.

Don't, I told them. *Whatever it is. Don't do it.* They closed their eyes like the rest, and I kept a light mental connection on them, the equivalent of placing a hand on their shoulders.

"Everyone feel a ball of energy in your chest. Give the energy a color or a scent and allow the ball to expand so it covers your shoulders and arms, working its way down your back to your hips, thighs and down your legs."

I sent them through the relaxation exercise as shields formed around me. Then I had them work on strengthening their shields for fifteen minutes. I tried to scan the kids, forcing my Gift through their shields.

Some of the shields disintegrated immediately, and I carefully withdrew from their thoughts, while others were strong enough to block me.

At the end of the hour, some of the kids had significantly stronger shields, at least for a little while, while others still needed a lot of work. Using shields was similar to keeping a muscle flexed. It took years to develop the strength until it was instinctual. It was why so many Wilds without training struggled.

The Level Twos filed in after the Level Ones went to math. It had been a fun class. I'd forgotten how much I liked teaching. But too many of the kids' opinions were about Stephen and how they didn't like him very much. The telepathy teacher always learned secrets, like who the kids had crushes on, and how many times someone had masturbated the night before, things embarrassing to the teens. They needed to trust him to relax and learn telepathy, and right now they didn't.

For the Level Twos, I partnered the class up and put the partners on opposite sides of the room. One partner was to start a conversation, writing down a thought or a phrase and then telepathically send the words to the other. Then the receiver was to write down what he thought he heard. They went back forth for the whole hour talking about anything they wanted, but had to turn their papers in.

This was one of my favorite telepathy exercises and I loved watching the kids. Some of their faces were tightly screwed up, eyes closed in concentration, mouthing the words of the conversation, while others looked serene. I walked around, looking at everyone's sheets. There were some with cuss words, some gossip, some conversations about internet shows.

I stopped two groups who had hijacked another's conversation on accident and then sent the groups on to math. Stephen hurried in right before the third session started.

"Thank you," he said. "All good?"

I looked at the third years walking in. "All good. But can we talk later?"

"Of course. Did something happen?"

"Nothing like that. I'll see you."

I went into Kaya's office, remembering she had a break for her grading in the third period. I had so much work to do but wanted her advice.

I hear you had to sub for Stephen, she thought, as I sat down on the tiny loveseat, she used instead of a visitor chair.

Breaks up the day, something a little different to do.

She went back to the paper she was grading, while I used my Gift to open up her mini fridge and steal a bottle of water. Kaya's walls were covered with pictures of students, friends, family and random events taped directly onto the walls. Some were old and yellowing, their corners curling up, and others were brand new from a few days ago. The room was full of moments in time.

She looked up when I didn't say anything. *Sweetie, I'm not trying to be a bitch, but I'm really behind. Did you need something?*

Do you think Stephen's a good teacher? I asked.

She closed her screen. *Yes. His students have learned not only telepathy but when and how to use their Gifts. He's teaching them ethics, which we neglect here.* She tossed her head, her dangling earrings catching in the light. *And he's a Rune. He's the smartest and the bestest at anything he does.*

Bestest? Thought you were an English teacher.

I can make up words if I want. She poured a cup of coffee from a steaming pot and offered me a cup, which I accepted with thanks. *The students seem like they're where they should be,* she continued. *Shielding is getting better and they're starting to cheat on exams. That's right for three months in. What's this about?*

They don't like him.

Kaya's eyebrows shot up. *This shouldn't come as a surprise, but they don't have to. Being liked helps, but there are good teachers not liked by their students.*

I know. I'm not explaining it right. I stood up and paced to the window. It was a different view of the rock garden then out of my office window. *He had all the desks in formation. He wasn't teaching them to relax before they started the class. I'm not saying his way is wrong, but the kids don't like it.*

And it's not how you learned?

Is that the problem? It's different for me?

Talk to him, Kaya thought. *See what he says.*

I frowned. I didn't want to. His comments from last night kept running through my head. I should get some distance from him. Or as much as I could considering he lived next door to me. Besides was his way really wrong if he was getting results?

"Just ask," Kaya said out loud. "It can't hurt."

"Maybe."

Everything else good? You seem really tired.

I tried to smile. *Yes. I'll let you get back to work.*

CHAPTER TWENTY-THREE

THAT EVENING, Stephen knocked on my office door frame as I juggled the supply order against our budget against what was actually in our bank account. My eyes were grainy, and a low-grade headache radiated into my skull from the back of my neck. We'd just come out of our meeting, with PowerPoints this time, and my hands shook from too much caffeine and exhaustion. I was too old to work this much on two hours of sleep.

How'd this morning go? he asked.

I pulled off my headphones.

Easy. The first and second levels are good groups. I used games, so they had fun, but they worked hard. A few of your Level Ones actually established some shielding and Leo's tentacles are full shields. These kids are really impressive three months in.

Stephen leaned on the doorframe, stubble on his cheeks, dark circles under his eyes and a coffee stain on his sleeve, looking nothing like the Quality Breds we'd been around last night. He looked like the rest of us, working eighty-hour weeks, trying to make things just a little better.

God, I was tired.

Tentacles? He asked. *Leo has tentacles?*

I grimaced. *I see people's shields in shades of color and movement. I can... see their emotions rather than feeling them. Weird, but I'm not the only one.*

I've read about that, but I've never met anyone who describes shields that way. Most people just feel a wall.

I shrugged. *Must be a Wild thing.*

What are my shields like? He raised an eyebrow, daring me.

I smiled, seeing the blues, greens and turquoise circling his thoughts. "Like the ocean." *They change color based on your moods. When you're happy they're turquoise and when tired, gray, like a storm.*

I can tell when people's emotions change based on how they smell.

I laughed, a huge laugh, surprising both of us. "You're shitting me."

"Nope. When I told my dad I could tell he was lying because he smelled metallic, he called the doctor."

"Smelling shields sounds very Wild. Are you sure you're a Bred?"

He rubbed his chin, the stubble scritching. "Pretty sure." *I have to admit, one of the most fascinating things about the Warehouse is how abilities vary from student to student. We had that at Seagull's Landing, but to a lesser degree.*

Quality vs. Value Breds.

Those are horrible terms and we shouldn't be using them. It leads to stereotyping.

Is it a stereotype if it's true? I asked.

He flung himself into my visitor chair, just like he had last night. Jesus, the Wild kids were rubbing off on him.

Even if it's true, we, as teachers, should be setting an example and not using derogatory terms. We have a responsibility to our society and to these children.

Dude, all we're trying to do is teach these kids to survive and not kill anyone with their Gift.

We should be striving for something bigger though. I mean, there's no research on Wilds and how you can do all the things you do. There's no research on why you have odd physical characteristics Breds can't duplicate. You're not weaker or worse than Breds. Wilds and how they're, how you're treated, has societal implications.

Says the Quality Bred.

The oranges and reds swam to the surface of his thoughts. I

shouldn't have said that. Stephen ran his fingers through his hair, taking a deep breath.

"Sorry," I said out loud. "I'm tired and wasn't thinking."

He was quiet, the only sound a ticking from my clock, while the fish swam beneath the surface of his thoughts. I could just see his exhaustion, his thoughts of how hard he was trying, of how much harder this was than expected.

He wasn't going to last.

Is there anything I need to know about today? He finally asked. *Did you follow the lesson plan?*

Mostly, though I did it through games. Some of the kids are getting good, which is impressive three months in. I winced. I was repeating myself.

Well, this was awkward.

He nodded and stood. *I'll let you get back to your evening then. You look tired, try not to work too much more.* He smiled, but it was forced.

I did notice one thing though. The words were out before I even realized. What was I doing? He wasn't in the mood to hear this.

Of course you did. He lowered himself back into my chair. *What Warehouse exclusive rule did I break now?*

Warehouse exclusive rule?

Yes, something only Wilds do, that only Wilds know. Or maybe something the rest of the faculty knows except me.

Wow. The water in my glass spun slightly.

It's small, I responded. *Not really a big thing and not something to stress about. Let's just talk in the morning. We're both pretty tired.*

No. Now's a perfect time.

I looked at the whirlpool forming in my glass and took a deep breath, tucking my Gift away. "Now's not a good time," I said out loud. "You're not in a good place to listen."

As soon as I spoke the words, I wanted to take them back.

His shields spiked, like a tsunami coming at me. "Hate to break it to you, Wild Princess, but I won't be in a better mood tomorrow, or the day after so you'd better tell me."

Wild Princess? Was he serious? And he couldn't come up with a more imaginative insult?

"Fine." Fucking-Bastard-Neanderthal. FBN, that was my new name for him. And it was more imaginative than his.

"The kids, especially the Level Ones, are tense. I heard them thinking about too much detention, too many rules. You're too strict with them. The desks were perfectly straight for fuck sake."

He raised an eyebrow, the wave of his shields cresting even higher. "And it's a problem...?"

"If they can't relax, they won't be able to learn to shield or send thoughts." Mother-Fucking-Jack-Off. MFJO.

"My style is very effective. I've taken students who ranked in the bottom twenty five percent in their first year and had them at the top eighty percent within six months. And their shields don't break at the first sign of stress."

"Those are Breds. Not Wilds."

"You said yourself some of the students have effective shielding. That it's impressive where they're at."

"But it's at the expense of their self-esteem. They don't like you."

They don't have to. This isn't a popularity contest. Whether or not I'm liked doesn't bother me or change my teaching style.

Lie. I saw it below the surface. It bothered him he hadn't been able to connect with any of the students.

"As you said," he continued. "Survival is the priority and I'm teaching them to survive. It's more important than making the kids like me."

I threw up my hands. "I'm just trying to help, but whatever."

He breathed loudly, in through his nose and out through his mouth. "Fine. What do you recommend?"

I didn't want to tell him. I wanted to fold my arms and refuse to talk to him. He was such an ass. But that wasn't going to help the kids. Fucking-A, I was tired.

"I started them with some relaxation techniques," I said. "Daniel starts his classes with them too."

"I don't have the time if I'm going to turn these teenagers into functioning adults. They should know relaxation techniques already."

"Wilds don't grow up knowing they're going to be Wilds. We don't learn meditation at home or in school. Fucking-A, Stephen. Half of the kids have no communication with their families. Relaxation hasn't been high on their must-do lists."

He stood up and paced away. *Fair point.* The tsunami in his shields receded, just a little. *I'll add it to the curriculum.*

There's one more thing. What was wrong with me? I should've stopped when I was ahead.

Only one other thing I'm doing wrong?

The water had almost completely spun out of my glass.

Have fun with them. They're good kids, most of them. Play games—it'll help them learn a little differently. These are teenagers.

Moronic Neanderthal.

Fun? We don't have time for that. We only have five years and unless they work very hard, and are lucky, they're not going to achieve anything. They'll continue at minimum wage jobs, barely using their Gifts or hiding them completely. I mean, we're killing ourselves so they can have a chance to work a job at a place like Mt. Olympus. Trying to guess drink orders from Breds who think Wilds are pieces of furniture or less.

He was right. I knew that, I really did. I'd said similar things at staff meetings. Being a Wild meant less opportunities and more work for everything. But I still saw red. *Then why are you here? Why even try? Let's just be done with Wilds in general. We don't matter.*

That's not—

Lock us up. Use our genetic code to make better Breds.

"Are you done?" His shields swirled in a mess of yellows, reds and oranges, but his voice was patient. Like he was calming an upset teen mouthing off in his class.

My water glass shattered.

In fact, just exterminate us at birth. I couldn't stop, the words hissing out from my mind too quickly to control. *Offer tests for parents to predict whether or not their unborn baby is a Wild. Abort it or just have someone there to take the baby away. Claim it died.*

I'm not talking to you when you're—

Why don't you Breds—

He closed the channel, teleporting away and slamming up his shields so quickly my brain felt bruised. My office window cracked into a star pattern, like someone had thrown something against it.

Mother-fucking-son-of-a-goddamn-bag-of-fucking-shitheads.

My hands shook.

Breathe in. And out.

Breathe in. And out.

I couldn't afford to replace the window. I was an adult, not some teenage Wild who couldn't control their Gift.

The framed picture of my friends cracked. Fucking-Bitch-Balls.

I focused on five things I could see, four things I could hear, and three things to touch until my breathing calmed and my desk stopped vibrating.

I wanted to go upstairs, hammer on his apartment door and scream until I lost my voice. He didn't know. He just didn't understand.

Tears pricked at my eyes.

This world wasn't fair, and I was so tired of seeing my kids only get the bare minimum of a life, regardless of how powerful, smart or kind they were. I was tired of the eighty-hour workweeks and of slicing the budget to squeeze money out of empty accounts. I was tired of turning kids over to the Guardians for not being teachable. Tired of protestors, of mobs chasing us, of Guardians who didn't help because of who we were born to.

I put my head on my desk and wept.

CHAPTER TWENTY-FOUR

I WAITED FOR HIM, my feet washed by warm surges of water. Foam fizzled on the damp sand, and broken bits of shells glinted in the sun. I faced the horizon where no boats, birds or whales broke the perfect line. When his shadow approached from the beach line, I turned to smile.

"I've never been to the ocean, except in these dreams," I said. "It's so different from the internet and books. I should go sometime. It's an easy teleport."

"My family's estate is built on an island, so I grew up surrounded by the ocean." He stood behind me and snaked an arm around my waist. I rested my back against his body. He felt good, warm and solid.

He ran a finger along a shoulder, and I shivered, delicious goosebumps popping up. "Not everyone likes the ocean. Some find it too violent or cold." His lips murmured close to my ear. My breath shuddered as desire echoed through me. "Others don't like the sand or the bugs living in it."

I stepped away to pick up a handful of sand. "No bugs."

"I try to make things perfect here, because nothing is perfect in the real world.

"No, it's not."

I turned around and rested my hands on his shoulders. "I think I'm mad at you in the real world."

He grinned, that grin I loved on his unshaven face. "I think I'm mad at you too."

I ran my fingers over his shirt. I couldn't believe how real this dream was—I could actually feel the texture of the shirt, soft against his warm skin.

"We'll get over it," he said.

"And then we'll fight again."

He touched my chin, running a hand to the back of my neck to pull me in.

"Why am I here?" I asked, my lips close to his. "Why do I keep coming?"

"You're not perfect," he whispered, his face so close to mine, the green in his eyes bright, with tiny flecks of gold.

I pulled away, just a little. "Excuse me?"

"Perfect is boring. It's been my entire life and I'm so bored." He leaned in, his lips just brushing mine, but I laughed and pulled away, slapping his hand away.

"More lines. You'll have to do better. I'm not easy." I looked around at the perfect beach, the perfect moment. "And this is a little too perfect."

"I love a challenge."

The scene changed. We were at a fancy bar, surrounded by blank people, without thoughts or shields. It was like something out of the fifties, with glittery chandeliers, carved crown moldings and waiters in tuxedos holding martinis and tiny trays with even tinier foods.

He'd put me in a purple silk dress with a flirty skirt, hitting just above my knees. A mirror over the bar showed my white hair swept up into an elegant knot. Diamonds glinted at my neck and ears. I looked down. My shoes were silver needlepoint heels, my toes and fingers painted the same color as my dress.

Stephen turned away from the bar, two drinks in his hands, a Cosmo with a cranberry floating in the bottom and a clear liquid over ice with a lime. He tried to hand me the Cosmo.

"You really think this is me?" I took the drink over ice and took a sip. Cold, sharp gin hit my tongue.

He put the Cosmo down.

"Then you choose."

I concentrated and we were in a bar I'd played a few sets in when my band was still playing gigs. In real life, the space was dark, with the drink bar against one corner and the tiny stage in the other. I used the dream to clean it up, polishing the scuffed floor until it gleamed and adding twinkling candles everywhere. I set up a band playing folk rock, and blank people listening and dancing around us.

I changed into jeans and a peasant blouse, with leather boots laced over my knees. I'd left him in the suit he'd worn in the bar; he could change his own clothes if he wanted to.

He glanced around and was suddenly wearing jeans and a casual button-up shirt. I leaned against him, my back against his chest to watch the band. He wrapped his arms around my waist again. His breath on my ear, he murmured, "Better?"

The goosebumps were back. "Much," I said. I turned around and he slid his lips down to mine.

CHAPTER TWENTY-FIVE

"You wanted to see me?" I asked Miriam.

"You've been avoiding me," Miriam said. The flowers on her desk this morning were orange, red and white, the insides of the vase crystal clear. She must have just gotten them.

"Not intentionally," I lied. I leaned on the doorway, my screen clutched against my chest. "There's a lot to do."

"And it's definitely been noticed. I can't believe how much you get done on a daily basis. You're the glue holding Phillip's Academy together and I can't say enough how much I appreciate you."

What the—?

"Have a seat." Miriam came out from behind her desk and sat in one of the visitor armchairs, gesturing for me to sit on the couch. This was new. Normally only parents sat in the visitor chairs lately. The last few years, she'd preferred to keep her desk between her and her staff. "Do you want some water? Tea?"

"No thanks." I stared at Miriam's shields trying to figure out what was going on. They were dark, which was nothing new, not lately. She'd tightly wrapped them around her thoughts, and I couldn't catch a glimpse of anything. Miriam herself had circles under her eyes and new worry lines in her forehead and bracketing her mouth.

I'm fine, Miriam thought. *Just a little tired. No need to poke at my shields.* She switched back to her voice.

Something was definitely up. I'd never had a one-on-one with Miriam like this before.

"Oh, and I have your backdated paychecks," she said. "I didn't realize I was so far behind and you have my apologies." An envelope flew out of her desk and I caught it. "It's only five of the seven—"

"Eight," I interrupted without thinking.

"Eight," she said, a magenta burst in her shields signaling her frustration at being corrected. Her voice didn't change though. "But I will get you the rest as soon as I'm able."

I glanced at the number inside the envelope and teleported it to my apartment. "I really appreciate it. Christmas is coming and I'd like to buy some presents."

"It's only a few weeks away. And I'm sure you have your eye on some sort of instrument, too."

"I do." A smile stretched my lips. "I was thinking of getting another cello. It's my favorite instrument, but mine is about to fall apart."

"You still have the one I gave you?"

My first year at the Warehouse had been horrible. I'd had so much difficulty controlling my telepathy and psychokinesis despite all the private tutoring from Daniel and Ruffalo, the telepathy teacher at the time. Like Becca, I was terrified I'd be expelled if I made one more mistake. So I'd gotten into the habit of sneaking into the admin building before it was locked to hang out in the empty rooms and get away from everyone. I'd been in the admin conference room, scrunched in a corner between a file cabinet and the wall, when Daniel had teleported a mess of donated instruments for him and Miriam to sort through. The instruments were in bad shape, chipped, cracked and broken with holes in the wrong places. Violins missed their bows, guitars had smashed tuners, and there were way too many drumsticks and no drums. But with the instruments, the room had felt different. It was like I'd been trying to breathe underwater and had suddenly grown gills.

I'd climbed out of the corner, and gone straight to the cello, somehow finding its bow in all the mess. I'd drawn it across the strings, creating perfect notes on the chipped instrument, by pure instinct.

The cello was Stephen's favorite instrument, a voice whispered in my head.

Jesus-Christ. What was wrong with me? Maybe I should invest in an accordion or a banjo. He'd probably hate those.

"I definitely think you should buy another cello, then," Miriam said, breaking through my memories. "I've been hearing you at night. You've been playing it a lot."

"I'm sorry," I said. "I thought I was playing quietly enough."

She waved it away. "I've been up late the last few nights. It's the only reason I've heard you. Otherwise, I don't think anyone else does. Maybe Stephen?" She frowned. "Has he mentioned it?"

Uhhhhh...

"Yeah, but he says it doesn't bother him." The trick to lying was to just leave things out. I added another layer to my shields, keeping my face still.

"Changing the subject," Miriam said, folding her hands in her lap. "You're not expected to work seven days a week, week after week," Miriam continued. "Please take at least one day off. You're starting to look tired and pale. And I'm really going to need your help in the next few months."

"What's going on?"

She paused, the gray streaks in her shields spreading even more.

I reached forward and touched her hand. "Did something happen?"

She met my eyes and smiled, but there were tears. "Of course not. I just think things are going to get busier, so take some time while you can. I worry Phillip's Academy is turning into a fishbowl for you. You need to get out and have some other interests."

"I know," I lied. I didn't know why everyone always went on and on about needing days off. I was as happy as I was going to get. And if I didn't work, what else would I do? My band was dissolved, and I hadn't played a gig in years.

"Maybe I'll go out with Seiko this weekend. He's probably performing at some comedy club."

"That's a really good idea—maybe we should all go. Or maybe all of you can go and I'll stay with the students."

I agreed to set it up and Miriam continued, "But I did have something else to discuss. Chanelle, the social worker at Sedona's Institution for Wilds, contacted me. Remember her?"

I nodded.

"She has a potential Wild for us that might be a good fit. The girl was picked up for stealing but hasn't spent a lot of time on the streets. When the Guardians contacted her parents, they told the Guardians they didn't want her back."

When did it become okay to refuse to take care of your own child? Oh! I remember. If they were a Wild, you were supposed to refuse.

"Chanelle says she's clever and it would be a waste to see her locked up for the rest of her life," Miriam said. "We could fill Dharma's spot with her." Dharma was a fifth year, whose parents had pulled her after the mall incident.

"But Dharma's parents paid tuition. We can't afford to take on another freebie."

"That's the great part," Miriam said with a smile. "I just worked out a plan with the Office of Gifted where we're going to get an allowance for each child we house here who would otherwise be in an institution. So all the students without families, like Becca, we're actually going to get paid for. It's not as much as we'd get from charging tuition, but it helps. And they're going to give us a lump sum for all the students we currently have not paying tuition."

"That's amazing!"

Miriam's shields turned luminescent. "I've spent weeks on this. It's going to make all the difference."

"What's the catch?"

Her shields darkened. "You're too smart."

"No. Just been around the OOG for years. What got traded?"

Miriam straightened her stapler and picked a dead leaf off her flowers.

Miriam?

All of our students go on the Registry.

"All? Even the ones paying tuition?"

"Yes. It's not that many students. And the Registry is just a list of Wilds. It doesn't impact things much. Not everyone checks it."

Was she that out of touch? Our graduates struggled to find jobs, even if they weren't on the Registry. Why would Miriam make it harder?

"This is part of the big picture thinking I need you to do."

"I get it." But she was wrong. Putting all our Wilds on the Registry was only thinking about today.

"But I didn't bring you here to talk about that. We need to focus on the Wild." Miriam pressed a few buttons on her screen. "I just sent her info to you."

I scanned it. The teen was thirteen years old, lived in Phoenix and had poor grades from her middle school. I read her thin psych and personality screenings. She'd been tested and "observed" by some exhausted and underpaid Wild or some bored and overpaid Bred. She was intelligent and Gifted in psychokinesis and telepathy. They noted she had shields, could move small objects with effort, but couldn't speak telepathically.

"It'll be hard to start three months into the school year," I started. "But if she's a good fit and tries hard, she'll probably be fine. We've had other students start even later."

Miriam inclined her head. "We have."

I sighed, looking at the girl's picture. Her eyes told the world to fuck off. Her hair was bleached blonde with blue tips, and she'd pierced her eyebrows, ears, and lip with bits of metal. The picture showed her with a black eye and bruised cheek. Someone had hit her, probably getting her into custody. She'd had it rough.

"We haven't taken on a child that's been arrested and has a record in a while," I said. "They don't usually work out."

"True."

Part of the reason Miriam had been so upset about Becca was because the last three Wilds we'd taken off the streets had been disasters. Wilds who did whatever it took to survive on the streets had problems adjusting to the rules and structure of the Warehouse. The last one from two years ago, Mercy, had stolen, and gotten into fights. She'd finally threatened to kill another student and Miriam had called the Guardians. Then, Mercy used her Gift to turn anything not bolted down into projectiles. We'd had to sedate her, and she'd fought against the sedation. It took three syringes to completely knock her out.

"Why'd you accept me?" I asked, and then wondered where the question had come from.

She sighed. "Instinct. The same instinct you had about Becca and Leo. But it's up to you after you speak with her."

I looked at the picture of the girl again. There was emptiness behind her eyes. She didn't expect anyone to help her, ever. Her life was done, and she knew it. All because of her genes.

My heart broke. "Her name's Cassandra Lopez," I said, reading off the screen. "Prefers Casi." Like naming a stray pet, she was ours. "I'll contact Chanelle and plan to pick her up tomorrow."

I grabbed my screen and stood up. "Anything else?"

"There is," Miriam said, taking off her glasses and polishing them on her skirt. "I want you to take Stephen with you."

"Why? I don't need a babysitter."

"Part of your write-up was you would take another faculty member when recruiting."

I thought the write-up was behind us. She'd just told me what a great job I was doing.

"Fine," I said. "I'll take Kaya. Or Seiko. He hasn't ever gone to one of the institutions."

"No. You're going to take Stephen. There's a multitude of reasons," Miriam said, raising a hand to my protests. "First, I want him to evaluate Casi as well. If he thinks she won't fit in, she's not to come with you. Understood?"

Awesome. "Yes," I said.

"Second, he needs to understand how Wilds are treated in the outside world, so he can understand how to help them."

I thawed a little. "Agreed."

"And third, the building was shaking last night, so I need the two of you to get along. I can't have my staff arguing so much the windows rattle."

"Fine," I muttered.

"We need him," Miriam said. "Who do you think helped us get the money from the OOG? Please do your part so he's not blaming you if he goes back to Seagull's Landing."

"Fine. I'll try. But he's so—"

"I don't care. Help him to succeed here."

I threw up my hands. "That's what we fought about. I was trying to help."

"Not correctly. Fix this. He's trying and we can't afford to lose him. Tell him I'll sub for his classes."

"I know he's trying," I muttered. And his dream self kisses really well, the traitorous bitch inside my head whispered.

Outside Miriam's office, I strategized. Should I just knock on Stephen's door and apologize? He'd brought me flowers after our first argument. Should I do the same? What was a good apology present for a guy? A cake? A plant? Were either of those things at the Warehouse or was I going to have to leave, buy something, come back, and then apologize?

There was light streaming out of Stephen's open office door.

I was stalling.

Opening up a desk drawer, I grabbed a chocolate bar and a half empty bag of granola along with two waters. I knocked on his office door frame, the snacks balanced with my Gift. He looked up from his screen, and his turquoise shields wrapped themselves further around his mind. He was still mad. That was fine. I was mad too.

Did you have dinner? I have some snacks if you're hungry.

He nodded toward a half-eaten tray of food from the kitchen. Tonight had been meatloaf, mashed potatoes and a side salad. He'd eaten the salad and left most of the meatloaf and mashed potatoes.

Wow, his Quality Bred palate still needed to adjust.

I tucked the thought behind my shields before he could see it. I didn't want to argue again, and the idea was mean. And he'd lost weight since starting at the Warehouse, I realized. He'd been the perfect weight for his frame, his shirts and pants nicely filled out. Now the sweater he wore sagged slightly on his arms and shoulders.

He pointed at the pile of junk food. *Your dinner?*

I often forget to eat. Hence the snacks in my office.

Hence, he repeated.

I took a deep breath and spoke out loud. "I'm sorry for last night." *I was way out of line and overreacted,* I continued telepathically. He didn't say anything, but his shields lightened a little, green working their way through them. *I was tired and get so upset about the way Wilds are treated. I'm sorry. I know you're not like others.*

I wish you'd stop trying to get me to leave. It's hard, but I really do want to make a difference, as clichéd as that is.

I know. I gently touched his shields with mine. *But you're teaching like the kids are Breds and they're not.*

I'm trying. He leaned back, his sweater lifting up just a touch and showing a band of tanned, muscular ab. "Come in and sit down with your tiny and unhealthy dinner."

I sat down in his leather visitor chair and melted into the soft upholstery. This wasn't standard issue from Miriam. He must have brought it from home.

I offered him the half-eaten bag of granola and he took a handful.

"I do need your help for a project. Miriam thought you'd be a huge help," I said, trying to be diplomatic. It was a weird sensation.

He laughed, but not like anything was funny. *Of course. I should've known you'd need something.*

God, I was a horrible liar. What was I supposed to say? I would've apologized even if Miriam hadn't ordered me to do so? I wouldn't have. I'd just avoid him until we both forgot about the argument.

I am sorry. Really. Even if Miriam hadn't asked me... I swallowed. *I'd still be sorry.* I wished I'd never gotten into a fight with him.

He stood and went to the window, looking at the reflection of his office. He ran his fingers through his hair. "I'm not being fair to you. And my last comment was out of line. And I shouldn't have called you a Wild Princess yesterday."

I shrugged. "I came up with some really good names for you too, and then I turned them into acronyms. Like MFJO."

He frowned and tried to puzzle it out. "Mother-Fucking...Jell-O? I'm terrible at acronyms. What did it stand for?"

"It's a secret. Are we even, at least?" I crossed my fingers, holding them up so he could see. He laughed again, this time with more humor and sat back down at his desk, taking another handful of granola.

"I guess so. What did you need?"

Miriam wants you to come with me to an institution tomorrow. A social worker in Sedona thinks she has a Wild who'd be a good fit. Miriam will sub for your classes.

Two subs in three days, my students will rejoice.

He'd known his students didn't like him before I opened up my mouth. Of course he had. He was the telepathy teacher.

"Want to come over to my apartment and watch a movie?" I asked. "You can eat more of my crappy granola. I have cheap bourbon. And only one chair, that broke, but Daniel fixed it. But I can sit on the floor." Great. Now I was babbling. Like this afternoon couldn't have gotten any more embarrassing.

He smiled, his shields expanding around him, the turquoise color brightening. I loved the way the blues and greens melted, merged and then separated when he was amused.

How about I invite you over tonight since you only have one chair. I'll invite the entire faculty.

That would be fun.

"Meet you upstairs in an hour?"

"Sounds perfect."

———

I brought the bourbon. His apartment was clean and tastefully furnished in blues and browns with hints of green. There was a faint ocean theme between the blue green colors and other items he'd picked out, like the distressed wood and expensive looking beach prints on the walls. "You really like the ocean, don't you?" I asked.

"It's my favorite place."

We watched two old comedies, Daniel, Kaya, Seiko, Stephen and myself crammed into his living area. We ate popcorn and drank hot chocolate seasoned with a few drops of Bailey's, laughing, quoting the dialogue and talking with our mouths full.

We had such a great time, we talked about setting up a monthly schedule to sit in each other's apartments and watch movies.

"Except Kendle," Daniel said with a sneer for me. "She doesn't even have furniture."

"I have some," I said. "You're welcome to come over whenever you want. The floor is clean. We can set up blankets and pillows on it."

"Do you even have a big screen?" he snapped, his honey shields dark, like amber. I wondered how much Bailey's he'd poured into his hot chocolate.

But he was right. I didn't normally have people over. There was no point. I stopped working late at night and was too tired to socialize. I didn't watch many shows, so I didn't have a screen big enough for others to watch.

We said our goodbyes and I walked the few feet to my apartment, pressing my palm to the lock to unlock the door and stepping inside.

I'd switched the bedroom and living room three years ago after Seiko complained my music kept him awake. Now when you went into my apartment, you stepped into a kitchen and bedroom combo. In the beginning, I'd put up a folding partition to separate the bedroom from the kitchen, but it had broken, and I'd never replaced it.

My bed was a basic queen covered with different colored blankets against the winter drafts. I only made it when I changed the sheets. I didn't even have a headboard. I'd painted the walls of the entire apartment a sage gray when I'd moved in and hadn't touched them since. There were scuff marks in some places and the baseboards were faded and dingy. I vacuumed the carpet weekly, but it had been old when I moved in and was now thin and stained in spots.

Daniel had fixed the leg on my armchair, but it still wobbled, and I hadn't fixed the rip along the back. And that was it for my furniture. A bed, a bedside table and the armchair.

I went into my music space, what should've been the bedroom. It held wall-to-wall instruments, including the cello I'd saved all those years ago. Two ukuleles hung on the walls. I picked up my favorite guitar, one I'd found in a used bookstore of all places, noting how thin the wood was getting where my hand hit it while strumming. I compared my apartment to Stephen's well-decorated space with its expensive furnishings. His belonged to a grown up. Mine belonged to a Wild.

Kaya touched my shields. *Don't let Daniel get to you. Your apartment suits you perfectly.*

I haven't changed anything since I moved in. Haven't I changed? I put down the guitar and went into the kitchen to pull open a drawer and fish out a joint. It was almost gone but was enough to help me sleep.

Let's do a girl's day out on Saturday. Maybe pick up some paint, some art for your walls. Have lunch out.

Sounds good, I lied. I'd just make sure there was some crisis and I wouldn't have to go.

I changed into pajama pants and a sweatshirt, lying down in bed with a novel on my screen. But the fiction about a giant, fencing, miracles and true love didn't keep my interest. I went into my music room and picked up my guitar again. I picked out a song, the music vibrating off my fingers.

Thank you for tonight, Stephen whispered across my shields. *Most fun I've had since I've been here.*

You're welcome.

You going to play for a while?

For as long as the music wants me to.

Then I'll listen until it stops.

CHAPTER TWENTY-SIX

"MAY, LIKE THE MONTH," I said to the Guardian who couldn't find my name on the approved list. "Starts with an M." We were at Sedona, going through security to get inside the building. The Guardian swiped his screen, his olive-green shields lazily moving. He thought this job was beneath him.

He finally found my name and checked it off his screen. When Stephen said his, the Guardian straightened a little, his shields darkening with surprise and recognition. Guess Stephen had a fan.

Stephen smiled, but the orange and red thoughts appeared beneath his shields. He was annoyed. Maybe that's part of what had drawn him to the Warehouse; not being worshiped everywhere he went because of who he was born to. I sighed. Things were so much easier when he was just a Rune that wasn't going to last at the Warehouse. And I'd had another dream about him last night. We'd been at the ocean again, making out on a blanket and talking about our childhoods. I'd told him all about the two-bedroom apartment I shared with my mom and grandmother and the kitchen cupboard I'd hide in, pretending I was on a pirate ship. My mother had always smuggled me rations—oatmeal raisin cookies warm from the oven. I'd woken up so ridiculously happy and relaxed.

At least my dream libido was getting a workout, I consoled myself.

The Guardian finished checking off our names, his smile only for Stephen. He reached into a box and pulled out two dark gray bands.

"I'm sorry, sir," the Guardian said to Stephen. "But anyone who doesn't have a security clearance must wear the bands when on the premises. Though it's ridiculous for someone like you, and I deeply apologize—"

"It's all right," Stephen said with a small smile. "You're just doing your job. And I wouldn't want you to get into any trouble."

Have you ever worn bands before? I asked him.

No, but I've seen them in use. They just dull Gifts, right?

Right, but they're really painful.

Painful?

Meanwhile the Guardian instructed Stephen how to clip the bracelet around his wrist, ignoring me completely. Stephen complied, jumping as the bracelet turned red and then green. "Something poked me."

The Guardian turned white, and stammered, "I'm so sorry. I should've warned—"

I cut through the drama. "The bands take a blood sample of your genetic code to make sure you're Gifted. The needle stings a bit if you're not prepared for it."

The Guardian's expression didn't change, but orange leaked into his olive shields. He didn't like that I'd dared contradict a Bred. I was only a Wild.

"Once it's on, you can't take it off, unless someone unlocks it," I said.

"Any side effects?" Stephen asked.

"Absolutely not," the Guardian said. "It's been well tested."

I shrugged. "You hear stories. Some Wilds report difficulty using their Gifts for a few days afterwards. I haven't had any problems though and I haven't heard about any Breds with problems."

"Sir, I apologize," the Guardian said. "I can assure you the use of the bands make this building safer and they themselves are completely safe."

But Stephen was inspecting the band around his wrist. "Let me see your arm," he asked me.

"Why?"

Not everything needs to be an argument.

Jesus. Fine. I held out my arm, knowing what he was going to do. He pushed up the sleeve and compared the scars on my wrists to the band on his.

"If they can cause scars like this, they don't seem safe to me," he said to the Guardian.

"Sir, I assure you, if you don't use your Gift, there's nothing to worry about. The bands do tighten incrementally over time if you use your Gift, but it's barely noticeable. Unless you're using your Gift because you're trying to escape or are fighting the Guardians. Then they'll cause that kind of damage."

"You do know Wild gangs use them as punishment, right?" I said. "Or illegal Gladiator Rings? Or Wild traffickers?"

"Wilds shouldn't be on the streets. Otherwise those things wouldn't happen."

"Of course not." I clipped the band onto my wrist and winced as the needle bit. The bracelet turned red, then blue. Stephen and the Guardian's shields faded away. I felt numb and off balance, like my legs had gone to sleep but I still had to walk on them. Now that I couldn't sense his shields, I noticed the Guardian's blonde surfer hair and tanned skin. And I noticed how good Stephen looked in his suit, though it, like the rest of his clothes, sagged a bit on his frame. And he had a day-old beard and dark shadows under his eyes. On anyone else, he'd look ill, but he looked like he'd pulled an all-nighter saving the world.

Stephen grimaced and I heard the faintest whisper of telepathic thought from him. He winced and glanced at the band.

"Wow, these are terrible," he said.

"If you don't use your Gift, you'll be fine," the Guardian said. "And you won't have to wear it for very long." He pressed a button and the front doors swung open. "Welcome to Sedona's Institution for Wilds. Have a good day."

"What were you going to say?" I asked, as we walked into the building.

"Why is yours blue and mine green? Wild vs. Bred?"

"Security threat vs. not. I have a record."

"For what?"

"Stealing. I was never arrested or anything, but they issued a warrant."

"Was this while you were at the Warehouse?"

"God no. It was before. Miriam found me in Vegas where I'd escaped from one of those underground Gladiator rings where they pit Wilds against Wilds and bet on the winners."

"Wait, what?" He stopped and tugged on my arm. "Are you serious?"

I took off my sunglasses and stuffed them into my bag. "It's not..." I stopped. It was a big deal. "I don't talk about it. But after I escaped, I didn't have anywhere to go, so I and some other Wilds stole from the Vegas tourists."

"And then Miriam found you?" He stared at me and I couldn't tell what he was thinking or feeling. I really hated wearing the bands. I wished I hadn't said anything. My past was over and done and I didn't like to talk about it.

"Pretty much." I started walking down the hallway again. "So that's why my band is blue and yours is green."

By this point, we'd reached a darkly varnished desk manned by a Bred receptionist, her icy blonde hair pulled into a bun, her high cheekbones giving her an elfin look. I wondered how much money her parents had poured into her appearance.

"We have an appointment to see Chanelle," I said. Like the other Guardians, the receptionist wore black, but it was a black dress instead of a uniform. It felt so weird not to see her shields.

The receptionist nodded and typed onto her screen. She eyed Stephen, giving him a big toothy smile. He smiled back, automatically, his lips closed. I congratulated myself, realizing my brain no longer stuttered when I looked at him.

"She'll be right up," the receptionist said, her voice breathy, like a forties movie star. I wondered if her parents had added it to her genetic code too. She invited us to have a seat, but before we could, a tall Bred with straight and shiny hair hanging down to her knees approached us.

"Chanelle," I said with a smile, holding out my hand. She glanced at me, ignored my hand and turned to Stephen.

"New teacher?" She literally purred. I tried not to roll my eyes, but probably didn't succeed.

I'm not taking you anywhere ever again, I started to say to him, but the band tightened again. Wonderful.

"Stephen Rune," he said. "Telepathy."

"What on earth are you doing at Phillip's Academy?"

"Teaching."

"Wilds? Why aren't you at Seagull's Landing?" She stood too close to him, her head tilted coquettishly to the side.

"I like Phillip's Academy."

She ran her tongue over her lips, and then tapped a fingernail against them. "I think I just read an article about you. The picture didn't do justice."

"I ignore the media." His green eyes had darkened, and a flush worked its way up his neck. I wondered if he always flushed when he got frustrated. I was too used to looking at his shields and had never noticed.

"Chanelle," I interrupted. "These bands are terrible. Can we get this done, please, so we can go home?"

"Sure," she said with a shrug. Then she moved down a hall, her ass waggling.

I raised an eyebrow at Stephen as we fell in behind her. "I can't help it," he mouthed to me.

"Does this happen a lot?" I asked, trying to ignore Chanelle's ass.

"Yes," he muttered, running his fingers through his hair. His eyebrows twitched and he looked down at the bands with a sigh. "It was my parent's choice to make me look like this."

We passed through tunnels of industrial halls, painted a cheap gray, broken up by forgettable art with a desert theme deemed appropriate and neutral enough for the workers in the building. After being buzzed through multiple locked doors, we finally reached the detention area.

The girl we'd come for sat in a ten-by-ten room surrounded by thick one-way glass. There was no furniture, and she sat against the glass, her arms around her knees, her head resting on them. She wore glowing red bands on each wrist. The skin around them was reddened and swollen. She didn't have good control and was inadvertently using her Gift, without being able to stop. But the bands just kept tightening.

"Can I scan her, please?" I asked Chanelle. I held out my wrist so she could take the ridiculous band off.

She paused.

"You guys have let me do it before," I said.

"I know." But she didn't unlock it. I mentally cursed, but kept my face neutral, while Chanelle thought. Miriam would never allow this girl to come unless I scanned her. I needed to know what was beneath her thoughts.

"He can do it," Chanelle said. "He can scan her."

"I'm just tagging along," Stephen said, raising his hands.

"He's new. He doesn't know what to look for," I added.

Chanelle looked from me to him and stepped forward to unlock Stephen's band. The flirting was gone. "He's a Bred," she said by means of explanation.

The band tightened so much my hand went numb. The glass around the cell vibrated, just once.

I took a deep breath, hating every part of this day.

"I'll be registering a complaint with your supervisor," Stephen said to Chanelle.

"Why?" She legitimately didn't know.

"You're making it impossible for Ms. May to do her job. You're risking the lives of her students...our students," he corrected, "if we can't get a proper reading."

"And we're condemning this girl if we choose not to take her," I finished. "You've been helping us for years. Why now?"

"I can't break the rules," she said.

"Fine," I said. "I'll talk him through it."

We walked around until we faced the girl's back.

"Have you done a scan on anyone before?" I asked.

"Of course." He put his hand on the glass, right above the girl's head and closed his eyes. Thirty seconds later he straightened.

"This could be so much easier if I could show you," he said, running his fingers through his hair so it stood up.

"Well you can't," I snapped. I moderated my tone. "Sorry."

"I know. No offense taken. But this girl is pretty messed up."

"Most Wilds in her position are. Did you see violent tendencies or anything else?"

"Not really though she's scared and angry. I didn't go too deep, but I think her thoughts are normal for someone that's been through..." He rubbed his head again. "God it was terrible." He held my eyes with his. "What happens if we don't accept her?"

"She stays here or a place like this, because her parents don't want her."

His lips pulled down new lines forming.

"In the end she will die here or a rehab facility like this one," I said. "And if she's lucky, she'll only live for a few years. But as Miriam keeps reminding me, you can't let that impact your decision. We have to protect our students too." I really missed telepathy.

He just stared at me. "It's instinct," I said. "Becca and Leo were instincts." I threw up my hands. "They're doing fine now, but...I don't know."

He'd run his fingers so many times through his hair, it looked like he'd been electrocuted. "So how am I supposed to make the decision?"

"Miriam and I already mostly decided to accept her. This is the final test. What does your gut say?"

"We take her."

"Okay," I said, before he could ask me if it was the right decision.

CHAPTER TWENTY-SEVEN

"I GOT HER FROM HERE," I said to Stephen once we were finally home and breathing through the vertigo from the transport pad. "I'm going to give her a tour, show her to a room and introduce her to her room-mates. You'll see her tomorrow in your class." It was only Wednesday; I couldn't believe it.

Will she be okay? he asked as he held the gate open for the two of us and we moved down the path toward the buildings.

I don't know.

The things she's been through...

Are the same as many Wilds. Our students have been so fucked by life, simply because of who they were born to. Go eat some chocolate or something. There's ice cream in back of the walk-in freezer, under the frozen berries.

I couldn't distract him though.

Life screwed you.

God, I wished I hadn't told him about Vegas. *Yep. Before Miriam found me.*

I looked up at the buildings, my home for the last fifteen years. It was a few weeks until Christmas and the ground was frozen, a cold wind blowing off the lake. The tiny vegetable garden was clear; the plants either dug up and transplanted into pots to live in various buildings or allowed to die. *I still have nightmares sometimes,* I thought.

If you ever need company in the middle of the night, just knock on the wall.

Excuse me? Was he hitting on me again?

That came out wrong, he thought. I meant, never mind... I'm going to go relieve Miriam from teaching. I'll see you around.

He teleported away instead of walking. It was almost three and classes were nearly finished for the day. It was better to let Miriam finish rather than interrupting.

And what was his comment supposed to mean?

I shook my head and focused on Casi, pushing Stephen out of my head. Like Leo, Casi had arrived with just the clothes on her back, so there was nothing to drop off in her room.

"Ready to go on a tour?"

She shrugged, looking around at the four buildings, her eyes shaded from the bright winter sun. Casi had the skinny look of someone who'd lived on chips, candy and processed foods. She probably hadn't had a vegetable or fruit in years. Her shields were a charcoal gray shot through with reds and oranges. I wondered if they'd be more of a silver color once she relaxed.

"There's about seventy students here," I started, as we started toward the dorm. "Everyone knows each other by sight if nothing else, so they'll know you're the new kid, but most are really nice here. They won't haze you."

"How long do I stay?"

"The curriculum is for five years, and most of our students start when they're twelve or thirteen, but we've had some Wilds join us when they're a little older. It kind of depends on your skills, and what you came here with. Most stay until they're seventeen or eighteen."

"And then?"

"And then they try to get a job, an apartment. We can help with that too. A lot of people from the Warehouse get apartments together in the beginning."

I pointed out the classroom building so she'd know where to go in the morning. "In addition to school, we have clubs on the weekends and evenings. There's a club for everything anyone is interested in. Books, sewing, baking, Anime, Harry Potter."

"DnD?" Casi had watched an older sibling play Dungeons and Dragons when she was really young. She'd idolized him and had wanted to be just like him when she was older. Watching the game was one of the highlights of her childhood.

I gently withdrew from her thoughts. Stephen was going to need to catch her up on her shielding.

"We haven't had a DnD club in a bit, but we could get one going, if we have a decent Dungeon Master. There's probably other kids interested. I'll suggest it and let you know if we get one started. Sound good?"

"Whatever."

We walked to the dorm warehouse. It was three stories high with an open middle running up to the tin ceiling. Built like a rectangle, it reminded me of an old-fashioned hotel with hallways of doors on each story. The right side of each story was for the girls, the left for the boys. The bottom had a large common area full of couches, chairs, tables, food and board games. We were constantly under attack from ants and last year mice moved in. And Mr. Sparklebutt was no help.

I led her through the sliding glass doors into the building and down the girl's hall on the first floor, showing Casi how to use her palm print to unlock her door. The other kids in the hallways and in their rooms twisted their necks to see her but didn't say anything. I felt the echoes of telepathic communication as the kids gossiped about Casi. Her face hardened, but she raised her chin as we walked into her new room.

I had put Casi with Becca and Helen. Helen had sweetly agreed to give Casi the single bed and had moved to the bunk bed with Becca on top. Becca had been doing extra chores for spending money and now had several stuffed animals and throw pillows on her bed. The framed pictures of her parents still took center stage on her desk, but there was a figurine of a popular action figure she hadn't had before.

Helen had been enrolled by her parents into the Warehouse and paid the most expensive tier of tuition. A strong Wild, with rainbow shields, she held straight As, had learned sign language and was friends with nearly everyone. Her part of the room was pretty, with red and blue throw pillows matching the new bedspread where a stuffed cat sat. Stapled to the walls were pictures of friends and sunny tropical places. There were a few bare patches waiting for Casi's things.

I introduced Casi to Helen and Becca and showed her where her uniform was.

"Uniform?"

Casi rolled her eyes at Helen, hoping for an ally.

"They're not that bad," Helen said.

Casi focused her eyes on mine. She was probably trying to speak telepathically but hadn't figured it out yet.

"Do I have to?" she finally asked.

"Yes. We require uniforms. It's easier to get dressed in the mornings. Helen and Becca will show you how to wear or sew them, so they look better on you, right?" I asked, signing to Becca. They nodded, but I could tell they weren't too impressed with Casi.

"What else do you need?" I asked her. "Shampoo, deodorant, even makeup, you have."

"What if I want to go shopping or leave by myself?"

"You can't right now. It's not safe for Wilds and we're in charge of your safety. We had an incident recently, so we're not taking anyone anywhere."

She nodded. "Something at a mall?"

What the hell? She must have seen it on the news. She totally seemed like someone who would watch the news, I thought sarcastically to myself.

"Something like that," I said. "There's a chore chart in the dorm building with money posted next to it you can earn." Becca tapped Casi on the arm. *I'll show you where it's at.*

"'K," Casi said.

"Can I let Becca and Helen show you around?" I signed to Becca.

"'K," Casi said again, but red seeped into her charcoal shields. She was nervous.

"I'll see you later," I said to Casi. "My office is on the first floor of the admin building if you need me, and I'm always around."

Outside of my apartment a huge box of chocolates sat against the door. There was a note folded on it, reading, "You could use some chocolates too." I went inside and put the box onto the counter, opening it. I bit into a candy, closing my eyes as the chocolate melted on my tongue, leaving a faint flavor of nuts and caramel.

Somehow, it did make things better.

CHAPTER TWENTY-EIGHT

MY BARE FEET walked across the sun-warmed boards of the pier, the thick rusty bolts nearly the same color as the wood. The moonlight reflected on the seawater beneath. I heard and smelled the ocean and a faint mist touched my skin, bringing out goosebumps. The moon was full, and stars painted the blue-black sky. Up ahead, a building on the edge of the pier beckoned, flickering light spilling out from the open door and windows. Jazzy music played complete with the faint catch of the needle on the vinyl. Inside were candles, dozens of vases filled with colorful roses and rose petals on the ground; all the clichés. Stephen held out a champagne glass.

"Of course the champagne's not real," he said. "But I couldn't do the roses and candles without champagne." I took a sip, the sweet grape flavor exploding on my tongue. Maybe we could just live here for the rest of our lives, not letting the real world interfere.

"Are you trying to seduce me?" I asked.

He leaned in, his lips close to mine. "I've been trying for weeks." He ran his hands down my shoulders to my waist. "Is this going to work?" he whispered.

I licked his lips, taking a quick nip.

"Yes," I said.

He tossed me onto the suddenly appearing bed, silk sheets puffing around me. I laughed as he ripped my sweater over my head, his hands quickly sliding beneath my bra. "For someone who worked hard on seduction—" I gasped when he pinched my nipple, his lips on my neck. "You're in a hurry."

"I'll slow down when it gets to the good part," he promised.

I sat up and slowly unbuttoned his shirt, flicking the buttons out of their holes one snap at a time. I leaned in to nibble down his neck, letting my tongue follow my hands.

I pushed him down and straddled him. He ran his hand up me and I captured it, bringing it to my lips. I kissed the tips and slipped off my bra, a black lacey one I'd never in my life bought or owned.

"You're beautiful," he said.

"That's just 'cause I'm straddling you."

He sat up, flipping me over so I lay on the soft, thick pillows. "No, it's not." His lips traveled down to suckle on my breasts.

I reared up, my nerves electrified. He pushed me back down.

"From the moment I saw you, I thought you were the most fascinating person I'd ever seen. From your hair and eyes, to your shields. I wanted this from the moment I saw you, a warrior goddess."

He paused at my waist to slowly pull my shorts and panties off. I noticed they matched my bra, though weren't an uncomfortable thong. It was getting harder to think, harder to do anything but feel what he was doing.

He touched me gently, withdrawing when I gasped. "I'm no warrior goddess," I hissed out. He grazed me with his fingers again, his eyes on mine, drinking up my reaction. "I'm just a Wild." The words were getting harder to say.

"You're my goddess," he said and somehow with only a few more touches I flew away.

CHAPTER TWENTY-NINE

I sat up in bed, my body vibrating from multiple orgasms. What just happened? Had I just had crazy, mind-blowing sex with a co-worker in a dream?

Kendle you awake?

I blinked, trying to force my brain and body away from the dream. Holy shit, that had seemed so real. I'd never had a dream that intense before. *I'm up*, I told Seiko's voice. *What's going on?*

It's seven a.m. Wall inspection time. Get up, you lazy ass.

Had I really slept that late? *Rude.*

Come on, girl. I'll get you some tea. Meet you by the gate in five minutes.

Once a month, Seiko and I walked all the way around the wall, inside and out. We made sure there weren't any cracks, holes, or words graffitied on the outside. We also shooed off the homeless Wilds camping along the wall, using the numbing metal in the wall to hide or soothe their abused and exhausted Gifts. Because we weren't complete monsters, we also handed them food close to expiring, though I suspected Miriam wouldn't be happy if she knew.

Seiko handed me a giant to-go cup when I met him at the gate.

"You okay?" he asked. "It's not like you to oversleep."

"Just tired," I said, taking a giant sip and scalding my mouth. "Let's go."

We walked along the inside of the wall, our arms crossed against an icy wind off the lake that managed to cut through our clothing layers. I loved and hated the numb feeling of being close to the wall, so similar to getting high or drinking too much.

"I'm looking for another job," Seiko whispered, out of nowhere.

"Why?"

"It's just too much. Too many hours, too much stress. Too much I can't help. And I keep getting in trouble with Miriam."

"For what?"

"Small things. She doesn't like how I'm teaching math. She doesn't think the kids know enough when they graduate. I think it's Stephen's fault."

"No. I'm—"

"I'm not college educated," Seiko said. "I'm just good at math and I follow along with the lesson plan out of the book."

"What's wrong with that?"

Seiko stuffed his hands into his pockets. "The kids should have someone who has a degree. She's right."

"But then our math teacher won't be a Wild. None of us have college degrees, unless we somehow managed to sneak through online."

"It's not just that. I can't do these hours anymore. I want to be a stand-up comedian. I can make a living at that, if I get good and I can't get good working eighty-hour weeks, seven days a week."

"But Seiko, the kids—"

"I won't do anything until the summer, assuming I can even find a job. Probably something I can do on the internet with a company that doesn't check the Registry. Maybe sales or... I don't know."

His emerald striped shields were more black than green. I put my arm around him. "Give it more time. It's always hard this time of year."

"It's more than—"

We jumped when something hit the wall next to us. It sounded like a thrown rock.

Ms. May? The connection was spotty, like someone was standing next to the wall.

Becca?

Another rock hit the wall. *Ms. May?* I could just hear her thoughts whispering.

Becca? Are you outside the wall?

"Fuck, fuck, fuckity-fuck shit balls," I said.

"What's wrong?" Seiko asked.

"I think Becca's outside the wall."

"What? By herself? In this neighborhood?"

I teleported to the gate while Seiko started running.

I typed in the code to open it, waiting for Seiko as the gate slid along the rusty track. "I hate it when you do that," he panted.

"Learn to teleport."

We jogged along the wall. There were a lot of homeless, a lot of garbage and human waste along the wall, more than I'd ever seen. Things were getting bad for Wilds. We found Becca, barefoot and only wearing pajama pants and a t-shirt. Her lips and toes were a pale blue. A homeless man waited with her.

"I kept the others away," he mumbled at us.

Jesus, it was Theo, a Wild that had gone to the Warehouse a few years ago. "I knew she must be one of yours," he continued.

"Thank you, Theo," I said.

Becca took a few painful steps, Seiko assisting with an arm around her waist and his psychokinesis, lifting her into the air to protect her feet.

"Get her to the infirmary," I told Seiko. I turned back to Theo. "We're going to have to clear you all out today," I told him. "Maybe tell the others?"

"Will there be food?"

"Yes, I said. "And I'll get you an extra box for helping with Becca."

He nodded at me and I caught up to Becca and Seiko.

We were too close to the wall for telepathy, so I signed to Becca. "What happened?"

She signed back, "I don't know. I was in the dorm room and Mateo scared me. Just a joke and then I was outside. I didn't know how to get back in."

Tears ran down her face.

"Let's get you warmed up," I signed back. "We'll figure out what happened."

———

That evening, Miriam glared at Mr. Sparklebutt curled in my office visitor chair. He yawned, stretched and meandered out the door, like he didn't care what she thought of him.

"Sorry," I said. "I never know where he comes from. He just appears out of nowhere."

Miriam sat down in the vacated chair, circles deep under her eyes and graying hair falling out of her ponytail. Her cheekbones looked pronounced and her shields were nearly black, with only a thin strip of magenta left.

Becca was still in the infirmary. She'd been so upset to have accidentally teleported outside the wall, Jasmine had to sedate her. Hours had passed, classes had started and ended, and I was tired. It had taken Seiko, Daniel and I hours to clean up the trash and run the homeless Wilds off of the wall. We'd run out of near expired food quickly and then it got even harder to get them to leave. This weekend, we'd have to take some time to paint over graffiti on the wall with paint we didn't have the money to buy.

"Do we know how Becca got out?" Miriam asked.

"I checked on her once she was more coherent," I said. "She said she accidentally teleported to the roof of one the high rises we can see from the grassy area. Then she teleported to the street, tried to get back in, but couldn't get past the wall and the gate was locked." I used my Gift to pull two bottles of water out of the fridge and passed one to Miriam. "She's a scared thirteen-year old. She didn't think if she backed away from the wall, she'd be able to use telepathy to get in touch with one of us."

"So somehow she got out. Which shouldn't have been possible." Miriam took her glasses off, setting them on my desk and rubbed her eyes. "And I take it there's no money to retrofit the wall so she can't get out?"

I shook my head. "I have no idea how she did it. And I'm going to have to dig into savings to get paint to cover up the graffiti."

"If Becca can get through the wall, so can others. Our entire security plan just went out the window. And we need it right now. It seems our wall has become the 'in' place for the homeless."

"Some of them were our former students," I said.

Miriam closed her eyes. *I can't deal with that right now.* She stood up and paced to my bookshelves, looking at the cracked picture of my friends from the Warehouse.

"We need a plan to return Becca to the Guardians, since she can get out," Miriam said suddenly, her magenta shields near black. "Maybe Chanelle can help with that."

My stomach dropped and the water in my water bottle spun into a whirlpool. "What? After Jame—"

Don't say his name. Miriam's head bowed and her shoulders moved with several deep breaths.

"Miriam. You can't. She has no one. She's a sweet, scared child."

"I must protect the Academy. It's bigger than one Wild."

"Miriam—what if I work on her teleportation? I know Daniel tutors her weekly, but maybe we move to daily. And maybe Stephen can help too. We can all teleport and maybe each of us looks at it from different angles. Maybe one of those will click with her. Between the three of us, we can teach her some control."

"You sound like Daniel."

"He's a smart man."

She chuckled, but it was dark without humor. "You two don't generally agree."

We care about the students. As soon as I said it, I knew I'd screwed up.

"I care." Miriam moved back to my desk and picked up her glasses. She raised her chin and met my eyes. *I care more than any of you do. I started this school to help Wilds like you.*

"I know. You let me come here because you couldn't leave me on the streets in Vegas. You built the Wa—Phillip's Academy because you care." I didn't know what to say to get her to change her mind. "Please don't expel Becca. We've had worse and they've made it to graduation. I was worse for God's sake. She's trying and it should count."

Miriam bowed her head.

"Do you really think all Wilds should be locked up because we're a danger to ourselves and society? Becca's not a discipline or a behavior problem and deserves everything we can do to save her."

Miriam stared at a random spot on my desk.

Talk to her, I thought in desperation. *She doesn't mean to teleport so much and is trying so hard. And she's getting really good with her telepathy because she wants to communicate with everyone.*

I did. She let out a huge sigh, her entire face dejected. "Okay, but I want you, Daniel and Stephen working to fix her Gift. And if she ends up outside the wall again, she's gone."

"You got it," I said, promising to use others' time they probably didn't have.

"She's to work with one of you every day, including weekends."

"Of course."

"And there had better be improvement by Christmas, or she's out."

"Agreed," I said. If there wasn't, I could probably use the you-can't-throw-someone-out-at-Christmas as an excuse to buy more time.

She nodded once and turned to go.

I needed to talk to Daniel and Stephen before Miriam did. They were going to kill me.

CHAPTER THIRTY

WE LAY TANGLED in the sheets together, legs overlapping each other. I took a deep breath, like I did after a long run, trying to reset my breathing. I was sweaty, sleepy and sated. I wondered if I could fall asleep in a dream and if so, would I dream?

I asked Stephen. He curled into my shoulder, dropping a kiss on my bare collarbone.

"I don't know," he said. "Maybe this is reality and the Warehouse is the dream."

"Then we're spending too much time in the wrong place," I said.

We were back in the cabin on the water, but it was daylight and the slatted wood sides were open to a clear ocean horizon. Sleepy shadows filled the room, but the mix of sun and shade kept it the perfect temperature. The floor was glass and bright fish swam by in a forest full of coral. I pulled away from Stephen to lean over the bed and watch the sea. An octopus went by, followed by a giant turtle.

"I'm not sure that's accurate," I said, pointing at the two critters.

"It's whatever we want it to be," Stephen said, not looking at the ocean, but tracing a finger slowly from my shoulder to my bare hip and back up again. "Though I don't know which one of us thought of the turtle. I think mine was the octopus."

"It's too bad we can't do that in real life," I said, shivering a little with his touch. "Think of whatever we want, and have it come true." A giant ray went past, followed by a sunfish.

Stephen continued his patient tracing, outlining the skin on my back and hips, each sweep of his fingers tracing lower and lower before going back up to my neck. My skin tingled. I'd never had anyone touch me like this before, during, or after sex.

"What would you wish for?"

That was easy. "I would move the Warehouse."

Stephen paused in his tracing. "Where and why?"

"I don't know," I sighed and made a pillow with my arms for my head. I was growing bored of watching the fish but wanted Stephen to keep touching me.

"Seriously," he said. "What's wrong with Chicago?"

I rolled over onto my back. God, he really was handsome with his blue-black hair and pale green eyes. I smoothed his hair and then mussed it again. He'd taken to having a beard in the real world but was clean-shaven here. I ran my hand over his chin, and he kissed my fingers.

"I like the beard," I told him. "You look like Warehouse Stephen. Not perfect Bred Stephen."

"That we can fix." And his carefully trimmed beard appeared. I sat up to kiss him, run my lips down the tickle of hair on his face.

"Wait, wait, wait," he said. "I want to know what's wrong with Chicago."

"Nothing." I traced a quiet line with my lips and tongue down his cheek to his neck. I'd already found a spot he loved to be bitten just below his ear. I nibbled and he let out a slight curse. I pulled back and smiled. "I just think the Warehouse should be someplace quiet. Some place the protestors can't find us. Where we don't have to worry about the city and their worries, we're going to blow them up." I flipped back over to watch the fish and Stephen went back to tracing his fingers up and down my back.

"They're not actually worried about that."

"After Jameson, they probably are."

"What else would this Warehouse have? Money's no object." He dropped a kiss on my shoulder, his teeth nipping.

"I don't know. Someplace where the kids can have their own rooms or only have to share with one person. More like a home with lots of hanging out places. Gardens, trees, a separate building for clubs and after school activities. A stage for plays, a music room—"

"With a baby grand?'

"Yes." I rolled over again. "I've always wanted to play on one." He smiled a little but broke off eye contact. "You own one, don't you?"

"I do. I think I own two. Or I used to. What else would you have? A movie theatre? Bowling alley?"

"That's silly."

"Sillier than moving the Warehouse? Seriously, what else?"

"I would have stables."

"Like with horses?"

I couldn't believe I was telling him all of this. "And farm animals and chickens, and sheep and big dogs, that like...I don't know. Herd the sheep? Do dogs do that?"

He leaned down to kiss me again, a quick kiss. "Yes. They're called sheepdogs."

I kissed him back, a deep, deep kiss. He ran his hands down my breasts, his thumbs caressing the nipples. I leaned back.

"Where'd you come up with the stable idea?" he asked, continuing to stroke. I closed my eyes. God, he knew what he was doing.

It was getting hard to think. "It was Eeva's idea. She thought it would be good for kids learning telepathy, since we can sense animals and Eeva claims she can talk to them." The caressing stopped and I opened my eyes. Stephen stared off into the horizon. "That's a genius idea."

He went back to the careful caresses, stopping to trace his tongue over my nipple. "Do I have a place in your perfect school?"

"Of course," I said. "You can stay in my apartment and we can do this every night."

"Do what?" he dipped his head forward, feasting on my breasts.

"This type of thing," I groaned.

The ocean lit up, and then went dark. A huge clap of thunder sounded, and I opened my eyes in my apartment.

It was two weeks until Christmas, classes were dismissed and today we were getting up early to set up the tree. I closed my eyes, opening them again to another clap of thunder. Rain poured down on the roof and I stretched, feeling like a queen, my muscles loose and languid. And like every morning, reality set in. Every day, I swore I'd figure out a way to stop the dreams. Then I'd work too many hours, drink or smoke enough so I could sleep, and forget to remind myself to stop the dreams.

Why couldn't I have normal dreams with weird hallways stretching into nowhere, or teaching naked and forgetting where the cafeteria was?

CHAPTER THIRTY-ONE

CHRISTMAS WAS a trigger holiday for many of our students, some of who remembered holidays with families that loved them before their Gift manifested. Some students would go home during the winter break, but that brought its own stresses and worries too. A few of the teens returned before Christmas Day, tired and hurting, despite the best intentions of family. And others appeared the day after Christmas and booked an immediate session with a counselor.

We didn't force anyone to participate in holiday functions and incorporated other winter holidays too. In the past, we'd had students celebrating Winter Solstice, Kwanza and Ramadan, but had none this year. We did have a few celebrating Hanukkah, which I loved facilitating and we lit candles in the Menorah for the eight evenings, inviting all to celebrate.

The day the giant tree for the dorm went up, I organized ornament making stations in the cafeteria where the kids could make as many ornaments as they wanted out of whatever supplies I'd managed to scrounge up. Some of the resulting ornaments were museum quality, carved out of wood, or sewn together. Some were patchwork creations of bits of lace, fabric, glitter, wood and plastic beads, to make something beautiful and unique. Other ornaments were glued together hot messes of glitter, paint and pictures. Ornaments made in previous years and kept in dorm rooms during the year appeared on the tree along with candies, beads, tinsel, cookies, popcorn, candy canes and enough lights to cause complaints from the students on the ground floor about it beaming into their rooms under the floor cracks in their bedroom doors.

We didn't have pretty trees at the Warehouse—we had ones full of homemade ornaments and memories.

We were a whole five days before Christmas when I had told the kids they couldn't make any more ornaments. The tree was so full you couldn't see the plastic needles anymore and I worried about it falling. Of course, that's when Casi finally came to the table I'd set up in the cafeteria while I was using my Gift to move all the glitter into the trash. She walked by twice, pretended to inspect the snack shelves, and came back to pick up a thick piece of printed cardstock. I mentally rolled my eyes. NOW, she'd decided to participate?

I'd barely seen the girl since she'd come to the Warehouse. She hadn't joined any of the clubs or activities she'd seemed so excited about. I'd started a DnD club and expected her to be the first to sign up, maybe volunteer to be the Dungeon Master, but she was a no show, despite the notes I'd stuck on her dorm door. I wondered what she was doing with her free time because I'd seen her grades, and it wasn't studying. And she wasn't making friends, preferring to eat in the cafeteria by herself, playing on her screen. I'd have to bring her up in the next staff meeting. We might need a different plan.

The blue had faded out of her hair and her blonde hair looked greenish-gray and messy. But she'd put on some healthy weight in her arms and legs, lost her belly and the bags under her eyes.

Basic shielding circled her thoughts. It had only taken Stephen a week, but it was a light charcoal with orange and red streaks like lava running through it. Not a good sign. And she wasn't good at sending thoughts, tending to bruise shields with clumsiness.

"Hi," I said. "I was just cleaning up, but did you get a chance to make an ornament?"

"No," she muttered, putting down the cardstock.

"Feel free," I said waving my arm at the assortment of crafting supplies. "Take as long as you want. I think we can still find room on the tree." I hoped she'd make something, even if it was just glitter glued onto a Styrofoam ball.

Helen and a few other first years came into the cafeteria, grabbed some snacks and a board game, and headed to a table. Helen glanced at Casi, and Casi looked away. I really wanted to read Helen's thoughts, see what she felt about Casi, but it would've been invading her privacy.

Casi's shields grew darker.

I mentally groan. If Casi wasn't getting along with Helen, there was a huge problem. Helen was pretty mellow. That's why I paired them together. I wondered if Casi was getting along better with Becca.

Casi picked up a piece of ribbon, patterned with sparkling red and green gems and then some silver glitter. She touched a paintbrush.

"If you need some ideas, you can borrow my screen to do an internet search," I told her.

She shook her head, and I went back to my emails.

Casi pulled out a chair and sat down, moving other supplies in front of her. She was quiet, working with the glue gun and a tiny paintbrush.

Helen wandered over to watch Casi and within a few minutes, the other girls had joined them.

"That's pretty," Helen complimented Casi. "I like the glitter."

"Thank you," Casi muttered, but her shields lightened, just a bit.

"You guys can make more ornaments if you want," I told them. "I can always clean up later."

The other first years sat down around Casi, pulling out new crafts, laughing, talking and including Casi. Casi didn't giggle with the others, but the red and oranges in her shields softened and stopped flowing so dramatically through the gray.

"Ms. May?" Helen asked, holding up an empty container of green glitter. "Is there any more?"

We looked through the table, shifting things around, making sure a container hadn't been missed.

"There might be some in the storage room," I said. "But I don't remember seeing any." I stood up, my chair scraping on the concrete floor. "I'll go check."

After glancing outside at the slushy rain, I teleported to the other building and directly into the storage room. Two minutes later, with a box of glitter under an arm, I teleported into the middle of a fight.

"Knock it off," I said using my telepathic and verbal voice to break through the screaming. "You," I said, pointing at a tear-stained Helen. "What happened?"

"That's my necklace," she sobbed, pointing at Casi's neck. "My sister gave it to me."

Casi wore a gold and purple glass butterfly necklace with the purple stones making up the wings. I knew Casi hadn't come to the Warehouse with it and she hadn't purchased it.

"Casi?" I said.

Casi unclasped the necklace, passing it back to Helen with shaking hands. "I found it and put it on so I would keep it safe," she whispered. "I didn't want to lose it."

The red and orange color spread with the lie in Casi's shields. And yet, I saw an element of truth as well, a tiny glimmer of gold, like the necklace.

My head hurt.

"I don't want her as my roommate anymore, if she's going to steal," Helen said, folding her arms. The other first year girls folded their arms too. My heart broke for Casi.

"We'll talk in a bit," I said to Helen. "In the meantime, you have your necklace back. Go back to your dorm room."

"Isn't she going to get punished?" one of the other first years asked.

"Not your business," I said. "Casi, let's go to my office."

"By the way," Helen said to Casi. "Your ornament sucks."

I glanced at the complex knot of ribbons Casi had created and meticulously painted tiny patterns of snowman and trees onto. It was beautiful and so different from what I thought she'd make.

"Well yours sucks too," Casi said. "I mean, putting glitter—"

"Enough," I said. "Office, now."

Casi used her Gift to clumsily move her ornament to the trash can. Before it hit bottom, I teleported it to my apartment. She might want it later.

"Tell me what happened," I said, once we were in my office. "And please don't lie. I'll know it and then we have to deal with the lying too."

"I don't know," Casi muttered, picking at loose thread on the chair. She was dry-eyed, but the oranges and reds moved through her shields like lava.

I let her sit. I knew how to use silence.

"I just wanted to wear it for a little while," Casi said finally. "I could feel—I don't know. I knew her sister gave it to her. And her sister loved her." *It sounds stupid.*

I gently touched her shields. She was telling the truth. She'd wanted the necklace because it had been given to Helen with love and Casi wanted to feel a little piece of that.

"I was going to give it back," Casi muttered. She held my eyes with her blue ones. *I promise.*

I sighed. "Have you been borrowing other things?"

Casi's shoulder went up in a half-hearted shrug.

"Casi, you can't do that."

She shrugged again, her eyes on the floor.

"I mean it," I said with my voice and mind. "You can't steal or borrow items without permission. You have to ask."

"Doesn't matter," she muttered. "I know I'm done."

"Do you want to stay?"

Another half shrug, and half flip of her hair.

"If you don't, then let me know before I talk to Ms. Phillips."

Her shields surged, turning a pretty silver, before fading back to charcoal, with its rivers of red and orange.

"So last time I ask," I said. "Do you want to stay?"

"Yes."

"Then you can't steal or borrow anything. ANY. THING. If you do, you're out. And if—IF," I said the word again. "If Ms. Phillips lets you stay, then you're in detention with me for the next month. You'll be my assistant tidying up the storage room, organizing the theatre props and costumes and doing a deep clean on the classrooms. Okay?"

"Okay."

"Also, have you been seeing the counselor?" I knew the answer though.

Casi shook her head.

"I'm going to make it a mandatory part of you staying. You have to see her once a week."

Casi groaned. "It's stupid. All she wants to do is talk about my feelings and how things are going. I feel worse afterwards."

"That happens a lot in the beginning," I said. But it really works. It helped me when I first came here."

"Did you borrow things too?" Casi muttered.

"No. But I broke a lot of things because I was angry and scared. Talking helped me get control. My roommate got really angry my first few months, too. She's my best friend now."

Casi nodded, her eyes on the threadbare carpet.

"Just try it," I said. "Do the journaling and goal setting she's going to recommend."

Another half shrug, followed by a half nod.

I sighed. "Okay Casi. I'll go talk to Ms. Phillips and let you know. Head back to your room and apologize to Helen."

"What if she's still mad at me?"

"She's going to be," I said. "You're going to have to accept that consequence."

Casi didn't say anything, didn't move.

"Start with an apology and don't take her stuff again."

"Okay." She stood to go.

Thank you, she thought, her words painful through my shields.

You're very welcome. "Don't do it again."

She turned to go, and I picked up my screen. "Ms. May?" she said, coming back to stand in front of my desk.

"Mmmm?" I really needed to work on some emails. I had over fifty to deal with.

"I think I had a dream about you," she said in the way teenagers talk when they're embarrassed. She twisted her hands together, more red seeping through her shields.

I closed my screen. "Interesting. What was I doing?"

She shook her head and shrugged. "I just remember you were someplace else. It was snowing like here, but it wasn't here. It was up in the mountains and there were trees. Lots of trees."

"Was I doing anything?"

She shook her head, hard enough for her gray-green hair to flop. "You were in front of a building, like an old mansion, and walking into a snowy forest. You wore a red jacket."

"What do you think it means?"

She shrugged, her universal response to everything.

"I don't think dreams mean too much," I said, hoping I was right and not messing up some dream analysis the counselor was going to make her do. "They're just random firings of your brain, putting pieces of your day together." And apparently pieces of Stephen in a bunch of different places combined with leg-wobbling orgasms. I pushed the thought away and focused on the here and now.

I waited to see if she would tell me more, but she seemed to be done. "Head back to your room," I said. "I'll let you know what's going to happen after I talk to Ms. Phillips."

I called Helen in next, who wanted to come in with her entourage of friends. I shooed the extras out. It took me a few minutes, but I convinced Helen to give Casi another chance, with the agreement if Casi stole or borrowed again, Helen wouldn't have to live with her anymore.

Once Helen left, I got myself a cup of tea and sent a thought to Miriam, *Do you have a moment?*

I'm just finishing up with Stephen, but come to my office.

I grabbed my mug and knocked on Miriam's door frame.

Flowering plants Franny carefully watered and tended for Miriam grew in the sunlight from the window and scented the air, mixing with the spicy smell of a candle burning on a shelf. Miriam sat on her couch, with her screen on her lap, and Stephen in one of the visitor chairs with a cup of coffee.

A few years ago, I would've sat on the couch next to Miriam, curling up with my feet next to me as we planned what the next few weeks would look like.

Instead, I stood in the doorway, my mug in one hand.

Rough day? Stephen asked.

"Did something happen?" Miriam asked at the same time.

Caught Casi stealing, I thought to Stephen. *But cross your fingers and toes I can convince Miriam to keep her.*

I will. He touched my shields with his, giving my thoughts a turquoise cast for a second. I really wished he'd stop doing that. Things were weird between us. I really needed to talk with him, see if he was having the same dreams I was.

Bet that would be an awkward moment. 'Excuse me, Stephen, but have you been having erotic dreams about me, because I've been having erotic dreams about you?'

Yeah, I should totally put a reminder in my calendar.

"I'll let you two talk," Stephen said standing up. "Thanks for the help, Miriam."

Miriam moved to her desk, indicating one of the chairs in front of it. I sat down, put my mug on her desk, and took a deep breath. I hoped I wasn't going to get in trouble for asking to keep Casi.

"I caught Casi stealing," I said, jumping right into it. "Or borrowing, I guess."

Miriam made a note on her screen. "Then she's done," she said, not looking up. "We can't have thieves. It erodes all the trust among the students." She took off her glasses and rubbed the bridge of her nose. "Do any students know?"

I nodded. "Helen caught her."

"Then she's doubly done, and I know you're going to argue to keep her, but we can't have thieves," she repeated.

"I think we should give her another chance." I pretended she hadn't spoken. "We've made exceptions for others."

"And regret it each time."

"But remember Benny—"

"Most times, we regret it." Miriam rubbed her eyes.

"But Benny's doing fine now."

"He has a job under the table, gardening."

"He's contributing to society, has enough money to eat and a roof over his head." I thought of Jameson. "That's more than he would've had if we'd expelled him. Casi has no place to go. It's back to the institution for her. All the faculty say she's trying."

"Her grades are atrocious. Becca is trying. Casi is using us for a warm place to sleep and a meal."

"There's nothing wrong with that at her stage of integration. She's only been here six weeks and I've gotten flashes of her past. She was abused even before her family found out she was a Wild and kicked her out."

"Then she needs to see a counselor, which she's not even doing."

"If she stays, I'll make it a requirement."

"You told her stealing wasn't allowed? You did go over it with her, right?"

"Of course. But—"

"Then she's done."

"Can't we just do detention for a whole month? The rest of the year even? If she has klepto tendencies, then she can't help it, and it's up to us to try to help. I already talked to Helen; she's fine having her stay as a roommate."

Miriam's shields shifted and black veins threaded through them. "You already told Casi she could stay, didn't you?"

"I told her it was up to you."

"But you already told her the punishment, your punishment. Not mine. And then you convinced the roommate to let her stay."

My chest froze and I tried to breathe past the tightness.

"Kendle—"

"I also told her she'd have weekly counseling sessions to figure out why she has this desire to borrow. And I would work her to death as punishment."

"I want her expelled. I wasn't sure she'd work out after you and Stephen brought her here. She seemed traumatized."

"I couldn't scan her." The water in Miriam's desk vase with daisies started to shift back and forth. *They put the bands on me. And wouldn't let me take them off. Stephen scanned her. He had to. I told him what to look for. It's not his fault, but—*

Miriam put up her hand. "I understand there were mitigating circumstances and both of you did the best you could with the information you had." Miriam focused on the water in the vase on her desk.

I took a deep breath and the water stopped swaying back and forth.

"Kendle, you have got to stop thinking only of the individual and think about the school."

"I am. Look at Jameson. If we hadn't expelled him and had worked—"

Miriam paled, her shields going black. I'd gone too far.

"You think we should've kept a child selling drugs and alcohol to other students? Who wasn't even apologetic when he was in this office, and I was discussing it with him?"

"No," I said. "I misspoke."

"If we allow thieves to stay, it tells all the students they can steal too."

"Casi stole that necklace, was wearing it, because she knew the necklace was given in love and wanted to know what it felt like. Wanted to know if she could feel the love."

Miriam pressed her palms into her eyes. "That's the most depressing thing I've ever heard."

"We did get a stipend for her which we'd have to repay," I said.

"And we've already spent that money," Miriam said. "Has she stolen other things?"

"Not sure," I said. "She may be borrowing, but I think she puts it back."

Miriam looked at the picture of her husband, adjusting it slightly. "She can stay," she said after a minute. "But she's in detention for the remainder of the year and if there's any hint of stealing, she's out."

"Agreed. Thank you." I stood to go.

"We're not done." Miriam said. "Sit."

I swallowed and sat back down in her hard visitor's chair.

"Again and again we keep coming to this point," Miriam said. "You keep thinking only of the individuals and not the entire school. You should not have arranged to keep Casi here without my permission."

"I came here immediately to ask if she could stay. I told her it was up to you. She's waiting—"

"You already told her the punishment."

"But I told her it was dependent on you."

"I need to—" she stopped. "Any disciplinary issues are to be run past me before you make any decisions."

"Ok, but it's a change from what I've done in the past."

"Why are you arguing? I'm the director, you're not."

"I'm not trying to argue, I'm trying to understand why you're changing things." I needed to know so I didn't keep making mistakes.

"Because I need you to think about the school, not the individuals."

"But why are we here if it's not for the individuals? Wilds are rare in the general population. No one understands where we came from or why we can do what we can do. It makes sense to take everything on a case-by-case basis."

"It's helpful to know your stance as I'm making decisions about the future of this campus," Miriam said.

Wait. What?

"What kind of decisions?" I asked.

"As long as you're working for me, I need you to think of the whole school. I'm paying you and that's my requirement."

I had no idea what I'd done wrong.

"Yes, Miriam," I said.

"You may go."

I left, more confused than ever.

CHAPTER THIRTY-TWO

IN THE LEAD-UP TO CHRISTMAS, we kept the students busy. Without classes, we increased the clubs and activities and my work doubled. We broke down the cafeteria each day after breakfast for an indoor soccer game, hurriedly put it back together for lunch and then broke it down again for dance classes taught by Kaya. We had a movie night each night and a completely unplanned talent show Kaya, Seiko and I threw together over an afternoon. The weather didn't help either; it snowed a lot and drifts piled up against the buildings, preventing the kids from wanting to walk the track or spend time in the gardens. We kept the classroom building open, so the teens had places to go and hide from each other but had to patrol constantly to make sure they weren't breaking the rules.

Minor discipline issues I'd normally pass out detention or extra chores for, I ran by Miriam first. I couldn't risk her firing me for "not-thinking-big-picture". But I didn't know how to think differently about disciplining a horny teen caught in her boyfriend's room at eleven o'clock at night. Giving her and him a week of detention wasn't a big picture decision. But I still contacted Miriam, which was awkward to tell the kids I'd have to get back to them with their punishment. And checking with Miriam was making her angrier with me rather than less.

I had no idea what I was supposed to do differently. And questioning every decision I made was exhausting and stressful.

And I still hadn't dealt with Stephen, despite dreaming about him nightly.

Daniel caught me in the storeroom after the talent show as I inventoried costumes and props to make sure they were returned to the right places.

"Where's your helper?" he asked.

"Casi? She was too tired. I sent her back to her room."

"I haven't seen any signs she's stealing."

"Me neither. She's been spending a lot of time with the counselor. I think it's helping."

"Hope so. She reminds me of you."

"How? She's not destroying everything with her Gift. She's just scared."

"Exactly."

I checked the hat bin, making sure no one had stolen the hat shooting confetti out a hose down a sleeve.

"You're having a hell of a rough patch with Miriam."

I stuffed a petticoat into a garment bag. Daniel used his Gift to push the netting down and I zipped it before it could explode back out again. "It's been a really hard year," I finally said.

"For her too."

"I know. And I get money's tight and all of these kids...I mean Leo and Becca have Gifts we've never seen before. Never. How many other Wilds like them are out there? And Jameson. How didn't we know he was that powerful?"

Daniel leaned against a shelf, his hands in his back pockets. "That was a hell of a surprise. I taught him psychokinesis for three years. He was average. He shouldn't have had enough Gift built up to destroy a city block, even if he'd gone a year without using it. He's not you."

Why was everything he said an insult?

"I don't know, Kendle," he continued. "When Miriam and I founded this place, Wilds weren't as common as they are now. Things are changing and no one knows why. But outside of us, I don't think people are really aware of it."

"Because no one cares."

Yes. Stephen and I were talking about trying to get our Wilds tested, including us. He's betting that you and I and some of the students are stronger than most Breds. Daniel's honey colored shields turned a dark brown, the glints disappearing.

And then what?

I don't know. Maybe some research.

Experiments? On Wilds? On us?

He started to refold a stack of t-shirts that had been perfectly folded before. I rolled my eyes. Nothing was ever good enough.

That's how scientists learn, he thought. *There's been a lot of breakthroughs because of research and yep, experiments on people.*

Wouldn't it be unethical if it wasn't Wilds doing the research? And none of us can get money or grants to do that.

I don't know, he finally thought. *But someone has to learn more about Wilds. The Warehouse can't be the only safe place for Wilds. Something has to change.*

I guess.

"Back to the original subject," he said. "You don't have to ask Miriam."

"About?"

"Before deciding to give detention. Only if it's something big, like Casi stealing."

"She said—"

"I know what she said. She's under a lot of pressure right now."

"We all are. It's two days until Christmas and we're all trapped in the buildings with a bunch of telepaths and psychokinetics. But it's like this every year."

"Just go a little easier on Miriam. She has high expectations for you. We both do."

"Daniel, what's going on? Miriam's never been like this before." And neither had he. We'd never had a talk like this in all the years I'd known him. He was willing to help if you needed it, like with my chair, but he didn't share anything personal. I didn't even know what he did with his free time. I watched his shields, the honey color shifting slightly and the glittery fragments catching and repelling the light.

Don't pry, he thought.

Sorry. I'm just so stressed.

"I know. You're leaking a lot more than you used to. You haven't had this problem in years."

I sighed. "I'm trying to keep it under control."

"Try harder. You can't break. We need you too much."

I turned away to stuff a bunch of white shirts into the bag I was using for laundry, so he wouldn't see my eyes filling with tears. *I don't think that's true.*

You've been here seventeen years. He picked up a ripped pair of pants and put it back down. *That should mean you don't disappear at the first sign of trouble.*

What if Miriam makes me leave?

I won't let her.

"Don't mess up my organization," I said, as he put the shirts he'd folded into the wrong place.

He picked them up, looking around.

"Just give them to me."

"Nice talent show, by the way," he said, handing over the shirts. "We should do it every year, a few days before Christmas."

"I already put it on my calendar for next year," I said.

"Of course you did. He paused in the doorway. "Merry Christmas, early." And in his hands was a giant pot with a tiny sprout sticking out of it.

"This is different," I said, inspecting the pot. It was giant, silver, and had tiny etched flowers running in rows down it.

"I know. I thought you could use something more than tea and gin."

"I always like the tea and gin."

If you—

No, I like it. And I really did. "I'll probably kill it," I said.

"That's the beauty. It's a bulb. It'll grow on its own with no help from you, though you should water it. And then it'll die, and you can save the bulb for next year. Or toss it and put in a different one."

"Thank you," I said. "It's a nice change."

"Your office could use... It was a little bare last time I was there."

And there it was; a typical Daniel insult. I sent the pot to my office desk and transported his present to the storeroom.

"I didn't have time to wrap it," I said, holding out the expensive coffee I got him every year.

"Thank you," he said. "I always depend on it for Christmas morning."

"Merry Christmas," I said.

"Merry Christmas, Kendle." He looked at me for another minute. Well, this was getting awkward. Should I offer to give him a hug? I don't think I'd ever hugged him. Other than Kaya I'd never seen him hug anyone.

"Don't stay too much longer," he said.

"I won't."

He walked out, his coffee tucked under his arm.

That was weird.

———

Tonight the dream started with dancing, surrounded by flickering candlelight. We were all alone with jazzy music playing in the background. Stephen put one hand around my waist and pulled me close.

"Do you really think this place is me?" I asked, placing a hand on his shoulder.

"No. But it's me."

He twirled me around, my feet finding the steps, a red skirt flaring around my hips. I hadn't ever danced with someone like this in my entire life.

I tried again. "Dancing's not really my thing."

"Hush. It's an important part of seduction."

"Didn't that ship already sail?"

"Each time should be about seduction." He pulled me closer, his hand warm enough to feel through the thin dress, his breath close to my ear. "Setting the stage, for what's to come later."

My skin tingled. He was right. This was foreplay. He spun me and when I was back in his arms, I leaned up to kiss him. He kept the rhythm going, his hands on my hips even as his breathing quickened. I nipped at his lip and slid the jacket off his shoulders and let it fall onto the ground. I kicked it away with a heeled shoe.

He trailed kisses down my neck, stopping to nibble on that patch at my shoulder. My eyes closed, desire strumming through me. I stabilized myself against him when my knees buckled. He started to slip a dress strap down my arm, but I stopped him. "I want you naked first," I told him. He spun me out again and when I was back, I started to unbutton his shirt. He laughed, and kissed me, a quick happy kiss. He rested his forehead against mine.

"Where did you come from?" he murmured.

An annoying buzz sounded. I waved a hand around my head, thinking it was a bug, but it got louder. I opened my eyes. It was the phone we carried when we were on dorm duty. I yawned and pressed the button.

"What's going on?" I asked. The alarms hadn't gone off, so it couldn't be anything too serious.

"When's too early to open our gifts?" asked a voice on the other end. I looked at the clock. It was four a.m. on Christmas morning. We didn't put out the faculty gifts until eight. I was confused. "Do you have gifts already?" I asked the voice on the other end I couldn't identify until my brain woke up a little bit more.

"From my family."

"You can open those whenever you want. We'll be doing the big opening under the tree at eight. Breakfast starts at six."

"Okay."

"Do you have an emergency or anything?"

"Oh. No."

"Only call the teacher on dorm duty if it's an emergency."

"Okay."

"Merry Christmas."

"Merry Christmas," the first year responded.

I hung up and snuggled under the covers. But if I went back to sleep would I still dream of Stephen? And was that what I wanted? With a sigh, I threw back the covers. Merry Christmas to me.

CHAPTER THIRTY-THREE

CHRISTMAS PASSED and in that week of nothing between two holidays, we started planning the next event, New Year's Eve. New Year's Eve didn't have the triggers Christmas did, so we went all out, planning an all-night party.

I'd spent the morning of New Year's Eve reorganizing the cafeteria and splitting it into two sides. One side would play movies all night and the kids would set up their pillows, blankets and sleeping bags. I moved all the comfy couches and chairs I could find into the space. It was perfect for students that didn't want to be social or found it hard to be around a lot of people, but still wanted to celebrate with everyone. The other half I turned into a huge dance floor.

The school couldn't afford a DJ or band, but Kaya and Seiko spent hours asking the kids about music and designing a playlist. They worked to set up games and contests in case the kids seemed bored with the music. We even had a karaoke machine.

The kitchen crew outdid themselves building fancy-looking but cheap snacks holding to the New Year's Eve theme. And then there were bowls with the ubiquitous chips, popcorn and candy we normally rationed. But not on New Year's Eve. On New Year's I just bought everyone's favorites for them to gorge on.

On my way back to my apartment for a break, I almost collided with Stephen on the creaky admin building stairs. I stepped back, surprised. He'd shaved off his beard and wore a suit, the collar of his royal blue shirt open. He looked like a Bred. No, that wasn't right. He looked like a Quality Bred, like a celebrity on the internet. He was gorgeous, but not like Warehouse Stephen, with his beard, jeans, and sweaters with coffee stains on the sleeves from putting his elbow where his coffee cup had spilled.

He didn't look like my Stephen, whispered that voice in my head before I told it to shut up.

"Heading out?" I asked.

"Have to. Family thing." He ran his hands down the lapels of the suit and looked down. "Did I forget something?"

"What?"

"The expression on your face. Do you think I should wear a tie? I hate them but will if you think I should."

I shook my head. "Sorry. You just look different."

The colors in his shields shifted, turning more turquoise. "I used to think this was my normal appearance."

"You didn't wear a suit when you taught, I hope?"

"Of course not. But it was similar." *Do I look nice, at least?*

I laughed. "You're such a girl."

"Isn't that insulting to girls?"

"You're such a stereotypical traditional-role-of-a-girl-who-only-thinks-about-her-looks."

"Now you're just ruining it." He glanced at his watch. "I'm going to be late. Happy New Year."

"Happy New Year," I echoed.

He hurried away and I wished I'd asked where he was going.

I stretched out. *You do look nice.*

And I wish I were staying here tonight. I hate these things.

Next year?

It's a date and a promise.

I knew I imagined the faintest caress of his shields, but even the thought was enough to skyrocket me back into a dream and the feel of his body rising over mine, my skin tingling after—

Jesus Christ. What was wrong with me?

I sighed, letting myself into my apartment. I made a pot of tea, grabbed my screen and settled into my chair with a warm blanket over my legs. I opened a novel and lost myself in another person's world.

———

I just saw some pictures of Stephen on the internet, Kaya broke into my story about a changeling hero and his human love interest. Guess he's at some sort of fancy shindig.

I saw him on the way out. He looks good.

Did you see his date? Some Quality Bred. The internet is all over her. I guess she's often his plus one.

My chest froze and I had to breathe deep to get past it. *Good to know.* I went back to my book, refusing to take a peek on the internet. It didn't matter what he did inside or outside the Warehouse.

Are you seeing all these pictures of Stephen? Franny interrupted. *His date is so pretty. I love her dress!*

I wasn't going to look.

I wasn't going to look.

I wasn't going to look.

It didn't matter whether or not he dated. We were not dating. Or even having sex in the real world.

Come over, Franny continued. *Kaya is here; we're drinking wine and cyber stalking him.*

I think I'm going to chill here. Read my book. Have some alone time.

Oh come on, Franny responded. *He's our friend. How many other celebrities do you know? Seiko is coming over too.*

I'm really tired. Might take a nap.

You're always tired. Please? We never just hang out anymore. Remember how much fun that move night was?

I couldn't get out of it.

Five minutes later, I knocked on Franny's door.

Franny waved me in, and Kaya scooted over on the couch, handing me a glass of wine. Franny's apartment was full of plants, diffusing the winter light through the windows. During the summer, her apartment seemed like a solarium or a greenhouse.

I took a giant sip of wine before looking up at Franny's big screen, where they'd downloaded paparazzi photos of Stephen. They were all different angles of the same thing; him smiling down at some dark-haired woman. I knew that smile; I'd seen it often enough in my dreams. Franny's coffee table vibrated. I took a deep breath, another sip of wine and tucked my Gift away.

"Isn't she pretty?" Franny asked.

I had to breathe deep before answering. "That's Indira Dewan. She's the director at some hospital. I saw her with him at Mt. Olympus."

Seiko arrived with his own bottle of wine. Franny topped off our glasses and they pulled up different pictures of Stephen on Franny's screen as the paparazzi kept adding more.

"I've met Indira," Kaya said. "She went to Seagull's Landing with me. She's very powerful. And rich."

Seiko made a rude noise. "She's been his plus one to so many events. Look." He pulled up older pictures of Stephen and Indira on his screen for us to analyze.

"Think they're actually dating?" Franny asked. "Or just friends? I wonder how he met her?"

"Or she's one of his many fuck-buddies," Seiko said. "You know he has them."

This was horrible. They kept swiping through the pictures, laughing and showing different ones of Stephen putting his arm around Indira, her feeding him something off her plate, and both of them always smiling at each other.

My empty wine glass cracked, and I teleported it back to my apartment. I'd pretend I took it with me when I left and replace it with a brand new one.

Stephen was probably going to spend the night with her. Why wouldn't he? It would be a nice break from the Warehouse, a nice break from the rest of us. A nice break from Wilds and our imperfections.

And it shouldn't matter, I told myself. We. Weren't. Dating. I had a few erotic dreams. It didn't mean we were in a relationship.

Or that he liked me.

Like I liked him.

Oh. My. God. How had I let this happen?

CHAPTER THIRTY-FOUR

A FEW HOURS LATER, I stood in the back of the movie half of the cafeteria, the lights low. Students lay on blankets on the floor or curled up on couches or chairs. Leo, his purple shields wrapped tightly around his thoughts, and no hint of the tentacles, was practically watching the movie upside down, splayed across the arms of a chair, his now green spiked hair brushing the floor on one side and his feet brushing the other. Periodically a group of girls would glance at him and then each other. I could just see the echoes of their telepathy.

I felt the pumping bass from the dance floor, but the horror movie drowned most of it out. I used my Gift to tap on the shoulders of two students who had progressed from a gentle kiss, to groping, his hand under her top.

That's enough, I told them.

They could barely hide their contempt but separated. One of their thoughts was something along the lines of "can't even get laid."

I crossed the barrier into the other room and blinked. It was so noisy and bright compared to the darkness of the movie room. Kids danced, laughed and waved their hands in front of their faces to dry their sweat. The karaoke machine was a huge hit.

Everyone seemed like they were having fun, except me. I couldn't stop thinking about Stephen with his arm around Indira.

The dreams needed to stop. My mind and hormones had decided I was in a relationship, when I wasn't. I was sad, jealous, and angry with myself. I hated this feeling, especially when I'd been looking forward to New Year's Eve for weeks.

Seems like quite the party.

My heart leapt and I hated myself even more.

When did you get back?

Just now, Stephen thought. *Where do you want me?*

He had changed out of his suit and into jeans and a sweatshirt with a ripped seam in the sleeve.

Thought you'd be out all night. Why'd you come back?

I realized there wasn't any place else I'd rather be.

Liar. I saw the pictures. I tried to keep my tone light and teasing but wasn't sure I succeeded.

Pictures?

On the internet. At some bar with your brother and sister. And date, but I wasn't so far gone I'd say that.

I hate that stuff. What I do with my time is my business. The media only focuses on my looks and family. And I have no control over either.

Wow. Tell me how you really feel.

Sorry. He ran his fingers through his hair so it stuck up and gave me a little grin. *I got out of there as soon as I could. I know how hard you worked on this and wanted to help out, if I could.* He paused and touched his shields to mine. My stupid heart stuttered like it used to before I'd gotten used to his looks.

A snickering Leo called Stephen and my names' over the karaoke microphone. Teenagers always thought they were funnier than they were.

Stephen raised an eyebrow, and I smiled.

This should be interesting.

We climbed onto the makeshift stage to applause, laughter and catcalls. Leo passed out the mics, his smile huge, his shields a gentle lavender. The notes began, a silly song popular twenty years ago, one you think you know the lyrics to, but as you sing, you realize you don't.

"Who chose this song?" I said into the mic before the lyrics started. "It's not even a duet."

The kids shouted encouragement, brushing my shields with theirs. The lyrics blazed up on the screen, lighting up the words we were to sing. Stephen hit the first note and I tried to harmonize with him.

Fifteen seconds in, I stopped in shock. He couldn't sing.

What the—

He winked at me and missed a note completely. *The geneticists forgot to include singing ability. My mother actually sued.*

The kids' got louder, laughing and groaning. They began to clap along, singing the chorus with us. Those in the movie room ran over. We had a huge audience.

I gave up trying to make us sound good at all. He linked his arm with mine and we belted out the lyrics. We hit the instrumental section and danced, pointing at nothing, our butts and hips jiggling, our shoulders bobbing, our feet missing the beat entirely, doing the ridiculous dancing children do because they don't care.

Or adults do when they're really happy and have forgotten the rest of the world exists.

The music cut off and the countdown to midnight began.

Stephen and I used our mics to count it down, shouting "Happy New Year!" Stephen gave me a hug, his turquoise shields enveloping me just for a second. He kissed my cheek, one of those social niceties kisses you give to an aunt. Off kilter, I brushed my lips against his cheek and then pulled away, but not far. Our breath intermingled for one electric second.

Oh Lord. What was I doing?

He leaned in again, his breath tingling against my neck.

We could use you two on the dance floor, Miriam thought. *Or above the dance floor. Or something.*

I glanced up. Several couples had tried to escape the teacher patrols by floating themselves ten feet off the ground to make out with their partners.

Oh for— Get down here, I told them, opening a mental channel.

But they didn't listen and before another minute had passed, other students used their Gifts to lift their own bodies or their friends into the air. Handfuls of glitter, confetti, strings of streamers joined the floating people. It was like someone had hit the anti-gravity button in a sci-fi movie.

Anyone who picks up another student will spend a month in detention, Miriam thought through all the faculty and student shields.

Glad you came back? I asked Stephen, blinking to get the glitter off my eyelashes. *Or do you want to go back to your other life?*

Are you kidding? The turquoise in his shields was calm like the ocean at sunset. *This is my favorite New Year's Eve.*

CHAPTER THIRTY-FIVE

"I HAVE an idea I want to propose," Stephen said, during one of our weekly staff meetings a few weeks later.

Daniel leaned back in his creaking conference room chair at Stephen's comment, and stared at the ceiling in open annoyance.

Two weeks later I'd barely slept, had bought a black dress and heels and now stood in a line at the doorway of a fancy hotel, welcoming the people, the Breds, who'd paid three-hundred dollars a ticket for a chance to listen to boring speeches and eat dry and under-seasoned chicken.

Stephen had proposed a fundraiser for some quick cash. And somehow, we'd made it work.

All these Breds are here to see Stephen, Daniel thought after shaking another woman's hand. She wore a glittering dress of peacock purple, her eyes a sea blue no one saw in nature.

"Thank you for coming," I tried to tell her. She barely glanced at me, before clickety-clacking to where Stephen stood, at the end of the line, surrounded by other Breds.

Yep. They paid three hundred dollars to have a conversation with our Stephen just because of who his parents are, I responded.

Long as it helps the Warehouse, Daniel thought. *We need the money.*

I shrugged. *I guess.*

He likes it. You can tell.

I looked at Stephen, surrounded by Breds and smiling his gorgeous smile that made your heart stop. Seiko had been right, Stephen did look amazing in a tux, elegant and refined and so different than my Stephen. But his shields were a flat gray without color or movement.

He hates it, I told Daniel. *This crap he has to do because he's a Rune is part of the reason he came to the Warehouse.*

An hour later, I carefully ate my dry chicken and plain potatoes, finishing it up with a bland custard and thin coffee. We'd gone as cheap as we could for the food, and it was obvious. But we'd agreed to an open bar and the tab was going to be huge, I thought. I hoped we were making money. Chicago was going through a cold snap and we didn't have enough money to heat the buildings. We needed the money from tonight immediately.

There was a roar of laughter from Stephen's table. *Did you get a chance to eat?* I asked him.

I never eat at these things. I'll grab something at home. He broke away and I saw him laugh at something someone said. *Can you save me in five minutes if Miriam hasn't started the speeches? I can't take much more.*

Of course.

But at that moment, Miriam went up the podium and smiled at the crowd. Her magenta shields were still black streaked, but not as dark as usual. She launched into a story about why she, her husband and Daniel had wanted to start a school for Wilds but had lacked the funds. However, her husband's accidental death and his life insurance money had provided the seed money they needed. She explained the difficulties in the early years and why she'd finally chosen a bunch of warehouses in Chicago for her school. Around the room, people picked at their desserts, drank their coffee, had another sip of wine or stared with the glazed look of someone speaking telepathically.

I may have had too much to drink, Franny thought. *But her speech is really boring.*

It's factual, I responded.

Weren't they going to do a bunch of stuff about the students? They'd asked for pictures and I know Seiko filmed Daniel for some sort of video.

Video?

"To tell you more about our students, and the people you'll be helping with your donation, we put together this video," Miriam said. "Thank you again. My heart is full, and my staff are available for any questions you may have."

Daniel's voice sounded in my head. *I'm sorry. Please don't destroy the building.*

Wait, why? I asked.

The lights went down, the video started, and Daniel broke off the connection. His recorded voice started, overlaying still pictures of Warehouse students in classrooms, faculty pointing at screens and of course, floating objects while students concentrated. The video highlighted several students, explaining their back stories and what they were doing now, including Seiko, his love of math, and Eeva, her love of animals and maintaining a manager job at a popular nightclub.

Did they tell you about this? I asked Seiko who was back at the Warehouse making sure the kids behaved.

Are they showing the video? It's really cool. They didn't tell you?

No.

Ummm.... don't be too mad and destroy the building.

Why does everyone keep telling me that?

Then I was looking at a picture of myself at thirteen, right after Miriam had found me, my eyes huge and purple, my white hair shaved, lying in the Warehouse infirmary, hooked to an IV. My hair had been so matted, they hadn't tried to save it. The picture changed, showing my emaciated wrists right after Miriam had found me, the lesions from the bands I'd been forced to wear, still fresh and oozing. I touched the scars and regretted the sleeveless dress I'd bought.

Daniel's voice overlaid the pictures, telling how Miriam had spotted me on the street outside a diner in Vegas. Daniel explained I was newly escaped from an illegal Gladiator Ring, and slowly starving on the streets, glossing over the two months I'd spent stealing from anyone I could, how I'd physically beaten others to rob them and that eventually another Wild gang had kicked the shit out of me and forced bands on my wrists so I couldn't use my Gift.

Why are you showing this? I asked him.

You're one of our greatest successes. We couldn't leave you out of the video.

In the video, Daniel explained how I'd refused to go with Miriam, though I did accept a meal from her, a chocolate milkshake and hamburger. I could still taste it, if I thought back to that day. Miriam returned every day for a week, offering food in exchange for listening to her explain how the Warehouse could help me, if I could follow the rules. She did the same thing for me I'd done for Becca, Leo, Casi and countless others.

You should've asked me, I told Daniel.

You would've refused.

But that's my life. I should choose who knows about it.

Video Daniel went on to talk about how powerful I was and how little control I had at thirteen, especially when emotional. They showed pictures of me with my eyes closed, sitting in classrooms with a young-looking Daniel instructing me. He explained how the donated musical instruments had helped me so much, that we now had a program heavy in arts and music. The video continued to roll, showing other pictures of me, growing up at the Warehouse—doing a presentation in science class, staring at an hourglass, using my Gift to move the sand within, laughing with friends in the cafeteria, at graduation, playing in my band at Atomic.

I got up and left before he could explain how I'd taken the job at the Warehouse immediately after graduation.

I'd seen a bar on my way in and I headed there, ordering a gin and tonic and draining it before my Gift could turn it into a whirlpool.

Kaya sat down next to me at the bar, awkwardly draping the train of her expensive dress over an arm so she could settle onto the barstool.

She didn't say anything, just ordered a glass of wine.

He didn't tell you?

"Nope." I sipped the last little bit of my drink, the ice clinking against my teeth.

Asshole, she thought.

I didn't answer and tried to order another drink.

Kaya shook her head. "You can't have more, you have to go back."

"Fuck off," I said, the alcohol speaking for me. "I'm going home."

Kaya's shields turned smoky.

Sorry," I muttered. "I'm not mad at you."

The fiery colors of her shields surged at me. *At least go back to circle the room. You can't just disappear, or people will think the video was made up. Fifteen minutes max.*

Ten minutes and I'm not speaking to him.

That's fine.

Back inside, the video had ended, the band had started playing and everyone mingled at the bar. I helped myself to a glass of cheap champagne from a passing waiter. Kaya laced my arm through hers. "Let's circle to the left."

I tried not to look at anyone. I was so embarrassed. I couldn't believe every person in this room knew about my past. Breds met my eyes and smiled, but I felt their delicious curiosity and pity against my shields. Tears sprung up in my eyes and I pushed them back, thinking about how angry I was at Daniel.

You're doing great, Kaya thought. *Few more minutes.* Suddenly, Stephen was in front of us.

"Kendle, Kaya, I'd like to introduce you to an old friend of mine. Indira Dewan, these are two of the wonderful teachers I work with, Kendle May and Kaya Ethne."

I barely heard Kaya greet Indira. Stephen's hand was on Indira's elbow, steering her around the room. I used my Gift to lift another glass of champagne from a passing waiter and drank again, the room starting to spin as I forced a smile and a "pleased to see you again."

Indira reached out and grabbed a champagne flute. "A toast, to your wonderful story."

I forced my tight throat to swallow the champagne and coughed as it got caught. I wiped streaming eyes, my fingertips coming back mascara smeared.

Well, this was fucking perfect.

"I'm not sure you remember me," Indira said, after I caught my breath, her jewel-like shields glinting. At least the alcohol was numbing her ability to make me like her. "You came to my hospital once."

"Of course I do," I said. "Leo's father has cut off ties completely to his son because he works for you."

Stephen looked down at his old friend. "He did?" he asked.

The jewels in Indira's shields winked out. "I could've sworn I told you," she said, her fake English accent getting thicker. "I met Ms. May, Kendle, if I can call you that. After watching the video, I feel like I know you." She let out a trilling laugh.

Steady, Kaya thought. *She'll move on after two minutes. I know her.*

"Nevertheless," Indira continued. "I met the lovely Miss Kendle when she brought one of her students, or I guess not quite student," she said with a toothy smile. "To the hospital to speak with his father."

"And then you decided to fire your assistant for having a Wild child," I said.

Her shields shimmered in annoyance. "And you convinced me otherwise." She saluted me with her champagne glass. "And received a hefty donation from me. I think you won that battle in more than one way."

Play nice, Stephen thought to me. *She has lots and lots of money and can help us. And she's not that bad.*

I reminded myself I had no reason to be jealous. I took another sip of champagne. "And we thank you for the donation and for coming tonight." I forced a smile, hoping it didn't look too fake.

"Your story was fascinating," she said. "I can't believe you play the violin, cello, guitar and piano so well. You're phenomenal, truly phenomenal. Did you really never take a musical lesson? You just picked up an instrument and started playing?"

"Yes."

Stephen nudged my shields when I didn't say anything else.

"It's like my Gift," I continued. "One day, I just woke up and knew how to read minds and move things with a thought. The same thing happens with musical instruments. I just know how to play them."

"Kendle teaches classes on guitar, violin and piano at the Warehouse," Stephen said.

"I'd love to talk to you some more, at some point," Indira said. "After I met you, I realized how little research there is on Wilds. Your Gift and back story might make an interesting research paper."

"No, thank you," I said.

"I could pay you for your time. Or make a donation to Phillip's Academy if you'd prefer."

"I'm sorry, no," I said.

Kendle—

I shot Stephen a look and opened up a mental channel to Indira. *I and other Wilds are not laboratory projects. We're people.*

Of course you are, and we never forget that at my hospital. But wouldn't you like to better understand where Wilds came from? Society treats you poorly and understanding more about how your brain, how your gift functions might help.

"No," I said again.

She put up her hands. "I understand," she said, like she was talking to a crazy person.

God, I hated her.

"I do have a question though and I hope you don't think I'm being too forward with it. Let me know if I am."

"I will." I finished my champagne though my stomach swam with nausea.

"How did you end up in an illegal Gladiator Ring before being found by the director of Phillip's Academy?"

"Yeah, they left that part out of the video," I said, letting the champagne talk. "A social worker came to our apartment to tell me my mom was dead. I may have reacted—" I paused. "The way any Wild coming into her powers would." I'd nearly destroyed our apartment. "The social worker said she'd contact my father and bring me to a holding area for the time being. She promised to keep me safe until my father came. Then she sold me, and I ended up in a Gladiator Ring."

Stephen's shields went gray. "Who did that to you?"

"I don't remember," I muttered. My stomach heaved.

"No wonder you're so devoted to the school," Indira said. "Stephen tells me you work very long hours."

"I ask myself how many Wilds are out there that never found their way to the Warehouse. And I keep working."

Indira's face softened, her shields turning golden and beautiful. No wonder Stephen liked her.

"Thank you for sharing your story." She held out her hand. "I look forward to seeing what the next chapter is."

I took her hand and we shook, her jeweled shields touching mine in a typical Bred fashion.

"It was nice meeting you again," she said.

"You too."

She started to walk away and turned back when Stephen didn't follow. But he was staring at me and after a minute, when he didn't turn back to her, she moved on.

"I didn't know," he said.

I did so many horrible things to stay alive, I thought. *You have no idea.*

Miriam came over, smiling, her shields bright magenta, the black barely visible. "I came over to say congratulations, and to get you all out mingling."

"I need a minute," I muttered, the world toppling a little.

I got you, Kaya thought. She helped me to the bathroom, and I threw up. I just wanted to go home. When I was done, I asked her to help me to a transport pad.

Of course, she thought. *I'll tell everyone else you weren't feeling good and went back to the Warehouse.*

I squeezed her hand as she helped me up and out of the stall. *Thank you.*

Daniel waited for us, leaning against a sink.

"This is the girl's bathroom," Kaya said. "Get out."

"Don't care. She needs to get back out there."

"Fuck. You. You're a fucking shit-headed asshole," I slurred.

His shields darkened to amber.

"You used my past. Without my permission."

"Yes," he said. "To save the Warehouse. We are out of money and need this fundraiser to work. But I meant what I said in the video. You're one of the most powerful and smartest Wilds I know. You didn't let your past break you, and you care so much for our students. But you need to do your part. Talk to the Breds and smile so they donate more money."

"Didn't paying their entrance fee get us enough? Didn't the way you twisted my past help? The cute pictures of me with my head shaved and my wrists like some medical experiment?"

"I get you're pissed. And that's fine. But whatever you said to the Indira woman worked. She just agreed to donate one hundred thousand dollars. One hundred thousand dollars, Kendle! Do you know what we can do with that?"

"Holy shit," Kaya said.

I sat down on the floor, not caring how gross it was. I just couldn't do this anymore.

"Look," Daniel said, squatting next to me. "Don't let being pissed at me ruin the good we're doing."

"You took away my choice." *I'm going to have nightmares again. That stuff was gone. And now—* I couldn't explain. *It's all in my head again.*

Daniel paled.

"I'm sorry," he said, verbally and telepathically. He put his hand out like he was going to touch my arm but pulled back. *I didn't realize.*

I don't ever want to think about those days. I'm not some experiment that went well. You should've asked.

None of us think of you as an experiment. You were so broken when Miriam brought you to the Warehouse and I'm... he trailed off, his shields glowing with glittering bits. He held my eyes. *I should've asked. I'm sorry.*

Just go away.

As you wish.

The door swung behind him, and Kaya helped me to my feet. "Let's get you to the transport pad."

I looked in the mirror. My mascara and lipstick were smeared, my cheeks pale under the foundation Franny had applied. "I'm going back out," I said. "He's right. I should do more for the Warehouse." Plus I'd thrown up most of the alcohol and didn't like the sober feeling.

"You sure?" Kaya asked.

I nodded and brushed bathroom fuzz off my skirt.

Kaya pulled a tissue and lipstick out of her purse. "Let's fix your mascara."

CHAPTER THIRTY-SIX

Couples were on the ballroom dance floor now, the open bar fueling choices they'd regret in the morning. Other Breds sat at the tables talking, playing on their screens or eating a second dessert. A Bred wandered over and asked Kaya to dance. She refused, with a smile, but watched him go, her shields darkening just a touch.

Go ahead, I told her.

You sure?

I am. I feel better after throwing up.

When Kaya left, I pulled out my phone and played around for a second, before stuffing it back into the little purse I carried. I looked for my friends. Franny sat at a table, eating dessert and talking to another woman. Miriam stood with Daniel, nodding to a bunch of men in suits. Stephen was encircled by other Breds. As one they laughed at his joke.

Stephen touched my thoughts. *Please come save me.* There was another peal of laughter from the circle surrounding him. *Tell them there's some sort of an emergency. Then we can leave.*

Daniel says I have to stay.

What's he going to do? Scold you?

He had a point. *Where would we go?*

My beach house, just for a few hours. I need the ocean.

I've never been to the ocean.

I know.

I smiled. *Promise?*

Promise.

Are you still mad at me? Daniel's honey colored shields winked in my mind.

I'm not speaking to you.

Ken— I closed the mental channel and crossed the floor to where Stephen held court. I wormed my way into the group, waiting for a free moment when I could interrupt. "Sorry everyone. I need to borrow Stephen. Small Phillip's Academy emergency."

My apologies, he thought to the group. I glanced over my shoulder and saw the women ogling his ass in his tux.

Stephen grabbed my hand and pulled me onto the dance floor, just as a slow song started.

One dance.

He put one hand on my waist, and we linked fingers. This felt so familiar. Stupid dreams. My skin tingled through my dress where his hand touched, and goosebumps popped out on my arms. I strengthened my shields.

Daniel said we made a lot of money tonight. I needed to break up the silence.

Of course we did. And if Miriam sends out thank you notes with the video to a few interested people, she'll make even more. Things are about to get so much better for the Warehouse.

We swayed to the music, doing nothing more complex.

Did your social worker really sell you? He asked.

I stepped away, tugging my hand away from his.

No, no, no, he thought. *Where are you going?*

I don't want to talk about it. Ever.

Then we won't. Stephen pulled me back into his arms, holding me closer. I could put my head on his shoulder if I wanted. And I really wanted to. He took the hand off my waist and wiped away a tear. I hadn't realized I was crying.

I won't ask. I promise.

Thank you. I pushed the tears back and tried to smile, looking over his shoulder. Around the room people had their phones out, taking pictures of something. I frowned, wondering what was going on.

It was us. They were taking pictures of Stephen and me.

Stephen, people are taking pictures. I tried to pull away.

Fuck them. He pulled me an inch closer. *If they can't handle seeing me dance with a friend, fuck them. If I really wanted to blow their minds, I'd kiss you, but you'd punch me. No girly slap for you.*

Thought your parents made it so you can't get drunk, unless you try hard.

I'm not drunk. You look very pretty. That would be enough reason to kiss you.

Bet you say that to all the pretty girls.

Tonight, you're the prettiest one here.

The next cheesy line was mine. I was supposed to say something flirty. But I couldn't. I met his eyes and Stephen wrapped his shields around mine.

Can we talk, maybe tonight when we get home, he asked. *On the roof? Or the beach house. That would be the best.*

We're going to make an announcement about how much money we've raised. Miriam's voice in my head startled me, stopping anything I might have said. *Can all of you come up to the stage please?*

———

We got back to the Warehouse two hours later, all of us grabbing onto the railing around the transport pad as it spit us out. I breathed through the nausea. Drinking always made it so much worse.

Roof or beach house? Stephen whispered in my head.

But my heart dropped. It was nearly two a.m. and lights shown in the admin and dorm warehouses. Flashlights moved on the grassy area.

Kaya sighed. *Seiko? What's going on?*

You guys are finally back! I can't find Becca. And Casi is acting all weird. Tom, Weldon and Sam are all searching the ground for Becca. I'm with Casi.

I slipped the painful heels I'd been carrying back on. *I'm on Becca,* I thought. *How long has she been missing?*

Helen got up to get some water ten minutes ago and noticed she was gone. We already checked the common areas. Casi woke up when we were looking and started acting really weird.

I closed my eyes and focused on trying to find Becca's apricot shields. *I don't think she's on the grounds,* I thought.

I opened up the gate and slipped outside. Daniel followed while the others went to the dorm to deal with Casi.

Go away, I told him. *I can handle this.*

It's not safe in this neighborhood after dark, he thought.

Whatever. I didn't care enough to argue. I stretched out, trying to find Becca's shields.

"About tonight," Daniel murmured.

"We're not talking."

"I was trying to do what was best for the Warehouse. I wasn't trying to hurt you. I wou—"

Got her, I thought. Down the street and a city block away, I just sensed her shields, red and oranges streaking the apricot. I teleported to her and Daniel appeared next to me. Becca sat against a building, her knees up, trying to make herself as small as possible. She was still in her pajamas, her feet bare.

I didn't know where I was, she moaned. *And it's so dark. And I couldn't find the Warehouse.*

We're here, I thought. *Can you walk?* Becca shook her head and held out a foot. I fished my phone out of my little handbag and shone the flashlight. Her foot was badly cut, probably on the broken glass littering the street.

"I got her," Daniel said, lifting her into his arms.

Stop, Daniel. I'd been so tired; I hadn't noticed the other shields creeping up to surround us. Dark shapes, with ripped clothes and torn shields moved in until they were a few feet away.

I don't think I can teleport with Becca, Daniel thought.

I probably can, I responded. *If it comes to it.*

"We're from the Warehouse," I told the homeless Wilds. "We're just collecting a lost student."

Theo stepped forward, his olive and navy shields holey. "How about we let you go for two boxes of food a week."

"Let us—"

I stopped Daniel. "One box a week."

Kendle. There isn't enough for us.

They're starving. I'd give them the food anyway.

Miriam will kill you. We don't have the money.

Keeping us safe in this neighborhood is that big picture thinking Miriam wants me to do. I can find room in the budget, especially after tonight. She won't know.

"Agreed," Theo said. The crowd of Wilds melted back into the shadows.

I let out a deep breath.

We found Becca, I thought to the Warehouse group as Daniel carried Becca and I kept my senses open in case any Wilds decided to jump us.

Thank God, Kaya responded. *Where was she?*

A few blocks away. She cut herself pretty good though. We'll need Jasmine.

On it.

Is Casi okay? Becca asked Daniel and me.

Casi? Daniel asked the group.

She's back in bed, Miriam responded. *She was probably sleepwalking.*

She was muttering weirdly though, Seiko thought. *Kept talking about snow and a band and a house in the woods. She just kept repeating it.*

Casi's fine, I told Becca. *She's back in bed.*

We reached the Warehouse and Daniel took Becca to the infirmary where Jasmine waited to examine her foot.

I just wanted my bed. I didn't want to have an emotional conversation with Stephen. Not when I still needed to make sure Becca was okay.

Rain check on tonight? I asked Stephen.

Of course. It was a long night. Sweet dreams.

An hour later, Becca slept in the infirmary and I was finally able to peel off the little black dress and toss it into a heap in the corner of my living room. I rubbed a sore foot and wiggled my toes, swearing I'd never wear heels again.

A thought trembled on the edge of my brain.

Yes? I asked. I was so tired.

Did you guys make a lot of money tonight? Leo asked.

It's nearly three a.m. You should be asleep. And yes, it seems like we did very well.

Did you see my dad?

No, I'm sorry. But I talked to his boss for a little while. She mentioned you.

Did she say anything about him?

No. But maybe Ms. Phillips knows more. Or Mr.—

Yeah.

Send your dad an email. Let him know you were thinking about him.

Whatever. Good night, Miss May.

Goodnight Leo. I fell into my bed, not even bothering to wash the smeared makeup off.

CHAPTER THIRTY-SEVEN

I SHOT awake and winced in pain. My neck was completely locked, and I massaged out the kink. I'd fallen asleep curled up in my armchair watching a movie on my screen. Now my apartment was dark. I checked the time. Great—it was two a.m. and I'd slept for twelve hours straight. I wouldn't be able to sleep more tonight.

Miriam was so happy with the response to our fundraiser and I'd spent the day reconciling the donations, putting together thank you notes and paying the vendors. Thanks to Indira, we'd made enough money to heat the buildings and fix a leak in the classroom building. Then I'd assembled a report detailing our expenditures, who we'd used, who attended, etcetera, etcetera, etcetera. I'd also scanned social media for comments about the event and found they were mostly positive, though people hadn't liked the food, which was fair. Next time, if there was a next time, we'd serve better food.

I thought about trying to go to bed but wasn't sleepy. I made a cup of chamomile tea, lit a joint and settled back into my armchair with a novel, sending the pot smoke out the window with my Gift. I needed the break; during my social media search I'd found pictures of Stephen and I dancing. He'd looked great, smiling down at me, handsome in his tux. But each picture showed me mid-conversation, my mouth twisted in a weird shape, my mascara still smeared. And the comments were terrible. Breds, Regs and even other Wilds called me a bitch, a gold-digger, a GAFU, a slut and so much more. But it all came down to the same message. I wasn't good enough for someone like Stephen, not even as friends.

I took a long pull of the joint, holding the smoke deep in my lungs before releasing. I wished I had a picture of my mom, some connection to her on nights like this. I went to the window and looked out at the city lights, wiping away tears I couldn't stop.

Outside, a shadow in the moonlight moved, sitting down on a bench in the rock garden and tucking her legs underneath her.

Perfect. Casi had snuck past the dorm alarm.

At least it was something to do. I pulled on clothes, and teleported to the rock garden, my feet splattering the gravel.

The girl turned around with a strangled scream. "It's me," I said verbally and mentally.

Stupid, I told myself. I hadn't been thinking. A scared psychokinetic could cause a lot of damage.

"Ms. May, you scared the crap out of me."

"Sorry," I said. I went and sat down on a bench close to Casi, but not the same one.

"Whatcha doin' in this gin joint?" I said with a fake Texas accent.

I couldn't see her face to see if she smiled, but her charcoal shields lightened a bit.

"Couldn't sleep. And I didn't want to scare Becca and have her teleport away again."

"Insomnia sucks," I said. "That's why I'm awake myself. If it's really bad though, we can get you an appointment with the Nurse Practitioner. You need sleep."

"It's not often," Casi said. "And it's only—" she stopped, and I resisted the urge to look through her shields. "I don't know," she finally said.

"When your brain is chattering at you and you can't make it shut up?"

"No." She picked up a bit of bark and shredded it. "Kind-of, I guess. I don't know."

"Sometimes reading or watching a movie helps. Or I'll put in head-phones and listen to a show on the internet. Anything to keep my brain off of whatever is going on."

"I guess."

"Do you want to try one of those? Cuz, you know I can't leave you out here." I wasn't even going to address how she got out of the dorm room. "You can sit in the common area and watch a movie on your screen."

"I know. It's just—" She took a deep breath. "The walls are the wrong color."

Well that was a new one. It had to be a metaphor for something. "I'm old," I said with a smile. "I don't know what you mean."

She turned to look at me, her eyes catching the moonlight like something out of a paranormal romance novel. "In the dorm room, on the first floor. The walls are the wrong color. They should be gray, not beige."

The dorm alarm went off. Probably someone else out of their rooms after curfew, trying to sneak out like Casi was. Did everyone just wander around at night now? I'd have to bring it up at a staff meeting.

The third-floor alarm sounded and all the lights on that floor went on. Something had spooked one of the older kids. Then the alarm went off on all the floors, and every light in the dorm went on, patches of yellow lighting up the grassy area.

—*Help*—

—*joke?*—

—*cuate*—

Windows flew open and screams sounded.

"Stay here," I told Casi. "Do not move. Wait, run to the infirmary. Wake up Jasmine and bring all the emergency supplies to the grassy area." She gaped at the lights. "Run!" I yelled.

She ran and I teleported myself to the sliding glass doors.

—*Get out*—

—*blood*—

Through the sliding glass doors, I saw a tornado of flying objects caught in a whirlwind of psychic energy. Furniture stuttered across the floor. Students tried to get out, but retreated back into their rooms, slamming the doors shut. The building creaked.

God help us. Someone had imploded.

—*flying around*—

—*where*—

—*urt*—

—*I can't*—

Miriam's voice cut through the subsonic chatter.

All staff, immediately report to the dorms.

Someone imploded, I told the other faculty. *Hurry. The building is creaking, and it might collapse.*

The sliding glass doors slid open and three students ran out, releasing PK pressure. It felt like there were a dozen psychokinetics using all of their power at once.

Get the windows open, I thought in as open a channel as I could manage. *Or they'll blow.*

Windows hit sashes and a few shattered. But it was better than losing all the glass.

No one teleport yourselves out of the building, unless you're in danger and there is no way out, Miriam thought. *Evacuate through the main doors if possible. If not, go through your window. A teacher can help lift you to the ground if you need it.*

Thoughts pressed against my mind and I pushed them away. I needed to focus on what was in front of me. I went to help the students reeling in the sludgy snow. I pulled Samantha, Tom, and two other third years to their feet. Tom bled from a serious cut on his hand. "What happened?" I asked.

"Don't know," Samantha said. "Anything that's not nailed down is flying around, even in the dorm rooms with the door closed. I just grabbed whoever I could, put a shield up around us and got us out of there."

A few of the plastic objects that flew outside with the students, lifted sluggishly up into the air before falling again. This was bad. Something in the building cracked, the sound like a gunshot.

"Get to the infirmary," I said to Tom. "Make sure that cut doesn't need stitches."

The doors slid open again and more students came out, one holding her wrist against her body, along with a book shooting ten feet out and hitting the wall with an audible thump. Flying pages added to the chaos.

Jasmine came running, Casi jogging next to her. "I'm going to need a temporary first aid station out here," Jasmine snapped.

"I can help," Samantha said.

"Okay, do what she says," I told her.

"We're going to need a lot of supplies—take as much as you can carry out of the storage closet," Jasmine said.

Becca appeared beside me. *Everyone is trapped in their rooms. I can get them out.*

No way. It's too dangerous. The second-floor windows blew, and the lawn filled with screams and shouts.

Okay, I told her. God help me. I hoped she wasn't going to kill anyone teleporting them. *One student at a time. Take the injured ones. And if you start bleeding from your nose, or ears or get any hint of a headache, stop. Do not be a hero.*

Becca disappeared.

Stephen and Daniel appeared while the other professors ran out of the admin building. The screams inside were getting worse.

Any telepathic fifth years, we need a report, Miriam thought.

I slammed my shields up against the onslaught of thoughts and emotions.

—in my room with four other students. We can't get—

—my eye, oh my—

Miriam staggered, her hand over her nose as blood dripped. Blood dripped from Franny's face and ears.

Psychokinetic implosion on the first floor, Weldon's voice cut through the static. *Items and furniture are slamming around, even flying up the stairs and up the open middle.*

Any idea who?

No.

I can take over communications, Stephen said in our heads. Miriam's ears were bleeding.

Everyone, send your conversations through Stephen. He's the focus.

I met his eyes before he closed them.

Can you do this? I asked.

I don't think I have a choice, he responded.

Daniel and Kendle, find the source. We need the student sedated. Miriam's instructions filtering through Stephen came with magenta and turquoise tinges. *Franny help Jasmine. Kaya, Seiko, and I will evacuate the students through what's left of the windows. Kaya and Seiko, third floor, I'll take the second floor. Stephen, stay on the grassy area. Any students still in the building, get underneath or behind something and protect yourselves. Close doors if possible or get into a bathroom stall.*

—*pipes burst, bath*—

If the bathrooms are safe, get to them, Miriam amended.

Kaya, Seiko and Miriam used their Gift to float up to the second and third floors, helping students out the windows.

Franny grabbed sedation syringes from Jasmine and ran them over to Daniel and me. Her hands shook. "I didn't want to add to the stuff floating," she said.

"You're fine," I told her. "Help Jasmine."

"Ready?" Daniel asked.

"We got this."

We stepped forward, and the motion sensor tripped, opening the door. Our ears popped. It was like walking into a hurricane, even with all the windows open or shattered.

The common area was full of chaos, like from a movie with an angry poltergeist. Books, soda cans, pens, glasses, papers and parts of board games whipped around in cyclones or flew at random, slamming into walls or furniture. Most of the furniture was on its side or had been hit by flying objects and was scratched and gouged. Imbedded pens and pencils stuck out of couches and broken glass studded from the walls.

This is going to cost so much to fix, I thought. *It may break us.*

"That's why we have insurance." Daniel said. We crunched on the debris. The noise was terrible. Bits of metal, and plastic crashed into other and cracked or shattered and then other bits slammed into that and broke

Several students, first years, cowered under the giant table, holding onto the legs, physically and with their Gift, trying to keep it in place despite its sporadic jumps. Oniony panic scented the room.

"Get physical barriers up, get out of here," I shouted using my voice and Gift.

A bookcase slammed down a few feet away from the table. The kids screamed and moved further under the table. A pen whipped through the air, heading directly for them. One student dropped to the floor, barely avoiding it as the pen embedded in the wall behind him. He lost his hold on the table and it flew three feet up, before the others managed to yank it back down. They were too weak and panicked to deflect the objects or throw up a barrier.

Son of a fucking bitch.

We can't help them, Daniel thought. *We have to get to the student causing this.*

There are first years cornered in the community space, I told the other teachers through Stephen. *Can anyone evacuate them?*

Negative, was Miriam's voice.

I can get there in five minutes, thought Seiko.

I'm not sure I can even get to everyone on the third floor, Kaya thought.

The building shook, the walls vibrating and creaking. Doors slammed and screams echoed.

We need the student causing this sedated before the building collapses, Miriam thought. *Leave the others. We'll get them out as quick as we can.*

One of the kids under the table let out a yelp when a flying book struck them.

"I can't," I yelled to Daniel. "Go find the student. I'll catch up."

Hell no. "Create a null space around you where nothing can reach you," Daniel said, verbally and mentally to the students. A couch moved and slammed into Daniel and my barriers'. The impact vibrated in my mind. Daniel shook his head, trying to clear it.

If I get written up again for not following instructions...

His mind laughed, a panicked chuckle. *I got your back.*

We ran to the table, and I pulled the kids out while Daniel kept an extra barrier around us. We managed to get two out, before Daniel thought, *I won't be able to protect all of them at once. We'll have to make two trips.*

The four of us ran toward the door and it swished open. Samantha and Weldon ran to us, helping the two kids to a plastic awning in the grassy area. We ran back in and repeated with the other two kids before running back in.

My nose itched and I touched it. Blood. I was expending too much of my Gift. A pen whizzed by my ear and a book slammed into Daniel's barrier.

We got this, Daniel thought just as the bookshelf that had scared the students slid toward us. Even though we had physical barriers up, we both reacted by slamming our hands up and pushing the bookshelf back.

We got this, Daniel thought again. *We can do this.* He was chanting it, more to himself than me.

Have you found the student yet? Miriam asked us.

Not yet, Daniel thought. *We evacuated the other first year students.*

I think it's Leo, someone broke in, Stephen's turquoise shields coloring all the thoughts, making it harder to know who was talking. *All the other first years are out on the grass.*

It's a good guess, Daniel thought.

We turned down the corridor where Leo's dorm room was. The damage was much worse here, holes in the walls showing insulation, drywall dust floating through the air and coating everything. Water flowed out of the bathroom and down the hallway.

If anyone has a free moment, turn the water off to the building, I thought to Stephen.

Leo's room door was open, and a chair flew out, impaling itself into the wall.

Bingo.

We started down the hallway but stopped a few feet away. I shook my head. I had the strongest desire for a cup of tea and a cookie. My stomach rumbled. This was taking a lot of energy and I needed a break. I shook my head again and concentrated. Purple tentacles leaked out the doorway toward Daniel and me.

Daniel shook his head too. *I have way too much laundry to do,* he thought. *I really need to get it done.*

Get your shields up, I thought to Daniel. *Leo's trying to control us.* Daniel blinked but the desire to take a break was overpowering.

I'm really worried I left a load of laundry in the washer. I'll be right back.

I grabbed his arm before he could teleport away.

We have a problem, I thought to the group through Stephen. *Daniel really wants to check on his laundry.*

Truly, Daniel broke in. *I hate it when its mildew smelling. I'll be back in thirty seconds.*

And I really want a cup of tea and a cookie, I thought. *Like a shortbread cookie. And apples with caramel sauce to dip it in. But a red apple, like a Gala or a Fuji.*

I'll just go and check on the laundry. Be right back, Daniel thought, trying to pull out of my grasp.

They need a telepathic barrier, Franny thought.

It makes sense, came Kaya. *We told Leo he couldn't use his Gift.*

So, he imploded, Miriam finished.

I can put up a telepathic shield, Stephen thought. *I'm on my way.*

Daniel pinched my arm.

"Ouch," I smacked his hand without even thinking.

"Bitch," he hissed and pushed me. I hit the wall. My concentration broke, and my physical barrier went down. A bit of flying glass sliced my leg.

"Son of a fucking bitch," I yelled, putting the barrier back up. I pressed my hand against the cut. I'd liked these jeans.

Daniel disappeared, presumably to get his laundry. I really wanted to just sit down and quit. With milk and cookies of course. And an apple.

Stephen appeared.

We got this, he told me, wrapping my mind in his turquoise shields. I didn't want milk and cookies anymore. But I still wanted to quit.

Oh my god, Kendle. I'm so sorry, Daniel thought from outside the building. *As soon as I got to the grassy area—I realized—are you okay?*

I'm fine, I lied. Blood soaked my jeans. *Stephen's here.*

A book hit Stephen in the leg, and he let out a yelp. I extended my physical barrier around him. He took my hand and squeezed it.

I'm sorry. I should be—Daniel's honey shields were darker than I'd ever seen them.

It's okay. I meant it, too. *You can help with the next implosion.*

I left the channel open, just in case. Together Stephen and I held hands, walking down the hallway to Leo's room. His hand felt warm and comfortable in mine. I squeezed and he squeezed back.

We stopped a bullet together. We'll be fine.

Leo lay on his bed. Objects and furniture flew and jerked around the room. My hair whipped around my face in a wind caused by all the moving parts. We didn't have a lot of time. I was leaving a bloody shoe print and my eyes felt heavy. I wanted to curl up and sleep for a month.

Stephen tried to move into the room, but it was too thick with spinning, moving objects even with the physical barriers protecting us.

Can you teleport him out? Stephen asked. *We can sedate him outside.*

And maintain a barrier? Not possible, I thought. Leo's roommate's bed slammed into the ceiling and I cried out, my nerves as battered as my leg. My barrier dropped for a second and I was instantly battered with books, plastic and trash. A pen traced a line across my arm, drawing blood and a plate borrowed from the cafeteria rammed into Stephen's stomach. He dropped to his knees.

"We're going to have to merge again," I screamed verbally and telepathically.

I know.

It was already so easy between his telepathic and my physical barrier. We just slid into each other. Stepping as one, we pushed away the items flying around the room with ease, walking to Leo's bed. I injected the sedative while bending over the sleeping Wild.

Everything around us dropped to the ground. Our ears rang with the silence. We could hear water still flowing, until it suddenly stopped too. Someone had finally switched it off.

Ready, we asked each other.

Ready, we nodded.

I pulled my shields back into myself. It was sticky, like thick caramel, but possible.

My legs trembled and my butt hit the floor. I was so empty.

———

Ten minutes later I was in the infirmary getting my favorite jeans cut off and being numbed for stitches.

"How many were hurt?" I asked Dr. Evander. He was a Quality Bred, with bright blue eyes, tanned skin and bleached hair. He looked like every other word should be 'dude' and like he did triathlons in his free time. For all I knew, he did.

"Not as many as you'd think," he said. He hummed a little under his breath injecting the numbing stuff into my skin. The cut was long and deep. "This school does a great job of teaching Wilds how to protect themselves," he continued. "Most of the students could either place a physical barrier or were able to evacuate. He picked up the curved needle, already threaded. "Look away," he said.

Miriam had somehow convinced this Quality Bred doctor to donate his time to the Warehouse. He came out once a month for physicals, and prescribed ADHD medication, sleeping, anti-depression and anxiety meds to those that needed it. He was also an expert, as much as anyone was, on Wilds and how our brains operated. He felt that even though we could do similar things as Breds, we were using different parts of our brains, which is why so many thought we were inferior to Breds.

"How's Leo?" I asked to distract from the faint tugging of the needle.

"The boy that caused all this? Still sleeping. He'll be out for a while. I'll stay around just in case though." He hummed again a bit and then the forceps clattered into a tray. "Do you know what happened?

"No," I said. "Leo's a good kid. His Gift is...unique and he's been working hard to control it."

"Too hard, if he imploded," the doctor said, wrapping a thick bandage around my leg. "Though I've been wondering if there's an emotional element to implosions. Did anything happen?"

I sighed. "He asked me last night about his dad. I was at a fundraiser with his dad's boss. I think Leo assumed his dad had gone, and he could get news about him."

Dr. Evander nodded. "Perhaps thinking about his dad is what triggered it. You're done," he said, taping up the edge of the bandage. "You'll have another scar to add to your collection."

"Yay," I deadpanned.

"Get out of my infirmary,"

"Jesus, okay, okay." I awkwardly climbed off the exam table.

You do good work here—don't let this ruin that.

We'll try not to. See you around.

I limped out to the cafeteria, using my tired Gift to help support my weight so I didn't need crutches. My other cuts and bruises were minor, but I had to be careful not to rip the stitches out of my leg.

While I was in the infirmary, the others had set up the kids in the cafeteria with a movie and headphones for those that couldn't sleep and a quiet area for those that did. When I limped in, most were in the movie area, drinking hot chocolate and eating donuts someone must have gone out and gotten.

Seiko, Franny, Stephen and Kaya, my friends, sat in the back of the room, their shields gray and black with shock and exhaustion.

Hey guys, I thought, joining their open mental channel.

Hey you. You okay? Kaya asked, standing to give me her trademark hug.

Just a few stitches. I hugged her back gratefully. I knew she hugged everyone no matter what, but it felt so good, I held on for an extra few seconds. She touched my shields with hers when I released her.

The most embarrassing part was I hadn't shaved my legs in a while, I quipped.

Then we're grateful you put on some pajama pants.

Daniel opened a personal channel to me, though he wasn't in the room. *I'm so sorry,* he thought. *I can't believe I pushed you.*

Barely felt it, I lied. *And Stephen came and got a telepathic shield up. I don't think we'd be able to get to Leo's room without it.*

He saved the day. Again.

I teleported into the kitchen. Daniel was in the huge walk-in fridge, staring at the nearly bare shelves, the door hanging open. I limped in, my breath puffing white. The smell of old meat, veggies and fruit surrounded me. His honey colored shields were a muddy brown with no glittering pieces.

"It's okay," I told him, putting a hand on his shoulder. He jerked, just a bit. "I'm fine. No one was hurt seriously. Today could've been so much worse."

He turned around and I hugged him. He wrapped his arms around my waist and leaned his face into my hair. His shields glowed and then locked around his thoughts. He breathed out, a quick puff of air and released me.

He turned back to the fridge and grabbed our last gallon of milk. *Been a hell of a year. Are you still mad at me for the video?*

Yes. But we'll get past it.

We went back out, and Daniel made more hot chocolate.

How's Miriam? I asked the group.

She's in her office, contacting the insurance company, Stephen thought.

She wept when she saw the damage to the dorm, Kaya thought.

I remembered the holes in the walls, the broken glass and pulverized belongings.

How bad is it?

The burst pipes caused the most damage, but the boys' side of the first floor is trashed. We're going to need new furniture. And after we patch the walls, they'll need new paint. The carpet where it flooded is a loss, so we'll need new carpet at least on the boys' side. The common area took a huge hit too. The other floors aren't too bad. Most of the kids closed their doors. It helped, Daniel answered.

"Settle down," Stephen said to a bunch of whispering students passing a screen back and forth.

I should go help Miriam, I thought. *Anyone made coffee yet?*

Seiko saluted me with his cup, and I went into the kitchen to pour a big mug for myself and Miriam.

CHAPTER THIRTY-EIGHT

THE NEXT MORNING, we met in the conference room to decide what to do about Leo. He'd come out of the sedation poorly, jerking awake and immediately knowing what he'd done. I hadn't seen him, but Dr. Evander had shared Leo had turned his face to the wall and cried. Leo's Gift had protected him from the bumps, bruises and minor cuts most of us had, but Dr. Evander had recommended Leo stay in the infirmary for the next day or two for observation. Leo's Gift was pretty depleted, but Stephen and Daniel had both gone to talk to him, forcing him to use his psychokinesis and telepathy.

I sat down in my normal spot in the conference room, looking at all the faded post-it notes on the walls. So many ideas and so little time or money. Now the money we'd gotten from the fundraiser would go to rebuilding the dorm, instead of improving the school. We could never win. I picked at a bit of drywall under my nails, waiting for the meeting to begin.

I'm so tired, Seiko thought in an open channel to Kaya, myself, Stephen and Franny.

None of us had gone back to sleep. It was Monday morning, but we'd canceled classes and allowed the kids to move into the classroom building after breakfast so they could spread out. No one could go into the dorm building until we could get an engineer to look at it.

A giant carafe of coffee and a bunch of pastries from the cafeteria appeared on the conference room table.

You can go without food or sleep, Stephen thought. *Not both.*

My leg ached. I probably needed another pain pill. I rubbed a sore shoulder and felt someone's Gift press into it, digging into the knot. I could tell from the turquoise shields who it was.

Thank you, I thought on a private channel.

Anytime. The phantom hand moved to the back of my neck, finding knots and digging into them. I'd never really gotten a massage before.

"I've good and bad news," Miriam said as she and Daniel came in. They took their seats. "The estimate for the damage Leo caused to the dorms is nearly one hundred fifty thousand dollars and if we had to pay it, it would force us to immediately close our doors, despite the fundraiser. The good news is our insurance will cover a great deal and we can bring down some of the expense if we do the work ourselves. And we're going to have to tighten our belts."

I nodded. "We'll make it work. We always do."

"But we have a bigger issue," Miriam continued. "Leo obviously can't stay here. So please tell his father to pick him up tomorrow, Kendle."

Wait, what? We were expelling an imploding student without teaching him some control? Didn't we learn from Jameson?

"His father wants no contact with him," I said. "He wrote a letter to me right after Leo joined us, stating the boy was not to come home for any holidays or the summer."

"Then he goes to Sedona," Miriam said. "Next item. Does anyone know how to fix furniture or know anyone who will do it cheaply? Maybe a Wild who graduated from here?"

Seiko opened up a channel to the rest of us, minus Daniel who always sided with Miriam. *Is that what we're doing? We're expelling Leo? Into an institution?*

He did destroy our dorm, Franny thought. *I think he's too dangerous.*

He's too dangerous to let out without training him, Seiko thought.

But we have a responsibility to our students, Kaya thought. *We have to keep them safe. Leo could've collapsed the entire dorm, killing all of them.*

Many of our students could do it if they tried, Seiko thought. *Kendle could do it.*

But Leo actually came close, Franny thought.

But it doesn't seem right to just expel him, Stephen responded. *He's been a perfect student, and doesn't control people.*

Which is what led to the implosion, Kaya thought. *I get it. But we have to protect the students. We've never had an implosion here.*

But we've had a few near misses, I thought.

Franny started, *And those—*

"Perhaps Daniel and I should join the conversation you're all so obviously having," Miriam interrupted.

"I think we need to talk more about Leo," I said. "Some of us aren't sure expelling him is the best choice."

"He caused over a hundred and fifty thousand dollars of damage," Miriam said. "We have students with broken bones, students that will have nightmares. You yourself sustained a serious injury."

"I just needed a few stitches." I shrugged it off.

"What argument would you possibly have to keep Leo?" Miriam asked.

"He has no control of his Gift, making him a danger to society," I said. "He's our responsibility to fix."

"Actually," Seiko started. "Leo has complete control, which is why the implosion happened. He wasn't using his Gift."

"Wasn't he using it in telepathy and psychokinesis?" Miriam asked those professors.

"Of course," Stephen said. "But maybe controlling others isn't like his psychokinesis and telepathy. Maybe it's a totally different Gift. It's too hard to know without testing."

"You're saying he has to control people to prevent his Gift from building up," I said. "I mean, maybe Becca would be at risk of implosion too if we stopped her from teleporting."

Miriam sighed and took off her glasses. She massaged the bridge of her nose. "Point taken," she said. "And perhaps if we realized this before, we could've prevented this. But I can't keep a student here who caused this much damage. We're lucky no one died."

"But this is our fault," I said. "You just said it. We didn't realize he was just storing up his Gift and not releasing it. We need to teach him how to use it, or we're looking at another Jameson."

Miriam shook her head, her shields gray and black. There was no magenta left anymore. "This is the issue, Kendle. You're not thinking about the school, you're only thinking of the individual."

"No," I corrected. "I'm thinking about our reputation if another Warehouse Wild implodes and destroys a building. I'm thinking entirely big picture." And I was also thinking of Leo. I couldn't imagine telling him he'd have to go. And I was thinking of his Gift. We'd never seen anything like it. I'd never believed an institution was the right place for him.

"He controls people with his mind," Miriam said. "You and Daniel experienced that yesterday."

"That's true," Daniel said with a sigh. "And in full disclosure he forced me to do something I never would've done."

"Yes, go and check your laundry," I said. "The big meanie forced you to do the most boring thing ever." *Don't tell them,* I told Daniel in a private channel. *It wasn't a big deal and if we hadn't been under so much pressure, you would've never pushed me, Leo controlling you or not.*

You have stitches because of me, because there weren't two layers of barriers around you.

I'm fine. Don't tell them he made you push me.

"Leo could force any of us to do anything." Miriam had continued the conversation. "He could force us to empty our bank accounts, force a student into sex they don't want. He could use his Gift to get students to hurt each other. He's fifteen and like all fifteen-year olds, has no self-control."

"I disagree," Kaya said. "He knows he can control people. So, he stopped using his Gift. It had to be difficult."

"How would we get him to siphon off his Gift?" Miriam asked. "Take turns letting him puppet us around? Should we make it a part of the chore rotation? Let Leo control you to earn five dollars?"

Seiko snapped his fingers. "I got it. Maybe he could control animals. Get it, like some sort of animal control?" He looked around, trying to get a grin out of one of us, but we were all too tired. His black and emerald shields deflated a little.

"That's actually a good idea," Kaya said. "Look at Mr. Sparklebutt. Eeva told him to watch Kendle and he does. Perhaps Eeva controls animals, just a bit."

"Yes," Daniel said. "It has nothing to do with Kendle feeding him."

I rolled my eyes at him. "But maybe Leo could control animals instead of people to use his Gift."

"Kendle had this great idea about a secondary school for damaged or Wilds with unique Gifts," Stephen said. "She thought animals would be a great addition, like therapy dogs and stuff. And horses too, right, love?"

"Oh, come on," Miriam scoffed. "We barely have enough..."

Miriam's voice faded away. I hadn't had a conversation with Stephen about my idea for the secondary school with the stable and horses. I'd only told Eeva.

I dropped my head into my hands. Holy shit. I was really dream sharing with Stephen. Time slowed, and everything got crystal sharp. Darkness crowded on the edges of my vision and the table under my hands vibrated slightly. I strengthened my shielding.

Did he know? He couldn't. He would've said something. Right? Like I'd totally said something. Oh. My. God. Maybe that's what he'd wanted to talk with me about.

Fuck, fuck, fuckity-fuck me sideways and into next week.

Was dream sharing even possible? Maybe I'd told him about the school and the animals in real life and my mind had created the dream of us lying naked in the little cabin and replayed an entire conversation I couldn't remember having.

"Kendle!"

"What?" I looked up with the verbal and mental shout. Seiko was shaking my shoulder. I took a deep breath, darkness crowding my vision. I'd stopped breathing.

"Are you okay?" he asked.

I looked around the table at my friends, scooting my eyes over

Stephen as quick as I could. There were mini whirlpools in my water glass and the table vibrated slightly.

I tucked my Gift back where it belonged. "Sorry," I said. "I'm really tired. And the pain pills are probably messing with my control," I lied.

You okay? Stephen asked. Just as I knew he would. This was so embarrassing.

The whirlpool in my glass started up again. I took a deep breath and willed it away. I needed to focus on Leo.

Kendle? Stephen was worried about me; I could see it in the oranges and reds swimming through his shields.

I'm fine. Sorry. I managed to drum up a half smile for him, for the man I'd been having orgasmically good dreams with for the last six weeks. My cheeks burned and I triple checked my shields.

This must be why Regs hated telepaths.

"If we could return to the topic," Miriam said. "We don't have the money for a secondary school. We can add it to the post-it notes. And I hear what you're all saying, but my decision stands. Leo's done. Kendle, please contact his father and tell him. Stephen, please contact Chanelle because the probability is Leo will be joining her in Sedona tomorrow. Also, if Becca gets out one more time, she's out too, so Stephen, please raise the point with Chanelle as well. We can't protect Becca if she's getting past the walls, and she's going to get hurt. It's better she's somewhere that will keep her contained."

"No, Miriam, no," I said. "These are children's entire lives. They're the reason you built this place. To help advance Wilds. It's in the fucking name. We don't get to pick and choose who we help."

"We do if it's going to hurt the rest of our students," Miriam said, enunciating each word. Her thick and unmoving gray and black shields should've been enough to make me stop, but I couldn't.

"I say we vote. If the majority agrees an institution is the best place for Leo and Becca, then I'll stop arguing."

"This isn't a democracy." Miriam stood up, her chair scraping on the cracked Pergo flooring. "I'm your employer. And I'm happy to make that change whenever you want. In fact, I'm not even sure what I was thinking. You seem to be incapable of learning from your mistakes."

My world shrunk to her voice and my breath stuck in my throat. The water in my glass spun.

"Miriam," Daniel said.

"You are continually putting our lives and our students' lives in danger with your ridiculous decisions."

"Miriam," Daniel said.

I wouldn't lose control. I tucked my Gift back and put the lid tightly on it. I focused on the shields of those around me, watching the ebb and flow of the colors. I raised my chin.

"Think about each mistake you have made this year. Becca, Leo, Casi," Miriam continued. "They were all poor choices and have wreaked havoc in our home."

"Miriam!" Daniel's voice echoed around the room.

"No, I won't stop," she snapped. "We're always so careful about what we say, so scared someone will lose control if we speak the truth. Well I'm tired, and I'll say what's on my mind. You're destroying my school." Her shields swirled around me, black and terrible.

"That's enough, Miriam," Daniel said using both his mental and verbal voice. "This meeting is over. Miriam and I will talk further about Leo and Becca. I really appreciate all your feedback. I truly do. If you have any other ideas or points you want to make, please make an appointment to speak with me tomorrow."

I teleported to my office, seeing him help Miriam back into her seat.

Kendle, she's going—

I slammed the channel closed on Daniel's words.

From my office, I teleported to my apartment, burning off some of the excess power I'd built up. I was halfway into running clothes before I remembered my leg. I screamed in rage and the building vibrated. I had to get out of here, I had to siphon off my emotions before I imploded.

I teleported away, standing on the walkway of the Golden Gate bridge, the cold Bay Area wind whipping my white hair back. Regs walked or jogged past, their thoughts breaking on my shields. Some were tourists thinking about how long the bridge was and wondering whose brilliant idea it was to walk the entire Golden Gate Bridge. But under that, everyone worried about jobs, romances and families, things they couldn't change.

I opened the channel to Daniel back up. *Please don't let anything happen to Leo and Becca.*

Where are you?

Never seen the ocean before. A bubble of hysteria tried to break through. I couldn't believe I'd been sharing dreams with Stephen. I pushed it away. Becca and Leo needed to come first.

Please Kendle, Miriam's—hell—it's not mine to tell you. But—please come back.

Leo and Becca? Take care of them.

I won't let anything happen.

My hands curled around the railing. The water below looked hard and cold. Letters from kids to potential jumpers, telling them they had so much to live for, stuck out of the fencing. A cold wind cut through my layers and a seagull cried in the distance.

Kendle? I will fix this. Come back. Daniel's southern accent was thicker than usual.

A boat moved under the arches, far below me. I could teleport to that boat. Go where it went. Be a stowaway heading to far off lands.

I told myself to grow up. I wasn't seven, and the far-off lands were other countries that didn't allow Wilds.

I'll be back later. I closed the channel.

I breathed, trying to make my mind go blank. But instead, it alternated between what Miriam had said, and realizing Stephen was in my dreams. I'd told him things I hadn't told anyone. Tears leaked down my cheeks, and I wiped my nose on my shoulder.

How had I gone from being Miriam's right-hand person to someone she despised, in just under a year? Miriam and I used to be friends. I understood she needed to kick my butt sometimes as my boss, but I wasn't trying to destroy the Warehouse. I was trying to help.

My thoughts circled.

Stephen, Miriam.

Stephen, Miriam.

I teleported away again, to Portland, walking up the hipster streets, with its restaurants and cute stores, then Denver, Seattle and St. Louis, trying to siphon off my Gift, trying to get control of my thoughts.

I didn't want to go back to the Warehouse. Maybe I could just pack my things and leave. It wasn't like Miriam wanted me there anyway. Eeva would let me sleep on the couch until I could figure things out. I could get a break from Stephen. A break from Miriam.

Miriam, Jesus. I pushed off against a random building and teleported again, to Salem. It was getting dark on the Eastern side of the United States.

Come back, Kaya's voice was soft in my head. *You've been gone for hours. Miriam agreed not to expel Becca or Leo right now. Things will look better in the morning.*

We'll figure this out, Stephen thought.

He and Kaya must have been together.

Seiko, Franny and Daniel are getting really worried, Kaya thought.

Please come home, Daniel thought in a private channel. *Miriam is sorry. Her emotions are much calmer. She didn't mean what she said and owes you an apology. She wants to make this up to you. And so do I.*

I don't want to talk to her or you tonight. You're both—

I know. We've let you down. Tremendously. You're vital to the success of the Warehouse and we haven't been treating you that way.

No, you haven't. Between all the hours and no paychecks and then the video—

I know. We really messed up. We need to talk, but not tonight. Come home. Everyone is so worried.

I leaned on a random waist-high wall surrounding an area where they'd burned the Salem witches. I wondered if any of those women were Gifted. Maybe our genetics were all related to a woman murdered by a mob for being different.

Kaya says Leo and Becca won't be expelled, I asked. *Is that true?*

A sigh echoed across the connection. *They're going to stay under probation. But it's going to be a lot more work for you. Or one of us, I guess. But we need to look at giving you a break too.*

Now? After Leo destroyed the dorm? You guys need someone to coordinate with the contractors, the electricians, and the plumbers. Someone to figure out what furniture needs fixing, and what needs tossing. Someone to help replace all the destroyed kids' stuff.

We'll figure it out. In the morning. Just come home so we know you're safe.

God, I so didn't want to. I didn't want to deal with any of this. Why couldn't we go back to last year? To before I'd met Stephen, Becca and Leo?

The moon rose in Salem, looking like something out of a Halloween movie. I had to go back, had to make sure Becca and Leo were okay. There were decisions to make about Stephen. I'd been making a fool out of myself for weeks. My cheeks burned when I remembered how we'd danced at the fundraiser. I was such an idiot. He'd just wanted to talk to me that night. Explain this had been a misunderstanding. Explain he was a Quality Bred, a Rune and I was a nobody Wild. He would be kind, I knew that about him. But we had to figure out a way to stop the dreams.

CHAPTER THIRTY-NINE

"I DON'T THINK you've ever come to see me in my office," Dr. Evander said. "You usually see me when I'm at the Warehouse."

I'd gone back to the Warehouse and paced around my apartment, not sleeping, just circling my thoughts. When the sun came up, I'd called for an appointment with the Warehouse doctor and left. I hadn't seen the bright airy office with its trendy lobby, the ocean landscapes on the walls and comfortable exam room tables. My head and leg ached despite the painkillers I'd taken with my tea and stale toast that morning.

"What's going on?" he asked. "How's the leg?"

Over his shoulder, the blue cleaning fluid in a glass container with used instruments swirled. I took a deep breath and the swirling slowed. Was I ever going to be in control again?

"My leg is fine. It hurts, but it's healing."

"Need me to look at it?"

"No, thanks. I just wanted to ask about our Gifts. I've noticed some...weird...I don't know," I trailed off.

God I was so sophisticated. What would someone like Stephen see in me?

"What kind of weird things?" he asked, sitting down on a rolling stool, his comfortable forest green shields with glinting onyx bits, carefully tucked around him.

"Do you know anything about shield merging?"

He raised an eyebrow. "Never heard of it. Did you merge with someone?"

"Another teacher. Twice. And now things are weird."

"Was the merging intentional?"

"First time no. It was when we stopped that bullet at the mall."

"Ah," he said. "I was wondering how you pulled that off. You're powerful but stopping a bullet shouldn't have been possible. And the second time?"

"Two days ago with Leo. That was intentional. The building was going to collapse around us if we didn't get him sedated." I pulled my injured leg up onto the exam table, sitting with it folded in front of me.

"Same person you merged with at the mall? The Quality Bred? A Rune, right?"

I nodded.

"Interesting. And what was it like?"

I thought back. "It was like my thoughts were his and his were mine. Like if we spoke, it was both our voices, saying the same thing. Like some sort of creepy twin thing in a movie."

"Fascinating. Did you notice any side effects? Are you able to hear his thoughts easier or are you having thoughts that aren't yours?"

I shrugged.

"Ah," he said. "I take it that's why you're here."

"Kind of, I mean...yes. I mean, could there be side effects?"

"Absolutely. We don't really understand how telepathy and psychokinesis work, so naturally, we inserted it into the genetic code of our children, creating superheroes and demi-gods." He scrubbed his chin with his hand. "And then you Wilds came along, which we truly don't understand. So, to answer your question, yes, I would imagine if a Wild and Bred merged shields, there would be side effects."

When I didn't say anything, he nudged my shields. "So, what are you experiencing?"

"We've been sharing dreams," I said, figuratively ripping off the Band-Aid.

"That's really interesting." He seemed all excited like he'd discovered a new species under a microscope. "Truly fascinating. And it started after the mall?"

"Yep."

"It makes sense. You're probably instinctually blocking each other during the day, but when you go to sleep, if there's a shared connection, it's possible you'd see each other's dreams."

"Not see," I muttered. "Like share. Like control. Like changing the scenery, changing what happens. There's none of the weirdness with normal dreams, unless one of us want it."

"Can you describe one to me?"

"No."

He raised his eyebrows. "Because...?"

"It's personal and—No."

"Ah," he said. "Is it like fantasy fulfillment?"

"Sure," I said with a one-shouldered shrug so similar to Casi.

He was silent until I spoke again. "How do I get the dreams to stop?"

"I have no idea, Kendle. I've never heard of something like this. Things that prevent REM sleep may help. Sleeping pills, alcohol, etcetera. I can prescribe you something, but we need REM sleep to survive. Without it you'll be looking at other side effects such as increased depression, anxiety, irritation and metabolism problems."

"Oh."

"Have you spoken to him?"

"I only just figured it out and then Miriam—fuck." I took a deep breath when my eyes filled with tears. I was so tired of crying. "No. I haven't spoken with him. I just want the dreams to stop and everything to be normal."

"I don't think they're going to," Dr. Evander said, putting one hand in front of the other and adopting his 'I'm listening' pose. "But if you have control over the dreams, you both can set some ground rules."

I sighed. Maybe if I started with a bottle of gin and took it over to

Stephen's. Or maybe port. But would that be giving him the wrong idea? God, how had I let this happen?

"Can I be blunt?" Dr. Evander asked, looking up from his screen where he was taking notes.

"Sure," I said again.

"You look terrible. Your shields are ragged, and your Gift is leaking. You're not going to heal from your injuries. I'm pulling you from work for a week."

"Absolutely not," I said, hopping off the exam table, and then wincing as my stitches pulled. "Do you have any idea how much damage Leo caused? And it's not like we have the money or the staff to fix it. It's up to us. I shouldn't have even come. They need me."

"I do know. And a week off for one person, even if it's you, won't change too much. It'll give you space, too, between you and your Bred. You never know, you may be able to stop the dreams with some physical distance."

"But—"

"You're taking a week's vacation, or you'll collapse. Or implode."

The pain in my chest flared. I had been worrying I'd implode yesterday. I'd had so much power available. Was I putting everyone at risk?

"And," he added. "Before you tell me you've never imploded, I'm not convinced implosion is caused by not using your Gifts. I think it may be from too much emotion."

"Then why haven't we had an implosion before two days ago?"

"Because you're doing good work. But you won't be able to keep helping your students if you don't take some breaks."

"Fine," I said. I just wouldn't give Miriam the note.

"And I already emailed Miriam," he said, proving he knew me. "And I told her your week off is away from the Warehouse."

"But where am I supposed to go? What am I supposed to do?"

"See, the fact you're asking makes me glad I'm forcing you. Haven't you ever wanted to go anywhere? See anything? The ocean? The mountains? You can go anywhere in the world."

An image clicked into my head of Stephen's cabin surrounded by water, and him in all of his yummy nakedness.

Damn it! I slammed the thought away.

Dr. Evander glanced at the clock.

"You have more patients," I said. "Guess I'll figure it out."

I wasn't being sarcastic. Nope. Not me. Not at all.

"You will," he said. "And if you don't take the time, I'll force you to take two weeks. I've told Miriam in no uncertain terms your health is at risk if you don't take the week off, so she shouldn't give you too hard a time."

"I bet she will," I muttered.

"Then you should re-look at your employment," he said. "She asks too much of you and you're only human."

"She saved my life."

"And she shouldn't expect you to kill yourself for her."

"It's not for her. It's for the kids."

"And if you kill yourself, you won't be able to help them," he said. "Come see me if your leg gets more painful or you rip a stitch."

"Fine," I muttered, limping out the door and teleporting myself back to the Warehouse.

———

Miriam waited for me, outside my apartment.

I froze, my hand gripping my purse.

"I thought you'd end up here first," she said.

"What do you mean?" I felt nauseous. What was she going to do? Was she here to fire me?

"I owe you an apology," she began. "And I truly mean it, but I also want to give you a chance to go on vacation without...increasing your stress level."

"Okay."

"We'll talk when you're back." She turned to go, heading toward her apartment.

"Will I still have a job?" I could barely get the words out.

She turned back. She took off her glasses and cleaned the lenses on her ragged sweater sleeve. "Always." *I'm sorry. Things have... I think a break is a good idea. You've never taken a vacation in all the years you've worked here.* "Is there anything pending that can't wait for you?"

I'm not trying to destroy your school.

I know. You're trying to make it better, in a different way than I would. But — "We'll talk when you're back. Where's your to-do list?"

"It's on my desk. My biggest priority is working on the budget for the dorm and ordering whatever we need to replace. And the grocery ordering. And the regular supplies, toilet paper, paper towels, that type of thing. And all the clubs owe me an attendance sheet and the presidents or kings/queens, vice admirals, or whoever is in charge owe me a one-page write-up on what they've been working on, though I guess it can wait until I get back."

"Vice admirals?"

"I let them pick their titles."

She nearly smiled, her gray shields with magenta streaks lightening. She pulled out her screen to take notes. "What else?"

"I think electric and water bills are due. And the handyman was upset about the fake rat he found." I went through my list with Miriam, standing in the hallway outside my apartment, noting what could wait and what someone else had to take care of for the week.

"So, what are you going to do?" she asked, when I'd run through everything.

"I don't know," I said.

"Well, have fun. Rest. We're really going to need you in a week."

I went into my apartment and pulled up my bank account. Miriam hadn't paid me in a month, and I'd bought a used cello with the last money she'd given me. I didn't have much and needed to save what I could in case Miriam fired me while I was gone.

The thought hit me, and the windows rattled.

I didn't believe her. I didn't believe I'd always have a job at the Warehouse.

I had to sit down; my legs were too wobbly.

This was Miriam, the woman who'd saved me in Vegas when I had no hope left. The woman who'd given me a job when I couldn't find one. She'd given me a place to live, Wilds like me to help. I owed her all I was.

And I didn't trust her.

What was I going to do?

I took a deep breath and opened a channel to Eeva.

———

Eeva was happy to have me stay with her for a week. I started packing for the cool bay area in February, stuffing sweaters, scarves, jeans and beanies into my overnight bag. I debated taking my cello, but opted for a violin instead, propping the case next to my overnight bag. I could always teleport back to the Warehouse to grab another instrument if I wanted it.

Stephen's turquoise shields filled my mind. *I hear you're taking a week off. Where are you going? Are you okay?*

I'm fine. I went to ask Dr. Evander a question and he pulled me from work for a week.

Bastard. Maybe I need to go see him too.

I couldn't stop the chuckle and sent it across the channel. *Maybe.*

You can use my beach house if you want. No people, other than the maid and gardeners. And even they're barely there.

It sounded like a perfect place for Quality Breds to take a break from their lives. But I wasn't a Quality Bred.

I'm going to go hang out with my friend Eeva in San Francisco.

She runs Mt. Olympus, right?

Right.

That'll be fun too. Let me know if you change your mind or if you and she want to spend some time in the house. Maybe we could all join you one night.

Maybe.

Have fun, be safe. We'll miss you.

He broke off the connection but was back a minute later. *Can I take you out to dinner while you're gone? You still owe me.*

For what?

I can't remember. Honestly, I probably owe you something. So how about I pay you back with dinner? I'm not on dorm duty on Friday night and I know this amazing English pub. Gifted friendly and they have the best fish and chips.

God, he was such a flirt. And it didn't mean anything, I reminded myself. He was a flirt with everyone.

We did have to talk. Might as well get a meal out of it.

Okay, Friday it is. I'll see you then.

I had until then to figure out what to say to him. Figure out what ground rules we needed for the dreams. Figure out how to ...break up with him? But we weren't together.

Fuck my life.

I grabbed my bag, but before I went, stopped by Daniel's office, knocking on the doorframe.

"Hey there," he said, looking up from behind his desk. His office was utilitarian, and super clean with a large wood desk and soft gray walls. He preferred paper to the screen and had filing cabinets full of random documents and notes. Otherwise, he had the ubiquitous plants from Franny and nothing else.

"I wasn't sure if you wanted..." Daniel stumbled. "If I'd get to— where are you going?"

"San Francisco. Eeva's letting me crash on her couch."

"Oh perfect. I was going to loan you some money for a hotel or whatever. Sounds like you're good."

"I think so."

He paused and I sensed him choosing his words. "Did Miriam apologize?

"She did."

She's going through a hell of a lot. You have every right to be angry. At both of us. And I know I keep repeating, but I'm truly sorry. Just try to have a little patience with Miriam.

What's wrong with her?

He shook his head. *It's not for me to tell you.*

But you know?

Some of it.

I didn't have the energy to worry about her. God, I was so tired. "You promise Leo and Becca are safe?"

"You have my word. And I will contact you if things change. They will still be here in a week. I promise. And we, all of us, will figure out what to do."

"Thank you."

He picked up his pen and I turned to go.

"One more thing," he said. "I'll feed Mr. Sparklebutt for you, by the way."

But you hate him.

But he needs to be fed. "Enjoy your time with Eeva. Try not to think about work. See you when you get back."

"See you when I get back," I echoed.

CHAPTER FORTY

I PUT my overnight bag on Eeva's couch. She ran around her tiny,
shadowy apartment trying to curl her hair and put on make-up in an
entry mirror before heading to work. All while talking.

"Are you good with the couch? I guess I can try to find a blow-up
mattress or something. Or maybe someone has a military cot, but I
think it'll be less comfortable."

The couch is fine, I interrupted, because I knew I wouldn't be able to
get a word in edgewise. "Why are you doing your hair out here?"

"Because the light in the bathroom is terrible. Go look."

I flicked the light in the tiny room holding a toilet, a sink without a
counter and a shower so small you practically had to stand on one leg
to fit in. I glanced in the mirror and did a double take, letting out a
small yelp.

"Told ya," Eeva called from the living room.

In the mirror every line, every shadow on my face stood out. Good
god, I looked fifty. And like I hadn't slept in a year. My pale skin was
somehow a combination of shiny and yet dry and were those crows
feet?

I came out, vowing I'd never look in that mirror again. Eeva was using her Gift to curl her eyelashes and hair at the same time. "Do you have any plans?" she asked. "Sightseeing? People to see?"

I thought about my...meeting with Stephen. "Maybe something on Friday, when you're working, but otherwise, nope. Dr. Evander told me to take a break, so I'm taking a break. Thanks for letting me crash."

"Of course. I'm sorry I have to work, but I think I can take tomorrow and Thursday morning off. We'll go to Golden Gate Park, Pier 39—all the touristy stuff. And then Sunday night Mt. Olympus is closed. I have to go in for a few hours that morning to deal with orders, but we'll be able to have a nice dinner somewhere."

"Don't worry about me. I can entertain myself." Doing what, I had no idea. I really needed to check my email. Just to check off a few work things so no one else had to.

"And don't think we're not going to talk about why you look like hell, are limping, and on a mandatory break." Eeva tapped her eye shadow brush and carefully applied the glittery color.

My eyes filled with tears. I blinked them away hoping she hadn't seen.

"I'm fine, just need some sleep." I played with the tassel on a bright throw pillow. My living room at the Warehouse could fit Eeva's entire apartment in it. But Eeva had filled her home with bright furniture and throw pillows, Middle Eastern tapestries and candles stuck into wine bottles. And if you didn't look, you wouldn't notice the fridge with a rust stain leaking from it and the crack in the window taped over with bright duct tape.

"And you have your volunteering at the animal shelter, too. I don't want you to miss that."

Eeva's sky blue shields darkened and she ran a brush over her blush compact, then carefully tapped the powder off.

"They don't want me there anymore," she said, leaning close to the mirror to apply the pink color. "They found out I was a Wild."

"How?"

"Apparently they ran everyone's name through the Registry."

"For a volunteer job? Ridiculous."

She shrugged. "You know how it goes." She pulled out eyeliner and leaned close to the mirror. "Which reminds me." She turned around and pointed her eyeliner at me. "There's a multitude of Wilds getting attacked now. Breds too. The Regs hate us and want all Gifted gone. And everyone is trying to teleport now. There's been a ton of accidents."

"Teleportation isn't hard." I braided the individual strings of the pillow tassel. "You just have to practice a lot."

"Well I'm not trying it," she said. She used her Gift to throw her makeup into a bag and grabbed her purse. "Gotta go. Get some sleep and remember, if you go out, go to tourist places and make sure you wear a hat and sunglasses."

"I have my contacts."

"That's right. And if you cover your hair, you'll be fine. Just don't do any psychokinesis and telepathy."

"I can't help the telepathy," I said with a sigh. "I'll probably just stay here. Read or watch some internet show."

"Sleep. You look like hell." *Or maybe you need a really good cry.*

I cried a lot yesterday.

"Then sleep. Love you."

"Love you too," I said.

She blew me a kiss with perfect lips and wiped the lipstick off her hand. "If you're still up at two a.m. come by Mt. Olympus. I'll buy you a drink."

"Thanks," I said.

"And if you want to smoke or play your fiddle—"

"Violin," I corrected.

She grinned. "Whatever. But if you want to smoke or play, please go up the roof. The walls are really thin, and I don't want to piss off my neighbors."

"You got it." I made finger guns at her until she laughed and closed the door.

———

An hour later, I was climbing the walls. Miriam had changed the password on my email account, and I couldn't access it, no matter how many different passwords I tried. My book was boring, and I couldn't find a good show or movie on the internet.

I'd tried to play my violin but banging from above and the wall on the right forced me to stop. Eeva wasn't kidding about her neighbors.

I opened up a channel to Kaya, Franny, Seiko and Stephen. *How are things going there?*

Good, good, good, Seiko responded, his words ragged from the distance.

All's good, Kaya thought, with a little too much cheer. *Why, what have you heard?*

I haven't said anything, Seiko thought.

I didn't contact her, Franny added.

What's going on? I asked. *Do you guys need help? I could come back, just for a few hours.*

Absolutely not, Kaya responded. *It's nothing we can't handle.*

We just miss you, Franny thought. *You always know where everything is and who to call and what to do.*

What do you guys need? I can be there in less than five minutes.

No, Stephen thought, speaking for the first time. *We're fine. There's a bit of learning curve, but we're fine. Enjoy yourself.*

But—

Take a nap. Go for a walk. Hang out with your friend.

But—

No, Kendle, he thought. *All is fine. Do not come back.*

Okay. I literally felt my shoulders drop. *See you all soon. Contact if you need me.*

We will. Stephen closed the channel but touched my shields gently with his. *Miss you,* whispered across the connection, so faint I wondered if I imagined it.

No, I told myself. I had definitely imagined it.

Cranky, I pulled up my book. How did people relax if they didn't have work?

CHAPTER FORTY-ONE

STEPHEN WAITED for me on the beach, the sun slowly sinking into the horizon, the sand warm beneath my feet and dolphins playing in the waves. He smiled, his green eyes lighting up. I took his hands and he pulled me into a quick dance to the sounds of the ocean.

"Told you before," I said, swaying with him. "This romance stuff doesn't work on me."

"Yes, it does."

He stepped away and suddenly held out champagne glasses. He beckoned to a candlelit table set on the beach, just as the sun set and stars appeared. In our dreams, the laws of space and time didn't matter.

I took a glass and stepped close to touch his chin with my other hand, feeling the rasp of his beard. "God, I love this beard. It's more Warehouse Stephen." But something tugged on my memory, something I had to do.

His beard scratched my cheeks when he bent to kiss me. I slipped my tongue inside his mouth and his breath hitched. His lips traced a line along my chin to my ear, then down my neck. My knees stopped working and he wrapped his arms around me, holding me upright while his lips and teeth nibbled my neck.

But there was something I had to do...

Wait.

Fucking-A. I remembered.

I pushed him away. "No," I said.

He grinned and raised a hand. Suddenly we were in a rooftop garden, overlooking a city. The lights below us sparkled in contrast to the glittery stars. I could see all the way out to a river and a bridge.

"London," he said, passing me a perfect rose. "Or as near as I can remember. We should go sometime."

"No," I said. "This—"

I shot up, not sure where I was, as Eeva turned the key and came into her apartment, heels in hand.

"Did I wake you? I'm sorry. I was trying so hard to be quiet."

Kendle?

Go away, I told Stephen. *Just leave me alone for a little while.*

And he said the most perfect thing, *Okay. I'm here if you need me.*

I burst into tears. Eeva cuddled with me on the couch, despite having worked a fourteen-hour day making sure rich Breds had the perfect alcohol-fueled experience at a fake speakeasy. She offered cup after cup of tea each laced with brandy. The brandy warmed me and helped with the tears, but the more I drank, the less sense I made. She just listened and offered tissues, asking an occasional clarifying question when she lost the train of my disastrous life. Finally, I couldn't cry anymore. My eyes felt heavy and grainy.

"Sorry," I said, getting up and going to the bathroom to wash my face and blow my nose. I let out a little squeal at the red nosed, red eyed old lady in the mirror.

Eeva laughed, though her blue shields remained cloudy. "I warned you about the mirror."

"Too late." I flicked the light off behind me and let out a mock shudder. "I do not cry beautifully."

"No woman does. Are you feeling any better?"

"Don't know," I said. "I'm numb."

"Wanna watch a movie? Some dumb comedy?"

"Not a romance?"

"Absolutely not," Eeva said.

"You need some sleep."

"I was planning to go in late anyway. Long as I get a few hours, I'm fine." The screen flicked on and Eeva used her Gift to pick some dumb comedy about two wise-cracking women. They were mistaken as cops and then decided to go to the police academy together because their boyfriends were jerks. It was ridiculous, but it made me laugh and forget, just a little.

When the movie was over, she gave me a hug and went to bed. I curled up on the couch, my mind still buzzing. I gently reached out with my Gift, a feather touch. It was nearly four a.m. here, which meant six a.m. there. He should've been awake, but I had to make sure. I didn't want to dream with him anymore and I wasn't ready for a conversation.

He was awake and...I focused, forgetting I didn't want him to know I was reaching out. He was in the shower. My libido hummed in appreciation before I cut the connection.

Kendle?

Fuck.

What's up? I kept the tone light and breezy. *Did you guys need anything? I thought I felt someone reach out with a question.*

I didn't. But maybe one of the others?

I sensed his confusion through the connection. Smooth, that was me. Totally smooth.

Are we still on for Friday? he asked.

I sighed, my brain buzzing with alcohol, emotion and sleep deprivation. *Yep. Just let me know where to meet you. Eeva has to work on Friday.*

Sounds good. He paused. *Did you want to talk about anything?*

Nope. All is good. I broke off the connection, feeling like a teenager who had dialed their crush and they'd picked up.

CHAPTER FORTY-TWO

"TELL ME MORE ABOUT THE DREAMS," Eeva said, linking her arm with mine like we used to at the Warehouse. She'd only gotten the hang of using telepathy our last year as students. Today, just like in our pasts, she leaned close, her breath tickling my neck as we walked through a trail between giant trees in California.

"Do you really want details?"

"Of course. At least one of us is getting some action."

"Is dream sex real sex?"

"I'm not the expert you are. Normally, I'd say no, but I think this is different."

"I guess."

When I didn't say anything else, she pinched my arm. "So details?"

"Well this one time we went to this cabin on the water with this giant bed. And the floor was glass and we could see—"

"Girl, I'm not talking those kind of details."

"I know," I said, with a laugh. "But those are private. Come on, I've never gone into that kind of detail before with you."

"At least tell a little. For example, is he as good looking with his clothes off as on?"

"It's a dream, for fuck sake. I don't actually know what he looks like with his clothes off."

"At least tell me if it's full on orgasms?"

"Eeva, it's...orgasm."

"Multiple orgasms?"

"Some nights. Haven't you had sex dreams?"

"Of course. My favorite is—"

"I don't want the details," I told her, and she laughed, her breath hot on my cheek. "I thought they were just dreams. I mean they are dreams. We could have sex on the beach and not worry about sand...everywhere."

"That's why I refuse to have sex on the beach," Eeva said.

We passed giant sequoias, the sunlight filtered through the branches and our footsteps muffled by fallen leaves on the path. A few Regs moved past us, but for the most part, it was quiet, other than bird song and the breeze through the leaves.

"So now what?" she whispered. "Did you dream with him last night?"

"Until you woke me up."

"Ew. You were having dream sex on my couch?"

"No." I chuckled, the ridiculousness of it breaking through my depression. "I realized I was dreaming and told him no. But he knows we're dream sharing. So that'll be a fun talk."

"What did you do when he reached out?"

"Burst into tears, as you saw."

We stopped to read a sign proclaiming the tree in front of us was over eight hundred years old, older than the United States. "It makes total sense," she said. "You were in a relationship with him. Of course you were upset."

"There's no relationship. We're sharing sex dreams."

"Did you talk, I mean beyond pillow talk? Like about your pasts and how your day went and other small stuff that means everything?"

"Fuck." I had to sit down on a bench. "I told him my plans for a sister school. And he told me about his family, stories about them learning how to use their Gifts, and growing up as Quality Breds."

"That's a relationship."

Eeva sat next to me to stare at the ridiculously tall trees. We watched birds flit from branch to branch. A hummingbird flew over us, chirping and thrumming. Eeva watched the bird with a small smile. *Do you like him?*

He's my friend. But a Quality Bred. You know how they are.

Eeva grinned. *I've had a little experience.*

"So you know how they're perfect at everything, and you feel like you can never be good enough to be around them? But Stephen grew this beard and not because it was fashionable, but because it takes work to shave every day and he doesn't have the time. He works the same crazy hours we all do. And he really cares about the kids. And us. He'll do anything for us." And me. I knew that. I picked up a little bit of bark and peeled some of it back. "When he's at the Warehouse, he's not a Quality Bred. He's just...Stephen."

"Wow. You've never talked about anyone like this before."

I chucked the bark into the woods, like I was pitching for the Cubs. "Did you see the pictures after the fundraiser?"

"What fundraiser? The one you guys did a few days ago?"

Jesus, was it only a few days ago? I used my phone to show her the pictures of Stephen and I posted all over social media.

"You look so pretty," she said. *And look at his smile. Sweetie, I think he really likes you.*

"Read the comments."

Eeva read them, sighed, rolled her eyes and handed me back my phone. "Just typical Wild stuff."

"But dating him would be like that all the time. Pictures all the time, so thousands of people can comment on how ugly I am, how I'm just after him for his money, that I'm just a Wild."

"Every relationship has its irritations. You'd spend most of your time at the Warehouse. I know it bothers you, but it's not a big deal. I think—"

A child screamed. Not the I'm-not-getting-my-way scream, but a primal one. Another child let out a wail. Eeva and I ran toward the sound, rounding a corner on the trail to a small clearing where a man lay. He was trying to get up, trying to fight off two large rocks pounding into him. Blood pooled beneath him. A little girl, about five in pigtails with a pink blanket dragging behind her, stood in front of a stroller, screaming, but with her arms out trying to protect the baby inside.

I threw a physical barrier around the man, stopping the rocks from hitting him, though they continued to hit the barrier. The man reached out toward the girl, rolling onto his stomach and commando crawling toward the stroller. He protected the back of his head with his hands, not realizing I'd stopped the rocks.

Get the children out of here, I told Eeva. She grabbed the stroller and scooped up the girl, sprinting out of the clearing.

He let out a yell.

"She's just taking them away from the rocks." I mentally searched through the trees, trying to find the Gifted abuser.

There! Through the trees I sensed sickly yellow and green shields, moving like infected mucus.

Got you, fucker.

I wrapped a barrier around the Wild, keeping him in place. He fought me, but I ignored him, releasing the physical barrier around the beaten man. He was still conscious, though bleeding from cuts on his head, lip, nose and arm.

"Stay where you are," I said. "I'll call 911."

"Bring back my kids," he gasped. "You can't take them."

"I'm not," I said. "I'll have my friend bring them back. Now that I have the guy, she can bring them back."

I winced and closed my eyes when the Wild mentally stabbed into my shields. I poked him back.

Knock it off. I forced a channel between us. *I'm stronger than you and you're not going anywhere.*

His shields were disgusting; angry and hate filled thoughts about Regs floating beneath the surface. The Wild was tired of losing jobs, tired of never having enough money to get the things he wanted, the things he deserved because he worked so hard. The woman he'd been dating had found out he was a Wild and kicked him out by throwing his stuff out a window and then turning the sprinklers on while he begged her to take him back. Then he got soaked trying to—

Nasty colored rainbows shot across my closed eyes and I fell, not feeling when I hit the dirt.

CHAPTER FORTY-THREE

MY HEAD HURT. I kept my eyes closed, though my throat was so dry, my mouth caked with the taste of old blood, I almost choked. I stretched out with my telepathy.

Nothing.

No shields, no echoes of telepathy. I was completely numb. I tried my psychokinesis, hoping to get a feel of the room, but it was like holding water. My heart hammered and sweat broke out on my forehead. I slowly opened my eyes, confused when one stayed closed.

I lay on my side, on a floor. I saw dark metal bars, the metal that blocked Gifts. My shoulders ached because my hands were handcuffed behind my back.

I slowly sat up, my head spinning. I threw up, I couldn't help it, and heard groans around me.

On top of everything else, I wasn't alone. And I had no idea who these people were, what their shields looked like or what they were thinking.

I wiped my mouth on my shoulder. Tears sprung up and I blinked them back.

"Sorry," I muttered to the room. Someone moved next to me.

"Flop over onto me," a female voice said. "I'll help you up. But don't throw up again."

I did what she requested, and together we moved away from the vomit. I realized her hands were handcuffed too, but they were at least in front of her. She helped me up onto a bench, where I laid on my side, the room spinning and not in the good way like when you have a bit too much to drink.

"Thank you," I said. I tried to focus on her, but all I got was the impression of blonde hair and pale skin. I'd had the shit beaten out of me. The nausea swam up again and I swallowed down bile.

I think I passed out again because when I opened my eyes it was darker, but I felt better.

I sat up, slowly. My shirt was a mess of blood and my face itched—a sure sign of the blood caking off. My shoulders and head ached so much, my eyes filled with tears.

I wiped my cheeks on my shoulder.

My memory was hazy. I remembered a man getting hit by rocks I was trying to help. A Wild was attacking him but I had stopped it. Right? How had I ended up here?

The barred metal door swung open. A Guardian walked in, her black suit darkening the room even more. My brain took in the blonde hair braided in tiny braids and shaved on the sides. It was Amanda-the-Ogress-Hag. Of course it was—she'd be only too happy to see me like this.

"Let's go," she said.

I tried to roll to my feet, but the world swam too much.

"Now," she said, wrenching me up and letting me go so I fell. I managed to turn so my shoulder took the hit instead of my face. I squawked. I didn't think I'd ever been in this much pain. She pulled me back up again and darkness crowded around my vision.

I couldn't pass out. Not in front of her.

She marched me into a room with ugly gray walls, one-way mirrors and a table and chairs bolted to the floor. Miriam and Kaya stood when Amanda threw me into a chair.

"Oh my God," Miriam exclaimed, rushing over and touching my face.

"She needs a doctor," Kaya said to Amanda.

Amanda shrugged. "One examined her when she was taken into custody. She'll heal."

I threw up again, barely managing to turn my head to avoid throwing up on myself. My empty stomach cramped.

"She's concussed," Miriam said. "Get a doctor."

Amanda stared at Miriam. I knew they were communicating telepathically, and my heart ached. I hated feeling so numb.

"Just have me see Dr. Evander when I get back to the Warehouse," I muttered. "When I'm home."

Miriam took my hands, her eyes full of tears. "I can't help," she said. "If you were recruiting or out with students, the lawyer would be able to help, but you were on leave and...I'm so sorry. You're going to have to use a public defender."

"Stephen's already contacted his lawyer," Kaya said.

I couldn't deal with that right now. "Is Eeva okay? Those kids?"

Miriam glanced at Amanda who stood in the doorway, listening to every word. "Your concussion is really bad," she said. "Eeva was at home. You were out walking by yourself."

I nodded, understanding, though it made my head hurt worse.

"Can you at least handcuff her hands in front of her?" Kaya asked. "Her fingers are blue, and her shoulder is going to dislocate."

"She's within parameters," Amanda rumbled.

"She can't do anything with the bands on," Kaya argued. "Even if you put them on one wrist, she wouldn't——."

I lost track of the conversation as blackness crowded in. "Eeva," I repeated. "And the kids. They okay?"

"See," Kaya said. "She's concussed and confused. She needs to see a doctor."

"As I said," Amanda enunciated each word. "One already——" The blackness took me back under.

———

When I came to again, people were yelling, making my head hurt even more. My shoulders felt terrible, but my hands were tingling. I must still be in the bands. I didn't know who was in the room.

"Miriam," I croaked.

"Here," she said. Someone touched my tingling fingers.

I saw Stephen through my one good eye. I closed it again as the world spun. I concentrated on my butt in the chair, trying to convince my mind I wasn't actually spinning.

"Home," I said again. I couldn't focus on anything beyond that point.

"We can't," Miriam said.

"I'm getting you a doctor, right now," Stephen said.

"Home," I said. "I want to go home."

"Oh sweetie," Miriam said.

I wanted to ask what happened, where I was, what was going to happen, but I couldn't get the words to work.

"Okay," said a sharp female voice. "Do you remember what happened? Can you tell me what symptoms you're having?" My good eye was peeled open and a light shined into it.

"Home." It was all I could say.

"Definitely a concussion," she said. "We need to move her out of here, do an MRI, get some fluids in her and figure out how serious her other injuries are."

Amanda's voice whined, "—rous Wild."

"She's not doing anything wearing a band," Stephen said.

"Home," I said again.

"Unfortunately not," the female voice said. "I'm not comfortable taking you through a transport pad," she said. "But we'll get you to a place where you'll be comfortable."

The voices faded and then there was nothing.

———

When I woke up again, my head hurt a lot less and the room had stopped spinning. I tried to reach out with my Gift, but the band on my wrist, and only one wrist, thank God, tightened, cutting into bruises and old scars.

Oh goody.

My mouth tasted like someone had died in it, but a floaty feeling told me I was on some good painkillers. I tried to open my eyes. Both opened, though one only partially. I was in a hospital room. Sunlight streamed in through a window and the cool whites and blues of the rooms were a huge improvement on the interrogation room I last remembered. Machines beeped and booped softly. I moved my arms, feeling the tug of the tape holding an IV in place.

"Hey there," Miriam said, moving to sit on the bed.

"What happened?" I asked. My voice was creaky.

"That's better," she said. "Last time all you could say was home."

It's because it was all I wanted. I wanted to feel my crappy mattress under my head, get bumped by Mr. Sparklebutt's hard head and curl up in my armchair with a screen to read some silly romance novel. My eyes filled with tears. I wanted home more than anything in my life. I tried to blink them back, but some leaked out. Miriam held up a cup of water with a straw and I sipped, feeling a little better.

"What happened?" I asked again. I closed my eyes. "There were children. Are they ok?"

Miriam nodded. "Eeva sent the kids back to the dad, but because the Guardians were already there," Miriam took a deep breath. "She took off. She feels horrible."

I stomped on the quick feeling of betrayal. "I get it." I instinctively reached out to Eeva to tell her not to worry. I winced as the bracelet tightened again. "Eeva has to protect herself. She could get fired if she was arrested."

"She contacted us immediately and we were able to get to you as soon as they brought you in."

I nodded, grateful. I'd only been locked up for a few minutes, maybe an hour before they'd moved me to the interrogation room. It had been the concussion making me feel like I'd been in jail for hours.

"How'd I get here?"

"Your injuries were more severe than...they cared about. Stephen came with a lawyer for you and became...a Quality Bred." Miriam's fingers squeezed mine. "I can't describe it. Everyone in the room wanted to do whatever he wanted, just to make him happy. He's paying for the doctor and hospital room. Now his lawyer is working to get your charges dropped, without involving Eeva. The man you rescued thought you were the one hitting him with the rocks. So he hit you with rocks."

That explained the concussion.

I nodded. "He didn't see the other Wild. But why would I suddenly stop and stand there so he could hit me with a rock?"

Miriam nodded. "That's our argument. Stephen's lawyer thinks everything will work out. He's been busy."

"How long has it been?"

"Two days. Your concussion was pretty bad, and your other injuries contributed, though they're mostly just bad bumps and bruises."

A knock sounded on the doorframe.

"Can we come in?" Stephen and another man poked their heads into the room.

I didn't want Stephen to see me, bruised and bloodied with the whole dream thing still hanging there.

Great. Just peachy keen. Swell even.

I tried to smile at them, and my lip split.

Son of a bitch.

Miriam handed me a tissue and I dabbed at the blood. I felt the echoes of telepathic thought and the band tightened again. "Doesn't this thing have a stopping point?" I muttered, jiggling my arm so it clacked on the metal of the hospital bed.

Stephen winced. "My fault," he said. "I forgot."

I looked at the stranger. He had dark chocolate eyes, tanned skin and dark hair. His ears stuck out a little too much—his parents must have missed that option when checking boxes. I wished I could see his shields.

"Mathew Paddock," he said. "I think we're going to be in good shape. They've got nothing. You were helping and got beaten instead. We could probably press charges against the man that beat you, if you wanted."

"Oh. You're my lawyer," I said, like a dork. "And I don't. Want to press charges I mean." God, words were apparently hard. "And I appreciate your help. But I can't afford you and I don't—"

"Don't worry," he said. "I owe Stephen a favor. And this isn't a hard case."

"But—"

"It's done," Stephen said.

"But Stephen..." I wanted to argue he shouldn't have to pay for the hospital room and call in a favor with the lawyer just for me. But the band tightened again, cutting painfully. I cried out. Then Stephen was there, sitting on the edge of the bed. "What happened?" he asked.

"It's this stupid band." A tear leaked out of my eyes. He wiped it away, his eyes holding mine. And once the tears started, I couldn't stop them. Miriam sat on the edge of the bed and put her arms around me as I wept.

"It's okay. Everything will be fine," she said over and over.

Stephen laced his fingers with mine, which made me cry even harder.

They waited until I calmed down to hiccupy breaths. "I'm sorry," I said to the room. My tissue had disintegrated, and Miriam placed the entire box on my lap.

"It's okay," Miriam said, as I tried to mop up my face. "You've been through a horrible few days. You're entitled to cry."

"And I just got good news that will make you feel a thousand percent better," Mathew said, his eyes refocusing. "My office just told me the guy you saved is going to drop the charges. He now believes you didn't attack him."

"Why?" I asked.

The band tightened again around my wrist as I felt the rumble of telepathic conversation. It was too bad I couldn't just turn off my Gift like I was apparently supposed to.

"It's okay," I said. "Whatever it is."

"The Wild that attacked the man, attacked another Reg family the next day," Mathew said. "Same MO. Beat them with rocks. The Guardians caught the Wild, but..." Mathew stopped and I knew why.

"He killed someone?"

Mathew sighed, glanced at my beeping monitor and nodded.

"I had him," I muttered, more tears leaking out. "Completely contained."

"Not your fault," Stephen said.

"I had him," I said again.

I felt all of them reach out toward my shields, trying to comfort me the way Gifted did whether they were Wilds or Breds and the band tightened again. "I fucking hate these bands," I said. I wiped my face and my tissue came back with old bloodstains. I must be a wreck.

"Time to leave," the nurse said, coming into the room. "She needs to rest, or she won't heal." She looked at my wrist. "And I need to loosen that."

"You can?"

"Of course." She inserted a little metal piece and turned, until the band loosely encircled my wrist, but not so loose I could take it off.

"You're really strong," she said. "It'll keep tightening, because you can't help using your Gift, but I'll try to keep it loose."

"Thank you," I said. "You're the most amazing person I've ever met."

Miriam and Stephen laughed, but it was forced and louder than it should've been.

"Hey," Mathew said. "I'm still right here."

"You're amazing too," I said. "Thank you for getting the charges dropped."

"Happy to do it. I don't like owing Runes' favors."

Stephen winced but before I could ask, the nurse clapped her hands, my head pounding with each one.

"Time for you all to leave."

Anxiety punched me in the chest and one of the monitors beeped louder. I didn't want to be left alone. Miriam forced a smile, squeezing my hand in hers. Stephen leaned over with a kiss to my cheek, smelling of sweet sweat and peppermint. I'd never noticed his smell before.

"Nice to meet you at last, Miss May," Mathew said, waving and heading out the door.

"Twenty-four hours," Stephen said. "And you'll be home."

The nurse injected something into my IV. "Something to help you sleep, sweetie," she said, patting my shoulder.

"Can someone stay, please?" I asked the nurse. "Just until I fall asleep."

The nurse gave us a stern look, her hand on her hip. "Okay. One can stay, but has to leave when you fall asleep," the nurse said. "It'll be under ten minutes. I gave you a strong dose."

Miriam and Stephen looked at each other and Stephen grabbed the chair Miriam had been sitting in. Miriam gave me a last smile before leaving with Mathew.

I tried to smile at him but was getting sleepy already. It had been a really hard two weeks.

"Thank you," I said to Stephen. I felt like I was saying it a lot.

"There's nothing to thank me for. I'm glad I was able to help."

Like a Band-Aid, I thought. "I have to tell you. The dreams—" I stopped. "You know how we've been..." Jeez, this was hard and embarrassing even on painkillers. "I didn't know until a few days ago."

"Oh." He scrubbed his hands through his hair and across his beard. My eyes wanted to close.

His cheeks flushed. My mouth came unglued from my brain and I said, "I thought flushing when you were embarrassed would've been taken out of your genetic code."

"Good to know you'll be fine," he said with a frown.

"Sorry," I murmured. I couldn't stay awake, no matter how much I wanted to. We had to talk, had to figure out the dreams.

"We'll chalk it up to your IV." He leaned over me and kissed my lips, just a quick peck, so quick I didn't even respond. "We'll talk when you're better. Sleep for now. I won't bother you in your dreams."

"I did like the dreams," I murmured. "I just didn't know. Assumed they were just fun."

He chuckled, a quick breath of air.

"They were my favorite part of my day. That and listening to you play. Sleep. We'll figure this out. We have all the time in the world."

We didn't though. Things were changing. I could just see it on the horizon. I closed my eyes but reached for Stephen's hand and linked his fingers with mine.

CHAPTER FORTY-FOUR

FOUR DAYS AFTER COMING HOME, a week after I'd been beaten, I went downstairs to my office, even though I still had a few days on my leave. I opened the door and flicked on the light. The room smelled musty, and I muscled a window open. My plant, the one Daniel had given me for Christmas, needed water. I patted the plant, happy to be back, and took a seat in my squeaky chair.

You're not supposed to be down here, Stephen thought.

No one had watered my plant.

Lies, I watered it myself.

I smiled. I'd missed this.

You were in my office?

We all were. It's not a sacred space.

Stephen had been a perfect gentleman in the dreams since I'd come home. We still met on the beach, but he'd toned down the romance. There were no more dolphins, sunsets or picturesque rocks. It was just white sand, warm water and a gentle sun. He'd lie down next to me on the sand and talk about nothing, our childhoods, the kids at the Warehouse, even our co-workers. We gossiped more than we probably should to pass the time. Sometimes, he'd touch my hand, reaching out to lace his fingers through mine, before withdrawing.

My office should be a place of worship, I responded. *You should've all left offerings of tea and gin.*

He laughed across the connection.

"It's good to see you back," he said, appearing outside my door and leaning on the door jamb. His beard needed trimming and his hair stuck up in crazy angles. There was a coffee stain on his sleeve and a patch of mud on the calf of his jeans. "It's where you belong. But don't let Miriam see. She'll get angry."

I shook my head. "I doubt it. She'll just put me back to work." I looked around my office. I thought I'd missed it so much, but it seemed smaller, darker and a little shabbier than I remembered. Maybe I should use the time off to do some cleaning.

You feel up to talking? Tomorrow night maybe? Maybe with dinner? Away from here and not in a dream.

I'd been thinking so much about what to say to him, how to break things off in a way that didn't destroy our professional relationship. Or our friendship. I needed his way of seeing the world and helping with our daily problems. I loved how he handled any problem with calmness. And I didn't want him to leave the Warehouse. Not because of me. We needed him too much.

Stephen—

Stephen glanced down the hallway and smiled at someone. "Hi Casi," he said. "You coming to see one of us?"

"I heard Ms. May was in her office."

"Wow," Stephen said. "News travels fast."

"We are in a school of telepaths," I said. "I'm not technically working, but come on in, Casi. Do you want some water? I think there's still some left as long as no one raided my mini fridge."

I used my Gift to open the fridge door on empty shelves. I mock glared at Stephen who held his hands up.

"Not me," he said. "Blame Daniel."

"I always do." I winked at Casi.

Tomorrow night, please? he asked. *Dinner? My treat.*

Roof. Tonight.

His shields darkened, just a touch. *Agreed. See you there. Seven?*

I nodded.

He bowed to Casi, like a knight out of a movie, as she stepped into my office, and closed the door after her.

"Grab a seat," I told her. "What can I do for you?" My chair squeaked as I shifted my weight.

Casi shoulders were hunched, her hands stuffed into pockets. She sat down, still hunched, and I smiled, trying not to worry about tonight. My head was starting to hurt. I probably shouldn't have come downstairs.

"Glad you're okay," she said. "A Reg hit you with rocks, right?"

"He assumed I was threatening his kids." I hedged the question. "I can't be mad at him for protecting his family. And I'm fine, just tired."

Casi picked up my stapler, fiddling with it, before putting it down. *How's your telepathy?* I tried. *Would it be easier to talk like this?*

She shook her head and put my stapler down. Then she fiddled with my desk lamp, turning it off and on.

"Did something happen, Casi? Are you okay?"

"Fine," she muttered. "I've just been having these thoughts."

"Like what kind of thoughts? Thoughts you can't control?"

She rolled her eyes. "These are different. They're like someone else's."

"That can happen sometimes when people are learning telepathy. You're probably picking up on someone else's thoughts. Are they bad?"

She shrugged. "I don't know," she muttered. "They're like...dreams, only I'm not asleep and I'm not in them. Well, sometimes I am, but it's like I'm watching them, like a movie. They're like, first person shooter, like in video games. But I can't walk or talk or anything. I'm just..." she trailed off and shrugged.

"Witnessing?"

"Yes, that word." She pointed her finger at me. I let the silence stretch for a few minutes.

Casi fidgeted and then said, "It's just images." She stuck a piece of her faded gray hair into her mouth. "Other people's thoughts are words with some images thrown in. Know what I mean?"

I did. Most people thought in a mixture of words and images jumbled together that tended to jump all over the place.

"Have you spoken to your counselor? Or Mr. Rune? Maybe this is a weird Wild thing." Or she was hallucinating, but I wasn't going to tell her.

She shrugged, continuing to chew her hair.

"What are you seeing?" I finally asked.

"Like I told you before. You in the woods, with snow, and there was this old house like out of a horror film, but it was happy, not scary. Like how you can tell buildings are happy or tired."

"Sure." I had no clue what she was talking about.

"And I've seen buildings on fire and things in the street, like there was an explosion. And then Guardians walking together, in perfect step, like out a history book, their eyes closed. And all these kids crying. And I saw you playing a guitar and wearing a purple top on a stage. And I saw Samantha yelling at some man, her hands on her hips. And a hospital room. People crying; I saw you crying. And more fires and a reporter talking and crying and people holding signs and—"

My desk vibrated.

Oh god, not again.

"Casi," I said verbally and mentally.

Casi kept muttering, her words disconnected. "Smoke, and the ocean and dogs, lots of dogs and a hand with green nails..." Her eyes rolled up into her head and my desk slid a foot.

"Casi!" I ran around the desk and grabbed her arm, shaking it hard, but she kept muttering. The glass in the window shook.

"Building on fire. Mr. Rune in black and Samantha with a bloody baby and..."

What's going on? Seiko asked. *Is someone imploding again?*

Anyone have eyes on the student? Miriam asked.

It's Casi in my office. I'm sedating her, I thought, using my Gift to lift a syringe out of my desk and injecting Casi.

The glass stopped shaking, but Casi on kept muttering, "— wedding, cake, yellow flowers, purple car, broken—"

Seiko ran into the room, followed closely by Miriam. Casi slumped in the chair, her eyes rolled up, still muttering.

"I've sedated her," I said. "It's like she went into some trance, but—"

The plant on my windowsill tipped over.

"Give her another quarter dose," Miriam said. *Jasmine we need you.*
The other faculty crowded in the doorway.

"I'm putting a physical barrier up around the room," Daniel said.

"Good," Miriam said. "We can contain any damage in here."

I injected Casi again and she slumped further over, still muttering slightly.

Jasmine hurried into the room. "We gave her a dose and a quarter," I said. "But she's not quite sedated." Stephen and Daniel leaned in the doorway.

Jasmine peered into Casi's eyes. "I can't see her pupils. They're rolled too far up."

"She did that right before I sedated her."

Jasmine held onto Casi's wrist, counting her pulse. "Her heart is still racing. Give her the entire rest of the dose."

I did. Casi went limp, like a stuffed animal. Jasmine lifted Casi into her arms, using her Gift to help. "I'll get her to the infirmary. Let you know when she wakes up."

Why are you down here? Miriam demanded.

I came to water my plant. Casi wanted to talk and I didn't want to say no.

You need to rest. You still have two days off and I won't be responsible for you relapsing.

I know. It's too early. My head hurts and I'm still tired.

"Are we good?" Seiko asked. He was asking more than just whether or not they could leave. He was asking if the other teachers should leave me with Miriam.

"I think so," I said. *I'll let you know if I need back up,* I told him.

Don't let her push you around.

I won't.

They left and Miriam rubbed the bridge of her nose. "What happened with Casi?"

"She was telling me about these images she'd been getting. I think they were frightening her. But she said..." I stumbled, not sure where I was going. "They were really dark images. Lots of fire and people crying and Guardians marching in the streets."

"Hmmm...maybe her brain is turning other people's thoughts into images? She needs to talk to Stephen."

"She did but says that's not it."

"Maybe Casi is bipolar and hallucinating somehow. Like a waking dream. Probably need to have someone evaluate her."

"Probably."

"I can see your headache in your shields. You should go back upstairs."

"I will."

Miriam left and I watered my plant. *Are we good?* She suddenly asked.

That was all I was going to get out of her? No discussion of the horrible things she'd said to me?

Yes, I responded.

Good. We can't wait to have you back again. Things have been difficult without you. She closed the connection, ending the conversation.

I went back upstairs and curled up in my armchair, a blanket over my lap, feeling numb and off kilter. Golden shields full of twinkling jewels touched my mind, asking for a quick conversation. What on earth did Indira Dewan want?

Good afternoon, I answered the polite summons.

Hello, Kendle. Are you picking me up okay? I know it's difficult for Wilds at times to hear long-distance telepathy.

I rolled my eyes but resisted letting it creep through the channel. God, I really hated her.

I know Wilds who can transmit better than value Breds, I responded. *I can hear you just fine.*

I'm so pleased. Her fake English accent put my teeth on edge. Hundred-thousand-dollar donation, I wrote on a piece of paper over and over. Without that donation, we wouldn't have survived Leo's destruction of the dorms.

Can I help you with something? I asked, in my most helpful voice.

I hope so. After hearing your story, I started to do some research and found little has been done on Wilds. It's shocking.

No one has really cared to.

From what Stephen has shared and what I learned at the fundraiser, many of you are not weaker than we are. In fact, from what limited research I can find, your telepathy and psychokinesis come from a different part of your brain than with Breds. And then there are the fascinating physical changes, like your hair and eyes.

I wondered where she was going with all of this.

Do you remember I told you I'm in charge of research at my hospital?

Yes. Even my Wild mind could remember things. *I do,* I thought, keeping my mental voice sugary sweet.

I was wondering if your students and the other Wild instructors would be interested in participating in some research.

What kind?

I'm not quite sure yet. I'd have to draw up the proposal. Definitely some observations, some testing, some DNA analysis. Maybe some basic experiments.

Experiments? Like with lab rats?

Her mental laugh tinkled. *Of course not. It might look like bringing some of the kids to a lab setting and seeing what happens. Maybe for a week or two, over the summer, like a summer camp. There would be payment, of course.*

Of course, I echoed.

I sense you're less than pleased with the idea.

I am. We're not pieces of equipment or animals to experiment on. We're people, same as you are.

Of course you are. No one is saying differently.

Breds do when they say we should be separated from the general public and locked away. Do you know what happens in institutions?

But if we understand you, Wilds, better, it may not be necessary. Or we'd have the tools to help prevent the need for institutionalizing Wilds.

I'll say something to Miriam.

I do appreciate it. I'll check back with you in say, a week?

Sounds good. And then I vowed to be too busy if she contacted me again. There was no way I'd go to Miriam with this.

———

A few hours later, I crept back to the infirmary. Jasmine looked up when I crossed to Casi's bed and pulled up a chair.

"She should be waking up soon," Jasmine said, her spring-like shields clear and gentle.

Casi's eyes flickered.

"Casi," I said softly, ready to put up a physical barrier just in case. She sat up.

"You're okay," I said verbally and mentally. "You're in the infirmary." Casi looked wildly around, then relaxed, redness fading from her charcoal shields.

"What happened?" she asked.

"We were talking about the weird things you're seeing and then you went into a trance. The other teachers and I were worried you'd hurt yourself or someone else, so we sedated you."

"Oh."

"Do you remember?"

Casi pushed her hair off her face and shook her head. "It's like a dream."

Interesting.

I patted her arm. "We'll figure this out. But get some rest. You didn't hurt anyone or break anything." I stood up to go.

"Can you stay?" she asked. I remembered how I didn't want anyone to leave when I was in the hospital.

"Of course," I said. "Don't tell anyone though. Especially Jasmine."

"I know nothing," Jasmine said, not looking up from her screen.

Want to watch a movie on my screen?" I asked Casi.

Casi nodded and smiled, just a little.

CHAPTER FORTY-FIVE

I WAS early to meet Stephen for our...? I didn't know what to call it. Conversation? It was definitely not a date.

There was a lot of dirty snow up on the roof, half melted and refrozen. I unfolded a few lawn chairs and teleported a pair of gloves for my hands. Early March in Chicago was cold. I sat down and looked up at the stars I could barely see, thanks to air and light pollution. I looked for Jupiter but couldn't spot the bright star.

I lit a joint and breathed out.

Hey you. Are you feeling better? I haven't seen you at all.

"Kaya," I said, struggling to stand without getting eaten by the lawn chair. She gave me a huge hug, both arms wrapped tightly around me, rocking me slightly back and forth, while her gentle fire-like shields touched mine, warming me.

"Heard you had some excitement today with Casi. What happened?" She sat down in the chair I'd pulled out for Stephen.

"It was so odd," I said, glancing at my watch. I'd have to get rid of her soon, but I didn't want her to realize it. "She went into some sort of trance. Said she'd been getting all of these images, but they weren't hers."

"Thought transference and she didn't realize it?"

"She said no. And when I went to talk to her in the infirmary, she didn't remember the images."

"Odd."

"Yep." I glanced at my watch again. Five minutes to seven. Should I tell him to come at seven thirty?

"Kaya, Kendle, two of my favorite people."

"Stephen," Kaya gracefully stood and hugged him.

Sorry, I thought.

We should've done dinner. Too many people here, too many interruptions.

I didn't know what to say, so I just shrugged.

"Kendle was just telling me about Casi."

"Yeah, that was strange," Stephen said. "I'll keep working with her. I'm betting it's thought transference. You Wilds are definitely a challenging group to figure out."

"We try," I quipped.

"Well, I'm interrupting something," Kaya said.

"No you're not," Stephen and I said at the same moment. I almost added, 'jinx', but that was immature. And I was too tired and worried to play a game. What was I going to tell him?

Kaya laughed softly. "Whatever you say. Have a good night." *It's not my business, I know,* she thought only to me. *But he really likes you.*

Why? I asked. *There's nothing special about me.*

Oh sweetie. Ask him why he adores you.

He doesn't know me.

Kaya's shields touched mine, similar to her hugs. *Let me know if you need some girl talk tonight. I'm around.*

She touched Stephen's hand, and I felt the echoes of telepathy from their conversation, before she climbed down the ladder.

"Got you a chair," I said, pointing at the one Kaya had just left.

"Thank you. It's a lot colder out than I believed it would be," Stephen said, gloves and a scarf appearing. He wrapped the scarf around his neck before sitting down. "Here." A throw blanket smelling like Stephen appeared over my legs. "You're still recovering," he said.

"Thank you."

"Happy to help. How are you feeling?"

"Fine," I said. "I had a headache today, but it—" *So when did you realize about the dreams?* I asked, tired of the small talk and wanting to get this over.

About the dreams?

I nodded.

Stephen took his time answering, teleporting a bottle of wine and pouring a glass.

"Want some?"

"No thanks." It was probably expensive, and I wouldn't appreciate it.

He took a small sip. "It's not a port."

I laughed. It was forced, but I tried. "Okay," I said. "Just a small glass."

He poured some and I took a sip. Smooth and spicy grapes hit my tongue, so much better than the five-dollar bottle of wine in my apartment.

"This is a pinot noir," he said. "It's a more unique grape than the grape used in cabernets or zinfandels."

"Ah." I took another sip. It was good, but I'd never learn how to tell the differences in wines. And no reason for me to learn.

Stephen leaned back in the chair, staring at the stars.

I realized about the dreams around Christmas, he started. *You made some innocent comment about the ocean or the beach or something.*

I don't remember.

As I said, completely small and innocent and in the course of a conversation. I'd been suspecting maybe they were shared for a few weeks. The dreams were, are, so regular and so—

Undream like?

Exactly. When did you realize?

When you brought up the other school in the conference room.

Before or after Miriam went all crazy, to quote our kids?

I think, right before. Like, boom, boom. We're sharing dreams, and then Miriam said...what she said. Which is why I got so upset.

I took another sip of the wine. It was nice. Not as bitter as other red wines I'd had. We kept staring at the stars, not looking at each other.

I thought you knew the dreams were shared. I assumed you knew by the fundraiser at least, if not New Year's Eve. But either way, we're long overdue for this talk.

They did fade like dreams do, so it was easy, during the day, to pretend they were just dreams.

Do you think the merge caused it?

I took another sip of wine. *Probably. I did ask Dr. Evander about them, he'll keep it confidential, but he's never really heard of shield merging.*

I doubt many can do it.

We were quiet for a few minutes.

So now what? I finally said. Stephen's shields rolled back and forth like waves on a stormy day.

I really would like the opportunity to date you, Stephen thought. *Really date you, not in dreams. You're like no one I've ever met, and I would like to explore that further. I think we're compatible—*

Compatible? That's romantic.

He let out a puff of air, a half laugh. *I didn't realize I'd be so nervous.* He turned his head to look at me, his face perfect. Exactly what his parents designed. He took my hand, interlaced his fingers with mine and raised it to his lips. My skin tingled, and our interlocked fingers felt comfortable and right.

You've made my life at the Warehouse so interesting, he started. *I love listening to you play music, love talking about the kids with you and how we're going to help them. I think*—he bit his lip. *I think there's a lot of chemistry.*

You think?

A kiss would tell for sure. He stood up and leaned over me, waiting for me to meet him halfway. When I didn't, he leaned back and went to the edge of the roof, his hand in his back pocket.

Stephen, I began.

Starting with my name isn't a good sign.

I—I broke off. I adored him, I realized. Could probably call it love if I had another reference. Being around him made me happier than I'd been in a really long time. But I had to think. There was no way a Bred like him would stay with someone like me. I couldn't handle a broken heart on top of everything else.

I think...you're a Quality Bred, I thought. *I'm a homeless Wild with two hundred dollars in the bank account and owed paychecks. You have millions at your disposal. Do you have any idea how many pictures were taken of you and Indira on New Year's Eve? How the social media people were analyzing each look, each bite of food she fed you, noticing and commenting on how you didn't feed her and what that means. And then the pictures of us at the fundraiser. What people said about me. There was a Top Ten Things Not to do When Dancing with a Rune article based on me. Do you know how many people said I didn't have any eyelashes, my hair was ugly, and I had fat thighs they couldn't even see in my dress?*

He winced. *Why do you think I wanted to come here? And we don't have to go to events like that. And I'm not rich.*

You're a Rune.

My family...was unhappy with my decision to come to the Warehouse. They made it so I didn't get much of my mother's inheritance.

What about the beach house you keep mentioning?

Yes, I still have the beach house. And I still have investments and money in savings. But I'm not rich like I was. He turned around. "Does that matter?"

"God no," I said. "I don't care about money. I work here." *But I care about the media. I care about your family hating me because you're avoiding all events where there might be paparazzi.*

He came back to sit next to me, flinging himself into the chair.

I don't care what they think.

They're your family. I won't destroy those relationships.

You wouldn't. I don't care about my brother.

He's family.

He's an asshole. Especially since—

Since you came to the Warehouse, I finished for him.

He wanted me to get hair and blood samples from the "unique" kids. Said to ask them, he would pay them. When I said no, he said to take it. Actually go into their dorm room and riffle through their stuff for random hairs. And when I said no, he made my inheritance disappear.

Sounds like an awesome guy. What about your sister?

Roberta would be fine with you.

Isn't she running for a second term as a senator? Do you really think her campaign manager would recommend her brother start dating a Wild? It's going to be hard enough with all the Regs hating all Gifted.

That's her life, not mine.

But she could say she can't see you.

I doubt it.

He was so sure of his sister's support.

You don't know what it's like not to have any family. Not to have that connection to share stupid stories about your childhood with or go to if you need help. You can't destroy that relationship because of me.

He poured a large splash of wine into his glass. He knew I was right. I could see it in the stormy gray of his shields. *We're assuming too much. We don't know what the future will hold. I think you're worth it.*

It was my turn to stand up. I leaned over him, not waiting for him to meet me halfway, and touched my lips to his, tears slipping down my cheeks. *I love this Stephen. My Warehouse Stephen.* I touched his beard, the words "love" and "my" slipping out before I could stop them. *But I can't handle Quality Bred Stephen.*

That's your choice?

I had to take a deep breath. He reached up and touched my cheeks, wiping the tears away with fingers roughened from helping to rebuild the dorms.

Yes. I moved away and paced to the edge of the roof, looking down on the path between the buildings. It was only a four-story drop onto concrete. I wrapped my arms around myself. I was so cold.

CHAPTER FORTY-SIX

"LOOK UP," Kaya said.

"You keep saying that," I bitched. "I don't want to go anymore."

"So not sorry," Kaya said. "You haven't played in years and we're excited to see you."

I wiped my sweaty hands on my jeans. Eeva had felt so horrible about leaving me in the forest, she'd planned a gig for me as a surprise, a week after I'd returned to work. She'd found two of my old band mates and begged and probably bribed them to play a gig with me. Then she'd set up the whole thing at Atomic, the Wild bar in Chicago the other teachers and I sometimes went to.

"Just let me go with my bruises. It's dark there. No one will notice."

"I'll notice," Kaya said, twirling her foundation brush in make-up. "And stop talking. You're messing things up."

I sighed and looked up.

"I like this dress," Franny said, coming into my apartment without knocking. "I didn't like the one you wore to the fundraiser," she said. "It didn't suit you at all. Who picked it out?"

"I did," I said.

"Stop talking," Kaya said. "Jeez, you're a telepath."

What's wrong with my little black dress? I asked them. *It's traditional and safe.*

Not for you, Kaya thought.

It made you look old, with your white hair, Franny thought.

Why didn't you tell me? The dress was a simple black sheath that covered my collarbones, so my breasts didn't spill out. I'd believed the dress was classic and elegant.

We didn't realize it until an hour before the fundraiser, Kaya thought. *But it wasn't a big deal, really. You were fine. We just want to help you look...*

Better than fine, Franny thought, waving the yellow dress she'd brought. *Like you'd look in this. Though it's not like Stephen didn't like your dress at the fundraiser,* Franny thought with a sly smile.

Stop. We're not having this conversation. Stephen hadn't spoken with me since the roof, other than the basic niceties as we went through our intermingled life. He wasn't mad. Not exactly. More just wanting space. And we hadn't shared a single dream. I didn't know how he figured out a way to stop them, but he had. Maybe we both needed to be willing partners.

We should've talked months ago.

I missed him.

Kaya and Franny exchanged a glance, followed by the echoes of telepathy. Kaya popped open a few containers of eye shadow and mixed them on the back of her hand.

I'm not going to do a smoky eye, she thought. *It wouldn't suit you. But I'm going to make your purple eyes pop.*

Whatever, I thought. Stephen was only a room away, but it felt like I'd broken something that couldn't be fixed. I rubbed my cold chest. *How'd you know about Stephen?* I asked Franny.

"Everyone knows," Franny answered out loud.

How?

"You could tell at the fundraiser," Kaya said. "How he looked at you. And then he was so upset after you got hurt. He went straight to his lawyer, while Miriam went to try to get you out. Then he harassed the lawyer, forcing him to stop working on all of his other cases, until the charges against you were dropped."

Oh.

"We were all so worried," Franny said. They touched their shields to mine.

I'm okay, I thought.

You were lucky, Kaya thought. "Things are getting horrible. I almost don't want to let these kids graduate. What kind of a world are we sending them into?"

We were silent until Kaya said, "Done." She held up a hand mirror.

The bruises were gone, and as advertised, my purple eyes popped. They stood out in my face, big, sharp and unusual. But new lines pulled my lips down despite the makeup. I sighed. I wished Eeva hadn't put together the gig. I wasn't in the mood.

Why'd you tell Stephen no? Franny asked. *It was so much fun watching the two of you.*

I got up and paced away into my kitchen. I made cups of tea manually, just so I could get some distance from my friends. *I just couldn't do the Quality Bred thing,* I finally responded. *You know, the Rune thing. The family events and pictures in the news.*

I handed the two women cups of tea not caring whether they wanted them or not.

Okay, Kaya thought with a glance at Franny. She passed me a tissue. *Dab it into the corner of your eye to absorb the tears. That way you don't destroy your make-up.*

"Let's talk about clothes," Franny said, waving the yellow dress.

I shook my head. "No way," I said. "That's too fancy. I'm going to wear jeans. I always wear jeans at gigs."

Franny groaned. "What top then?"

"This one," I pointed at the simple black tank top I wore. "I'll put my fake leather jacket over it."

"No, you're not." She went running out of the room.

I rolled my eyes and Kaya laughed.

Have you asked Stephen to go tonight? She leaned forward to wipe a smudge from my chin.

Do I need to? Aren't we all going except Daniel and Miriam?

Kaya shrugged.

What are you trying to do?

She stood and gave me a hug. *I support all my friends when they hurt. And you both are hurting right now.* She passed me another tissue. "Corner of your eye, sweetie."

I dabbed with the tissue. I couldn't seem to stop crying. *Is he okay?*

"He'll be fine." *I think he'll be better if he hears you play. He really loves it.*

"I know," I murmured.

I took a deep breath and focused on the turquoise shields I sensed in the next room. Except they were a quiet gray, like the ocean on a foggy morning.

Hey, I thought to Stephen. *Were you going to come tonight?*

Hey you. I hadn't decided. I could sense him moving around his apartment. *Do you want me to?*

It...if you want...I mean, we're still friends, right? I mean, I get you're...after some time? We can still be friends? Wow, that was awesome. Totally smooth and cultured.

What the fuck did he see in me?

I jumped when Franny barged into the room. "I got it," she said, waving a lavender peasant top around. "This is perfect for folk rock. And it'll go great with your eyes and hair. I mean, I couldn't have designed a better top for you."

I fell in love with it immediately, one of those gut punches you sometimes get with clothes. The top was a pale purple with poufy sleeves cut with slits and tiny silver flowers embroidered around the neckline, sleeves and hem. It was cut tight, so I wouldn't look like I wore a tent, but the slits in the sleeves meant I could still move my arms and play.

"It's perfect," I told her. "Thank you for loaning it to me."

"Keep it," Franny said. She waved a bottle of wine. "Want some?"

"Sure," I said. It would help with my nerves.

I'll go, Stephen thought to me. *At least I can see the blouse everyone is exclaiming about.*

Are you eavesdropping?

I think Miriam in her office downstairs heard Franny.

I laughed and Franny demanded to know why.

"Nothing," I said, accepting the glass of white wine and telling Stephen, *thank you.*

He touched my shields, a quick embrace, and then disconnected.

Kaya and Franny clinked their glasses to mine.

CHAPTER FORTY-SEVEN

AN HOUR LATER, I stepped onto the stage at Atomic, holding my guitar, the one with the worn patch from where my hand hit the strings, the second instrument I'd ever owned. The one that had come with me on dozens of gigs and played thousands of songs.

The bar was half-full of Wilds standing and holding beer bottles or fruity drinks in red cups. But they cheered and hooted when Ruben, Henry and I stepped out. I didn't know what Eeva had promised Ruben and Henry to get them away from their jobs, but I was grateful. We started with a big hug and then Ruben and I plugged our guitars in while Henry took his place behind the drums.

Ready? I asked them.

Yep, Ruben responded while Henry knocked his drumsticks together.

We launched into the first song, a folk-rock cover. It was rough. We hadn't had any time to rehearse and we didn't immediately remember how to play together. But the audience singing along, bobbing their heads and shoulders or outright dancing evened us out and by the third song, we remembered how to use our telepathy to anticipate what the others were going to do.

On the start of the fourth song, I reached out to Eeva, the connection weak with distance. *Thank you.*

You're welcome. Someone had better be recording it. My heart broke a little that after all her work, she hadn't been able to come tonight.

They are.

Hopefully it's the first gig of many. Break a leg.

Henry started another beat and I played the opening chord. The crowd cheered, instantly recognizing it.

I don't have time to do this a lot. There's just too much work at the Warehouse.

You need to change something. I love you and while you're on stage isn't the time to tell you this, but you need to get out of the Warehouse. Need to get away from Miriam. She's not healthy for you.

Now? She wanted to start this argument now?

Love you. We'll talk later.

Love you too.

———

The crowd got louder as they drank more. We were only playing covers, which allowed the crowd to sign along. There were points when Ruben stopped singing and let the audience carry the song, mostly because he couldn't remember the lyrics. We were rough, but no one cared. More and more Wilds showed up, their shields merging into a colored mist of purples, greens and blues of happiness.

God, you're phenomenal, Stephen thought.

I caught his eye and smiled, reaching out with my shields to touch his before I remembered and pulled back with a sigh. I took a puff off the joint I'd brought with me and passed it to Henry and Ruben.

Want to head back to my place after this set? Ruben had small abilities in psychokinesis and telepathy and tried to pass for a Reg, managing to hold down a normal job. He was one of the lucky few Wilds not on the Registry. His shields were basic, a cobalt blue. He'd been a few years ahead of me at the Warehouse and we'd reconnected after I'd graduated to form our band.

Wow. Not even a pretense at getting a drink afterwards or something to eat.

Did we ever need that?

Sometimes, I responded. But he was right. We'd had sex at his place numerous times, heading directly there after gigs. There'd even been a few times when we'd had sex backstage, I remembered with chagrin.

No thanks, I thought.

You guys ready? Henry asked. *Count of ten?*

Sure, Ruben thought to Henry. *I mean, we can do dinner if you need that.* His shields hadn't even changed with my refusal. He really didn't care.

No thanks, I answered, hitting the first chord of a popular country song. The crowd roared. *But I'm not interested.*

Whatever, he thought, stepping up to the mic and starting to sing.

I slid into the song, trying not to think about my past and the mistakes I'd made. Three songs went by before I slid back into the groove.

Guys, Daniel thought. *We have a problem.*

I missed a note and looked into the crowd. Kaya was frowning and Seiko's eyes were closed.

Casi is...kind of in a trance, Daniel continued. *But not like before. She's insisting a bomb's about to go off at Atomic.*

I missed another note and Ruben frowned at me, continuing to sing into the mic.

How would she know? Kaya asked.

Is Kendle wearing a purple top? On the right side of the stage? Is there a big banner over the stage? With a pool on it?

I looked up. I hadn't noticed it, but there was a banner advertising a pool cleaning company—the bar owners attempt to make a few extra bucks.

I lunged for the mic, opening up a mental channel to anyone who could receive.

Evacuate now. Teleport if you can. But get—

The world went red and yellow.

CHAPTER FORTY-EIGHT

I COUGHED INTO MY HAND. There was smoke, fire and rubble everywhere. I'd thrown up a physical barrier at the last second and while the blast had knocked me to the ground, I wasn't hurt.

I got to my knees and then up to my feet. My ears rang horribly.

Kendle?

I'm okay, I thought to my friends from the Warehouse. *Anyone hurt?*

Seiko was helping Kaya and then Franny to their feet. I couldn't see Stephen. My heart stopped. I'd assumed I knew what that felt like, but I didn't. My heart didn't beat, didn't circulate oxygen and I had to gasp for air.

Stephen? I felt for his turquoise shields.

I'm here. I must have instinctually teleported out. I called the Guardians and the regular police. The front door is completely blocked.

I looked for my bandmates. Ruben and Henry had managed to put up physical barriers too, but Ruben laid still, an arm flung across his face, while Henry crawled to his feet, bleeding from dozens of cuts.

I dropped next to Ruben, feeling for a pulse and then breathing a sigh when I found one. He was probably concussed.

We'll get people out the back, Kaya thought. *Before the Guardians get here and arrest the Wilds.*

I pulled myself to my feet, looking around, trying to see how I could help. I figured I had ten minutes before I had to leave too.

I used my gift to smother tiny fires, putting them out before they caused more damage. Some Wilds got to their feet, moaning, crying and reaching out for their friends and family. Henry jumped into the crowd, pressing his hands onto a Wild woman's lacerated arm.

I used my Gift to pull a collapsed portion of the bar off a bartender whose leg was caught.

"Thank you," he told me, his weak green shields tinged with black and gray like all of our shields were. He scrambled to his feet, despite his obvious broken leg and limped to the back door, trying to get out before the Guardians found a way in.

I walked around, helping where I could, pressing shirts and scarves against cuts, and pulling Wilds to their feet. I glanced toward the stage where Ruben had been. He wasn't lying there anymore. I felt around through the chaos for his shields, but they were gone.

Coward, I thought to him.

Guardians are coming. I can't risk it. I'm a Reg in my normal life.

I wanted to be angry with him, but I couldn't. I got it.

Kendle and I should leave, Seiko thought in an open channel to everyone from the Warehouse.

Probably a good idea, Kaya thought. *Stephen, Franny and I have this.*

Seiko and I hurried out the back door, just as the Guardians and paramedics hurried in. A few Guardians split off, chasing the Wilds scurrying down the streets.

Dude, you need to learn how to teleport, I told him as we ducked into alleys and sprinted up and down streets at random.

I couldn't be arrested again. They might not let us go this time.

Finally, we reached the Warehouse gate, out of breath. My chest hurt and I rubbed it. I punched the code and we went in, closing the gate behind us. Seiko flopped to the grass and I joined him, waiting for my breath to calm.

We made it, Seiko thought to the other three. *Where are you guys?*

We're walking back now, Franny thought. *The Guardians weren't interested in us because we're Breds. They took down our names and said they'd stop by for our statements later.*

I looked around at my home for the last twenty years. Had everything always been so run down?

Can we go up to the roof? I need a drink and I'm not ready for bed. Kaya asked, as they came in through the gate.

Sounds perfect, Seiko thought. *I can't imagine going to bed. Fifteen minutes? After a shower?*

I see all of you standing out there, Miriam told us. *Emergency meeting immediately.*

Or we could have a work meeting, Seiko thought. *And then get drunk.*

We need thirty minutes, Stephen responded. *To shower and change.*

Thirty minutes then. She broke off the connection.

CHAPTER FORTY-NINE

WITH A SIGH, I teleported to my apartment. My beautiful top, the one Franny had insisted on giving me, was soot and blood stained, the sleeves ripped into fluttering pieces. I used my Gift to turn on the shower and threw the top into the corner of my kitchen, along with my bra, jeans and panties. I stepped into the shower and tried not to notice the water running off my body was dark with soot and blood. But none of the blood was mine. I was fine.

How many weren't? Had anyone died? I hadn't seen bodies, but maybe I'd missed them in the chaos.

I picked up the soap, leaving more dirt streaks on it. I washed my hands until they were pink and wrinkled. I shampooed my hair three times hoping the smoke smell was out.

You okay? Stephen's mental touch was gentle, tentative. I did a final rinse and turned the water off.

I don't know, I answered. I hadn't cried. Shouldn't I have? Someone had set off a bomb in a Wild bar just because they hated us. It didn't seem real. Why would someone want to do that? They didn't know who we were. We weren't a threat to anyone. We just wanted a normal life.

I couldn't believe how horrible the last few weeks had been.

Stephen? Come over. Please.

Be right there.

I looped a towel around myself and used my Gift to open my apartment door a crack. He slipped into my main room, the one I hadn't wanted him to see, all those months ago.

I wrapped my arms around him, burying my damp head into his chest. He smelled of soap, his skin still damp from the shower. His shirt was partially unbuttoned, and I loved the feel of his skin against my cheek. I breathed his scent in, feeling warm and calm with his arms around me.

We all could've died. You could've died, he whispered in my thoughts.

I lifted my head and standing on tiptoes, which I swore I didn't have to do in dreams, kissed him. He kissed me back, his lips soft at first, then stronger, demanding. I gave and took as well. The numbness retreated.

You're only wearing a towel. His lips broke away from mine to nibble down my neck just as I liked it.

That should make this easier.

He stepped back and for a moment thought he didn't want me anymore. That the last week had changed his mind completely.

"Are you sure?" His voice was soft and he touched my bare arms, running a calloused thumb up and down.

"Yes," I whispered. I let the towel fall and he lifted me to him. I wrapped my legs around his waist.

———

Afterwards, we lay in my queen-sized bed, not touching, just staring up at the ceiling. His shields had been a brilliant blue, like the ocean on a sunny summer day, but now the storm crept back into them.

Stephen propped himself up on an elbow. He ran a finger over a scar on my belly, and another on my arm.

So many scars.

I tried to withdraw back into myself. I shouldn't have slept with him in the real world. What had I been thinking?

That's what a Gladiator Ring will do to you.

How long were you there?

Few weeks. Not long. I touched the scars on my wrists from all the bands. *My bands were defective, and I was able to get them off. I teleported away. It was the first time I tried.*

Lucky you didn't kill yourself.

I wasn't going to last much longer in the Gladiator Ring. It was either dying there or teleporting.

He ran his fingers up and down my belly and shoulder, like he did in the dreams.

You have a tattoo. He moved my hair out of the way. *Hummingbird?*

We all got them our third year. At home job. My fifteen-year-old self had been proud of it. Adult me was glad we hadn't gotten Hep C or worse.

Hummingbirds are symbols of rebirth and new hope. They're one of the only birds who hibernate in the winter and come out in the spring. It's perfect for you.

I shouldn't have slept with him.

So Casi—he trailed off.

Can see the future, I thought. *It makes sense. Those images that frightened her were things from the future.*

That's a really scary skill.

People will want it. The government. Foreign governments. Geneticists will want her DNA to figure out how to recreate it. Your brother would pay millions for it.

We'll have to keep her safe, Stephen thought.

We have to teach her to use it.

Between Casi, Leo and Becca, our school has become full of superheroes.

You guys coming? Seiko asked Stephen and me. *We're waiting for you in the conference room.*

I'm still getting cleaned up, I responded. *All of us showering at the same time used up all the hot water. Ten more minutes.* I climbed out of bed and went to pull on clothes. Stephen watched from the bed.

I want a redo.

I let out a shout of laughter surprising us both. *Forget the romance, the seduction in the dreams. We have sex and you say, "I want a redo."* I climbed into a pair of yoga pants and an old sweatshirt with the Warehouse logo we'd never changed in all twenty some-odd years on it.

He made a face. *You're right. I would've preferred a different route. But a bomb went off. So I want a redo. I want to be with you.*

What would that even look like?

To start, I want to take you out on a date ending in a hotel room. Maybe a whole weekend away. Just to be together without all of the normal chaos.

I went into the bathroom to grab a comb for my damp and tangled curls.

We've been through this, I thought. *I can't do the photographers taking our picture everywhere we go. I can't have them follow us around, wondering who I am. They'll dig up my past. There'll be commentary and analysis of what I did to survive in Vegas. Of what I did in the Gladiator Ring. I'm sure there's videos.*

Hell, there may even be charges. I rubbed my painful chest. I wished Stephen and I could just live in our dreams.

It'll be fine, he thought. *We won't go anywhere. Just stay here and the beach house. And I'll have my lawyer sue journalists for slander.*

The idea of never leaving the Warehouse with Stephen didn't sound as good as it would've a few months ago. I gave up on my curls and tied my hair in a headband, letting the mess fall where it was going to. I sat on the bed, next to Stephen, and laced my fingers with his.

Please, Stephen thought. "I think I'm in love with you." His voice seemed to echo in my room. *I've never said that to anyone,* he continued. *Relationships are work and it's not going to be easy, but I want to try. Being around you makes me happier than anything and I think I make you happy too.* He touched his forehead against mine. "You don't have to tell me you love me back," he whispered. "I just want to try."

He made me happy too. Happier than I'd ever been. I'd almost died twice in the last three weeks. At this rate, I wasn't going to last until the end of the school year. What was wrong with being happy, even if it was just for a little while?

I took a deep breath. *Okay,* I thought.

Okay what?

I had to take another deep breath. I'd just ignore what anyone said. We both would. Totally doable.

Let's try.

Really? His shields were turquoise, cool, deep and beautiful.

Do you want me to change my mind again?

No. I just—really?

Really, truly, absolutely. I laughed. Everything felt right and perfect in the world. *Yes, I want to try this. We'll figure out your family and the media and the Warehouse and Miriam and...*I trailed off. "All the moving pieces. We'll just make it work." *I think it'll be worth it.*

I kissed him then, a promise for the future. We didn't know what tomorrow looked like, but we could try. His shields were such a beautiful turquoise. No matter what happened, I would always remember that.

We're still waiting for the two of you up here. Some of us want to go to bed. Daniel's voice was harsh in our heads.

"God, what an ass," I said, pulling away from Stephen.

Stephen gathered up his clothes and kissed me again, like he was worried I'd disappear. He interlaced his shields with mine, filling my thoughts with oceany blues. "You really don't know why, do you?"

"Because he's always been an ass?"

He smiled, his lips nearly touching mine. "For a school full of telepaths, we keep a lot of secrets. I'm going to take a quick shower and see you downstairs in five minutes." He kissed me, long and deep.

CHAPTER FIFTY

I TOOK my normal seat in the conference room, looking at the curling sticky notes on the walls. The colors were faded, the ink hard to read. We'd planned so much. Buying a new warehouse with a separate library and a space for cooking classes. Creating a partnership with junior colleges for online classes for our graduates, hiring more teachers, hiring more help in general. All the ideas we'd never been able to do because we didn't have the time or money. It had been five years since we'd had the project manager in for a multi-day brainstorming session. We'd come up with over fifty ideas broken into various columns. And had only completed six. In five years.

I wanted to rip off the notes.

This wasn't working anymore.

It was time to start over.

"Where's Stephen?" Miriam asked.

"He's not here yet?"

God, that was the stupidest question I'd ever asked. Of course he wasn't.

Subtle. That was me.

Stephen appeared, sitting in his normal spot, his shields glowing with happiness. Exuberance. I touched his shields and he grinned only for me, sliding his shields next to mine, like holding hands. I couldn't believe I had him, for this moment.

I was so scared.

Oh yay, Kaya thought to both of us. *You two worked it out. I'm so happy for you. You're going to be so cute together.*

Almost blowing up helps with priorities, I thought.

"Now that Stephen's here," Miriam said. "We need to talk about Casi."

I wrenched my thoughts back to Casi's Gift.

Miriam nodded at Daniel.

"Becca reached out to me, saying Casi was really upset," Daniel started. "I went over to the dorm. Found Casi pacing back and forth in the common area. She was walking fast, muttering to herself."

"I've seen her do that," I said, putting pieces together. "When she came to see me before I sedated her, she was twitchy too."

"I got Miriam," Daniel continued. "And a syringe ready in case I had to sedate her."

"What was she saying?" Seiko asked.

Daniel pulled out a notebook. "I tried to write it down." He flipped through the pages. "Fire, wedding, babies, people marching in the streets. Guardians, a happy building, a building on fire..." He flipped another page.

I nodded. It was all the same stuff she'd told me earlier. I was glad Daniel had written it down.

"Then she focused, and said you all were in danger, something would happen at the bar. I asked how she knew," Daniel flipped another page. "And she said to please, please make y'all leave. Then she described Kendle's shirt and where she was on stage. I figured I should say something. Worse case, she was just wrong."

"And even with her warning, we were too late," I said.

Kaya shook her head. "I think those that could, got shields up in time. I'm not sure there were any deaths, which is a miracle."

"So can she see the future?" Seiko asked.

"Seems that way," Daniel said.

"Ask her what the winning lottery numbers are," Franny quipped.

"Seriously," I murmured. "But I don't think she has good control."

Miriam nodded. "It's probably a bit like a flashlight on dying batteries coming and going. But that brings me to my next point. And there will be no discussion or debate. I expect my instructions to be carried out to completion or you won't work here anymore."

Daniel dropped his eyes to the floor, his shields turning thick and gooey, the glitter disappearing.

"Effective immediately, children identified as a risk to this facility, its employees and other students will be expelled and returned to their families or institutionalized. This means Becca, Leo and Casi," Miriam said.

"What?" Kaya said, half standing up. "She saved our lives. Her skills are valuable. We can't repay her by expelling her."

"We agreed we would continue to work with these kids," Seiko said. "Or we run the risk they'll become a danger to themselves or others. We're here to help them."

"That's not our issue," Miriam said. We cannot continue to support these individuals. There are too many risks to this school, its faculty and our students. What if one of these students kills another? Could you live with yourself? I couldn't."

"Miriam," I said. "You can't do this. Institutions are horrible places. They'll be drugged and wearing bands for the rest of what's left of their lives. And Casi—it's not her fault she can see the future. I mean, that's not dangerous."

"She shook the building a few days ago."

"Yes, but now we know why, and we can work with her. She's not the first to shake the building. I shake the buildings sometimes. Are you going to expel me next?"

"I was clear when I started this meeting. There would be no discussion. If you can't carry this out, then you're not employed here anymore."

I swallowed, the water in my glass swirling. "But Miriam—"

"No discussion." *I mean it Kendle. This isn't an idle threat. My top priority is to protect this school and the children within.* She switched back to verbal. "And I can't do that with children who have these Gifts."

"You can't—"

"You're done." Miriam said. "I'm terminating your employment immediately. Collect your things and leave." Her shields may have been black, but they were hard and strong and without movement.

The entire room froze, like the second before lightning hits during a storm. Then everything vibrated, just once, and I had no idea who did it.

"No. You're not," Daniel said. "Everyone calm down. We'll talk about this."

Please don't fight her, Daniel thought to me. *I will fix this. But I can't right now. I'll do what I can to protect Leo, Becca and Casi. Put them in a temporary holding or something, until I can get Miriam to change her mind.*

What if she doesn't?

Then you'll still be working with kids that need you. The Warehouse needs you. It'll cease to function if you leave. Then we'll have to close, and all the kids currently here will have no place to go. We. Need. You. Please, Kendle. Don't push this. Now's not the time. Be patient. I'll fix it.

Be patient? She's expelling three students and firing me.

She's not thinking. She's very...you don't know...it's been a hard year. His thoughts rolled together, his words coming fast. *I can't do the admin stuff. I'm a teacher and that's where my strength is. Not in schedules and storage closets and ordering and all you do.*

This is wrong. Becca and Casi aren't threats and we can't just expel Leo. He's been trying so hard.

Casi scared her. She told Miriam...it doesn't matter. I'll get this fixed. But you leaving does no good. If you go, the others will too. And the Warehouse will close.

I couldn't worry about that. Becca, Leo and Casi were my priority at this moment. I needed someone to give the kids a safe place to work on their Gift and get control. And the Warehouse wasn't safe for them.

Or me.

I reached out, way out, looking for golden shields with jewels embedded within.

Indira?

CHAPTER FIFTY-ONE

INDIRA OPENED her office door to my knock and invited me in, past what was presumably Leo's father's assistant desk. Her office was surprisingly comfortable, furnished in whites, grays and greens. I'd expected something more ostentatious. Colored art looking like someone had flung paint on a canvas broke up the gray walls.

"Sit down," she invited, pointing at a hard-looking green couch. I melted into the soft leather. I wanted to sleep here.

She touched her jewel like shields to mine, greeting me, Gifted to Gifted.

Kendle. It's so good to see you again. How can I help you?

I pushed back my exhaustion and I tried not to notice how rested, healthy and pretty she looked in a black cocktail dress, at one o'clock on a Sunday morning. However, she had kicked her red heels off and the soles of her feet were dirty, her toenail polish chipped. It was pitiful how cheery that made me.

You'd mentioned wanting to learn more about Wilds and what we can do. You'd wanted to bring Wilds into a lab setting and perform tests, experiments. Set up cameras, watch what we do.

I had. She leaned back in her chair, one arm over the back like she was posing for a magazine cover. *And you seemed less than willing,* Indira continued. *Has that changed?*

There are three students at the Warehouse at risk of expulsion. Their Gifts are unique, and it makes them dangerous. I tried not to throw Miriam under the bus. *Miriam feels we...*the tightness in my chest spread out, numbing me. I had to do this. The Warehouse couldn't be my home anymore.

They feel having them at the Warehouse increases the risk to the other students.

And you disagree?

I think we shouldn't throw children out like garbage because they're difficult and different. They should be taught how to control their Gifts so they're not a risk to others. Not locked away.

Interesting. And you're asking for what?

A place where I can teach them control. Food, resources, that type of thing.

In exchange, you'll let me study them?

I rubbed my chest. I had no other choice. *If they agree to it.*

More jewels winked into Indira's shields and she rubbed her lips together. Her screen flew through the air to her lap and she started taking notes. *After our meeting in February, I was fascinated by Wilds. There was a great deal I was unaware of. After you refused us, I found Wilds and brought them in for observations with some tweakable parameters.*

Experiments?

Observations. You yourself told me no one really understood Wilds. And you were right. Our observations indicate Wilds are very different from Breds and can likely do things we can't. Frankly, I'm shocked it's taken this long for someone to notice.

"They have," I answered out loud. "But instead of studying it, they've taken our genes and tried to insert them into Bred genetic codes or use us to create new Bred abilities."

"Mostly unsuccessfully," Indira said. She stood up and started pacing, while her screen kept typing. *I'm not a geneticist, but I'd theorize there's some sort of genetic mutations with Wilds. And as the lines blur between Wilds and Breds, we have to ask what their combined offspring will look like. We need to understand Wilds better, to help them, especially as our society turns its back on Gifted in general. Regs have the numbers on their side and we, Breds, need to change how we think about Wilds or we'll be a footnote in history. A cautionary tale for the future.*

She was good, I thought. *But?*

But we're finding the lab is tainting our results. So I'd already planned to set up a living situation, a house basically, for Wilds. It's very isolated so safety's not an issue and we won't have outside influences flummoxing our results. I can give it to you. Private bedrooms, a full kitchen, room for studies, money for online classes, staff to cook and clean.

Animals? I asked. *I'd love to have space for animals.*

Like dogs and cats or farm animals?

Both?

That's a fascinating idea, Indira thought. She grinned and, like Stephen, suddenly seemed human. *Do you think there's a possibility Wilds can control animals?*

I might know someone who can.

A child?

No. An adult, I thought.

Would they be interested in coming with you? That's an intriguing facet.

I shrugged. *I can ask, but she already has a job.*

There's an old barn on the property. We could have it refurbished for horses. It would be a fascinating addition to my research plan. What do you think of the rest of it?

I couldn't screw this up. *It has potential.*

I'm being rude, she thought. *It's late and I'm sure you're hungry.*

A tray with a coffee pot, water bottles and a bowl of pastries appeared on her desk. My stomach let out a rumble and her lips twitched.

I was going to hate working with her. She was so beautiful, smart and perfect. Had Stephen never told this queen he loved her? How was it only me he'd said those words to?

I pushed the thought away. I had to focus on helping Becca, Casi and Leo. And Indira could do that.

I used my Gift to pour a cup of coffee and bring it and a pastry over to my seat. I bit into the flakey sugar dough and downed the coffee. My brain cleared.

So what do you get by doing research? I asked. *Does that make money for the hospital?*

She let out a tinkling laugh. *There's a great deal of money in research. Papers, articles and our observations would easily pay for you and your students' room and board.*

Does the additional money go to paying salaries?

She smiled and I felt like I'd won a prize. I smiled back without realizing it and strengthened my shields. I wasn't going to let her manipulate me with her Gift.

I'd be happy to provide a salary for your help with our research. She passed her screen over and my tired brain stopped. I hadn't made that much in five years at the Warehouse, assuming I was actually paid.

You're trying to bribe me.

Yes. I know you're not happy with this. And I'm buying your good will. I'm buying your help with the experiments and our research gathering. And I would want to study you too.

Me?

You're a Wild, with unusual abilities.

You'd experiment on me? I was embarrassed my mental voice had a squeak to it.

Research. You'll have to get the vocab right.

What kind of research then? I asked.

Testing to see what you're all capable of, to start. You would have the option of choosing which tests, though, especially if you're on our payroll. Then we'd observe. I want to start with seeing what Wilds can do, see how you interact with each other.

*Would I get to choose things like...*my brain didn't want to work. *Like where the cameras would go? Like if I said, no cameras in the bathroom?*

Yes, I agree. No cameras in the bathroom unless there's interesting things happening in there.

She looked at me and I felt like I'd given something up, not gained anything. I was too tired for this. I didn't understand what I was doing.

Can I get everything in writing, before it happens?

Of course.

And can I have someone else review it?

Possibly. They'd have to sign some non-disclosures, but perhaps.

There had to be more I was missing.

"What's your hesitation?" she asked.

My laugh startled me. "You're asking me to allow teenagers to be experimented on. And I don't know you."

I think you're missing a bigger piece of this.

Oh goody—someone else telling me I wasn't thinking big picture.

And that is?

The amount of good you're going to do for Wilds with this research. I know you're focused on the three students you want to save, but this research could change the course of Wilds in society. And you get to be a part of that.

That was a frightening concept. I just wanted to help Leo, Becca and Casi. Not change the course of history.

"Can I scan you?" I asked. "Just to find out if you're telling me the truth? If you're going to be ethical?"

She raised a perfect eyebrow. "No. That's not a possibility. You'll have to trust me."

"Can I put a clause in the contract that states we can leave, if I feel the need?"

"Perhaps. If certain parameters aren't met, you might be able to break the contract."

"I want promises you're not going to sell our DNA to R&E or any other genetic company."

"That would defeat the purpose of my research. But I'll put it in the contract."

Hours later, I stood up. We'd gone over so many details and my brain refused to function anymore. I was amazed I could still walk. "Can you just send all of this to me in writing so I can read it after I get some sleep?" I asked.

Indira stood up too. "Of course. And then later today, do you want to examine the facility?"

God, all I wanted was sleep. *Yes. Two o'clock work? And can I bring some other people, maybe another Wild, to review the location and the contract?*

She glanced at her calendar. *All that should be fine. I've cleared my schedule for the next two days to work on this for you. I understand your reluctance, but I only want to help Wilds.* She was telling the truth, but I worried her version of helping us was different than mine.

"One thing more," she said. "No Breds on the premises and no Breds living there or even spending the night. It might change our results."

Oh. I hadn't even thought about what moving to her facility would do to Stephen and my relationship. But it wasn't like I had a choice.

I teleported back to the Warehouse and looked at my watch. It was seven a.m. I'd been up more than twenty-four hours straight.

And I still needed to meet with Daniel and Miriam. Explain the plan.

Do you both have a few minutes? I asked them.

We can meet in fifteen minutes, Daniel responded and closed the connection.

I went up to my office and stared at my gibberish notes. There was no way I could do this.

Seiko ran into my office and closed the door behind him. "So what's going to happen? Did you save them?"

I dropped my head into my hands. "I think I just agreed to be a part of an experiment. I mean, research project. With Casi, Becca and Leo."

"Research?"

"In exchange for room, food and a salary, I'm going to let Stephen's ex-girlfriend do experiments on me and the kids."

"Salary? Can she do experiments on me too?"

I laughed and once I started, I couldn't stop. He handed me a water and I tried to calm down.

I don't know about this, Seiko thought.

I know. I wiped my streaming eyes and realized I was crying. "Do I have another choice?"

"Not if you don't want the kids to go to the Guardians."

We sat in silence.

So does that mean you're leaving? he asked.

"Miriam fired me." I said it both verbally and telepathically, trying to wrap my brain around it. I was going to leave the Warehouse. It wasn't my home anymore.

If you go, I go.

You can't. Someone has to stay for the kids.

He pressed his lips together, his striped shields dark. *I'll stay until the summer. I'm already looking. It's time to go.*

Maybe things would be different by then. Maybe he'd change his mind. I stood up. "I have a meeting with Miriam and Daniel in five minutes. I have to tell them."

"Good luck," he said. We didn't have a hugging relationship, leaving that to Kaya, but he wrapped his arms around me, giving me a huge hug. *It'll be okay.*

"How do you know?"

"I don't. But it's what you're supposed to say."

Thank you.

He turned to go. "Oh! Girl, you and Stephen. Seriously? And you don't tell me?"

I chuckled, because it's what he wanted. "It was kind of a secret. From me too."

He is a Quality Bred. I think in the end, you're giving up more than him.

He makes me happy.

Is that what you want?

Isn't that all we want?

Seiko stuck his hands in his pockets. *I worry you'll end up more lost and broken.*

Thanks for the vote, I responded sarcastically.

But I'm here to pick up the pieces if that happens. "See you around."

I pushed that worry aside. I couldn't deal with it right now.

———

Five minutes later, I stood with my hands behind my back in front of Miriam's desk. Miriam sat with the desk separating us and Daniel stood behind her, his hand on her chair. The flowers she always kept on her desk were wilted, the water dark, and mold floating on top.

I raised my chin and as concisely as I could, explained my plan.

"You think having a hospital perform experiments on them is better than..." Miriam petered out, her lips tight.

"Then having children handed over to the Guardians to be drugged? Placed in bands? At least with Indra and me, they're safe."

"This is a terrible idea," Miriam said. "And I take it you're resigning?"

"You fired me."

Daniel's eyes closed, his shields a dark amber, but he didn't speak.

"What if I don't sign the children over to you?"

"Indira said her lawyers would take care of it."

What if I let them stay?

Daniel touched his shields with mine. *She won't,* he whispered in my mind. *I think you've made the best out of a horrible choice.*

Really?

Yes.

I have to check out the facility at two. Will you go with me? And review the contract? I just want to make sure I'm not missing anything.

You don't want Stephen?

Apparently, everyone knew about Stephen and me.

I just...I want a Wild to look at it.

Happy to. Just let me know where.

"You won't let them stay, not really," I said to Miriam. "And I won't stay either. It's done. We're done." God, my chest hurt, and I had to will the tears back.

"Then I want you gone immediately," Miriam said. "Packed and no longer here within an hour."

An hour? But it was seven hours until I met with Indira. And the contract wasn't finalized or anything.

"No," I said. "I need twenty-four hours to put everything in place."

"I said an hour. I want you gone."

"Twenty-four hours is fine," Daniel said.

"Fine, then," Miriam repeated, her shields darkening even more. At this rate, Daniel wouldn't have a job either. "Then by morning I want you and the three students gone by seven. And I don't want to see you again."

Darkness crowded on the edges of my vision. Was that really what she wanted? Miriam, the woman who'd saved me in Vegas, who'd given me so much, never wanted to see me again?

"Miriam," Daniel breathed out. "Think this—"

"She made her choice." Miriam turned to me. "You can leave."

I nodded once and teleported to my apartment. I looked around. Other than my instruments, there was little to pack. I could do this quickly and help Leo, Casi and Becca gather up their things. Not that they had a lot either.

Stephen touched his shields against mine. *Can I come over?*

Yes.

CHAPTER FIFTY-TWO

A FEW HOURS LATER, I climbed out of bed. Stephen tried to pull me back, but I pushed him away with a laugh. "I have so much to do. And I have to meet with Indira at two to check out the facility."

"Want me to go?"

"I don't think you're allowed. It's Wilds only." I said it as a joke, but Stephen frowned.

"Interesting," he said.

"Please tell me Indira isn't bullshitting me or something."

"No." *Not in the way you mean. But the research is paramount to her. You can trust her, but to a point. And she's not your friend.*

Got it. I sat back on the bed and Stephen ran his fingers up my bare back. I wiggled away from him and wrapped the sheet around myself. "Stop that," I said.

His Gift tried to push me back onto the bed. I pushed back with a laugh.

What does this do to us? I asked.

You leaving? He shrugged. *I'm not sure it's a bad thing. We can actually go on dates, have weekends away. It's probably a healthier way to develop whatever we have.*

Are you going to leave too?

He frowned. *Daniel asked me that. I don't know at this point. What Miriam did to you and to Becca, Leo and Casi isn't acceptable. But if we all leave, the school closes. And I'm not sure I can let that happen. But there's one thing.* He touched his forehead against mine. "I don't plan to let you go."

And we still have the dreams, I responded.

———

At two, Daniel, Casi, Becca and Leo stepped off the transport pad with me. We were deep in Colorado's mountains, surrounded by a forest. Indira waited for us, looking refreshed and beautiful, her golden shields bright. She pointed out the giant house, like we would miss it if it weren't for her, babbling like a real estate agent.

"It has six bedrooms and four bathrooms. One of the bedrooms is a large master suite, perfect for Kendle. There are multiple common areas, including a library, study and even a billiard room. Plenty of space to study and hang out with others or by yourselves."

Contractors carried wood, furniture and pipes inside the main house and all I heard was banging and electric saws. But once they left, it would be quiet and peaceful.

What do you think? I asked Daniel.

It's isolated. He studied the contract on the screen he'd brought with him. *I can't find any problems with this. I think you've done a good job of setting boundaries with the research group. As good as you can. But you should try to get out of here. Quickly. I can't see this being good for you or the kids, long term.*

I sighed. I just wanted to rest for a little while. I needed to think.

Agreed, I told him. *I'll figure something out.*

Mountains rose out of the distant forest. Fog broke across the peaks, snaking down. In an hour, we wouldn't be able to see them anymore and the fog would wind between the trees.

Do you like it? I asked Casi, Becca and Leo.

"It's the happy house," Casi said, pointing at the building. She signed to Becca and I wondered when she'd learned sign language. "This is where I always saw you," Casi told me. "I'd never seen you at the Warehouse. You didn't belong there."

Oh.

Indira raised an eyebrow. *This is going to be fascinating. I can't wait to see what you all can do.*

A chill snuck up my back and I shivered.

What do you guys think? I asked Becca and Leo.

Whatever keeps me away from the Guardians, Leo responded, with a flip of his green hair.

Becca?

Casi says it'll be fine. And we belong here.

Okay, then.

Can we name it? Becca asked. *A better name than Phillip's Academy for the Advancement of Wilds?*

Sure, I responded. *How about May's Home for the Betterment of Wilds?*

Becca laughed silently and Leo groaned.

So ideas? I asked.

"The Borough," Casi answered.

"That's an odd name," I said. I kind of liked it though—a safe home, secure and hidden away from everyone. "Where'd you come up with it?" I asked.

"Because you named it that," she said.

Oh god. She was going to make my head hurt.

"The Borough it is then," Indira said. "I'll add it to the paperwork. And you, sir," she said to Daniel. "As another Wild, you're welcome to come here whenever."

"If Kendle will have me." *I'll go anywhere you need me to. I'll leave the Warehouse and come here if you want me.*

Wait, what?

"You're welcome anytime," I said. His shields glittered at me. *Someone has to keep us out of trouble,* I thought to hide my confusion.

We looked up at the house, our new home. A flock of humming-birds swirled around us.

God, I hoped I was doing the right thing.

ENJOYED THE BOOK?

PLEASE LEAVE A REVIEW

Reviews are the best way to thank an author for the months, and sometimes years of effort that it takes to create a good book for your reading pleasure.

ACKNOWLEDGEMENTS

Warehouse Dreams was either a year in the making or over ten years, depending on how you look at it and Kendle's evolution. (Steph: I know you still have an early copy; burn it!). While the action and romance are a large part of this story, it also asks the question--if we can create genetically perfect people, should we? And what would that do to our society and our children? I wish I knew the answer, but like all good sci-fi, Warehouse Dreams allows the reader to explore that concept. I hope. At least that's the idea. Or it's just a good story. I'm fine either way.

I have to thank my family and parents who, when I said I wanted to be a writer, asked how they could help, and bought me tickets for writer's conferences and became cheerleaders for each step of this story's evolution.

Thank you to Stephanie who read an early copy all those years ago and in facing her own mortality, forced me to face my own. You are one of the most amazing friends I can have and the strongest person I know.

Thank you to the other Semi-Sages, Sarah, Molly and Morrigan for your friendship, support and advice. I would not be sitting outside, on my patio in 2020, during a quarantine, writing this, without the three of you.

Thank you to those who read early drafts, Izabela, Leah, Jessica, Stephanie and Chris. I would not have been able to complete Warehouse Dreams without you.

Thank you to Chris Bannor who was one of the first people I called when I decided to take this writing thing seriously. Our chats to and from the Writers' Coffeehouses and our Write-ins have been invaluable and I cherish our friendship.

Before I forget, thank you to H. for loaning me the name Mr. Sparklebutt. It makes me snicker each time.

Finally, I can't say enough thank yous to my boys and my husband, Brad. You have taken on so much so I can eke out a few extra minutes a day to spend writing. Thank you for sacrificing so much so I could follow my dream. Brad, without your support, love and friendship I wouldn't be who I am and I'm so incredibly grateful to have you as my partner in this insane world.

Thank you all for reading Warehouse Dreams. Any errors are mine and mine alone and feel free to find me on my social media platforms to debate them with me.

ABOUT THE AUTHOR

Theresa Halvorsen has never met a profanity she hasn't enjoyed. She's generally overly-caffeinated and at times, wine-soaked. The author of *Warehouse Dreams* and *The Dad's Playbook to Labor and Birth*, Theresa wonders what sleep is. When she's not writing or podcasting at The Semi-Sages of the Pages, she's commuting through San Diego traffic to her healthcare position. In whatever free time is left, Theresa enjoys board games, geeky conventions, and reading. Her life goal is to give "Oh-My-Gosh-This-Book-Is-So-Good!" happiness to her readers. She lives in Temecula with her amazing and supportive husband, occasionally her college-age twins, and the pets they'd promised to care for. Find her at www.theresaHauthor.com and on Twitter and Facebook.

Made in the USA
Monee, IL
14 January 2024

50844555R00192